HAPPILY NEVER AFTER

A CLAIRE HARTLEY ACCIDENTAL MYSTERY

MADISON SCORE

That's What She Said Publishing, Inc.

Happily

NEVER

After

ISBN: 979-8-88643-953-3 (ebook)

ISBN: 979-8-88643-954-0 (paperback)

madisonscore.com

110124

To Lucy. For being the best big sister and for proving that the impossible is possible.

CHAPTER ONE

To Do:
- Call caterer
- Groomer appointment for Rosie
- Email city of Los Angeles

"Absolutely not. I said buffalo plaid, not tartan plaid. Yes, there is a difference. I was very clear when I spoke to Janice. Is she available?"

On hold, Claire Hartley tapped her foot against the Italian floor tiles in her kitchen. The sun was beginning to set on the cool April evening, sending long shadows across the acres of impeccably manicured yard that had been freshly mulched in near-freezing temperatures the week before. She straightened the Jell-O shot Battleship station at the breakfast nook.

The line picked back up. Claire took a deep breath and collected her thoughts. She was letting the stress of the day

1

get to her. Being shouty and rude was unprofessional and unkind.

"Listen, I know you're just trying to do your job. I respect you as a caterer, and I know you're capable of wonderful service. But if the waiters don't show up in the agreed-upon buffalo plaid bow ties, it's going to compromise the entire party aesthetic. They won't match the napkins."

Maybe she was being a little extra. But this was the first of Luke's birthdays they would celebrate as a couple. He deserved a perfect day.

Janice muttered something apologetic on the other end.

Movement in the foyer drew Claire's gaze. "Oh, Mindy, can you put those on the back table in the ballroom, next to the whiskey fountain? Thank you."

Mindy, Claire's assistant and one of her best friends, plucked a case of snifters from the island and disappeared down the hallway. The smell of hibiscus and spearmint gum lingered in her wake.

The hold music resumed. Apparently being polite wasn't going to work either.

"Caterer not cooperating?" Nicole Collins asked, new diamond wedding band sparkling on her ring finger. An expensive camera was slung around her neck, partially obscured by her waterfall of chestnut-colored hair. Kyle, her husband as of two months ago, seemed to be attached to her hip. He was dressed for the occasion in a sport jacket and loafers. Nicole glowed next to him in her strappy, amethyst cocktail dress. They were both tan, fresh off a plane from their two-week Caribbean honeymoon.

"I told you not to use them again. Not after the McCaffery proposal." Nicole paused to bring her camera to eye level and capture the plaid-and-burlap birthday banner Claire had just finished hanging in the foyer.

"Caviar at a vegan proposal," Claire muttered, shaking her head. "I stretched the party budget too thin. They were the only option left. If they don't show up in buffalo plaid, they're going to get a less than enthusiastic review on Yelp."

The hold music ended. "Hello, yes? Oh, hi, Janice. I understand. Thank you so much for taking care of it. I appreciate the discount. The chefs will still be here within the hour? Wonderful. Bye."

With a sigh, she crammed her cell phone into the sweetheart neckline of her emerald-green, floor-length dress. It was a crime that formal dresses didn't include pockets. She left Nicole and Kyle in the kitchen, where they had huddled into the breakfast nook to canoodle in that extra smug newlywed way.

She started down the wainscoted hallway, eyeballing the floor for stray hair. Spotting several clumps undoubtedly left there recently by her absent corgi Rosie, she swore and twisted the knob on her office door. It was locked, but she hadn't been the one to lock it. A flutter stirred in her belly, and she rubbed at the scar on her wrist. Surely they wouldn't sneak into her house during a party. They'd been silent for months.

It took standing on her tiptoes to reach above the doorframe. Her pinky brushed against the tiny silver key. She crammed it into the small hole in the knob. *Pop.* The door swung open.

Something crashed to the floor. Her heart leapt into her throat. She flipped the light switch on and stormed into the room, grabbing the nearest weapon—a wrought iron lamp.

"Oh, hey, Claire," came a voice from the floor.

She glanced down. Mindy lay flat on her back on the rug. The cap of a pen seemed to be stuck in her mane of raven hair, and the neckline on her black cocktail dress was

3

crooked. Her green eyes sparkled in amusement. As disheveled as she was, she looked like a portrait that belonged in a museum.

"Seriously, Mindy? There are five bedrooms upstairs. Sawyer, you might as well come out," Claire called into the room. Where could the mammoth-sized man possibly be hiding?

A pair of chocolate-colored eyes peeked over the edge of her scrubby, shabby-chic desk. It had been a hand-me-down from her mother. And now it was soiled. A moment later, six feet and seven inches of steel and sinew appeared.

"Hey, Claire. Great party."

"It hasn't even started yet." She crossed her arms. The man may have saved her from a serial killer last spring, but that didn't mean he got to exchange bodily fluids on her desk. "Can you take this party upstairs before you give someone else a heart attack? And Mindy, I could use your help with coordinating the—is that yours?"

A hot pink, lacy thong that she had most certainly not left there dangled from the picture frame that housed her business degree.

"I don't know how that got there. I'll dispose of it for you." Mindy stood and stuffed it into her clutch.

Claire set the lamp back down and leaned over to pick up their robot vacuum, shaking her head as she shut the door and turned it on. It chugged merrily down the hallway, banging haphazardly off the molding and sucking up clumps of dog hair. Where was that dog, anyway?

Her phone dinged with a notification, and she glanced down then nearly dropped it. *Shit.* Luke's flight was arriving twenty minutes early. He refused to check a bag, so there would be nothing to slow him down once he exited the plane.

She scrolled through her recently dialed numbers and found the limo driver.

"Ted! Hi, it's Claire. Listen, Luke's flight is landing twenty minutes early. Oh, you are? That's great. Thank you so much. Tito's outside with the sign, right? It's not checkered, it's plaid. It's part of the party aesthetic. Listen, just pick him up, okay? Shoot me a text before you leave the airport, and then again when you're about to pull up the driveway."

Thank god she had told the driver the wrong time on purpose. Luke landing at the airport with no ride was *not* part of the surprise party.

She hung up and opened the French doors to the ballroom. It was almost perfect. Pictures of Luke growing up were artistically arranged on tables that were soon to be covered in his favorite foods. A whiskey fountain bubbled merrily in the corner, next to a display of miniature pies—Luke hated cake—that stood nearly three feet tall. A bartender set up glasses at the bar in the corner. At least Mindy had managed to take the snifters to the ballroom before getting busy.

Stepping out onto the stamped concrete patio, Claire waved at George, the plump, middle-aged videographer who worked for her proposal planning business when Luke wasn't available. He was testing out the projector, which was hooked up to Luke's video game console.

Cornhole boards and ladder golf stood a few feet away. Cocktail tables were scattered across the backyard under the stars, and a bartender was beginning to set up at the wet bar next to the pool. If anyone walked away from this party hungry and/or sober, it was their own fault.

Was that the tip of a snoot poking out from beneath the banquet table? She strode over and lifted the edge of the tablecloth.

"Rosie! Drop the beanbag," Claire scolded.

Her elusive corgi clamped down even harder on the plaid beanbag and sprinted out from her hiding place, rocketing toward the edge of the yard. Her nails scrabbled over the dance floor that had been erected over the pool. Claire threw her hands up in the air and crossed the patio back to the house. That furry asshole was as stubborn as she was adorable.

Mindy rushed into the ballroom, nearly slipping on the marble tiles. Her dress was still crooked. "You invited Luke's mom? Are you insane?" she hissed.

"What? Rachel? I didn't—"

"Hello, Claire," a cool voice said.

Her shoulders bunched up like someone had just run an icicle down her spine.

"I came by to drop this off for Lucas, but I see you're otherwise occupied." Rachel eyed the tinkling whiskey fountain and buffalo plaid coasters as if they were going to leap off the table and strangle her. If only.

She stiffly held out a small, lapis-colored gift bag.

The odds that the bag contained a live snake were low, but not zero. Claire took it like it was a bomb and gingerly set it on a cocktail table. "Thank you, Rachel. Luke's flight hasn't landed yet. We were just having a small get-together to celebrate his birthday. You're welcome to stay, of course. He'll be so surprised." Because she wasn't invited.

"I suppose I could stay for a few minutes. Just until he gets here," she said, already trailing off as she spotted the bar outside.

"Oh—okay." Claire barely had time to blink before Rachel's Manolos had clacked across the marble tile and disappeared.

"At least your boobs weren't out this time," Mindy said,

picking up Rachel's gift bag and moving it to a table in the corner. It had been several months since Claire's first meeting with Rachel, during which she had fallen into the pool and lost her top when Rachel arrived unannounced at Luke's house. Rachel had also briefly served as a defense attorney for the man who tried to kill Claire, so they were definitely even now. They hadn't made much headway since.

Claire's phone vibrated, and she pulled it out to see a picture and text from Luke. His childhood sports hero, Tito Corona, held a plaid sign stating "L Islestorm."

Luke: *Is this for real??*

"Look." She shoved her phone at Mindy, who was rearranging the pies on the display. "He's on his way."

"He's totally fan-boying." She picked up a pecan pie and took a bite. "What did he play again? Baseball?"

"Professional wrestling." Claire smiled. Mindy's interest in sports did not extend beyond how the players looked in their uniforms.

"Huh. How did you find him, anyway?" Mindy stepped back and surveyed the display as she munched.

"Donna from the flower shop dated him in high school. He lives in Philly."

"Damn, Donna. Can I ask an insensitive question?" Mindy polished off the mini pie.

Claire raised her eyebrows. "Is there any other kind of question with you?"

"Shut up. How are you affording all of this? With our plan coming up and everything, I mean."

Claire glanced around the ballroom. She didn't want Rachel snooping in her business, and definitely not in her financials. Luke didn't even know about her and Mindy's plan. "I just wanted to have one last celebration before we really buckle down. I want him to know how important he is to me. And besides, I'm paying for this mostly with ad revenue from people streaming the proposal videos, actually." A dozen proposal videos on their YouTube channel were pulling in a surprising amount of cash.

"Didn't you look at last week's paycheck?" she added. "We had a huge bump in traffic."

Mindy shrugged and reached for the mojito the bartender had just set down. "It's direct deposit. As long as the rent's paid and my checks aren't bouncing, I don't really pay much attention."

Claire shook her head and dragged one of the cocktail tables an inch to the right.

A gaggle of Luke's friends walked into the ballroom, and she waved them into the backyard. Despite a strict no gift policy, she had now added two six packs of beer and a Cuban cigar to the table with Rachel's gift bag. Scanning the ballroom and the yard showed that everything was under control for the moment. There already seemed to be a rousing game of flip cup happening near the eastern tree line.

The catering team arrived, sending the smell of smoked ribs wafting down the hallway. They set to work in Luke's kitchen, making his favorites—miniature bacon cheese-burger sliders, smoked ribs, mac and cheese, and soft pretzels.

"I'm not complaining, but Luke eats like a toddler," Nicole observed, snatching a cup of mac and cheese from a passing waiter.

Claire shot her a dirty look before glancing at her phone. "Oh shit, he's here! Kyle, get everyone from the back.

To the living room. And lights off, please," she said to the chef, who sighed and moved his pan to an unlit burner.

Twenty people piled into the living room, ducking behind furniture and stumbling over each other in the dark. Rachel refused to crouch and instead stood behind a coat rack, sipping a dirty martini and inspecting her nail beds.

A pair of headlights wound up Luke's serpentine driveway. The lights flashed over a shape, and Claire's breath hitched. What the hell was that, a hunchback? Her heart rate skyrocketed. The lights shifted, revealing a clumpy bush that bore an undeniable resemblance to a stooped human being.

She exhaled noisily. *Get it together, girl.* She definitely would have remembered if one of the members of ESA, the group of murderous frat boys who had tried to kill her the summer before, was a hunchback.

Sawyer crouched next to her on the floor. He put a reassuring hand on her shoulder, and she relaxed. Even if there was a murderous hunchback in her front yard, she was well-equipped to handle them. Six months of self-defense lessons with Sawyer, who owned a private security company, had turned her into a machine.

It had been almost a year since she had been drugged, kidnapped, and nearly murdered in a newly constructed hotel owned by one of her clients. Barely three months later, she and her friends almost single-handedly took down a local ring of kidnappers and serial killers masquerading as a fraternity, Epsilon Sigma Alpha, at her alma mater. Night mares about that night still plagued her—her father's blood swirling into the moonlit lake, sweaty, meaty arms wrapping around her from behind. The crunch of a broken nose.

Even though ESA had fallen silent, she still looked over her shoulder every time she walked the streets of West

Haven. Her brain incessantly scanned for danger, cataloging all the men in a two-block radius. Prickles of fear caused her to turn around abruptly in grocery stores, trying to catch the person she was certain was staring at her, tracking her. Last week, an abrupt about-face had startled an old woman so much that she screamed and dropped a glass jar of pickles.

The local chapter of ESA may have been taken down, but there were more. A quick Google search had revealed two dozen chapters spread across the United States. Fraternity details had been wiped from university websites after the West Haven branch had been shut down, but that hadn't stopped Claire's research. Barney Windsor and his cronies were just the tip of the iceberg. Something told her this silence wasn't going to last for long.

The limo pulled to a stop, and Tito slid out first, followed by Luke, who didn't seem to notice that his side yard was full of vehicles. The two appeared to be deeply involved in conversation as they came up the walkway, Luke enthusiastically gesturing with his toned arms. He raised his hand to the keypad, typing in the code and pushing the door open.

"*Surprise*," everyone yelled as he flicked the light on.

"*Fuck*." He juked to the side and covered his junk with one hand.

Everyone laughed and clapped while Luke leaned against the breakfast nook, hands on his knees.

"Happy birthday, handsome," Claire said, sidling up next to him and giving him a kiss on the cheek. "You didn't think I would forget, did you?"

Luke unclenched one hand to draw her close. "You're insane."

"Yeah, yeah. I love you too."

He dipped her suddenly, kissing her deeply. The

muscles in his back rippled as she gripped them for balance. Her heart swelled in her chest, and all thoughts of ESA vanished like they were wiped from a whiteboard. Warmth spread from her fingertips to her toes. Did he really need to be present for his birthday party? Nobody would notice if they disappeared upstairs for a few minutes, right? They had just replaced the comforter and pillows but had yet to break them in. An arm with a snake tattoo reached between them and startled her out of her hormone-fueled thoughts. His friend Andy never did have a grasp on personal space.

She stepped away and let the throng of friends and family descend on him. Luke smiled and laughed as he shared anecdotes with each of them. He was a grumpy pain in the ass at least sixty percent of the time, but she loved him anyway.

"Great party, Claire," Kyle said through a mouthful of ribs. "The whiskey fountain is a nice touch."

"Thanks." She picked up a glass of white wine. The surprise was over. Luke was having a great time. Finally she could relax and enjoy.

Kyle took a step closer to her and lowered his voice. "Do you have a second to talk? It's about the case. I know it's not the best time, but I think you should hear it from me first. You know, rather than on *Marnie in the Morning*."

So much for relaxing. She set her glass down more forcefully than she intended to on the granite countertop. What was it this time?

"Okay," she said reluctantly, and followed Kyle back down the hallway.

CHAPTER TWO

To Do:
- *Yelp reviews for party vendors*
- *Give Luke the envelope*
- *Fake sick to get out of dinner with Jack*

It was hard to take Kyle seriously as a lawyer when he had a barbecue sauce stain on the collar of his white polo.

Claire closed the door of her office and took a deep breath. She backed into the corner and straightened the hem of her dress. A jolt shot through her elbow. Damn bookcase. It was the third time this week she had banged some part of her body on it.

Kyle took the seat behind the desk.

"So. The trial." She crossed her arms over her chest. Maybe if she squeezed tightly enough, she could suffocate the anxiety out of herself.

"You recall that I told you Barney is under new counsel."

He leaned back in her chair, crossed one ankle over his knee, and pressed the tips of his fingers together. Was he practicing lawyer poses? This was not the time.

"Yes, and I'll certainly miss Rachel calling me a deluded alcoholic in front of the entire nation."

He nodded. "Right, well, his new attorney reached out to me this afternoon. There's been a change in the plan."

She pursed her lips. "I already hate where this is going."

There was a series of sharp knocks on the door. "Come in," she said, even though the suspense was drawing a wedge of pain between her shoulder blades.

Rachel bustled into the room and shut the door behind her, a fresh dirty martini gripped in her pterodactyl-like claws. What the hell was she doing here? Maybe the bar had run out of olives.

"Mr. Collins," she said pointedly. Her nostrils were flaring, and for the first time since Claire had known her, she seemed to be shaken. Maybe it was just the vodka, but her perfectly coiffed hair had several escaping strands, and dog hair clung stubbornly to the hem of her pencil skirt. Ha.

"Rachel," he said cordially, nodding in her direction. It was bold to call your best friend's mom by her first name. Especially when he had thrown up Four Loko in her den as a teen.

She set the martini on the desk and crossed her arms. "You've heard?"

"Yes," Kyle said slowly.

"And you've told Claire?"

"I was about to. How do you know?" He narrowed his eyes.

Rachel waved one hand. "I have many connections. Well, get on with it."

He eyed Rachel before leaning forward and addressing Claire. This couldn't be good.

"The DA's office contacted Barney's team. They're offering a plea bargain."

A bowling ball dropped into Claire's stomach. "A plea bargain? What does that mean for the trial?"

"There won't be a trial."

Heat shot through her. Static burst into her vision. Her heart galloped like she was running away from Barney all over again.

"With a plea deal, he can plead to a lesser charge and negotiate for a better outcome," Rachel clarified.

Claire was silent for almost a full minute. Rachel and Kyle looked at each other.

Taking a deep breath, Claire pinched the bridge of her nose between her fingertips. "So you're telling me that the man who stalked me, chloroformed me, and stabbed me with the intent to bury me in his parking garage will be allowed to take a lesser sentence?"

Kyle's eyebrows knit together. "Most criminal cases end in a plea deal. There are some good features. You won't have to be involved with a lengthy, public trial. The press will back off sooner rather than later. There won't be a jury for him to manipulate or pay off. He'll have guaranteed jail time. He won't be able to flee the country. And the time he spends in prison will give the FBI time to build a case against him for the other victims."

She collapsed into the purple flowered accent chair across from Kyle. "There's only *one* body. We don't even know that they'll have enough evidence to convict him. How is he going to plead?"

"Guilty to one count of second-degree felony aggravated assault. But we won't accept that. He almost killed you."

"I don't understand. So he wouldn't be charged with attempted murder? How long would his sentence be?"

Rachel laid an ice-cold hand on Claire's shoulder. Claire jumped and reached up, then paused in midair. Months of self-defense training had led her perilously close to flipping her potential future mother-in-law over her head. She lowered her hand and tried to refocus. If Professional Stick-up-the-ass Rachel Islestorm, Esquire was comforting her, the next words out of Kyle's mouth were going to be catastrophic.

"Ten years in Pennsylvania," he said. "They're asking for five. But we won't accept that. We can't. I can make a recommendation to the judge of first-degree felony and the maximum sentence of ten years."

No way had she heard that correctly. Her stomach clenched. Was the room spinning? She jumped to her feet, throwing Rachel's hand off as though it were a damp towel.

"Ten years? *Ten* years? Are you fucking kidding me? He'll be thirty-eight when he gets out. So what, he serves a few years, gets out early on good behavior, and returns to stalking and murdering his ex-girlfriends?"

Her airways constricted. Never had she dreamed that she could see Barney on the streets of West Haven again. What would stop him from stalking her again? From taking more victims?

Kyle cleared his throat. The tension in the room was tactile. "The judge has to accept the plea bargain too. She could sentence him more harshly."

Rachel spoke from the corner of the office. "You'll have the opportunity to give a victim impact statement before the judge officially announces sentencing. It could result in a greater sentence for Barney."

Claire stared at the ceiling. It was up to her to convince

the judge to keep Barney in prison for as long as possible. If she failed, Barney could get out even sooner. More women could be in jeopardy. How was that fair? How was *any* of this fair?

Kyle stood quickly. He shifted from one foot to the other and put his hands in his pockets. "We can talk more about it tomorrow. Maybe at brunch? And give you some time to process."

Process. There was no processing something like this. Between the insane California proposal she had just taken on and Tuesday's meeting with the bank, her mental band-width was already gone. Her hands shook, and she clenched them into fists.

Kyle paused with a hand on the door. "It's our best bet, Claire. There's no telling what he's capable of." He squeezed her hand and wrenched the door open, then turned at the last second. "There's one other thing."

What else could there possibly be? She was going to lose it.

"The hearing is this coming Thursday." He lobbed that grenade and walked out of the room.

Perfect. Less than a week to write a statement that would hopefully send Barney to prison for the maximum sentence. As if next week wasn't going to be stressful enough already.

Claire and Rachel were silent for a long moment before the older woman walked to the door. She turned around at the threshold, the martini sloshing in her hand. "He's right, you know. Mr. Windsor is very wealthy and very connected. The plea bargain is the safest way to make sure he stays in prison, and the best way to keep other people safe." She shut the door behind her.

Claire sat, frozen in her chair. Laughter and the sounds

of chanting came from the kitchen, but she didn't move. She couldn't.

Seconds later, somebody kicked the door open. She was too numb to react.

"What are you doing in here alone? Weirdo. Here." Mindy stormed in with a mini cheeseburger and a fresh glass of wine. She handed both to Claire and stared pointedly at her until she got to her feet.

An hour later, after a third glass of wine, Claire decided to put all thoughts of the trial behind her. And she certainly wasn't going to think about her meeting with the bank on Tuesday. Her mop of curly blonde hair was twisted back and bound by what felt like a thousand bobby pins. The night air was cool as she viciously hurled a beanbag at the cornhole board. The bag slid up the polished wood surface and dropped cleanly through the hole.

She cheered and triumphantly looked around. It had only taken her twenty-six attempts to get it in the hole. Where the hell was everyone? Rosie, who was rolling in something sure to be smelly, seemed to be the only being left outside.

"Guys?" Claire called, but no one answered. Her shoulders tightened. Surely the party guests hadn't all been abducted and murdered while she was ten yards away. There was no need to be nervous.

The bartender shrugged and offered her a glass of water. She took it and walked, bemused, back into the house. The ballroom was empty. The hallway was empty. But voices came from the kitchen.

"Oh, Bri!" Claire nearly shouted, setting her glass on the island and racing to embrace her famous actress half sister, Brianna Hartley, who appeared to have just arrived.

Brianna squealed and drew Claire into a tight hug. The

remainder of the party attendees stood at a small distance, wide-eyed and seemingly sneaking pictures with their phones.

"I'm so glad you could come!" Claire returned the hug eagerly, delighting in its warmth. "How was your flight? Do you have the—"

"Yes, he's here. This is Jeremy," Brianna said, gesturing to a tall, lanky man with the posture of a thirteen-year-old who was glued to a video game console.

"You must be Claire? Luke's agent?" He shook her hand firmly.

"Yes, that's me," she said seriously, smoothing her hair back and transforming into business Claire. The third glass of wine might have been a mistake. Maybe he wouldn't notice. "You brought the documents?"

Jeremy handed over a thick manila envelope.

"Great, thank you so much. Why don't you enjoy the party while I have our lawyer look these over?"

"Aren't you going to introduce me to Luke?" Jeremy raised his eyebrows.

"Soon. It's kind of a surprise."

He nodded and moved in the direction she gestured.

She beelined for Kyle, who was hanging slightly back in the living room, but was keeping an eye on Brianna.

"Kyle, I need you to do something for me."

"Only if you introduce us to your sister."

"You met her at Christmas, remember? She brought that awful gluten-free fruit cake?"

"Yeah, but that was months and like two of her movies ago. She's an important person—I'm sure she doesn't remember."

Claire threw up her hands. "Fine, but after you do my thing. Take this and go in my office."

The envelope thwacked into his outstretched hands. Kyle eyed it. "What is it?"

"A contract for Luke. I know it's not a ton of time to do a thorough inspection, but I just want to make sure they're not taking advantage of him."

He grumbled and disappeared down the hallway, envelope in one hand and cup of mac and cheese in the other.

Forty minutes later, after Tito and Luke competed for the cornhole championship trophy that Claire had molded out of beef jerky (Luke won), Kyle reappeared and drew her aside.

"Luke's going to shit himself." He handed the envelope over.

They walked into the ballroom. "We're good?"

"All good. They were surprisingly generous with the terms. They must really want him."

"All thanks to Brianna," she said, smiling at her half sister, who was by the bar, exclaiming and pointing at Mindy's (admittedly adorable) strappy heels.

"Speaking of which..." Kyle prompted.

"All right, get your wife."

Claire approached her sister moments later with the newlyweds in tow.

"All good?" Brianna asked. Her blue eyes—definitely inherited from her bohemian mother, Tanya—sparkled.

"All good." It was close enough to the truth. "Bri, you remember my friends?"

"Kyle and Nicole! Of course. How was your wedding day? Tell me everything." Brianna grabbed Nicole's arm and led her to a cocktail table.

Claire turned to find Luke, who had just lost a game of "chubby bunny" against Sawyer. "Can you come with me for a second?" she asked.

"Thure," Luke said through the mouthful of marshmallows. "Do you hath thome water?"

She grabbed a bottle from a passing waiter and handed it to him.

"Man," he said when his mouth was free again, "I haven't played chubby bunny since high school. Sawyer's mouth is huge. I think he had an unfair advantage."

"Yeah, yeah. So, I need you to come to my office."

He paused. "Is there a spider? We're in the middle of a party. It can wait."

"No, there's not a spider. Just come on."

"Not until you tell me why you need me to go." He leaned against a banquet table and crossed his arms over his chest. Of all the times to be a stubborn asshole.

"I was going to suggest we do that thing you mentioned, but if you're not willing to—"

Luke shot away from the table, grabbed her hand, and immediately crossed the ballroom, thrusting the double doors open and dragging her behind him like a rag doll. He twisted the office door handle and had one hand on his belt when he apparently realized there was a man in the room.

Luke jumped, again covering his junk with his hand. Claire smiled and directed him into the chair in front of her desk.

"Luke, this is Jeremy."

"Okay," he said slowly. "Thanks for coming to my party, Jeremy who I've never met."

She elbowed him.

"Mr. Islestorm. I'm Jeremy Lewis of Streamster Incorporated. I work in content acquirement. I've been in contact with your agent, Claire."

Luke sat up and then froze. The wooden arm of the chair creaked under his fingertips.

"Nice to meet you." He recovered and reached across the desk. They shook hands.

"I'm here representing Streamster. We are interested in acquiring your finished documentary and securing a relationship for the one in progress."

Luke cocked his head. "You want my documentaries?"

"We do." Jeremy slid a stack of documents across the desk to Luke. "I know you've done well with releasing it independently. But true crime is a tremendous market right now. If we streamed your documentary, it would reach millions. I'm confident that it would be a very lucrative relationship."

Luke reached toward the documents, then snatched his hands back. He folded his arms and stared at Jeremy. "Would I be giving up any creative control?"

"None. We're not interested in micromanaging our creators' content unless there's something egregious we can't ignore. Our content manager loved *The Suburban Hustle*. The network would provide you with access to a team of people to help finish the new documentary— animation, camera crews, story editors, whatever you need. We would also give you the funding you need to finish. It's all in the contract."

Luke was silent for several seconds. Was this some kind of negotiation tactic?

"Can I think about it?" he finally asked.

Claire's eyes bulged, and she kicked Luke. He winced but didn't react.

"Of course," Jeremy said, standing up and sliding his blazer back on. "We'll need to know by Friday. My card." A black-and-silver embossed business card slid into Luke's hands. Jeremy nodded at them and left.

The second the door closed, Luke collapsed back into his chair.

"Streamster wants my docs," he said simply.

"They do." Claire slid an arm around him and perched on the arm of his chair. "Why do you want to wait on it?"

"It's a big decision." He wiped a hand over his face. "Probably not one that I should make while buzzed from Battleship Jell-O shots. Not to mention a blood sugar level of 3,000 from chubby bunny."

She nodded. "That's a good point. Are you excited, though? Happy? Pissed at me for interfering?" The wheels were definitely turning behind those stupidly beautiful green eyes. Maybe this whole thing had been a mistake. He didn't love surprises, and this evening had already been full of them.

"Just surprised." He turned to her. "I can't believe you did this for me."

She flippantly waved a hand. "It's nothing. I just had to impersonate an agent, ask Brianna to introduce me to some- one, and coerce Kyle into looking over your contract. It's solid, by the way."

"I am a little disappointed, though." His hand slid over hers.

"Why's that?"

"You said we could do the thing we talked about, but instead all I got was a contract."

"Well, it is your birthday." Claire stood, keeping her eyes on Luke as she locked the door with one hand and unhooked her bra with the other.

Hours later, Luke and Claire collapsed into bed full of carbs, booze, and love.

She curled up against his bare chest, breathing in his sweet, outdoorsy smell. He yawned and gathered her close.

Rosie, who had had a late-night bath in Luke's whirlpool tub after inexplicably rolling in barbecue sauce, snored lightly in her dog bed.

"I almost forgot, there's one more thing." Claire sat up suddenly and withdrew an envelope from under her pillow. A wax seal was stamped on the back, and Luke's name and address were written in calligraphy on the front.

He shook his head. "Have you been taking calligraphy classes again?"

She scoffed. "Please. I'm a calligraphy master. I don't need more classes."

He pulled out a thick cardstock envelope and hand-written invitation in the same loopy handwriting.

"Holy shit." He dropped the envelope on the bed.

"What?" she asked. She already knew after probing the depths of the internet, but this was Luke's news to deliver.

"*The Suburban Hustle* was nominated for an Emmy." His voice was barely more than a whisper.

"Holy shit," she echoed, snatching the envelope and scouring the contents. "Luke, this is crazy! How are you not ripping your shirt off and running screaming into the hills right now?"

He took the envelope from her and laid it gingerly on the nightstand. He flipped off the light and collapsed heavily onto his pillow, turning away from Claire.

Her heart dropped. Of all the things that could have pissed him off this evening, it was getting nominated for an Emmy?

"What's wrong?" she asked quietly in the dark.

"I didn't earn this." His voice was muffled.

"What do you mean?"

"I'm assuming Brianna orchestrated the nomination too?"

She rolled him over so he had to look at her. "Of course not. Don't you think if Brianna had any control over the Emmys, she would have like six of them by now?"

"You didn't ask her to say anything?" It was hard to tell in the dark, but he didn't look convinced.

"No, Luke. This was a complete surprise. I suspected what it was because I Googled what an Emmy nomination looks like and I hid it from you. I may have broken a federal law or two. I figured it was the best thing you could receive on your birthday."

He sat up and looked at her. The frown slipped from his face, and his eyes sparkled. Moonlight fell across his six-pack. It was awfully distracting.

"You earned this nomination. One hundred percent on your own. You're an Emmy-nominated director."

He threw the comforter off and stood on the bed. Rosie popped her head up.

"We're going to the fucking Emmys." He grabbed Claire's hand and pulled her up next to him.

"We're going to the Emmys!" They said together as they laughed and jumped on the bed. Rosie barked like crazy and propelled herself onto the bed to jump with them. Luke picked Claire up and whirled her around before sealing their joy with a lustful kiss.

He threw a dog treat out the bedroom door and snapped it shut before tumbling back into bed with Claire.

CHAPTER THREE

To Do:
- Write victim impact statement
- Thank you note for Jeremy

"I WILL NEVER EAT AGAIN." MINDY PUT HER FORK DOWN AND pushed her syrup-covered plate away.

"Same. At least not for another two hours, anyway." Kyle stretched an arm around Nicole and leaned back to look at everyone. "We have some news."

Claire's fork dropped to her plate, splattering hollandaise sauce onto the tablecloth. Surely it must be bad news. This week was full of it. Were they moving? Was someone sick?

"Maybe we could cheers?" Nicole suggested to Kyle.

"Perfect idea." They lifted their glasses, and everyone else followed, clearly confused.

"To Baby Collins." Kyle smiled broadly.

An explosion of noise came from the table. Everyone began talking at once.

Claire leaped out of her chair, knocking it over and sending it crashing to the floor. Heads turned in the restaurant, but she was already embracing Nicole. Tears streamed from her eyes as she pulled back, grabbed her best friend by the wrists, and looked her in the eyes.

"Nicole, you are a wonderful human being. You are so smart, so beautiful, and so kind. This baby is the luckiest baby on the planet, and I would die for either of you. I have two thousand questions for you, but I will wait."

Nicole laughed and flicked a tear away.

"Scoot." Mindy shoved Claire away to embrace Nicole.

After congratulating Kyle, Claire sat back down and watched her friends celebrate the newest, tiniest member of their group. Luke squeezed her hand under the table. Wow. Her best friend was pregnant. In less than a year, there would be a tiny, screaming human at their brunches. Nicole couldn't do margarita nights anymore. The very foundation of their friendship had just shifted ever so slightly.

"When are you due?" Luke asked as everyone settled.

"Early January. It's very early," Nicole said, clearly noticing everyone mentally counting backward. "We thought about waiting until the first trimester passed, but we both suck at keeping secrets. And if something...unexpected happened, we knew we would need everyone's support."

Claire reached over and grabbed Nicole and Kyle's hands. "I'm glad you told us. I know nothing is guaranteed, but you're going to be the most amazing parents. I just know it."

Hours later, Claire's mind was still buzzing with the news about Baby Collins as she paused at a red light on Broad Street. She glanced in her rearview mirror. The white van that had followed her for ten blocks idled behind her. A knot grew in her stomach and goosebumps ran down her arms. Just because it was a creepy white kidnapping van didn't mean it belonged to ESA, but the thought didn't ease the tension in her shoulders.

It was a good thing she was headed to dinner with her biological father, Jack. He was an FBI agent and, until recently, had been estranged from Claire for twenty years. He had abruptly re-entered her life when he discovered she was marked with a symbol associated with ESA. It wasn't the best way to re-meet an absent father, but they were making some headway.

The van drew her eyes again. What had he said about vehicle counter-surveillance at their dinner last week? Oh, right. Drive like an asshole. Claire sped forward at the green light and turned right without signaling.

Her phone rang, and she answered it without looking. "Hello?" In her rearview mirror, the van continued along its straight path. Worried for nothing.

"Claire. It's me. Tell me you watched *Stepwives of Seacaucus* last night." Ah. It was Charlie, Claire's sister who lived in Los Angeles. She was a publicist to the stars, adept at spinning embarrassing stories and covering up dirt. They didn't have a ton in common, but they did share the occasional obsession with trash TV.

"No, you know Luke's party was last night."

"That's right. Shoot. Call me when you've watched it. How was the party?"

"It was great," Claire said with a smile. "Luke freaked out over the Streamster deal. Brianna was such a huge help with that. I'm on my way to dinner with her and Jack, actually. Did you want me to pass on any messages?"

"Yeah, eat shit and die," Charlie said flatly.

"Charlie," Claire warned. After Jack had taken a bullet for Claire the previous summer, their mother, Alice, had finally forgiven him for abandoning their family. Charlie, on the other hand, would rather get a root canal than reconcile with her father.

"Sorry," her sister said. "It's not Brianna's fault. She didn't ask to be born. Jack can still eat shit and die, though."

"I'll pass that along." Claire shook her head. "I'll call you after I watch the episode, okay? Love you."

"Love you too. Bye."

Charlie was the bossiest, most fearsome woman she knew. It would take a miracle to get her to have a civilized conversation with Brianna, let alone Jack. She had only survived Thanksgiving at Claire's by hiding in the basement with their stepdad, Roy, and drinking wine.

With the impending trip to the West Coast, surely Claire could sneak in some quality sister time and start changing her heart. Something had stirred after Jack and his second family abruptly re-entered her life. She couldn't shake the image of a perfect Christmas, blended family, chaos, and all.

After driving through another two miles of quaint, suburban houses and well-manicured parks, the yards grew, and the houses became less frequent. She pulled to a stop in front of an unassuming Cape Cod-style home with a burgeoning garden.

Claire tapped a code on the keypad that controlled the gate. The gate slid open silently and allowed her Audi SUV to crawl up the driveway.

Oh, hell. A full-body shudder nearly jerked the car into the grass. Tanya, Claire's stepmother, stood completely nude in the backyard. She waved at Claire and bent over to sprinkle water onto some green buds that were just beginning to emerge from the soil. Jack had casually mentioned this springtime habit, but seeing it with her own eyes was another thing entirely.

"Hi, Tanya." Claire climbed out of her car with her eyes almost completely shut. She bumped into her fender and felt her way to the far side of the car.

"Claire, darling, you're early! Brianna hasn't arrived yet." Tanya's voice was like honey.

"That's okay, I'll just step inside and see if Jack needs any help with dinner." Claire stumbled over the curb as she headed for the front door.

Rosie ran ahead of Claire into the house and immediately found Jack, who stood in the kitchen with a towel slung over one shoulder and a wooden spoon suspended over a bubbling pot of red sauce. She jumped and put her paws on his knees in her customary greeting, and he patted her obligingly on the head.

"Thank you for coming." An almost-smile crept across his usually stoic face as he immediately washed his hands.

"It's the second Sunday." She slid her purse onto a dining room chair and reached down to scratch Rosie behind the ears. An awkward silence followed. They had been doing once-a-month dinners for at least six months now, and she still didn't know how to talk to her father. Jack wasn't much of a talker, but since he wasn't trimming rose bushes in the nude, he was the lesser of two evils.

He set his towel down and walked over to an overhead cabinet, then ducked to look underneath it and fit a key into a virtually invisible hole. A hidden panel swung down, revealing several firearms, ammunition, and electronic devices.

Claire sighed and handed over her bag. Jack picked up a device that looked like a stud finder and waved it over her purse.

"Shoes," he said, and she grumbled as she kicked off her flip-flops and handed them to him. He set them on the kitchen floor and carefully ran the device over them.

"All set?" It was the same song and dance at every family dinner. Despite the months of radio silence from ESA, he insisted on scanning her accessories for tracking devices and bugs.

"Almost." Jack waved a piece of bread at Rosie until she approached. He scanned her collar, fed her the treat, and replaced the device in the secret panel. When he turned back to the stove, he winced and rotated the shoulder that had been shot the previous fall.

"No bugs this week?" Claire asked.

"No. Can't be too careful." He calmly stirred the sauce.

She turned away, too, and studied a ceramic of a nude woman. Gold streaks mimicked stretch marks around the rotund belly. Tanya had many hobbies—gardening, ceramics, joining various pyramid schemes. She had never once made Claire feel unwelcome or uncomfortable, and yet their house didn't feel like coming home.

She was an intruder in decades of family history she had never known. Pictures of Brianna gleamed in frames on the wall—dressed as a witch for Halloween, standing on stage as a lanky teenager, arm-in-arm with a Brad Pitt-lookalike at her junior prom. A picture of Claire had appeared on the wall since her last visit, but the frames didn't match. Brianna's had a weathered, well-loved quality, and Claire's had clearly been chucked into a Costco cart right next to a five-pound bag of lentils. Maybe she didn't belong here, but they were trying. It was something.

"Nude gardening is starting early this year," she commented, helping herself to a glass of water. Jack and Tanya didn't allow wine at Sunday dinner. Strike number two.

"Once the temperature hits sixty, she has to be out there." He had used his FBI influence to make a number of indecent exposure charges disappear before convincing Tanya she could only garden in the nude in the backyard, where an eight-foot privacy fence obscured her from the neighbors' view. "She says it allows Mother Nature to speak to her in her purest form."

Claire shuddered and slid the curtains closed.

"How was your week?" Jack continued. Ah, time for small talk.

"Fine. Busy." The news about Kyle and Nicole's pregnancy was on the tip of her tongue, but she kept it inside. She usually only shared work-related news with Jack.

"And yours?" She clapped at Rosie, who jumped and stopped licking the trash can.

"Quite eventful. I think we're getting really close to an answer."

Claire looked intently at her father. His hair had a touch more gray than it did when he first broke into her apartment and introduced himself the previous fall. There was more sadness in his eyes.

"You figured out who William Hickory is?"

"We have a lead. Our best people are working on it."

That was a common refrain. She pulled her phone out of her purse and stared at the handwritten riddle Barney had presented to her father the week before. Apparently he had grown tired of waiting for her to visit him again, because he had abruptly changed tactics to handing riddles over to the feds.

"It's been almost a week. I can't believe they don't have anything yet. 'Where William Hickory paid the ultimate price.'" She had Googled the phrase a thousand times over the last week, but so far the internet had failed her.

"He assured me it's another body location." Jack dipped a spoon into the sauce and grimaced before twisting a salt mill over the bubbling pot.

She pursed her lips. What kind of monster murdered innocent women and then made the feds solve riddles in order to lay them to rest?

Her stomach hitched. She had nearly forgotten about the impending sentencing hearing. If she couldn't show the judge what he had cost her, he could end up with the minimum sentence. He would be knitting underwear blankets and dumping bodies again before the feds ever had time to build a case.

Rosie whined and licked her ankle.

"They're doing what they can," Jack added. He turned to look at her, and there was a flicker of worry in his brown eyes.

"Are you sure he's even telling the truth?" Claire asked. "That he's not just wasting your time? He's not exactly known for having a stellar reputation. I've Googled this phrase a hundred times and can't find mention of anyone with that name."

"He didn't lie about Kayley's remains. We're not sure if this will really lead to Jennifer, but if there's even a chance that this will lead to closure for another family, we have to figure it out."

He opened the small pantry door next to the refrigerator and pressed another hidden button. An LED screen flickered to life on the back of the door. Jack tapped the screen repeatedly, and eventually a map with a blinking red dot appeared.

"Oh, good, your sister's almost here," he said before snapping the door shut.

"Brianna really doesn't care that you track her like this?" Claire raised her eyebrows.

"I only do it with her consent. She wears the tracker on a bracelet, and she could take it off at any time. She's a public figure. She knows how important personal safety is, unlike some of my other children." He pointed a sauce-covered spoon at her.

"Oh, there are more of us? Good to know, I was hoping I wouldn't have to wait for my genealogy report to come back to learn about your second secret family."

"Will you set the table?" The ghost of a smile was back.

"Sure." She opened a cabinet and drew out a stack of cobalt-colored plates.

Rosie barked and charged the front door.

The door popped open and a moment later, in a cloud of Marc Jacobs perfume, Brianna appeared.

"Claire!"

She gave her half sister a tight hug despite the fact that they had seen each other less than twenty-four hours ago.

"Daddy," Brianna added, giving him a kiss on the cheek and a hug from behind. "Where's Mom?" She stooped to pick up Rosie and held her on her hip like a baby, rubbing her behind the ears.

"Naked gardening," Claire and Jack said together.

Brianna grimaced, revealing a set of sparkling white, perfectly straight teeth. "That time of year already, huh?" She set the dog down and took the plates from Claire. They barely made a sound as she arranged them on the table. This irritating gracefulness must have come from Tanya, as

Claire couldn't even walk through the kitchen without rattling the china cabinet.

"Guess what?" Claire said conspiratorially as they crowded around the small, square table, folding paper napkins and laying cutlery.

"Luke proposed?" Brianna gasped and grabbed her left hand.

Claire laughed. "No, but he did get nominated for an Emmy."

Her sister let out a shriek. Jack dropped his wooden spoon and, with blinding speed, unstrapped the 9mm handgun he always wore on his ankle.

"Relax, Dad." Brianna grabbed Claire's hands and jumped. "This is huge! I'll send a congratulations gift basket. Is he a scotch or whiskey guy? Whiskey, right? Never mind, we can talk about it later. Tell me everything!"

Being around Brianna was like standing next to a ray of pure, comforting sunlight. Everything about her exuded life. Her skin glowed, her blue eyes sparkled, and she was tan despite it being mid-April. Her flip-flops, discarded by the door, were from Target. She flung her no-name purse on the back of a chair. Her chestnut-colored hair was drawn back into a simple ponytail, and she didn't have a stitch of makeup on. And still she was radiant. That bitch.

Dinner passed without incident, except for Rosie leaping onto an unoccupied chair and running off with a piece of garlic bread.

After finishing his spaghetti, Jack laid his fork down and cleared his throat.

"Claire, there is some family business we need to discuss."

Crash. All four of them jumped when Claire's fork fell out of her hand. She surveyed the scene and found red droplets littering the front of her sweater. Great, she had ruined her cashmere sweater.

"Daddy," Brianna warned.

Tanya, who had deigned to put on one of her iconic flowered muumuus for dinner, reached over and clutched her daughter's hand.

"Oh god, what is it? Are you sick?" Claire's hands clenched into tight fists. The blood chilled in her veins.

Jack shook his head. "No one is sick. Brianna, would you like to start?"

Brianna glared at her father and turned to Claire. "You know that new movie I wrapped up in the fall?"

"*Private Sarah*? With the badass lady soldier who joined the Union Army and dragged a ton of men off the field and saved their lives?"

"Yes. The premiere is scheduled for next month, and it's getting some attention that we didn't expect," Brianna said.

"What do you mean?"

"Attention from ESA," Jack interjected.

Claire froze. The napkin slid from her lap and puddled on the floor. Rosie scampered over and lay on top of it.

"You're being targeted?" The words felt like ice chips.

"Targeted might be too strong a word." Brianna smiled and flicked her ponytail over one shoulder, but the candles on the table quivered from her foot tapping on the floor.

"Threatening notes were sent to her fan mail PO Box," Jack said quietly.

"Bri." Tears welled in Claire's eyes. Was the room tilting? Her clammy hands fisted as she braced for impact.

"I'm not worried about it." Brianna reached over and grasped Claire's limp arm. "People send me threatening fan mail all the time. Just last week someone told me I was going to hell because of that scene in *Dumb Summer* where I ate a steak with my hands on a boat."

"I was hoping you could talk some sense into your sister," Jack interrupted, looking at Claire. "She refuses to get a bodyguard."

Brianna's cheeks flamed. "I don't need a bodyguard."

"What did the note say?" Claire interrupted. "Are you sure it was from ESA?"

"Women don't belong on a battlefield. Kill the movie before you end up like your sister," Jack quoted apparently from memory.

A shiver racked Claire's body.

"I'm not killing the movie," Brianna said, stacking her plate on top of her father's and taking them to the sink. "It's a powerful story that deserves to be told. I'm not going to let some dummies intimidate me."

"It was a Los Angeles postmark, so it's not any branch of ESA we've dealt with so far," Jack said quietly.

"Can the FBI do anything?" Claire asked. The initial shock had worn off.

"My task force is investigating, but I'm not convinced we'll find anything." He rubbed the spot where an ESA brother had shot him the previous summer. "There are four million people in that city. It would take a miracle to track down the sender."

Claire pursed her lips and leaned back in her chair. "Great. I'm glad our tax dollars are being wisely spent." Whatever energy she had before she came had been zapped by this conversation.

"There's one other thing too." He glanced uneasily at Tanya.

Awesome. What were the odds that the "one more thing" was he was planning to buy a family beach house? Though

36

if Jack was buying, it was more likely to be a tactical nuclear bunker.

"I—" he stopped.

Claire and Bri exchanged a worried look before. Jack had never been lost for words before. What was he about to divulge? The suspense was killing her.

Tanya cleared her throat. "Your father thinks it's his fault."

"What's his fault?" Brianna narrowed her eyes.

"He thinks ESA is targeting our family because he's in charge of the task force." Tanya's voice was barely above a whisper.

Claire's heart leapt into her throat. She had always assumed ESA was pissed at her because she had put one of their members in prison. And then of course they had used her for their heinous training program for new recruits. But did it go even deeper than that? Were they punishing Jack for trying to take them down?

It was almost a relief to have someone else to blame.

"My partner's daughters also received some threats. They're not the type usually targeted by the group, so we know it's personal. I'm sorry." He had found his voice at last.

"It's not your fault," Brianna piped up. "Scumbags will always be scumbags." She smiled, but it didn't reach her eyes.

Claire bit her lip. What was she supposed to do with this new information? If ESA was targeting Brianna, it was only a matter of time before they crept back into her life. She had been responsible for shutting down an entire branch of their organization, after all. She was a dead woman walking. It wasn't over. It was *never* going to be over.

"We want you to have these," Tanya said. She reached

under the table and drew out two midnight blue velvet bags. *Thunk.* The mystery contents must have been heavy.

"Crystals—uh, helpful as they may be—" Jack said with a glance at Tanya, "are no replacement for a bodyguard."

Brianna sighed.

"Did you tell Charlie your concerns?" Claire blurted out.

He shook his head. "She won't take my calls."

"I guess I'll pass along the message." Claire stood up from the table. Charlie was likely to be unfazed, but Alice was going to flip shit. It was time to leave before he could divulge anything else that would permanently threaten her blended family fantasy.

After half a dozen prayers of protection from Tanya, Brianna and Claire were released. They staggered down the driveway, weighed down by a pound of vegan spaghetti apiece and their bags of mystery crystals.

"Hey," Claire began, searching the fence line for an enemy that probably wasn't there. But now that Brianna was being targeted, she couldn't be too careful. "I know Jack is being a little intense about the whole bodyguard thing. But you really should consider it. I think you know how big of a deal this is. ESA isn't some crazy fourteen-year-old who's in love with you. They're organized, they're connected. If they want you, they will try to take you. I had a police officer tailing me most of the time, and a single sociopath all by himself was able to kidnap me. You need to keep yourself safe. If not for you, then for us."

Brianna sighed and leaned against her car, head tilted toward the sky as though she were looking to the stars for answers. She pulled a cigarette from her purse and lit it in the darkness, sparks from the lighter illuminating her face. Suddenly her younger sister seemed years older. The sunshine was gone, replaced by a world-weary woman just trying to get through the day.

"I thought you quit." Claire helped Rosie into the back seat. She would never expose her tiny lungs to secondhand smoke.

"I did. Then I got the letter."

Claire approached and laid a hand on her shoulder. The smoke tickled her throat. "I know that hiring someone means admitting that all of this is real. That you're in real danger. I know how tempting it is to keep pretending like everything's normal. Hire a bodyguard. Please. Don't make it easy for them."

Brianna sighed, exhaling a long, thin stream of smoke. Not even Mark Jacobs could cover up the casino bathroom smell. "I will. As soon as I get back."

"Good. I'll be in LA in a couple of weeks for Brad's proposal. I'll visit. I love you." Claire leaned in and squeezed her sister, praying that it wouldn't be the last time.

She shuffled those thoughts to the back of her mind as she got in her car and began to pull a three-point turn. As she passed her sister, she rolled the window down.

"And throw those away," she said sternly, gesturing to the pack of cigarettes. "It's gross, and you're better than that."

"Yes, Mom." Brianna smiled for the first time since dinner.

CHAPTER FOUR

To Do:
- Background check on Nicole's obstetrician
- Call ice cream shop
- Review West Coast applicants

Dinner with her father had left Claire in a heightened state of stress. She had woken up that morning in the walk-in closet, one leg in a pair of Luke's cargo shorts while carrying a footlong dill pickle. If she wasn't careful, the sleepwalking was going to get out of hand again.

The air conditioning in the corner of the warehouse cranked noisily. It was only ten a.m., but the temperature had already hit the eighties.

Claire gripped the edge of the whiteboard and flipped it over, revealing notes on the upcoming Los Angeles proposal. Less than five weeks separated them for what promised to be the biggest, splashiest project of their entire career. That needed to be her focus; not whatever retaliation may or may not be coming from ESA.

"Did we get a response from the city about the permit?" She held her breath.

Mindy smirked. "Yes, as of this morning, we officially have a permit."

All the breath rushed out of her lungs. "You should have led with that. Thank god."

Mindy slid a pen into her topknot and leaned forward. "I can't believe you convinced the city of Los Angeles to let you change the Hollywood sign."

Claire smiled. "Only for one evening. Well, until Brad inevitably changes his mind."

"Brad," Mindy muttered with a groan.

"I'm going to start adding an extra dollar to our hourly consulting fee every time he alters the plan."

Much like the groom-to-be, every part of the proposal had been a colossal pain in the ass.

Brad was Claire's first (and if things continued to be this vexing, only,) non-local client. He had hounded her and the business for months following her kidnapping, offering larger and larger sums of money. She had only given in because he was Luke's friend. But his proposal grew more elaborate every day. Normally a proposal fit neatly into one three-ring binder. Brad's spanned six.

His bride-to-be was Karen Rager, a forty-year-old accountant for a Los Angeles hospital. Despite the memefication of her first name, she was a sweet, level-headed, lovely woman who ran charity 5ks and volunteered for Habitat for Humanity. It would be a second marriage for both of them. She grounded Brad, a fifty-year-old movie producer.

"It still bothers me that we couldn't observe them on a

date," Claire muttered. Happily Ever Afters had a rigid screening process involving intense social media stalking, sweeping for online dating profiles, background checks, and more. Being three thousand miles away from their latest couple had forced her to compromise.

Mindy whipped the pen out of her hair and chucked it at Claire. "Hey. Not everyone is a serial killer. Luke vetted him. You trust Luke, remember?"

"Yeah, yeah. So let's go over the order one more time. First, lunch at the restaurant where they had their first date."

"Check. Solar Flare. Pre-planned four-course lunch. They'll be the only ones on the outer deck of the restaurant. The chef confirmed the menu last week."

Claire put a checkmark next to Solar Flare on the whiteboard. "Great. Then, a limo ride to the Santa Monica Pier, where they will play Skee-Ball and then ride the Ferris wheel, where the bucket truck containing the a cappella quartet will serenade them at the top."

Mindy smiled broadly and clasped her hands. "Amazing. Then the gardens with the ice cream cones?"

"Yes, then they'll go to the Getty Gardens where an associate will deliver the absurdly expensive and obscure ice cream from Karen's hometown in New Jersey."

"And by an 'associate,' you mean you?"

"Probably," Claire conceded.

"Great. Then the horses?"

Claire nodded and pointed to the board. "I'm guessing the Los Angeles traffic will make the trip to the ranch excruciatingly long, which is why they'll be in the limo with a bottle of champagne and Karen's favorite movie."

"You really think she won't be suspicious with all this

trouble?" Mindy lifted her eyes from her tablet. One brow arched skyward.

Claire shrugged. "It's their dating anniversary, and Brad has a long history of over-the-top dates."

"'Kay. So, the horses," Mindy prompted again.

"Yes. They will then have a horseback ride through the hills of Los Angeles, culminating in their arrival at the base of the Hollywood sign at sunset where Brad will propose, surrounded by their friends and family and a lovely catered dinner. The props company we contacted sent confirmation that the letters are finished. They are each fifty feet tall, solar-powered and self-lit, not to mention insanely expensive. They will be dropping them in front of the existing Hollywood letters by helicopter on the evening of the proposal."

Mindy let out a low whistle. "This is insane."

"I know, right?" Claire whispered. Brad's proposal was already quadruple the cost of any they'd done before.

"So basically," Mindy said slowly, "the number of things that could go wrong is exponential."

"Exactly."

"Got it. Starting a new document for contingency plans." Mindy tapped on her tablet, then looked up. "What about backup transportation? You know, in case the limo breaks down or there's traffic gridlock?"

Claire pressed her lips together. If that happened, she would murder someone. "I reached out to a private helicopter tour company. I'm still waiting on the quote, though I don't think Brad will care what it is."

"I'm surprised he didn't suggest a helicopter himself."

"Same. Don't mention it to him. We're going to need a hell of a vacation after this. I wonder how long of a flight it is from LAX to Maui."

Mindy flipped the cover on her tablet shut. "You haven't taken a single vacation since we started the company."

"I know."

Aside from a few long weekend trips, Claire hadn't really taken any time off in a very long time. She had a million excuses—business was booming, her clients needed her. But really it was the stillness that she couldn't tolerate. As her new therapist had so helpfully pointed out, she had always thrown herself into work to avoid what was going on in her personal life.

She worked long hours in the early days of Happily Ever Afters to ignore the fact that her relationship with her fiancé was crumbling. She plowed through Nicole's proposal with singular determination after Jason cheated on her at her awards ceremony. Even focusing on Barney's proposal helped her forget that she had had to cancel her wedding.

Brad was annoying, but he certainly did a great job of distracting her from the trauma of the past year. As long as she kept moving, the ghosts of her past left her alone. But in the stillness, she was vulnerable. Nightmares and intrusive thoughts reminded her she was never truly safe. ESA was still out there, and now they were targeting her sister.

"Don't you have an appointment?" Mindy asked, glancing at the large, rustic-styled clock on the wall.

"I don't think—oh. Therapy." Claire deflated. Speak of the devil. "I guess I better get going. Come, Rosie."

She had conceded to therapy after developing a dangerous sleepwalking habit that culminated in her driving five miles while unconscious and spray-painting the side of a fraternity house full of homicidal misogynists. Sawyer, Mindy's boyfriend, had offered the services of his mother, Dr. Bernice Goulding. The sleepwalking hadn't entirely gone away, but at least it hadn't gotten worse.

"Mindfulness, girl," Mindy teased as Claire walked down the long aisle full of proposal props they stored, shuffling around a replica of the Eiffel Tower.

Claire groaned.

CHAPTER FIVE

To Do:
- *Fine tune presentation for bank meeting*
- *Impact statement!!*
- *Take donations to shelter*

"How do you feel when you finish a proposal?" Dr.
Goulding leaned back in her armchair and took a sip of
herbal tea. A bright pink blouse popped against her ebony
skin.

Her Ivy League doctorate hung on the wall, and it was
just the slightest bit crooked. There was a level on the multi-
tool in Claire's purse, but something told her Dr. Goulding
wouldn't appreciate the gesture.

Claire plastered a smile on her face. "Happy, of course. I
love bringing people together. That's why I made it my life's
work."

Why was she sinking so much time into therapy? She

could have been working on Brad's proposal this whole time. An hour wasted.

"And when everything is packed up, the couple's gone, and your work is finished, how do you feel then?"

Claire paused for a beat.

"Motivated to start working on the next proposal?" That probably should have been a confident reply rather than a question.

"You don't like to be still," the doctor observed. She looked too young to be the mother of a nearly thirty-year-old man. She swept her cornrows over one shoulder and shoved her cat-eye glasses back up the bridge of her nose.

"I like to keep busy," Claire conceded.

"Do you ever take a moment to be still? To stay in the moment, to appreciate what's happening around you?"

"I do yoga." She huffed. While listening to audiobooks about business management, but Dr. Goulding didn't need to know that.

"Mindfulness, Claire." The doctor capped her pen. "That's part of your homework for the coming week. You're living too much in the future. You're borderline obsessed with planning, with creating. All admirable skills for a business owner, and understandable considering your history. But you also need to learn to be okay when your plans don't come to fruition. You need to learn to look around, take a deep breath, and appreciate the moment."

"How do you want me to do that?"

"Get some drinks with your friends. Have a date night with Luke. Get in your car and drive somewhere you've never been. Or just do something spontaneous, something that feels very un-Claire. Wherever it is, whatever you're doing, don't think about the future. Don't think about the embarrassing thing you did in the grocery store—"

"I told you that in confidence!"

Dr. Goulding smiled. "Don't be bound by the cloudiness of your future or the hurt in your past. Just live, Claire."

Claire wrinkled her nose. This was the kind of advice she'd expect to get from her nude stepmother.

"And now, to completely contradict myself, we also need to talk about what's happening tomorrow. And on Thursday."

"Do we have to?"

"This is therapy. I wouldn't be doing my job if we didn't at least talk about it. You have a meeting with the bank tomorrow?"

Claire exhaled noisily. "Yes. We're trying to get a small business loan to help out with the cost of expanding."

"How does it make you feel to borrow that kind of money?"

She clutched a hand to her chest as her heart beat a staccato rhythm beneath her palm. "Awful. It feels reckless and irresponsible. My heart's pounding just thinking about it. But it's necessary. At least the analyst we hired thinks so."

Dr. Goulding leaned forward. "And what will you accomplish with the money?"

"Expand. Try things on the West Coast."

"And why now, after so much success in West Haven, are you interested in doing business three thousand miles away? In one of the most expensive cities in the world?"

Claire crossed her arms. "I thought you were on my side."

The doctor smiled. "I am. I'm trying to prepare you for questions the bank may have."

"Oh. Right. Well, I'm going to give the bank the numbers-and-projections speech. But I'm sure you're more interested in the emotional component."

Dr. Goulding nodded. "Go on."

"I think…" It was weird to even say this out loud. "I think I might be spending more time on the West Coast in the future. Charlie and Brianna are both out there. And Luke spends a lot of time there too. I don't like the idea of spending weeks and weeks away from him while he has to be at the studio. If I'm going to be out there anyway, I might as well be working."

The doctor smiled. "You're factoring Luke into your future. That's really nice to see."

"Yeah, well. As long as he doesn't dump me for my nemesis. Anyway, all of those emotional factors plus the potential for exposure and business growth kind of cemented the idea." She narrowed her eyes. "Is it totally crazy?"

Dr. Goulding's mouth twitched. "We try to avoid that adjective in the field of psychology."

Claire grimaced. "Right. Sorry. Is it irrational, then?"

Dr. Goulding shook her head. "I'm not a business consultant, but you've built a strong company. You are organized, disciplined, and diligent. Sometimes you have to take a risk in order to grow. Risks are scary, but they can lead to amazing things. I have faith in you."

"Thank you." Claire leaned back. As much as she hated to admit it, the crushing weight that had rested on her shoulders when she came in might have lightened by a couple of ounces. Maybe there was something to therapy after all.

"So. Thursday," Dr. Goulding prompted.

Damn it. She had almost forgotten. Claire frowned.

"Sawyer mentioned that Barney will be accepting a plea deal," the doctor continued.

Claire crossed her arms. "Isn't it unethical to discuss clients with your children?"

The doctor set her teacup down on the coffee table with a rattle. "He told me because he suspected you wouldn't. How do you feel about the plea deal?"

Claire inhaled deeply and made eye contact with the ceiling. She gripped an accent pillow with a pug on it and held it to her chest.

"To be honest, I feel betrayed. I've been trying not to think about it because the best-case scenario is Barney gets ten years in prison. Worst-case scenario is maybe five. And that doesn't take into account a year of time served. He took so much from me, and it feels like the justice system is failing."

Dr. Goulding nodded. "Ten years is not a lot of time."

"It isn't. In ten years, I hope to be married, maybe have a mini-Claire or two. How can I bring a child into this world knowing that that monster is still out there?" She gestured at the window, where a beady-eyed pigeon bobbed his head. "Not to mention that when I get married—if I get married— I'll officially fit the West Haven Widowmaker's criteria. What's to stop him from trying to kill me again? From hurting my husband or my children? And then the fact that he's not working alone—"

Wait. ESA was strictly need-to-know information. Her father would blow a gasket if she talked about ESA in a room that hadn't even been swept for bugs.

"There's a lot to be worried about," the doctor said. Her voice was like aloe vera. "How do you feel about facing him in court? Have you started working on your statement?"

Claire shrugged. "Facing him doesn't scare me as much anymore after my visit to him in prison." The FBI had pressured her into visiting Barney. As uncomfortable as it was, it had led to the recovery of Kayley Herrold's body.

"It makes me physically ill to look at him, to see the evil in his eyes and remember that night, but it's not as scary as it used to be," she added.

Dr. Goulding nodded and was silent.

Claire gripped the pillow harder. "As for the impact statement, I have sat down at my laptop half a dozen times the last couple days, looking for the words. How do you even begin to explain the 'impact' he's had on my life? And he'll be there when I read it. He loves rehashing his crimes. I don't want him to get some sort of sick pleasure from it."

The doctor's eyebrows knit together. "A victim impact statement is meant to be a way for you to show how the crime and the perpetrator have affected your life. He'll be there to hear it, yes, but he's not your audience. You're telling the judge how this has changed your life. Usually victims talk about how they have changed emotionally, financially. What did his actions cost you?"

Claire bit her lip and set her gaze on the window. The pigeon stared inquisitively back at her. In truth, Barney had nearly cost her everything. At the most superficial level, he had taken her one-of-a-kind wedding dress and her business reputation. Panties from her hamper. Her sense of security, faith in the basic good of humankind, her belief in herself. He had almost taken her life. He took what he wanted with no mercy or remorse. But he wasn't going to get away with it. She would write the damn thing, and she would land him in prison for as long as possible. And he would be there to see it.

Dr. Goulding glanced at the clock on the wall. "I'm afraid our time's up for the day. I'm more than happy to schedule another session before the hearing if you think it'll be useful."

Claire shook her head and jumped up. "I'll be fine. Thanks, Doctor."

When the door snapped shut behind her, Claire leaned against it and took a deep breath. All she had to do was take out a massive business loan, pull off the biggest proposal of her career, take down a ring of serial killers, and stare into the eyes of the man who tried to murder her. Easy peasy.

CHAPTER SIX

To Do:
- Pick up donuts for bank meeting
- Remember to breathe

CLAIRE EXITED THE DOORS OF FIRST FINANCIAL BANK ON Tuesday afternoon and ripped her blazer off. Adrenaline still sizzled through her.

Mindy collapsed onto the concrete stairs.

"I can't believe we did it." Claire sat down heavily beside her.

"One hundred thousand dollars." Mindy's skin was paler than usual. She clutched her stomach. "What the hell were we thinking?"

Claire blew out the breath she had been holding for half an hour. "We have to trust the analyst. Just think about what this will do for the business. A new branch, a West Coast rep. Exposure, growth, even more joyful couples."

"I have to text Sawyer," Mindy said, sitting up and pulling her phone out of her designer handbag.

Claire grunted as her stomach twisted.

Mindy's thumbs hesitated. She stared at Claire. "Don't tell me you didn't tell Luke."

"Of course I didn't tell him. He's going to be pissed that I didn't ask him first."

Mindy shielded her eyes from the sun with one hand. "Why didn't we ask him first? We would have gotten a way better interest rate. You could have leveraged blow jobs for a zero percent APR."

Claire wrinkled her nose. "I'm not going to take my boyfriend's money. I'm doing this on my own. We're doing it on our own," she clarified, gesturing between the two of them. "Happily Ever Afters is our baby. Besides, if he owned a stake in the company, he would start trying to boss me around and change the proposals. You remember the Barney incident."

Mindy raised one eyebrow. "Doesn't he do that already? And didn't you guys recently have a big conversation about the importance of honesty?"

Claire sighed and pulled out her phone. A text from her groomer appeared onscreen. "Yeah, yeah. I'll tell him tonight. I better go—Rosie's done at the groomers. Apparently she almost took one of the technician's arms off during the nail trim."

"Sounds about right. See you tomorrow morning?" Mindy stood and dusted off the back of her pantsuit.

"Yeah, see you at nine. Bring the binder with the LA applicants, please. I need to take another look before we set interviews."

Claire stood and walked to her car. Her purse was weighed down with a manila envelope full of loan details. It might as well have been an anchor. A one-hundred-thou-sand-dollar anchor.

Twenty minutes later, a freshly groomed Rosie panted happily in the back seat of Claire's new Audi SUV. Her little black convertible had been set on fire the previous year by ESA, so she had opted for a more business-friendly model. Rosie seemed to enjoy the extra cargo space.

"One stop before home, RoRo," Claire said as she swung into the parking lot of Tender Hearts Animal Rescue. She had adopted Rosie from the rescue almost two years ago. Rosie leapt out beside her.

Claire popped the hatch open and slung a forty-pound bag of dog food over her shoulder. The weight nearly knocked her into the gravel. She wrestled the front door open, and she and Rosie entered the building.

"Gloria? Sam?" Claire called out. No one sat at the reception desk. It must be dinnertime. She let the bag of food hit the floor with a *thunk* and popped open the door that led to the kennels.

A wiry-haired woman wearing overalls and gold hoop earrings set a bowl of kibble on the floor of a large kennel and turned around.

"Claire! Good to see you. You're just in time for the field romp."

"I wish I could stay," Claire said, glancing at her watch. She had an uncomfortable dinner with Luke to look forward to. "I just stopped by to drop off some food and towels. And to visit, of course," she said, poking a finger through a kennel. A three-legged boxer licked her. Rosie play bowed to him, stump of a tail wiggling.

"Thank you so much. We always appreciate the donation. We won't need any more, though."

Claire turned around so fast she got a crick in her neck.

"What do you mean you don't need any more?" Tender Hearts was a nonprofit. They subsisted almost entirely on donations.

Gloria sighed and propped another kennel door open. Rosie rushed inside to greet her favorite shelter friend, a blind pug named Winston. "We're closing down at the end of the month."

The bottom fell out of Claire's stomach. "Why? What happened?"

Gloria and her wife, Sam, had run the animal rescue as long as Claire had lived in West Haven. The shelter was always full of special needs animals and other unwanted cats, dogs, and birds.

Gloria stared into the eyes of a dachshund in a wheelchair. "We lost our main benefactor. We held on as long as we could, but it's the end of the road."

Claire drew herself up to her full height of five feet and three inches. "Who was your benefactor? I will personally go speak to them and convince them to continue supporting you."

"That wouldn't be a good idea," Gloria said as she dumped a scoop of food into another bowl.

"Why not?"

Gloria slowly turned around and raised her eyes to Claire's. "It was Barney Windsor."

The name hit her like a bullet. She staggered backward until she hit the wall. Her fingers fanned out over her breastbone. Her heart was galloping again. Was there any aspect of her life that Barney hadn't ruined?

"Barney was your benefactor?" The words barely tumbled out over her numb lips. Barney was selfish and ruthless. He had even admitted to killing animals as a child.

Why in the hell was he supporting the shelter? Was it just a tax write-off for Heirloom Hotels?

Gloria nodded. A flush had crept into her cheeks. "Apparently he set up the trust as an engagement gift to his ex-fiancée. But his assets were frozen after he went to prison, and we've slowly been running out of money."

Claire's stomach knotted. It was her fault. Well, technically it was Barney's fault. But she was the reason he was behind bars. She locked eyes with the blind Winston. What would happen to the animals?

Gloria smiled kindly. "It's not your fault. I can't believe a serial killer was financing our operation. Not a great PR situation. But it'll be okay. A few of the animals will be adopted by then. They won't all have to go to the shelter."

"The shelter?"

Gloria nodded. The chance of a special needs animal being adopted from a catch-all shelter was incredibly low. They would be first on the euthanasia list when the shelter filled up. Her ears rang like someone had just blasted a car horn. What could she do?

"I'm going to help set this right. I'll put together a benefit for the rescue. You can't close." Claire grabbed Gloria's hand.

"If we don't figure something out in the next two weeks, we won't have a choice." Gloria's eyes were red, and she seemed tired. She normally had the energy of a woman twenty years her junior.

Rosie trotted out of the kennel. Winston attempted to follow her but banged into the cage door.

"I'll take him." The words were out before she had even registered them.

Gloria looked up at her. "You want Winston?"

"Yes. Today, if possible." She couldn't save all the dogs. But she could save Winston. And besides, a friend for Rosie had been on her mind since moving to Luke's. It was such a big house, and they both worked a lot. How mad could Luke be? And more importantly, who could say no to that sweet face?

"I'll draw up the paperwork." Gloria walked to the front office.

Whoops.

CHAPTER SEVEN

To Do:
- New dog toys
- Throw together fundraising for shelter—gala?
- Caterer quotes for Brad

"I CAN EXPLAIN." CLAIRE DUMPED SHOPPING BAGS IN THE foyer. A new dog bed and a handful of toys tumbled onto the tile. Rosie skittered into the kitchen, Winston a couple of steps behind.

Claire approached Luke slowly, a bag of lo mein dangling from one wrist like a peace offering. Her stomach tightened into a ball. He couldn't be that mad. It was a blind pug, for Pete's sake, not a tiger.

"Who's this?" There was curiosity but also a hint of exasperation in Luke's voice. He ducked down to offer a hand to Winston.

The dog sniffed him apprehensively, then sat on his butt.

His head cocked to one side, and he allowed some head pats.

Claire took a deep breath. Might as well rip it off like a Band-Aid. "This is Winston. I kind of adopted him today."

Luke raised his eyebrows, then his mouth hardened into a line. "Claire, we talked about this. You can't buy a dog every time you have a bad day."

She narrowed her eyes. It was one time, and she had never *actually* gone to Wisconsin to get Rosie's biological cousin. "That's not it, I promise. I may be responsible for Tender Hearts Animal Rescue getting shut down."

He raked a hand over his face, then leaned against the kitchen island, arms folded over his broad chest. Winston, apparently annoyed that the attention had stopped, rolled over onto his back and exposed his belly, tongue hanging out the side of his mouth.

"And how exactly did you manage to do that? Did you sleepwalk there and steal all the dogs? Are there more outside?"

She raised her hands in front of her. "Just Winston, I promise. I talked to Gloria today when I was dropping off the food, and she said they have to shut down next month. Their benefactor is no longer supporting them. They're out of money."

"Well, that's bullshit. Who was their benefactor?"

"I'll give you a hint. He stabbed me last year."

Luke swore. "You're telling me that homicidal asshole funded a bunch of disabled pets? I'm not buying it."

She shrugged. "Apparently it was an engagement gift for Victoria. I guess his assets are frozen because of the investigation. Which means it's all my fault that these dogs are destined for a catch-all shelter where they'll inevitably be euthanized to make room for pets with the correct number of legs."

She turned away from Luke and sniffled. Her eyes watered, but she refused to cry. Barney was responsible for too many of her tears already. He had pretty much gotten away with stabbing her, but she was *not* going to allow him to send these pets to their doom.

Something tapped impatiently on the tile behind her. The wheels were already turning in Luke's brain. "How much do they need to stay open? I have some money put away that I was planning on using for a vacation for us."

She swiped a hand under each eye and turned back to face him. "I can't even imagine you on vacation."

"Right back at you. You'd be leading the tours by the end of the trip."

She ignored him. "I've decided to put together a charity event to benefit the rescue." She drew her arms tightly across her chest and turned to glance out the windows. The sun was setting. Shadows crept over freshly mowed grass. Winston got up and followed her, nearly bumping into the bar stool until Rosie nudged him in the correct direction. He sat on Claire's foot and panted happily.

Another sniffle escaped. There was so much on her plate, and so little time to do it. The hearing. Brad's proposal. Growing the business. And now the charity event. There were so many moving pieces, and if any of them failed, everything was going to collapse like a house of cards. There wasn't much time. She needed to get it together.

Luke tugged on her wrist and turned her around. She crumpled into him. "It's not your fault," he whispered against her hair.

"It kind of is," she said, voice muffled against the fabric of his T-shirt. The dread edged an inch away.

His fingers wound through her hair. "What kind of charity event are you thinking about?"

"Some combination of black tie, auction, and adoption event. If we could just train the dogs to serve hors d'oeuvres, we'd be in amazing shape. Do you think they make dog butler costumes?" She pulled back from the embrace and reached for her phone.

"I'm sure someone does. Is he blind?" Luke asked, eyeing Winston who was pawing at the coat rack.

Claire bit her lip. "Yeah. Most of the dogs at Tender Hearts are special needs. I'm sorry. I should have asked you if it was okay for me to bring him home." She sidled up next to him and put her hand on his arm. Did impulsively adopting a special needs dog count toward her mindfulness homework?

"I'll allow it. Once." He pulled her close and pressed himself to her. She yielded, opening her mouth as he kissed her deeply.

Crash. Something fell behind them, and they sprang apart. Claire grabbed the bag of Chinese and drew it over her shoulder like a shot put. If ESA had come to take her, they were about to be surprised by a face full of sweet and sour sauce. A quick sweep of the room revealed nothing amiss. She ducked around the corner of the island. A broom lay on its side. Winston huddled under the breakfast nook. A soft whimper escaped.

"Poor little guy," Luke said, picking him up. "Let me do some research. He'll be comfortable here in no time."

"I appreciate you." Claire snuck back in for another hug. Winston licked her cheek. Rosie whined at Claire's heels until she picked her up.

Luke grunted and kissed her again, more softly this time. Warmth ran up and down her like she was neck-deep in a hot tub. Shit. That was only one of the bombshells she needed to drop this evening. Maybe she should have led with the other one.

"There's something else I have to tell you."

"For fuck's sake. What now?"

"So Mindy and I went to the bank today. For Happily Ever Afters," she explained, turning away from him and walking to the fridge.

"Okay," he said slowly.

"And we took out a loan. For the business. To help with expanding out west."

There was silence. She pulled a bottle of wine out of the fridge and set it on the counter. Maybe some Côtes du Rhône could soften the blow. The storm in Luke's eyes had grown. Winston licked his chin.

"If you needed money, why didn't you just ask me?" There was danger in the growl of his voice.

She pulled two glasses out of the cabinet and poured the wine. "I didn't want to mix business up with this." She gestured between the two of them. "What if you dump me for a famous actress, and then I owe you a ton of money? Or what if I missed a payment and you started to resent me? And then you got some ideas from your true crime obsession and you started slipping cyanide in my wine?"

He glowered.

"I just needed this to be separate from us," she said hurriedly. "My own thing. Does that make sense?"

He drummed his fingers on the countertop. Winston panted happily on his lap. "How much did you borrow?"

Claire slid the full glass down the bar to him. "A hundred thousand dollars." She mumbled as softly and quickly as the words would escape her lips.

"How much?"

Damn it. "A hundred thousand dollars," she repeated. Her shoulders tensed, bracing for an explosion.

There was silence for another minute. Luke took a sip of wine. Claire took a sip of wine. Rosie whined. Was that the sound of blood rushing through her veins?

Luke cleared his throat. "I think it's a good idea. I've told you before you should think about expanding. But you should have asked me first."

Her grip on the wineglass tightened. "I don't need your permission to borrow money for my business."

He held up one hand. His posture was relaxed, not at all like he was going to throw a suitcase at her and send her packing. "Not like that. I just mean I could have helped. Fewer stipulations than a bank. Zero percent APR if you make Roy's empanadas recipe this week."

"Mindy said the same thing, only she suggested blowjobs as leverage."

"Mindy might be a business genius," Luke pondered.

Claire smiled. If he could joke about her stepfather's empanadas, surely he wasn't that mad. Thank god. "Thank you for understanding. I'm sorry for not telling you about it before. I'm going to make a conscious effort to be a better communicator." Dr. Goulding had been on her about it, anyway.

"How was your day?" she asked. "You seem grumpier than usual."

He sighed. "I really need to get out to LA. I had a conference with Streamster today and they're full steam ahead with setting up animators and someone to do the score. Someone's coming out here for photography at the end of the week."

"Holy crap." She pulled the containers of Chinese food

out and arranged them on the bar. "How do you feel about having all these other hands in the pot?"

He leaned back and his eyebrows scrunched together. "I don't like other people having a say in how I do things. Every frame of *Suburban Hustle* was mine. And the stakes are so much higher with this doc. I'm worried they're going to try to push for more Barney and less of the victims."

Claire crossed the kitchen and laid a hand on his arm. "Don't let them. You're the boss. This is your baby. And if you need me to scare them, you know I will."

"Are you going to pull an Alice and show up with a purse full of voodoo dolls and tarot cards?"

Claire's mother was a self-proclaimed psychic with her own television show and had been known to dabble in all elements of the psychic realm.

"You can't deny it's an effective tactic." She popped containers open and shoved her fork into some General Tso's.

They ate in silence, shoulders hunched and stewing in the mire of the day. Ready or not, Claire and Luke would both be in California in two weeks facing the biggest projects of their careers. Would this proposal propel her business to new heights, or would it be a disaster that would destroy everything she'd built in the last five years?

CHAPTER EIGHT

To Do:
- Research support for blind dogs
- Venues for gala
- Write statement!

"THIS IS INSANE," LUKE SAID, CRADLING WINSTON IN HIS LAP. Winston yipped, the sound reverberating in the warehouse.

Claire gave Luke the stink eye. This was why she didn't like to mix business and boyfriends. But alas, he was the best cameraman on the market. And Brad insisted on having the best.

"Sure, you thought about transportation for the couple," Luke continued, setting Winston down. Winston sniffed his way across the concrete floor and curled up next to Rosie in her dog bed. "But how are you going to ensure you'll be at the ranch in time? And the rest of the crew?" Luke leaned back in his chair and folded his arms behind his head. His eyebrows rose.

Claire and Mindy glanced at each other. Then they glanced at the whiteboard. Public transportation? It was one of the biggest cities in the country—there had to be systems in place to move those people around.

Luke tapped at his phone until a live traffic map of LA appeared on the flatscreen TV he had insisted on buying for reviewing his proposal videos. Red lines crawled across the screen like spider webs. "LA traffic is like nothing you've ever seen before. You're going to have to split up and have one of you in the hills and one of you handling all the downtown stuff. And you'll have to budget for at least one more cameraman. Frankly, this proposal is a huge risk. I'd give you an estimated success rate of twenty-five percent."

Claire threw her hands up. "He's your friend! This is what he wanted."

Luke stabbed a finger at the TV. "Your job as the proposal planner is to tell him what's possible. *This* is not possible. Did you at least get a private helicopter company for backup?"

She crossed her arms. "I'm still waiting to hear back from them."

He sighed. "Give me their contact information. I'll take care of it."

Grumbling, she thrust one of the six proposal binders splayed out in front of her at him. On second thought, maybe she should have beaten him with it. "You know I brought you here to consult on the videography, not to shoot holes in the whole proposal."

"Do you want the truth, or do you want warm fuzzies about the likelihood of finding eternal love in a second marriage?"

Claire's mouth dropped open. Mindy threw a marker across the conference table and hit Luke square in the forehead. "Brad and Karen scored a ninety on the compatibility test, they've dated for eight years and lived together for six of those, and neither one of them is a serial killer."

The toilet in the restroom flushed, and Nicole walked out looking green. Claire crossed to the small kitchenette and handed her a steaming mug of ginger tea and a packet of saltines.

"Did I miss anything?" Nicole collapsed into one of the swiveling conference chairs.

"Not really. We're going to need another videographer—two more, after I murder Luke—and we'll probably have to split up to make sure we cover all the bases in case of a transportation issue."

Luke might have been a pompous douchebag, but he knew LA better than they did.

Nicole groaned. "I better be vomiting less by the time the proposal comes around. This kid is trying to kill me." She splayed one hand over her still-flat belly.

Claire patted her back. "If you're not up to the trip, we can find someone else." It would compromise the artistic integrity of the entire proposal, but her nauseated friend didn't need to know that. There were more important things than business.

Nicole fervently shook her head. "I can handle it."

Luke glanced at his watch. "I have to go. I have a conference in half an hour." He bent over and kissed Claire on the cheek. "I'll take Winston and Rosie and let you know when the helicopter's taken care of."

"Thank you," she mumbled like a disgruntled child. She didn't need his help, but it wasn't worth the fight. She would figure out transportation alternatives for the crew. Plus the universe owed her. Surely it wouldn't smite the biggest proposal of her career.

"So he didn't kill you for bringing home a blind pug?" Mindy said as soon as the warehouse door swung closed.

"Surprisingly, no. He was more annoyed about us not asking him for the money. I probably could have adopted every animal in the shelter and filled the house to the rafters with cross-eyed cats and three-legged dogs. He seems really distracted with the documentary. I put on a French maid costume and walked around feather dusting his office for twenty-five minutes last night before he even noticed."

"What are you going to do about the shelter? Not that it's your job to save it, because it isn't. But I assume you have a plan?" Nicole munched on a cracker. Her color was returning to normal.

"I'm glad you asked. Who's up for a little pro bono work?" Claire pulled yet another binder from the bookcase behind them. She hit the stopwatch she was using to keep track of billable hours for Brad's proposal and added another hour to his total.

A flutter stirred her belly, and her heart rate inched up. There was so much to do, and now she was going to have to figure out alternative transportation for everyone. Was there enough time? Were they headed for failure, as Luke had suggested? She didn't need his negativity in her creative space.

Nicole set down her crackers and pulled out a notebook. Mindy tapped on her tablet.

"What do you need from us?" Nicole's pen was poised above the paper.

"Okay, so. The thing is...the gala is only nine days away."

Mindy choked on a sip of water. Nicole hammered her

on the back and raised her eyebrows. "Are you sure we have enough time?"

Claire shrugged. "I don't know, but I'm going to try. I can't just do nothing. Nicole, would you be willing to take some pictures of the shelter animals? Like this weekend? I'm thinking about making a calendar, but we have to put it together ASAP. Do people still buy wall calendars?"

"Sure they do," she said, scribbling some notes. "All three of us have one. Will there be costumes?"

"I think there has to be if we want people to buy them. And maybe we could tie in some local businesses and some tourism features of West Haven to get the Visitors Bureau interested. And make them pay for ad space."

"Genius." Mindy sputtered and walked over to the whiteboard. "Places first, then we can make the costume fit the location. What do we got?"

"Mario's Italian Restaurant," Claire said. "They have five Great Danes at home so they're definitely animal lovers."

Mindy pointed at her with the marker. "I love it. We'll dress up one of the dogs in a chef uniform in front of a bowl of spaghetti. Boom. Sawyer will definitely buy an ad too, so let's add Sanctum."

"Yee-Haw's," Nicole suggested. "Perfect for a Western-themed costume."

"Love it. Obviously the Rusty Rails. They have at least one game a season where you can bring your dog."

They kept going until they had twelve places that were likely to cooperate and four alternates.

Mindy capped the market and sat back down. "So in case this doesn't turn out to be a moneymaker, what are your other ideas?"

"A black-tie gala. Get local businesses to donate food,

auction items. Hundred bucks a plate, maybe more depending on what our expenses end up being."

Nicole nodded but Mindy frowned. "Where do you want to host this?"

"We have to go where the rich people are."

"The country club," Mindy decided. "Hopefully they won't have anything booked. I'll contact them. My uncle works there. I'll see if I can persuade him for a discounted rate or dig up some dark family secrets to threaten him with. Speaking of dark secrets, did you finish your thing for tomorrow, by the way?"

Claire flinched like she had been plunged into icy water. "No. I tried, but I have basically nothing."

"Go." Mindy jabbed a finger at the warehouse door. "You can't keep avoiding it."

"I'm not avoiding it." She was very much avoiding it. "I just don't know what to say."

"If you write it tonight, I'll take you to Sephora," Nicole offered.

Claire sighed. "Fine. I need new mascara anyway. Is there anything we need to discuss about Brad's proposal before I go? Luke's following up with the helicopter, I'll start working on the alternate transportation..." Was there something else she could bring up in order to delay?

"No. Go away. Love you," Mindy said, waving at her.

"I'll see you later," Claire grumbled.

She stepped into the afternoon sunshine. It was warm enough to take her sweater off. The sun beat down on her woefully pale skin. Green buds were starting to pop through the thin layer of mulch she had carefully spread around the warehouse the week before.

She stopped at the liquor store and bought her favorite

bottle of wine. If she was going to confront these feelings, she wasn't doing it without a drink in her hand.

Forty minutes later, she sat in her office with the door closed. There had been no sign of Luke and the dogs. Knowing Luke, he was probably pricing lumber to build custom doggie bunkbeds.

The cursor blinked on her computer screen, mocking her. What was there to say? She took another sip of wine and wrote *farts* on the first line, just to make sure the keyboard worked. Maybe she should blast it with that canned air just in case. In fact, her whole desk could stand to be wiped down. How could she write with a dirty desk?

An hour later, her desk and office were sparkling clean, and she hadn't written anything. She laid her head on her blotter and sighed. The wine was a quarter gone, and the blank screen was still staring at her.

How was she going to put this into words? What could she say about the man who stalked her, dressed her in her stolen wedding dress, and tried to kill her? She wasn't even allowed to talk about ESA because it wasn't relevant to the crime being charged.

Did she write about the little old lady she almost assaulted in the grocery store with a bag of frozen broccoli because her footsteps sounded just like Barney's? Or how she almost had a panic attack the first time she went into her parking garage after the abduction? How sometimes she swore she could smell his cologne in the middle of the night?

The thought of pulling up to the courthouse churned her stomach. Press was sure to be everywhere. They had hounded her for months after Barney abducted her, culminating in her climbing down her apartment's fire escape with Rosie just so she could pee. They were merciless in their pursuit of a story. Even with her friends and family accompanying her, climbing the steps to the courthouse was going to be almost as stressful as confronting Barney.

The cursor blinked. She pulled out her phone and called the first person she thought of.

"Everything okay?" Sawyer's rumbly voice poured out of the phone. He had been the one to find her the night of the abduction. If anyone could help her put that trauma into words, it was Sawyer.

"Yeah, no one's trying to murder me today. Not that I'm aware of, anyway. I'm trying to write my victim impact statement."

"Ah," he said. "How's it going?"

"It's not."

"I see." There was silence on the other end for a moment.

"You were there that night. And after, when things sucked. What do I say?"

Sawyer paused for a moment and seemed to consider his words carefully. "How about we make a list of questions, and then you can use that like a To Do list to write your answers?"

"Did your mom tell you to say that?" She should have known better than to call the son of her therapist for help.

"No, it's just how I usually approach things. I've testified a couple of times for work stuff. So one of the things they usually want to know is your recommendation for sentencing," he said.

"Oh, I have plenty of thoughts on that." She took another sip of wine and refilled her glass. "I think he should be sentenced to an eternity of sitting in a damp cave in a loincloth while a bunch of crabs pinch his feet and nipples for twenty-three hours a day."

"Damn. What happens the remaining hour of the day?"

"Mandatory calculus."

"You are a dangerous woman."

"You have no idea."

They talked for another half hour until she had a list to work from. All she had to do now was write a painful, emotional statement and pour her soul out in front of the maniac who tried to murder her.

Oh, and pick up her mother from the airport. The same mother who had nearly been arrested for trying to assault Luke's mom last time she had visited the West Haven courthouse.

And they would all be in the same car together.

Great.

CHAPTER NINE

To Do:
- *Emergency preparedness for LA*
- *Auction items for gala*
- *Pretend like hearing isn't happening*

"WHAT IS THAT SMELL?" LUKE'S MOTHER'S VOICE CUT LIKE A knife.

Rain pattered against the windshield as Claire glanced in the rearview mirror. Rachel was never one to mince words. There was a 200 percent chance she was complaining about Alice's perfume.

"Air freshener?" Luke grunted from the driver's seat. His knuckles were white on the steering wheel. Claire laid a hand on his thigh and squeezed.

The four of them had only been in the same car for twenty minutes since picking her mother up at the airport, and already Rachel and Alice had chided each other nearly to the point of Luke threatening to turn the car around. With the exception of a mercifully uneventful Thanksgiving, the last time Rachel and Alice had been in the same room was Barney's preliminary hearing, where Alice had been literally dragged out of the courtroom by the bailiff after verbally harassing Rachel.

Alice dug in her purse. "Is this the smell you're talking about?" She clutched a ziplock bag in one manicured hand and waved it under Rachel's nose. The car hit one of West Haven's infamous potholes, and Alice nearly shoved the bundle up Rachel's nostril.

Rachel recoiled as though the bag was full to the brim with Rosie's poo. She clutched a tissue to her face. "Yes, that's the smell. What is it?"

"Oh, it's just a cypress and lavender bundle."

Oh, boy. Shit, meet fan.

"What on earth do you use that for?" Rachel sounded as scandalized as if Alice had admitted to hoarding human cremains.

"This and that. Cleansing, evoking wisdom and calm."

Rachel scoffed. "Cleansing what?"

"Negative energy, of course. I didn't want to be rude, Rachel, but I believe you could really benefit from using some. Why don't you give this spray a try? It should help you let go of all that anger you're holding on to."

Alice held out a small spray bottle. Rachel didn't take it.

"I'm not holding onto any anger. Except perhaps at being in this car," she muttered, turning to glance out the window. She began tapping at her phone, as though she was going to call a Lyft in the middle of the highway.

Claire bit her lip. Things were getting a bit dicey. She didn't need the extra stress minutes before confronting the man who tried to kill her. Should she intervene? On the other hand, Rachel had represented Barney and publicly slandered her. Maybe she deserved to sweat in a car under Alice's watchful eye for a minute.

Claire dug through her purse for her phone. For once, no texts from Brad. She tucked it away, and her hand brushed against her victim impact statement in its sheet protector. Her chest tightened.

In the rearview mirror, Alice's face screwed up in concentration. Oh boy. That face either meant that she was trying to remember an obscure recipe for a tincture, or a member of the dead had come for a chat.

Alice set her baby blue eyes on Rachel. "He forgives you, you know. For the man from the convention. What was his name?" She raised her chin and paused, seemingly listening hard. "Skip."

Luke slammed on the brakes. They all lurched forward. "Sorry," he said after a moment. He lifted his foot from the pedal, and the car continued traveling west toward the courthouse. His eyes darted to the rearview mirror.

Skip? Who the hell was Skip? Claire glanced in the back seat. Rachel was as white as a ghost.

"Who told you that?" The pathologically cool and collected Rachel had a slight quaver in her voice. Alice tended to have that effect on people.

Alice placed the spray bottle on her lap. "He did. George. Lovely man."

Claire gripped Luke's thigh. George was Luke's deceased dad's name as well as his brother's.

"That's impossible," Rachel uttered.

"Nothing's impossible, Rachel. Like I said, he wants you to know that he forgives you." Alice paused and squinted again. She laughed, a strange sound in the tense atmosphere. "And the necklace you've been looking for is in a box marked 'George's Junk' in your basement. Next to the rocking horse you call Elvis."

Luke pulled to a stop at a red light. He and Claire exchanged a look. The courthouse was a couple of blocks ahead. The world's most awkward car ride was nearly at an end.

Rachel released her seat belt. "I believe I'll walk the rest of the way." She popped open the door and shimmied between their car and the one behind them. Stepping onto the sidewalk, she marched toward the courthouse as if she was going to battle.

"Ah, at least she took the spray," Alice said with a smile. "Poor dear."

Claire made a mental note to grill Luke about the Skip situation as soon as the hearing was over. Did Rachel have an affair? Was that why Luke's parents had divorced? She had never thought to ask, and Luke wasn't exactly forthcoming with his family drama.

The disastrous car ride was so distracting that she had nearly forgotten why they were traveling in the first place. The courthouse rose out of the fog. Evil waited inside, and she was going to have to face it head-on today. Even at this distance, the press was clearly visible crawling over the courthouse steps.

As soon as they turned into the parking lot, her stomach churned. A crowd of reporters crushed around them, their interest in Claire seemingly reinvigorated by the sentencing hearing. Her hand was halfway to her nose, primed for alternate nostril breathing, when she stopped and clenched it into a fist. Although the windows were tinted, they were definitely not dark enough to prevent the press from seeing her doing weird yoga stuff.

When Luke opened the driver's side door, the noise was

deafening. Alice reached forward from the back seat and gripped Claire's shoulder. She seemed to be muttering a prayer under her breath. Luke opened Alice's door, then Claire's.

He and her mother flanked Claire like a pair of soldiers. She ducked her head as the paparazzi swarmed, shouting questions from every direction. Raindrops plopped heavily onto her head and shoulders. She reached into her bag and pulled out her travel umbrella. There was barely enough room in front of her to open it. Where was Sawyer, her personal security detail, when she needed him?

"Out of the way. FBI."

The crowd parted down the middle. Jack Hartley's salt-and-pepper hair was molded perfectly into place as he marched over to the car.

"Tanya's inside already, but she wants to see you before the hearing. Ready?" he asked. Claire nodded and accepted the arm he held out. Luke took her other one, and the three of them surged through the crowd toward the courthouse. Claire glanced over her shoulder to be sure her mother hadn't been swallowed up by the press. Alice trailed behind, strategically banging her elbows into the more aggressive camera wielders.

A couple of feet in, the path widened dramatically in front of them.

"Move," a commanding female voice called. One of the reporters in front of Claire sidestepped and revealed one of her former couples—Tyler, a disabled army veteran, and his new fiancée, Ericka. They both held riot shields. Tyler's prosthetic legs clicked as he walked toward Claire.

"Claire," Tyler said, smiling at her before taking a position in front of her.

"Tyler! What are you—"

"Back off, you big lutz," a New Jersey accent interrupted from somewhere nearby.

"Ouch," a reporter called, and a very tan couple appeared in front of Tyler and Ericka.

Steve, another former client who had proposed to his girlfriend via Jet Ski the previous spring, held a boogie board in front of him, and his fiancée, Cassie, clutched an oversized tote bag like a battering ram.

"Hey, Claire," he said as calmly as though they had run into each other outside a local café.

She gaped at them. "What are you guys doing here? Aren't you getting married like—"

"This weekend." Cassie nodded and turned to the crowd in front of her. Raindrops came down on both of them, but neither moved to pull out an umbrella. Claire made a mental note to send their congratulations card out when she got home. "We weren't about to let the media make mince-meat out of you. Not after everything you did for us. I said *get outta here*," she demanded, shoving her purse directly into a camera. "Oh, and put this on." She pulled a scarf out of her purse and tossed it to Claire.

"What is it?" The fabric was shiny.

"Jane made it for you. It's high contrast apparel, so if the paparazzi use a flash, it'll blur your face. She and Aaron wanted to be here, but Jane had an exhibition in New York."

Jane was a talented painter. Her proposal video had gone viral, and Aaron wrote to Claire several months later to tell her that Jane was getting offers from galleries all over the country.

"I didn't realize you all knew each other." Claire tilted her head and ducked under a boom microphone.

"We didn't," Aaron said. "We connected online after you were abducted. We wanted to do something nice for you, but we couldn't agree on anything. That's why we're here."

Claire smiled and obediently wound the scarf around her neck. Between her FBI father, scowling boyfriend, and the four people wielding various objects in front of her, their path to the courthouse immediately became more manageable.

Déjà vu hit her like a Mack truck as she reached the building's exterior stairs. Everything felt exactly the same as it had on the day of the preliminary hearing. Climb the flight of steps to the front doors, pray that the metal detector inside didn't erase any of her proposal notes, hope her mother didn't try to bring any voodoo dolls or other questionable objects inside. As long as she thought of each step as an item on a To Do list, she could survive.

This time, instead of being sequestered, Claire was allowed to enter the courtroom. Her former couples broke off from the crowd with handshakes and hugs. They filed into one of the rows. Tanya pounced on her immediately and was, thankfully, wearing clothes today. Her tie-dyed romper and Birkenstocks were not conventional court attire, but for some reason, the sight of her zany stepmother was like a salve.

"Claire, you are an amazing, strong, beautiful goddess. Everything will be fine. How was your leftover spaghetti?" She clutched her hand like the outcome of her entire day depended on Claire's assessment.

Alice wrinkled her nose. Apparently Tanya's new role in Claire's life was getting under her skin.

"Uh, it was great," Claire said. "Luke enjoyed it too. Didn't you?" It wasn't really the time to talk about pasta, but maybe she was just offering a distraction.

"Hmm?" he asked. He had been scanning the front of

the courtroom. "Right. Yeah. I didn't even know you could make meat sauce without the meat. It was very convincing. We'd better go take our seats."

Alice managed a handshake with Tanya before whisking Claire away to a different row.

Kyle's growing bald spot was visible behind the counselor's desk. Mindy was already sitting in a row, tapping away at her tablet. Her raven-colored hair was gathered into a low bun. Sawyer's hulking shape sat next to her. Rachel was in the row behind them, as rigid as a two-by-four.

And there, in the front row, was Barney's mother. She was alone, head bowed. A woman defeated. No matter how this day ended for Claire, it would be worse for her. Her only son, a murderer. A chill ran down Claire's spine.

"Where's Coli?" she asked as Alice rushed to embrace Mindy. Focusing on Barney's mother wouldn't do her mental health any good.

"Bathroom," Mindy grunted through one of Alice's legendary bone-crushing hugs.

Claire sat on the worn wooden bench and pulled her purse onto her lap. She removed a binder, her victim impact statement, a roll of poo bags, a pen case, and a scrap of her wedding dress that she had brought for inspiration before finding a sleeve of saltine crackers. She bent forward and gestured at Kyle before tossing the crackers to him.

"Thank you for coming," she said to Mindy with a quicker and gentler hug than her mother had offered.

"Like I would miss the chance to stare daggers at that douchebag. It's great, by the way. You don't have to worry." Claire had forwarded her the victim impact statement when she had finally finished it at midnight.

"You get everything out that you wanted to say?" Sawyer asked as she hugged him next.

Claire paused. "I think so. We'll see if it makes a difference."

If her statement didn't make a difference, and the judge went with the minimum sentence, she was going to give up on America entirely and move to Canada. There was no way the Canadian justice system would let a dangerous idiot like Barney Windsor out after a paltry five years. She could totally make a living planning proposals in Canada. She just needed to learn more about hockey and publicly funded health systems first.

Nicole came back a few minutes later, paler than usual with dark circles under her eyes. She hugged Claire and collapsed onto the bench between Kyle and Luke. She took the crackers eagerly and shoved several in her mouth.

Alice stood and let out a little squeal, then nearly fell over Luke's knee as she rushed toward Nicole.

"Claire didn't tell me you were pregnant," Alice exclaimed, reaching her hands forward but snatching them back. At least she had the good manners not to rub the pregnant lady's belly.

"How did you know?" Nicole asked over a mouthful of crackers, placing a hand protectively over her stomach.

Alice immediately launched into a discussion about intuition and changes in Nicole's aura. Mindy scooted closer to Claire and offered her a thermos. The last time she had accepted a thermos from Mindy, it had been full of vodka. Claire shook her head. She needed a clear head for what was coming next.

Finally, after what felt like an eternity, most of the courtroom was seated. Silence gradually fell, and Claire's heart tripped in her chest. The yellowed walls seemed to be closing in on her. The clock at the front of the room ticked maddeningly. He was here. In the building. The man who had stalked her for months, chloroformed her in a hallway, dressed her in her wedding dress, and stabbed her.

The courtroom doors opened behind them. Was that the clack of chains? Luke and Alice simultaneously grabbed Claire's hands. She kept her eyes forward as the shuffling sound of footsteps approached. The courtroom was silent except for those shuffling steps.

Shuffle. Shuffle. Had prison seriously impacted Barney's ability to walk like a normal human being? Would it kill him to show some hustle? She could have been using this time to do another check of Pacific Park's policy on outside vehicles. Finally, the world's slowest felon hit her peripheral vision. His gaze bore into her like a drill, but she refused to look at him. He wasn't worth a single glance. The swinging doors opened, and she caught a flash of an orange jumpsuit before dropping her gaze to her lap. She dug the scrap of wedding dress back out of her purse and clutched it in her left hand.

Moments later, a door at the front of the room opened and the judge entered. It was time. Would justice be served, or had Barney managed to pay someone off despite his frozen assets?

The beginning of the hearing passed in a blur. People spoke at the witness stand, but it all sounded far away. After several statements from a parole officer, Kyle, and Barney's lawyer, the judge shuffled some papers on her desk.

"And now we'll be hearing a victim impact statement from Miss Hartley."

Claire stood on quaking knees. Public speaking didn't normally intimidate her, but this was something else entirely. She really should have peed again before coming into the room.

Her heartbeat thudded incessantly in her ears. It was so loud, surely the entire court could hear it. Her whole body was pulsating, telling her to flee. Even if her eyes were closed, she was certain she could have pinpointed Barney like a heat-seeking missile. Evil flowed out of him, billowed across the gallery like fog.

The scrap of wedding dress clutched in her fist grew damp as she entered the swinging doors and climbed the steps to the witness stand. The sheet protector with her statement crinkled in her hand.

She was going to be sick. She was going to throw up on the counselors. It would be in the news—*Hartley Hurls at Hearing.*

As she faced the court, she stared immediately into the steely, evil eyes of Barney Windsor. A shiver ran up and down her spine, but she barely gave him a passing glance before moving her gaze to her family and friends. Luke's arm was around Alice. Rachel looked more pinched and constipated than usual. Nicole was like a frightened baby deer with chipmunk cheeks full of crackers. Mindy crossed her eyes, put her fingers at the corner of her mouth, and stuck her tongue out. It was almost enough to make her smile.

Claire bent the microphone toward her, and a deafening shuffling sound emanated from the speakers. A couple of people in the gallery flinched. Nothing like making a good first impression.

"Your Honor, thank you for allowing me to present my impact statement today."

She turned to look at the judge, who nodded encouragingly at her. Everything rested on this moment. No pressure.

"How do you put into words the impact a violent crime has had on your life?" she wondered aloud. Her attention moved back to the crowd.

Alice smiled encouragingly while big, fat tears streamed down her cheeks.

Claire wrung her hands and picked up her paper. It shook in her hands. "Honestly, that night changed everything for me. My sense of security, my trust in my community and my judgment, my business, my emotional and physical health."

She took a deep breath and glanced up from her paper. Luke nodded.

"I had anxiety attacks. I had to take self-defense lessons to feel even a tiny bit of security. And still, I don't feel safe. I can't walk down the street without studying everyone in my path, cataloging all the men and what they're wearing. This scar"—she paused, patting the shiny mark on her chest where Barney had stabbed her—"it's a daily reminder of the worst night of my life."

She looked at the judge, but her face was unreadable. Claire's hands trembled, and for a moment she lost her place. A bead from the fabric of her wedding dress bit into her palm. She glanced at it. The day she wore this dress was supposed to be the happiest day of her life. Instead it had been a blood-drenched nightmare. Although, technically speaking, marrying her ex would have been almost as bad as getting stabbed by a serial killer in the long run. Maybe he had done her a favor when he cheated on her with her nemesis.

Shit, which bullet point was she on? She glanced up, and Mindy mimed someone taking a picture. Right, the press.

"He made me a spectacle. The press hounded me for months after the attack. I had to climb down the fire escape with my dog just to let her pee in peace. And my business suffered too. We built Happily Ever Afters to work exclusively with couples we genuinely believed were in love and wanted to get married for no ulterior motives. We had a one hundred percent success rate before Barney. My reputation in the business community was irrevocably damaged. I'm now the girl who planned a proposal for a serial killer. Who could trust such a special moment in their lives to someone who didn't see evil staring her in the face?"

She gestured at Barney. A smile curled his crooked mouth. "We've now incurred significant financial costs by requiring a federal background check for every applicant, but it still doesn't feel like enough. Evil doesn't always have a criminal background. Barney Windsor didn't."

A jolt hit her. Was her car door locked? She hadn't done her customary memory dance after shutting the door. But then again, she wasn't about to break out into the foxtrot with thirty reporters breathing down her neck. Surely Luke had locked it. She needed to focus. Another deep breath ballooned in her chest.

In her peripheral vision, Barney twitched in his orange jumpsuit, but she wasn't going to give him the pleasure of eye contact. Right, she should probably keep talking.

She took a deep breath and continued. "Even after being drugged, thrown in a trunk, dressed in my wedding dress, tortured, and stabbed, I didn't think I needed therapy. I thought I could handle it myself. Then the sleepwalking started. I would wake up with no memory of how I got where I was. I walked into a lake, woke up in the middle of a forest. One time I even drove my car. It made me a danger to myself and others. I started therapy a few months ago, and while it's been helpful, it doesn't stop the nightmares. It hasn't restored my sense of security or my belief that people are basically good."

Alice sniffed loudly from her row. At least she had

listened to Claire and left the voodoo dolls at home this time.

Okay, the end of her speech was approaching. She could do this. Just a few more minutes of baring her soul to the world, and then she could hide at home with a plate of enchiladas and a glass of sangria. Or maybe she would just run away. What was it Dr. Goulding had said? Her homework was to do something very un-Claire. Shirking her responsibilities and running away was about as un-Claire as could be.

"I carry the weight of what Barney did to me every single day. Even now, I'm trying to rescue an animal shelter he funded and abandoned. Twelve dogs—well, eleven, since I adopted a blind pug named Winston—and seven cats are destined for the euthanasia list in a catch-all shelter because of him."

There was a gasp from the court. Maybe she should have put out an empty guitar case for donations.

"Despite his best efforts, Barney didn't succeed in killing me. And because I'm standing here today instead of buried six feet underground, his expected sentence is dangerously, almost laughably light. Your Honor, this is a dangerous man."

She pointed at the putz in the jumpsuit before turning her attention back to the judge. "I implore you to impose the maximum sentence allowed for his charges. He's not capable of reform. The minute he gets out, he'll go straight back to stalking and killing. He's dangerous, and he's not alone."

Oops. Her dad was not going to be pleased that she just hinted at ESA. Oh well.

"Please do what you can to protect this community, Your Honor. Don't let the Widowmaker off easy. Thank you."

She stood and the chair made a farting noise as she scooted it backward. Please god don't let the entire court think she had too many beans at dinner last night. She hurriedly shuffled off the stand and through the swinging doors. Her eyes stayed locked on the clock in the back of the room as she passed by the man who had tried to kill her, but even without eye contact her skin crawled. How had she ever missed this stench of evil during their dress rehearsals? She tripped over Kyle's shoe and collapsed breathlessly back into her row.

Alice immediately threw her arms around her and rocked her like she was a child who had a bad dream. Luke squeezed her hand so hard it almost hurt. He kissed her on the cheek when Alice released her.

The judge banged her gavel, and Claire jumped. "The court will recess for fifteen minutes, after which time I will sentence the defendant."

Most of the crowd got to their feet. Claire stood, too jittery to be this close to Barney. Before anyone could follow, she stalked up the aisle, out the doors, and marched down the marbled hallway to the seating area where she had spent the first hearing. She pressed herself against the wall and took deep breaths. Her legs were Jell-O. The wall was the only thing keeping her upright.

A squirrel dangled from a bird feeder in the dreary courtyard. His mouth was full of seed. What she would give to be that squirrel. No one would ever make him relive his worst day in front of a hundred people.

There were footsteps in the hallway.

"Hey," a low, growly voice said. Luke appeared at her shoulder. "You did great."

"Thanks," Claire said flatly and closed her eyes on a sigh. "It was only the most humiliating thing I've ever done.

And that includes the time I streaked in front of my entire apartment complex. And the time I flashed my blood-drenched boobs at every first responder in the tri-county area. And the time I flashed your mom. Let's just include all nudity-related humiliations."

Luke's hand snaked around her shoulders. She opened her eyes. His rough thumb rubbed the side of her neck. She ducked her head and nestled into his shoulder, breathing in his familiar woodsy scent.

"Clairebear?" Alice's musical voice drifted down the hallway. Claire groaned.

"There she is. My darling, you were enchanting." Alice gripped her by the shoulders and stared into her eyes before pulling her into a suffocating hug. Then she moved back and cupped her chin in her hand. "So much pain. So much grace."

Nicole and Mindy appeared out of nowhere and surrounded her in a best friend hug. "I have tequila," Mindy whispered in Claire's ear. Aha. So the mystery thermos had been booze. Thank god she hadn't stumbled up to the witness stand smelling like Mardi Gras.

Claire shuddered. "Maybe after the sentencing. Come on."

She squared her shoulders and pulled away from the wall. Flanked by her friends and family, she had all the support she needed.

CHAPTER TEN

To Do:
- Breathe
- Pray

"WILL THE DEFENDANT PLEASE RISE?" THE JUDGE SLID HER glasses up the bridge of her nose and glanced at a paper in front of her.

Chains clanked as Barney climbed to his feet. He swiveled his head in Claire's direction. A cold, brutal smile cracked the unbothered marble of his face. There was no fear in his eyes.

Claire dragged her gaze from his and squared her shoulders. Her knees squeezed together like she was trying to hold a penny between them. Alice clutched her left hand. Luke held the other gently, running his thumb over her wrist in soothing circles in spite of the death glares he was shooting at Barney. Mindy had moved to sit behind her, and both of her hands were on Claire's shoulders. She was home base in an awkward, stressful game of tag.

The courtroom was quieter than a public library ruled by an iron-fisted librarian. Nicole unrolled a ginger lozenge and tossed it into her mouth, and the crinkle of the wrapper was near deafening.

This was it. The moment everything had been leading up to since Barney stabbed her in that parking garage. Was he about to pay for the hell he had inflicted on her? Or, like so many rich white men before him, was he about to get off with a slap on the wrist? She had all but bled on that stand. She had done everything she could. Was it going to make a difference?

Claire stared unblinkingly at the judge. Her expression was as unreadable as a blank legal pad. Seconds crept by. Was there a mandatory class in law school on how to create dramatic suspense?

The judge set her papers down and folded her hands. She stared at Barney. "Mr. Windsor, in all of my years serving this community as a judge, I've encountered a lot of criminals. I've seen things that would churn the stomachs of most people in this courtroom. I've heard accounts that would give almost anyone nightmares. But not, I suspect, you. Your cruelty and your cold, calculating nature are evident even though you didn't testify. I get chills when you walk into my courtroom."

Claire's mouth fell open. Mindy squeezed her shoulders. Could this be the wheels of justice grinding away?

"What you did to Miss Hartley is inexcusable. There was no emotional component to your crime, despite what your lawyer argued. What you did was what a hunter does to its prey. You stalked and tried to kill your victim. One failed date in college does not give you permission to take that woman's life. You're a dangerous man, Mr. Windsor. And because of that, I have no choice but to sentence you to ten years in prison with credit for one year of time served. I expect I'll see you again someday."

The judge banged her gavel and stood. The courtroom erupted in chatter.

Shockwaves coursed through Claire's body. Had she really heard the judge correctly? Mindy climbed over the back of the bench in her pencil skirt and stilettos and threw herself on Claire. Alice began sobbing. Tanya rushed from the back of the courtroom with a joyful shout. Jack offered a solemn nod with the ghost of a smile. Throughout the fray, Luke's hand stayed warm and secure around hers.

It had really happened. Against all odds, Barney was about to pay for his crimes. Although it was still bullshit that he was only getting ten years for almost killing her, he would be rotting in a prison cell. And now the FBI had time to build a case against him. Justice may yet be served for the other victims. Money could buy a lot of things, but for today at least, freedom wasn't one of them.

Barney's mother tearfully gripped a used tissue. She reached for Barney as he was led away, but he only had eyes for Claire. His steely gray eyes burned into hers. She raised a single eyebrow as he disappeared through the door. Stupid murderous asshole. Good riddance.

A breath she had been holding for what felt like a year whooshed out. "So, what should we do with the rest of our day?" she whispered to Luke over a mouthful of her mother's hair. The front of her blouse was damp from everyone crying on her.

"Drink?" he suggested. But then he glanced at his phone and furrowed his brow.

Before she had a chance to ask what was wrong,

everyone was pulling her toward the front door. It was just as well. Even after the sentencing was read, the sensation of the yellowed walls closing in hadn't left her. Shit. The press was presumably still outside. She wound the high contrast scarf around her neck and drew her shoulders back like she was about to dropkick her way out of here.

When Luke and Kyle pushed open the double doors, the sun shone through the clouds like spotlights. Warmth rushed into her cheeks. The rain had stopped, and a brilliant rainbow hovered over the dry cleaning shop across the street. If that wasn't a good sign, she didn't know what was.

Several steps down, a crowd of reporters surrounded Barney's lawyer. Her fingers curled into fists. Kyle had recommended she make a statement if she felt up to it, but the thought of speaking to the people who had hounded her for months made her skin crawl.

"Miss Hartley!" One shout was all it took for the press to abandon Barney's lawyer. They scrambled over each other like children on a jungle gym. Microphones hovered in front of her face as they jostled for positions.

"Miss Hartley, how do you feel about the verdict?" a man with a handlebar mustache asked.

A woman in a lime-green power suit elbowed her way in front of Claire. "Do you think the punishment fit the offense?"

Claire paused, and the caravan of people behind her bumped into each other as they lurched to a stop. If a few words now could stop the press from accosting her as she fetched the mail while wearing corgi pajama pants, it would be worth it.

She took a deep breath and looked into one of the cameras. "I'm relieved that justice was served today. It's the first step in gaining justice for the rest of Mr. Windsor's victims."

She turned on her heel and strode into the crowd without another word. Her heart was lighter than it had been in months, maybe even a year. She could have skipped all the way back to the car even with the handful of reporters shouting after her. The door handle was cool in her hand as she yanked on it.

Locked. All that worrying in the middle of her statement for nothing.

Luke unlocked the door and swung it open. She climbed inside and happily buckled herself in. A couple of members of the press stalked around the car trying to take her picture, but the horde had thinned. She closed her eyes and took a deep breath. Maybe things would finally go back to normal. Maybe the next time someone Googled her name, the auto-complete suggestion would be "Claire Hartley Happily Ever Afters" instead of "Claire Hartley Widowmaker."

The mental and physical scars Barney had inflicted would last a lifetime. But for the first time in months, their sting wasn't so sharp.

Alice slid into the back seat behind her, already jabbering about a family vacation they should take to celebrate the verdict.

Claire's eyes snapped open. "Mom, the last time we went to the beach you were arrested for performing a moon ritual."

Alice scoffed. "It was my own fault. I shouldn't have expected the Rehoboth Beach Police Department to understand the nuances of charging crystals. Maybe a mountain retreat instead. As long as there's running water nearby."

Luke paused in front of the car, frowning at something on his phone. Rachel was nowhere to be found. Perhaps that was the source of his frownyness. He slid into the driver's seat and fired up the engine.

"Home?" he asked.

Claire nodded. "Your mom's not joining us?"

Luke shook his head. So much for the maybe-future in-laws getting along. But there had never been much hope for that anyway.

"What's wrong?" Claire whispered over her mother, who had switched to expounding on the benefits of fresh maritime pine bark.

"It's probably nothing. I just need to check something out at the house."

His voice was calm, but Claire's stomach clenched. Happiness faded like a dying sunset. What was happening at the house? Was her pepper spray still in date? Should she grab the bat from the trunk?

Alice had apparently shifted her focus from the mountains to the Mediterranean.

"Ooh, this Airbnb has four bedrooms and a private infinity pool overlooking the sea." She shoved her phone into the front seat to show Claire.

"That's great, Mom. Do you really think the show will let you take off long enough to go to Greece?" There was no way this trip was happening. Alice was full of big ideas and very little follow-through.

"I'm the boss, darling. They'll do what I say. Did you catch the show last week?"

Claire didn't always watch her mother's TV show when it came on, but she usually tried to let it play while she cleaned the house. "I did. I got chills when you channeled that turkey farmer's mother."

"Poor dear. She just wanted to see her son happy."

"Do you think he'll reach out to Annabelle?"

"If he doesn't, Norma threatened to keep opening all the cabinets in his kitchen and slamming his doors. I told her there were more constructive ways to spend her energy, but she's a stubborn one."

"Pity," Claire said.

Luke sighed, making her smile. He didn't believe in much of anything her mother said and preferred to attribute all of her premonitions to a combination of coincidence and her ability to read people. He had been unimpressed by her interpretation of his tarot cards at Thanksgiving.

"Hey," Claire whispered to him while Alice babbled to herself about the Smoky Mountains in the backseat. "Did that name from earlier mean something to you? Skip?"

His mouth hardened into a firm line. "Yeah."

She waited, staring at his grumpy profile.

"Honesty," she prompted after thirty seconds of silence. Well, silence minus Alice expounding on Appalachian granny magic.

"He worked for a rival law firm. My mom went up against him a couple of times. She said they were colleagues."

Claire nodded. Colleagues who banged, apparently. "I'm sorry."

"Don't be. She and my dad weren't good together."

"Sometimes love isn't enough." She reached over and squeezed his hand. It was too bad the Happily Ever Afters compatibility checklist didn't exist when Rachel and George Sr. had found each other. But at least their disastrous union had produced her favorite person.

"I wish I could have met your dad," she added.

"Me too." He returned her squeeze, and silence descended again.

The clouds parted, and the sun gained strength as they

drove through the city. Luke skillfully avoided a series of large potholes on Market Street. They turned onto Beaumont Street and passed a large brick building. She turned, straining against the seatbelt as her former apartment building flew past them and out of sight. Some of the best—and strangest—years of her life had been spent there. And some of the worst. Now that Claire had moved in with Luke in the country, the apartment belonged to Mindy. Every time she visited, Claire was annoyed that Mindy had moved the coffee maker.

The smell wafting from Big City Bean Co elicited a loud growl from her stomach. Their chocolate croissants were almost as good as the ones she and Luke had shared in Paris. Nothing compared to the wide-open spaces of the country, but the bustling metropolis of West Haven had been a special place to call home. From her old apartment, she could step out her door and walk to a dozen restaurants. She had even done it while sleepwalking. Now she had to go to the grocery store an upsetting number of times each week. Ugh.

"Still hungry for empanadas, sweetheart?" Alice finally paused her diatribe on family vacations as they passed Claire's second favorite Mexican restaurant.

"They sound perfect. I wish Roy was here to make them, though."

Alice sighed wistfully. "He's stuck on a big job hooking up some HVAC for a new business. He said he'll call you tonight."

"Good."

Her mother abruptly decided to meditate, and silence filled the car as they drove past the city limits and into the countryside.

Claire laid a hand on Luke's thigh. He was gripping the

steering wheel so tightly that the leather audibly shifted under his palm. In her haste to figure out who Skip was, she had nearly forgotten that something was wrong at the house. Apparently he wasn't in a sharing mood.

What could have possibly happened? Did a pipe burst? Did Rosie get into the Doritos again and spatter the kitchen with doggie napalm? Claire took a deep breath and settled back into her seat. She would know soon enough.

They made a pit stop at the grocery store a mile from Luke's house when Alice suddenly remembered she had forgotten to instruct Claire to pick up green chiles. The defining characteristic of Alejo Empanadas was that the recipe was never written down. As a result, they were slightly different each time they were made. By the time Luke had pulled up to the garage, Mindy, Sawyer, Nicole, and Kyle were sitting on the front porch. They all looked pointedly at their watches as the car came to a stop. Luke grumbled.

The gang piled into the kitchen, dispersing to their usual spots. Sawyer's gigantic feet dangled from a bar stool at the island. He pulled out a laptop and checked his work email. Mindy sat next to him, entering data into a spreadsheet. Nicole and Kyle cuddled in the breakfast nook, where he rubbed her shoulders as she ate a piece of dry toast.

A cursory review of the kitchen and living room didn't reveal any chip-induced diarrhea or exploded pipes. Luke disappeared down the hallway, carefully avoiding eye contact. Something wasn't right. What the hell was he hiding from her? She moved to follow him but was trapped by Rosie and Winston's frantic embrace.

Alice picked Winston up and tucked him into the pocket of the apron she had just put on.

Luke stormed back up the hallway, hands balled into

fists, paler than he had been a moment before. Claire's heart leapt into her throat. He stooped down next to Kyle and whispered something to him. Kyle's mouth fell open, and he immediately pulled out his phone.

Luke stomped up the steps as though each one of them had personally wronged him. What fresh hell was this? Claire flew up the stairs two at a time, hot on his heels. When she arrived in the bedroom, he had already pulled one of her overnight bags out and was tossing clothing into it.

"What are you doing? What's wrong?" she asked.

"How many pairs of underwear do you need for a long weekend? Eight? Nine?" Piles of multicolor lace were wound between his calloused fingers.

A long weekend? This was hardly the time. There was cause to celebrate, sure, but her To Do list was practically endless.

"Well, it depends. Will I be peeing myself twice a day or only once?"

He grunted and shoved the whole lot in her bag. She touched his shoulder.

"Luke. You're scaring me. I need you to tell me what's going on."

"You're going away for the weekend."

Her stomach twisted itself into knots, and she gripped his shoulder tighter. "You know I can't do that. There's too much at stake with Brad's proposal. Every minute counts. And now I have the gala to plan, not to mention our next couples to pick. If we don't get all twelve pictures taken and to the printer by Wednesday, we might as well kiss the calendar goodbye."

"There are worse things." He opened the drawer where

she kept her jeans and threw three pairs in. It would take her ages to get the drawers organized again.

She groaned and threw her hands up. It was like talking to a brick wall. Maybe Kyle would explain.

She took the stairs two at a time. The kitchen was quiet. Everyone was gone. The back of her neck prickled. Where had they gone? And why the hell wouldn't anyone tell her anything?

She walked down the hallway, past her office to the ballroom. The double doors creaked as she threw them open. Empty. Her shoes clacked across the marble floors as she approached the window.

She came to an abrupt halt. And gasped.

Her friends were crowded around the edge of Luke's pool. This morning, the pool had still been covered. They hadn't planned on opening it until May at least. Now, however, the cover had been dragged away and the entire pool was filled with bright red liquid. It couldn't be blood. Could it?

Next to the pool, a message was scrawled on the concrete.

You'll pay for this.

Her knees buckled. She staggered and banged off the floor-to-ceiling windows that faced the pool. Her friends jumped. Nicole and Mindy rushed inside and clutched at her.

"It's okay. Everything is going to be fine," Nicole said, stroking Claire's hair.

"Who did this?" Claire croaked like she had smoked a pack a day for her entire life.

"You know who it was," Mindy whispered. She grabbed Claire's hand as if expecting her to disappear.

CHAPTER ELEVEN

To Do:
- *Email the Getty*
- *Consult with S&G on gala*
- *Bake laxative brownies for all of ESA*

THE LOCK ON THE HOTEL DOOR BEEPED AND FLASHED GREEN. Claire elbowed her way into the room and nudged her bags inside. Luke had insisted that it wasn't safe to stay at home, so now here she was. Completely alone in a Holiday Inn Express one block from the West Haven police department. No dogs, no boyfriend. Only her laptop and the file box full of binders she had lugged to the fifth floor would keep her company.

Out of habit, she dropped to her knees and peeked under the bed. No murderers. A pass with the RF signal detector Jack had given her found no bugs or hidden cameras. She really was alone. She flopped onto the bed with a dramatic sigh and immediately leapt off. What about bedbugs?

After searching all soft surfaces and declaring them bug-free, she opened her laptop. Her background popped up—a picture of her and Luke at the beach in Florida. They had visited Alice for Christmas. One of his eyebrows was cocked. She was nestled under his chin, the blue-green waters of the Atlantic behind them. Her heart fisted. Now he was in danger again just by being associated with her. Strangers had infiltrated his land, damaged his property. Something in her core told her it was only a matter of time before they hurt someone she loved. And there was nothing she could do about it.

She needed a distraction. Shallow breaths whistled past her nose as she opened the master list for Brad's proposal. The cursor blinked. Numbers stared back at her, but nothing sank in. She rolled her shoulders, pressed her palms to her eyes, and tried again. A knot formed in her stomach. How was she supposed to focus on a proposal when madmen had just filled Luke's pool with blood and threatened her? Again?

She strode over to the window and snapped the curtains open. Maybe something outside would distract her. Shoppers littered the sidewalks of Main Street. A woman in spandex yammered into a phone while pushing a toddler in a stroller. A donut was closed in his meaty little fist. Three young men crowded around a phone and erupted into cheers. Girls in Venor University sweatshirts passed out flyers. None of this was helpful.

A sign caught her eye. An office supply store. She rarely went there because they weren't dog friendly. Her fingers twitched. If she couldn't focus on work, maybe she could focus on something else. Revenge.

Forty minutes later, she burst back into the hotel room laden with half a dozen bags. She chucked them on the floor and went back into the hallway. A new rolling whiteboard slid smoothly over the hotel carpet. Much better. She uncapped a new marker and frowned at the blank canvas in front of her.

It was time to take back her life. Putting Barney away and shutting down the West Haven branch of ESA was a step in the right direction, but it was nowhere near enough. She wasn't going to stop until she found them all. There had to be a way. But how?

FIND PROFESSOR TAYLOR.

The first bullet on this particular To Do list was the most important. The only person she could definitively tie to ESA was still on the run. But with the advent of the internet, the world had gotten smaller. He couldn't hide forever.

A knock came from her door, and she gasped. The marker fell from her hand and thunked to the floor. She dove behind the bed and shoved both hands in her bag. A can of bear mace—a gift from Alice—tumbled out, and she clutched it like a lifeline. Was it ESA? Had they come for her?

"Claire?" a voice called at the door.

She crossed the room and wrenched the door open. "Mindy! You gave me a heart attack."

Mindy sidestepped into the room and tossed an overnight bag on the second bed. "I texted you like five times. I had to use the watch app to figure out where you were." She gestured at the GPS watch Claire wore, which Mindy had given her after she'd been abducted the previous year.

Claire peeked into the hallway, then snapped the door shut. "I'm sorry. Luke and Jack kept my phone. They wanted to sweep everything for bugs. I had to smuggle my computer out."

Mindy hopped onto the bed. "I see you've started without me." She pulled her laptop out of her bag and settled back against the pillows.

Claire crossed her arms. "You're not helping. It'll only put you in danger."

"Shut your stupid, beautiful face. I'm obviously going to help you. I see we have a 'To Do' list started. Now how do we find the professor?" Mindy twisted her hair into a bun and looked expectantly at Claire.

Claire sighed. Mindy was going to help no matter what she did, so she might as well lean into it. "Well, he's already on the Most Wanted list. But I don't know if that's enough visibility."

Mindy nodded. "Not everyone checks the list every week like us."

Claire slapped the marker against her palm. "Right. So I was thinking about that Web Detectives site. What if we posted some of his pictures there and asked people to watch out for him? They tracked down the Milton Murderer in three days flat."

"He probably changed his appearance, but it's worth a shot. That saggy ball sack can't hide forever. I'll get on that right now."

"Perfect. Can you go through the cache of the Venor websites and post all the pictures you can find?"

Mindy cracked her fingers. Keys clattered with ferocity.

Claire stood back and looked at the board again. She scrawled another item.

WILLIAM HICKORY.

If she was already going to be amateur sleuthing, she

might as well solve Barney's riddle as well. Lord knew the FBI wasn't about to.

"List of all ESA chapters" and "Missing Women" were added next. They knew that ESA was organized by fraternities and they had a pathological hate for high-profile women. If they could study enough cases, maybe they could figure out who would be targeted next. If they could save even one person, it would be worth it.

She was halfway through decorating a cover sheet for Murder Binder 3.0 when a knock sounded on the hotel door.

Mindy hopped off the bed. "It's probably Nicole. Please don't mace her."

Claire stood behind Mindy as she opened the door, Taser trained at the hallway. Nicole stepped through a second later, tugging a rolling suitcase behind her.

"I brought snacks!" She hefted a reusable shopping bag onto the second bed. Doritos and a jar of Nutella tumbled out. "Don't judge me. It's the only thing I can eat right now that doesn't make me projectile vomit."

Claire hugged her and went back to the whiteboard. "Did you bring your laptop?"

"Obviously." Nicole slung a backpack off her shoulder and unzipped it. A computer emerged, and she stationed herself at the table by the window. "Where do we start?"

"I need you to make a spreadsheet of all the chapters of ESA. Start with the ones in LA."

"Got it." Nicole slid on a pair of glasses and tucked her legs underneath her.

"And what are you doing, boss?" Mindy peered over the edge of her screen.

Claire picked up her computer and stationed herself across

from Nicole. "I'm going to comb through his social media and find places he's visited. Maybe he has an aunt in Nebraska or a vacation home in Aspen. He's out there somewhere."

"Let's nail this bastard." Nicole smashed a fist on the table, then promptly turned a shade of green and sprinted into the bathroom.

CHAPTER TWELVE

To Do:
- *Future fundraisers for shelter?*
- *New meditation mantra*
- *Track down ESA*

CLAIRE SLID HER KEYS OUT OF THE IGNITION AND RESTED HER forehead on her steering wheel. It had been a very long couple of days while the police and FBI had swept the house. A headache brewed behind her temples, fueled by the sleepless nights spent combing through Professor Taylor's online history. The man had spent a shocking amount of time playing Farmville in the 2010s. Beyond his penchant for flash games and annoying habit of checking in at Whole Foods, they had gleaned little from his discarded social media. He could be anywhere.

The ESA chapter hunt had also been a bit of a bust.

While there were still cached links sprinkled across the internet, there were no rosters, no social media pages, no way to contact the organization. Everything had seemingly gone underground. All they had was a list of colleges that once had chapters. What were they going to do, stake them all out and wait for a brother to sneak back in and grab his hastily discarded PlayStation?

Eventually, the three of them had run out of steam and devolved into lying in bed eating ice cream and watching rom-coms. They had a brainstorming session for the gala this morning, so the weekend hadn't been a complete loss. She hadn't had a chance to write all the ideas down before she left, so she had dictated into her phone the entire drive home. There were spreadsheets and presentations to make, but she was desperately ready to give Luke a hug and be stampeded by four-legged fur babies.

She pulled her suitcase out of the trunk and trudged to the front door. Her hand was raised to tap a code into the keypad on the door when she froze. Luke, Rosie, and Winston were all cuddled together on the couch in the living room.

Her heart lurched. They had forgotten all about her. The dogs were bonding with Daddy Luke, but Winston probably barely even remembered her. She added "bond with dogs" to her ever-growing To Do list and tapped her code into the deadbolt. It beeped angrily at her.

That was strange. She must have entered it wrong. She typed it again, more slowly this time. 1-2-2-3. Rosie's birthday. Her little almost Christmas miracle. The pad beeped at her again and flashed red. Maybe she had messed up the sequence. It had been a long weekend.

She entered the code one more time, and the pin pad

flashed solid red. An alarm wailed inside like a banshee on Red Bull. Rosie and Winston jerked awake. Rosie immediately barked and sprinted from one side of the house to the other and then ran back down the hallway. Winston tumbled to the floor and Claire waved. Oh, wait. He was blind.

Winston took several steps away from the couch, shuddered, and heaved his tiny body. A puddle of vomit appeared on the floor.

Luke, who appeared to have been in a deep sleep, jumped up like he had been plunged into icy water. He pulled a baseball bat from underneath the couch and stomped toward the front door.

Claire waved at him from the porch, and his expression changed from panic to sleepy, tousled joy. At that moment, his right foot landed in the fresh puddle of dog vomit, and he slid like a figure skater for two whole feet. The hem of his sweatpants tripped him up, and he crashed ass-over-elbow to the floor. Luckily, Winston had vacated the premises after panic-barfing.

Claire gasped and pulled on the door handle. "Are you okay?" she called through the glass.

Luke lay on the floor and groaned. Great, she had only been home for thirty seconds and already she had broken her boyfriend. What else could go wrong today? Would Rachel bring a caravan full of ESA groupies for a late Easter dinner? Would her bank burn down? Maybe Alice would decide to move back to Pennsylvania permanently.

After a minute, Luke crawled to his feet and disengaged the alarm. He opened the door. "Welcome home," he said, a streak of dog vomit on his sweatpants and hair sticking straight up.

She rushed into his arms. "I missed you."

"Missed you too," he muttered into her hair. "I changed the codes. Sorry."

"I figured. What's my new one?"

"Winston's homecoming day. 0-4-1-0."

"0-4-1-0," she repeated into his impressively defined pecs. She pulled back. "You love him."

He crossed his arms. "He's grown on me. But do not mistake that as permission to bring a dog home every time you feel bad."

She smiled. "Then you really shouldn't go look in the car. There's an entire family of chihuahua in the back seat, and they all have different skin allergies. Is the pool…"

"Dealt with. Everything's fine." One calloused thumb stroked her arm. Warmth crept into her cheeks. "How was your hotel stay?"

Something awakened in her downstairs department, but she didn't have time for romance. Not while a thousand ideas were buzzing around in her head.

"Listen, I—"

He smiled. "I know. Go get some work done. I'll bring you a plate for lunch."

Claire leaned in for another hug. "I love you." The words still sent a tingle through her spine when she said them. She had opened herself to him, petal by petal, over the last year. Despite her best efforts at maintaining a strict sex embargo after her ex-fiancé, Jason, had broken her heart, Luke had blown up her defensive walls with his dynamite smile and bossy attitude.

It was impossible not to love him, as grumpy and infuriating as he could be. He was like no one she had ever met. Ruthless in his pursuit of a story, a hurricane in the bedroom, stubbornly opinionated on everything regarding

Claire's career. And yet, he was an adorable, squishy marshmallow on the inside once she got to know him. He bought new dog beds by the dozen and insisted on changing her dressings every time she was stabbed, shot, or otherwise injured. He took her to Paris and made her an office.

He was everything she had ever wanted, and his intense gaze still brought heat to her cheeks. In spite of everything the universe had thrown at her, she was lucky.

"Love you too," Luke said, pressing a kiss beneath her right ear. Her body exploded into static. Maybe she had time for a brief romantic detour.

At that moment, something furry banged into her shin. Claire shrieked and jumped into Luke's arms. Was it a dog, or had she accidentally let in one of the monstrous, pot-bellied squirrels from the backyard?

She glanced down. Luckily, it was just Winston. His milky white eyes stared in her vague direction, and her stomach lurched. This was why she needed to get to work. Winston was one of a dozen. If she didn't pull off this charity gala and grow her business, all the special needs dogs in West Haven would be doomed.

"Hello, sweet baby," she cooed as she unwound her legs from Luke's waist and dropped to her knees. His fur was soft beneath her fingers. He put both his front paws on her knee and licked the air near her face. Something black was strapped over his torso. Did they make sports bras for dogs now?

"Poor guy. Let's get you strapped in." Luke walked into the kitchen and pulled a boxy apparatus from the island. Had he been playing with tinker toys while she was making murder spreadsheets?

"Luke," she said slowly.

"Hmm?" He bent down onto one knee and clipped the rig into Winston's harness.

"What's that?"

"It's to keep him safe," he said. There was a hint of defensiveness in his voice. "So he doesn't bang into things."

When Luke finished attaching it, a small halo surrounded Winston's head. He trotted off into the kitchen and promptly banged his shield into the island. The halo gently repelled him.

Butterflies fluttered in her belly. "You're amazing." She pressed herself against him for another sensual kiss. His hand fisted in her hair, and her hand slid down his chest to the waistband of his sweatpants. Then Winston knocked over the umbrella stand.

"Go." Luke righted the stand and put Claire's polka dot umbrella back. "We'll have dinner together at six. And I do mean six, not six fifteen," he growled.

"Thank you." She squeezed his arm and walked over to the kitchen sink. Ducking down, she rifled through the cleaning products. There was still dog vomit in the living room to deal with.

His hand closed over hers. "Leave it. I got it."

"It's my fault," she said, grabbing a roll of paper towels.

"No, it's not." He snatched the paper towels from her and gave her a kiss on the cheek. "Go save some animals."

She was clearly dismissed. Speaking of animals, where the hell had Rosie gone? A legendary scaredy-cat, she had clearly hidden after the alarm went off.

Claire's footsteps thudded in the hallway as she walked toward the back of the house, opening and closing doorways as she went. It wasn't likely that Rosie had learned to open doors since she had left two days ago, but stranger things had happened. Finally, the only door left was the ballroom.

A knot of apprehension grew in her stomach. The pool waited just beyond the windows of the ballroom. The latest physical reminder that ESA was still very much around and had a score to settle with her.

She swiveled away from the doors. Rosie couldn't have gone inside the ballroom anyway. One of the wooden stairs creaked as she crept upstairs. Her suitcase stood by the vanity in the master bedroom, already brought up by Luke. And there, on the floor beneath the king-sized bed, was Rosie. She was curled tight into a cinnamon bun, back end shaking.

"Come here, darling," Claire called, lying flat on her belly with her hand outstretched toward her beloved dog. "It's okay. Mommy's home now."

Rosie tentatively stretched her neck out and licked Claire's hand. Claire rubbed her snoot for a minute until the shaking stopped.

"Much better. Come with me," she ordered, shimmying away from the bed. Rosie crawled out and jumped at her, planting her feet on Claire's knees until she bent down for a proper hug. Warmth flooded Claire's body. Rosie hadn't forgotten her. She was home.

Five hours later, Claire's half-eaten sandwich was limp on its plate as she typed fervently. The smell of garlic wound its way seductively into the room, but she didn't have time to worry about food. Her calendar was filling up with meetings. A PowerPoint presentation with their newest applicants sat in her sent box. And then there were thirteen separate emails from Brad.

Her phone dinged, and she glanced at it. A picture appeared. Nicole stood in front of a wall, one hand on her belly. A sticker in the corner read eight weeks.

Claire sent a whole row of heart emojis and leaned back

in her chair. She pressed a hand to her abdomen. Alice had been dropping hints about fertility teas and rituals for months. She already had one grandchild in California, but she seemed determined to surround herself with them. Maybe, one day, Claire would be taking baby bump updates of her own. Of course, she would prefer to convince Luke to marry her first, but that was about as likely as Winston learning to surf. Not impossible, but statistically speaking, unlikely.

Next, she needed to tackle the latest accounting work for Brad's proposal. She scrolled to the bottom of the spreadsheet. The number of zeros at the bottom sent her heart into palpitations. She closed the spreadsheet and went back to the compatibility test Brad had filled out.

They were in love, weren't they? Like really, truly in love? Surely he wouldn't go to such great lengths to propose if they weren't. Was the magic of that one question getting bogged down in this insanely elaborate event? Ordinarily, she wouldn't think twice about the client wanting something huge. Big proposals were the reason she had a job. But this was next level, and the geographic discrepancy was preventing her from doing her in-person screening.

Part of her process was spying on her couples on dates, seeing how they communicated. But she hadn't had the opportunity to witness Brad and Karen on a date. Sure, they had been together for eight years and lived together for six of those, but were they really ready to get married again? And changing the Hollywood sign? Was this really all for Karen, or was it just so Brad could get on some morning shows?

Claire leaned back in her chair and pressed her palms over her eyes. Why had she agreed to do this? The entire future of their company now hinged on this proposal. News coverage from changing the Hollywood sign was inevitable. Every part of this project would be up to public scrutiny. If it went perfectly, maybe it would wipe the public memory of Claire as a proposal planner for serial killers. They could hire a West Coast staff member and take the first steps in growing Happily Ever Afters. If they succeeded, supporting the shelter was a much more attainable goal.

But if it failed, her reputation would be tarnished forever. Her entire plan to have a West Coast branch established so that she could work *and* spend time with her sisters and Luke would be destroyed. She would be all but shackled to clients who neglected to google her name.

The door to her office banged open, startling her out of her introspection, and Rosie and Winston flipped to their feet and barked.

"I said six." Luke put both hands on the back of her chair and wheeled her into the hallway. The clattering of dog nails on hardwood followed them.

"I didn't get to save my document—" She twisted in the seat and tried to stand, but Luke forced her back down.

"I've seen you type. You save your documents every fifteen seconds. Now it's time for dinner."

Claire crossed her arms as he pushed her to the kitchen. Didn't he understand what was at stake? Not everyone could make a living by exploiting the tawdry mystery of a serial killer for an audience of millions. Some people preferred to orchestrate beautiful moments for couples instead of celebrating the macabre.

Okay, that wasn't fair. Luke's entire documentary revolved around honoring Barney's victims and telling their stories. He had begrudgingly allowed Claire to watch the first episode when he was apologizing for asking her to be in it. She had refused to watch her episode, where she had finally consented to speak about her experience on camera, but she knew it existed.

He deposited her in the kitchen, and her stomach growled. Loudly.

"What is it?" She sniffed the air. Notes of garlic and lemon clung seductively to the air.

"Shrimp scampi." He steered her to a bar stool and dropped a bowl of pasta in front of her. A vase full of stargazer lilies stood on the island. Her favorite. "And after this, we're going to spend some quality time together and there will be no talk of work. Understood?"

"Yes, sir," Claire grumbled, twining some strands of pasta around her fork. The first bite nearly sent her into a full-blown mouthgasm. Of course he was amazing at cooking. With the exception of sorting laundry and practicing open and honest communication, there was nothing that Luke wasn't immediately awesome at. It was incredibly irritating.

"Now tell me about your hotel stay." He settled beside her. "I know Nicole and Mindy joined you."

She nodded. "We made a list of all the ESA chapters and snooped on Professor Taylor's online presence."

Luke sighed. "I wish you'd leave things to your dad. You already did your part. You got Barney put away for ten years."

Claire raised her eyebrows. "Do you really think he's going to stay in prison for ten years? I'm sure he's already started on his appeal. He'll find someone he can pay off, and then he'll be right back to murdering."

Mindy had helpfully pointed this very real possibility out during their long weekend. Appeals often took a while, but there was no guarantee that Barney was going to remain in prison. Claire's stomach twisted despite the delicious food. She set her fork down.

Luke stared off into space, eyebrows drawn together. For the first time in recorded history, he didn't seem to be in the mood to argue.

She took a deep breath and picked her fork up again. "That's why I also decided I'm going to figure out the William Hickory thing." It was a puzzle to solve, something she could control. Unlike Barney.

Luke put a hand over his eyes. His shoulders slumped. "You know the FBI has code breakers, right?"

"Yes, and they're doing a shitty job." She thrust one hand into the air.

His hand wrapped around her thigh. "Hey. It's going to be okay."

"I'm sorry, wasn't your pool quite literally just full of blood?"

"It was food dye."

"Right. That makes it way less scary that people stormed onto your land and tampered with your property."

He stood up and headed down the hallway.

"Where are you going? You barely touched your dinner. I can't be held accountable for what happens to it if you leave." She craned her neck, but he had disappeared. With any luck, he was setting up a sexy surprise as a distraction.

Rosie followed him back and sat outside her office. She sniffed the door and whined. What was he doing in there?

The door swung open, and he stepped out. "Come on."

"What?" Claire said, mouth full of shrimp.

Luke swore under his breath and came back to the kitchen, then picked her up like she was a rag doll. He deposited her in her office chair and wheeled her down the hallway to her desk. Her webcam was on, and someone was onscreen.

"Hello, Claire." Dr. Goulding's voice came through the speakers.

Claire jumped. This was not the sexy surprise she had hoped for. "What is this, a therapy ambush?"

The doctor leaned forward and pressed the tips of her fingers together. She was wearing the gold earrings Claire and Mindy had helped Sawyer pick out for Christmas.

"Luke told me he thinks you're having trouble processing what happened at the trial. He thought you could use a chat."

Luke ushered Rosie out and shut the door behind them. Traitor. Some work and a glass of wine were all the therapy she needed.

Claire frowned. "I'm not having trouble processing. We won. He's in prison. The end."

"Luke also told me about what happened after the trial. With the pool."

She crossed her arms over her chest. Why couldn't anyone just let her be? She didn't want to feel all her feelings all the time. It was exhausting. She just wanted to tamp them down into a nice little box and focus on something else.

"What do you want to hear? That I don't feel safe, even with him in prison?"

Dr. Goulding leaned back and hooked an arm over the back of her chair. "Don't you?"

"Of *course* I don't feel safe. Am I relieved he's behind bars and not walking the streets looking for more victims? Yes. But one good thing happened and immediately I faced retaliation from his idiot friends. There's no end to this, Dr. Goulding. I'm going to be looking over my shoulder for the rest of my life. One man in prison means nothing. There are probably a hundred more killers to take his place."

Dr. Goulding was quiet.

Claire drew her legs up in front of her and clutched them. "I just want to plan proposals, you know? Happily ever afters. I don't want to bring down serial killer rings and solve riddles and confront murderers in prison. I just want to do my job and live my life without being afraid."

"Everything you're feeling is valid. You did an incredibly brave and difficult thing," Dr. Goulding observed. "A killer met justice because of you. Why do you think you feel a responsibility to bring down the rest of them?"

"Am I supposed to just shut my eyes and pretend like innocent women everywhere aren't being ritualistically abducted and murdered? Just because they have the audacity to be successful?" Her arms swept out to her sides.

"It's not your responsibility, Claire. I know it feels like it is, but it's not."

Claire leaned back in her chair and heaved a sigh. Dr. Goulding was right about a lot of things, but this wasn't one of them. ESA was not going to go away. Her life would never be normal again until they were brought down. She couldn't stand by and do nothing.

She wouldn't.

"I know it's hard for you when there's something you can't control." Dr. Goulding spoke low and slow, like she was soothing a child. "But you can't control this. The only thing you can control is how you react."

Claire harrumphed and crossed her arms. Several seconds passed in silence.

"Have you given any more thought to starting the medication I mentioned?" The doctor's eyebrows raised.

Not the meds again. "The meditation and cardio routine are working just fine." Endorphins were better than drugs.

Dr. Goulding opened her mouth, then shut it, took a deep breath, and started again. Oh boy, now she was pissing off her therapist.

"Okay," the doctor said. "For now, let's keep working on our breathing exercises and meditations. You had a hard couple of days. Please make sure you do the exercises before bed, and maybe take some extra precautions."

That was fair. "Okay," Claire said. "I'm sorry. For being difficult. I just don't want to resort to medication if I don't have to."

"You have nothing to apologize for." Dr. Goulding had a ghost of a smile. "It's always your choice. I'm just here to point you in the right direction. Have a good night, Claire."

The screen went black. Claire closed her eyes and banished all thoughts of ESA. She emptied her mind and took long, slow breaths. Her heart rate settled. Her shoulders fell away from her ears. See? She didn't need medication.

She rose from her desk and stepped out into the hallway. Both dogs greeted her before sprinting to the kitchen. Luke stood at the sink with his back to her, kitchen towel slung over one broad shoulder.

"Hey," she said.

He turned around. There was definitely a hint of defensiveness in his eyes. "For the record, I didn't call her because I didn't want to listen to you. I thought she would be more help."

"It's fine. But no more therapy ambushes, okay?"

Luke nodded. He slid a glass of red wine across the bar.

"Want to talk about it?" His sea green eyes were laser-fixed on her.

She sipped from the glass and rolled her neck. "I really don't." Dedicating more mental space to the team of homicidal incels was not happening. She picked up the spatula from the drying rack and tucked it in its designated drawer. "Did I tell you Brianna invited us to the premiere of her movie? It's the weekend after we're supposed to leave LA, but we could come home in between."

"Nice," he said. He seemed to be relieved that she wasn't shouting at him. "Put it in our calendar. I'll have to see my tailor when we get to the city."

"That got me thinking. And this is not work related, I'm just curious. When will the premiere for your documentary be?"

Rosie came over and licked Luke's ankle as if to encourage him.

"Docs don't have premieres. Streaming parties, maybe. But probably not."

Claire stopped and turned to face him. "Nothing? They didn't do anything for your last doc?"

He shrugged. "It's not cinema."

She pounded a hand on the island. "Absolutely not. You are an Emmy-nominated film maker. We won't stand for that." She reached for her phone.

"You're about to plan a premiere for me, aren't you? Here in West Haven?"

She froze with her phone half pulled out of her pocket. "No."

"Is there anything I can say to stop you?"

Claire laughed. "I would love to see you try."

He frowned and stored the frying pan in the cabinet. "You shouldn't be adding another event to your plate. You already have too much going on."

She bumped her hip against him. "For you, nothing is too much trouble."

A hint of a smile appeared. "I still say don't do it. But because I know you won't listen, here's some ground rules. No Jet Skis or parades. Reserved seats for the victims right in the front row."

"Take all the fun out of it, why don't you? I notice you didn't say anything about fireworks, skywriting, or thrones made out of melted pieces of camera equipment."

Luke glared at her. She kissed him on the cheek and he drew her in for a hug.

CHAPTER THIRTEEN

To Do:
- *Practice mindfulness*
- *Confirm menu*
- *Email ranch*

"So, after four painstaking days of guilt tripping every business owner in town, this is what we have." Claire pulled a binder out of her purse and dropped it onto the conference table with a thunk. The sound reverberated off the warehouse walls. "In order from most exciting to least, we have a date with Brianna, followed by the tickets to her premiere."

Mindy scrawled the auction items on the whiteboard next to a group photo of the shelter animals taped to the corner. "Then we have a pre-owned Camaro from Budd's dealership. You'd think after all I went through with his proposal he could have sprung for a new car, but I digress."

Mindy turned around. "I know, right? We just finally got the smell of pigeon poo out of the warehouse. It's a miracle we didn't get toxoplasmosis."

"Honestly. Next, we have a year's membership to the country club, season tickets to the Rusty Rails, and then a bunch of miscellaneous donated stuff. A pot and pan set from Tidings, diamond stud earrings from Sable Jewelry, that watch Kyle got from his boss, restaurant gift certificates."

Mindy scribbled furiously as Claire spoke. "Is it enough?"

Claire sighed and collapsed into an office chair. A tension headache brewed behind her temples. Every time she closed her eyes, Rocky, the three-legged dog, and Pierre, the one-eyed cat, stared forlornly back at her. "I don't know. The auction items and the calendars are really bonus revenue, and what we really need now are the numbers. We barely have seventy preorders right now, and we only have four more days. I sent a PSA to all the local radio stations and emailed Marnie at *Marnie in the Morning*, but I can't guarantee she'll give us a plug."

Claire couldn't put her finger on it, but something in her gut said they were missing something for the gala. Something that would draw a crowd of people with expendable income. But what? Jell-O wrestling? Pie eating contest?

Mindy scoffed. "After what Wendy did to assassinate your character on her show, it's the least she can do."

Ah, yes. Wendy. Claire's (hopefully) former nemesis. Wendy was another West Haven area proposal planner, and she was as unimaginative as she was mean. Wendy had gotten so carried away with her professional war with Claire that she had seduced Claire's fiancé in a bathroom, which had led to Claire calling off her wedding. A fistfight had broken out at Nicole's engagement party, and Wendy had attempted to sue Claire. She only agreed to drop the lawsuit after Claire saved her from getting abducted.

"I had nearly forgotten about that twat," Claire muttered. "What's she up to these days anyway? Still getting paid to help people hide rings in restaurant desserts?"

Mindy shrugged. "Last I heard, she was doing some Caribbean proposals and Jason was tagging along."

Claire rolled her eyes. "I'm surprised a convicted drug dealer is allowed out of the country." Jason had been accidentally implicated in the case of Claire's missing roommate, Courtney Stevens, because he sold her marijuana on the morning of her disappearance.

"Anyway," Claire said, shaking her head to clear it of Jason nonsense, "I'm going to ask Nicole to make some graphics for us, and then I'll distribute flyers all over town. I don't want someone to be able to go more than ten feet without being bombarded with pictures of special needs dogs."

"You're going to make a lot of children cry," Mindy observed.

"If that's what it takes. Do you still think we should gamble on—wait." She stood up and gasped as an idea bloomed like a sunflower. "Gambling. Old people with money love to gamble! If we turn the gala into a casino night, we'll get busloads of old people. Excuse me. I have some phone calls to make."

She practically ripped the office door off its hinges in her pursuit of her vendor book. If she could pull this off, she just might save everything.

CHAPTER FOURTEEN

To Do:
- *Pack*
- *Ask Tanya about prosperity magic*
- *Emergency preparedness- firenado?*

"I wish you'd tell me where we're going," Claire said as acres of farmland flashed by her window. The roads on the outskirts of West Haven were much better maintained than the treacherous expanse of potholes that crisscrossed the city. "And why are we going to dinner at three p.m. on a Tuesday? I know we're getting older, but I don't think we're quite at the early bird special stage yet. Is someone at the restaurant going to chew my food for me?"

"Not far." Luke put a hand on her knee. "It's going to be very romantic."

Her mouth pressed into a hard line. The gala was in three days, and there were still so many details to be double-checked. If she forgot tablecloths or napkins because she was out at a romantic dinner with Luke, she would never forgive him.

"I can feel the tension radiating off you like a nuclear bomb," he said. "For someone who spends their entire life planning marriage proposals, you really hate romance."

"I don't hate romance," she said, perhaps a little too vehemently. "I just don't have a lot of free time right now and being away from a computer stresses me out."

Brad had changed his requested appetizers for the third time earlier that day and the local casino had had a last-minute snafu with renting out enough blackjack tables, which meant Claire had to drive to Wilkes-Barre to a different casino and beg the manager for help. Now two casinos were involved and it was impossible to pick which one had been more aggravating to deal with.

"You're spreading yourself too thin. I woke up last night and you had one leg off the balcony railing and a kitchen knife tucked in your leggings," Luke continued. "If you don't get rid of some of this stress, you're going to start sleep-walking into lakes and stealing tacos again."

"It was one time!" She groaned, throwing up her hands.

He raised his eyebrows as he made a right-hand turn. The turn signal clicked accusingly.

"Okay, it was like five times. I have control over it now. Dr. Goulding has been a huge help."

"Is that why you had a bottle of Fireball and half a pound of Lebanon bologna in your bra?"

She sighed. He had a point. "Fine. I'll schedule another appointment." But there was no way she was going on medication. What if she was so drug-addled that she missed an emergency client phone call?

"Damn straight." Luke squeezed her knee. He made a left turn and pulled into a parking lot.

"Wait, why are we at your bank?"

"Just a quick stop before dinner."

She glanced at her watch and crossed her arms. If she could have reached across the center console and murdered him in cold blood, she would have done it. They were never going to make it home at this rate. She settled into her seat. At least she could fire off a couple of emails while Luke was inside.

"Coming?" he asked as he climbed out of the car.

She gripped her phone like it had personally wronged her. "Why?"

He narrowed his sea green eyes. "They have the good lollipops here. Trust me, you're going to want one."

She lifted her gaze to the sky. Could she make it through this evening without strangling Luke? She couldn't pull off any of her upcoming events from prison, so hopefully somewhere deep inside was an untapped pool of self-control. She flung off her seatbelt and climbed out of the car. Anything to move this date night along.

They walked into the chilly foyer of the bank, and Claire hung back, tapping her foot on the floor. Taking a deep breath, she forced her hands out of tight fists. Dr. Goulding would probably suggest she practice mindfulness in a moment like this. Hmm. What would a mindful person think of right at this moment?

Don't think about the past, don't worry about the future. Whoever came up with the concept was clearly not an attempted-murder-victim-slash-proposal-planner.

She fixed her attention on Luke. Maybe the taut, round shape of his butt in those jeans would ground her in the present. Or the way the sinews in his forearms flexed when he reached across the counter. Great, now she was mindfully horny *and* pissed. Besides, there was no way a man was going to be the answer to a new, mindful Claire. That would have to come from within. Maybe on a less stressful day.

Luke leaned forward and said something to a teller, who came around the desk and escorted him across the bank. What fresh hell was this?

"Come on," he said to Claire.

She followed him wordlessly.

"Vanessa? Your three o'clock is here."

Who the hell was Vanessa?

A red-haired woman with a startling collection of porcelain angel figures littered across her desk looked up. "Oh, great! Come in, Mr. Islestorm. And Miss...?"

"Hartley. Claire Hartley." What was going on?

"So you want to open a joint checking account." Vanessa pulled her keyboard toward her.

Claire stared at Luke. He smiled. "Yes, that's why we're here."

Claire kicked him behind the desk. He had never once mentioned opening a joint bank account. They each had their own accounts, and it had worked perfectly well up to this point. They had only been together for a year. What if Luke broke up with her and ran back to California and she was stuck with a bank account with both of their stupid names on it? Crap, she was thinking about the future again.

"Great," Vanessa said. "Let's just get some of the paperwork done."

Forty minutes later, Claire walked out of the bank with a handful of temporary checks. They weighed down her purse like lead bricks. "You did this because you think I'm poor after taking out the loan," she accused as soon as they walked outside.

"No," Luke said, opening her car door and allowing her to step inside. "I did this because you insist on paying me rent, and it makes more sense for us to have a joint account to contribute to for household expenses. Especially while we're on the other side of the country."

She crossed her arms. "You're lucky I have my social security number memorized. You should have asked me first."

"You mean like when you asked me if you could bring home a blind pug?" He smirked.

He had a point. Dammit.

"One more stop before dinner," he said with a smile. He was clearly enjoying making her squirm.

"I love you, but I'm going to have to murder you. You've given me no choice." She pulled out her phone and flicked open the app they connected to their interior security cameras. Rosie and Winston were sleeping peacefully in the living room. Thank god.

"Can you wait until after the doc comes out, at least?" He shifted the car into reverse and pulled out of the parking lot.

"Ugh, fine." As they turned back onto the road, she stuck a hand in her purse. The checks were there, right next to her wallet, bag of dog biscuits, and Taser. She peeked at the corner and ran a thumb over the smooth paper. It was surreal to see their names right next to each other, the address of their first home below. Maybe she should finally spring for those personalized address labels.

Luke turned the music up—a hard rock band they had both listened to in high school—and they drove several more miles without speaking. She fought to fix her attention on the here and now, and the details that whirled endlessly in her mind like a sandstorm quieted.

When they turned into another parking lot, Claire sat

forward in her seat and looked around. There weren't any restaurants in this part of town. The only stores here were a bunch of tire and paint places and her second favorite spa.

"Is there a food truck somewhere?" she asked, leaning even farther forward.

"No. I lied. This is another pre-dinner stop." He pulled into a parking lot in front of Endive Spa. "Just a twenty-minute hot stone massage."

When she opened her mouth, he cut her off. "Don't pretend like you don't have twenty minutes. Let's go."

Claire glanced at her watch as she climbed out of the car. It was already four. He was really cutting into her evening prep time. How dare he be so thoughtful? And more importantly, how was she going to relax for this massage with a literal shitstorm of events hovering on the horizon like a hurricane?

Half an hour later, Claire waddled out of the spa feeling like she had just been cleansed from the inside out with pure, radiant sunshine.

"Better?" Luke asked when they got in the car.

She leaned across the console and kissed him full on the mouth. "I didn't realize how much I needed that. Thank you. For everything. I'm sorry for being a grumpy, stress-fueled nightmare."

He picked up her hand and kissed the back of it. "You spend too much time trying to take care of everybody else. Now I know you're antsy and ready to murder me, so we'll pick up some takeout and head back home. What'll it be?"

She considered for a nanosecond. "Greek."

"Greek it is." He drove off in the direction of downtown.

The two entered the restaurant and ordered at the counter. Minutes later, a teenage boy wearing a flannel shirt came out with a paper bag.

"Street taco!" he exclaimed.

"Jemarcus! I didn't think you'd remember me."

"It's not every day you run into a grown-ass woman eating a taco in her underwear in the middle of downtown."

Her face grew hot. She had last met Jemarcus during her first sleepwalking experience. "How are you? Almost done with school?"

"Yep. I graduate the first week of June, and I'm headed to MIT in the fall for robotics. It's the craziest thing, apparently at graduation I'm getting a $500 college scholarship from an anonymous donor."

"Huh." She brushed a dog hair off her dress, then took the bag from Jemarcus. "That is crazy. Congratulations! Don't let robots take over the world."

"See you later, street taco," Jemarcus called as she and Luke exited the building.

"Mysterious anonymous donor, huh?" Luke put a hand on the small of her back.

"Kindness deserves to be rewarded. Besides, it'll barely even be enough for his first semester's books." She shook her head.

Claire's heart was lighter when they pulled into the driveway twenty minutes later. The bag of kebabs had filled the sedan with the tantalizing aroma of tzatziki and basil. As a bonus, they were a portable food so she could totally eat and type at the same time. All she needed to do was feed the dogs and then—

"What the hell is that?" she asked. Luke tapped the brakes, and they both lurched forward.

"What?"

"Flowers. On the porch." Her grip on the bag tightened. While a colorful bunch of tulips wasn't a reason to upset the average person, Claire had been haunted by them since Barney had started stalking her.

Luke swore and his expression darkened. "Stay here. Let me check them out. Maybe they're from one of the families." The previous summer, the family of one of Barney's victims had sent flowers to Luke's house. Claire had nearly flung them into the yard.

He shut his car door and locked the vehicle.

Okay, there was no reason to panic. They were probably from someone else. People sent flowers for no reason all the time. Maybe a distant Hartley relative had died and Mindy had gotten a Google alert about it. They could be from the studio or a client—

Her phone dinged, and she glanced at the screen. There was a picture message from Brianna, and a group text between Charlie and Alice. She opened Brianna's message first.

Brianna: *So pretty! These from you? XOXO.*

The bottom dropped out of Claire's stomach. A nearly identical bouquet of tulips sat on Brianna's front steps.

Claire's hand trembled as she backed out of Brianna's message and opened the group text between her mom and sister. She already knew what she would find.

Alice: *Beautiful flowers! Your stepdad is so romantic.*

Charlie: *Weird, I got some too.*

Luke turned back to her as he approached the bundle of flowers. She shook her head and lifted her phone. It was already ringing.

CHAPTER FIFTEEN

To Do:
- *Flee somewhere off the grid*
- *Steel-toed boots for kicking ESA in the balls?*
- *Load decor*

CLAIRE WOKE UP THE DAY OF THE CHARITY GALA WITH HER heart in her throat. It was no big deal. Just the biggest fundraising event of her lifetime with incredibly high stakes. If she didn't succeed tonight, the shelter would have to close. And she was planning it all while she and her family were being targeted by a bunch of serial killers. Awesome.

Walter Smith, the long-suffering detective who had worked with Claire since Barney had broken into her apartment over a year ago, had confiscated the tulips. He had left with promises to contact the Los Angeles and Miami police departments. It wouldn't lead to anything. ESA wasn't stupid. There wasn't a spare second on her calendar to get involved in the investigation, but the mystery beckoned. The murder board from the hotel had been all but abandoned in the flurry of business events, but once she was on that plane to California, ESA was going down. Nobody threatened her family.

She whirled through her morning like a tornado full of razor blades and barbed wire. Casino deliveries and setup were scheduled to start at noon. She needed to check with the caterers and the bartenders and make sure the country club had used the right linens. And then there was the talent show, a last-minute brainchild of Mindy after an entire pot of coffee.

"Breakfast burrito?" Luke asked as she tornadoed into the kitchen. Bags hung under his eyes. Hopefully he hadn't spent the night watching the outdoor security cameras again.

She picked up her purse and a garment bag and kissed both dogs on the snoot. "I can't. I have to get going or I'll be late."

"You're mean when your blood sugar drops," Luke reminded her.

Damn it. She paused with one hand on the door. Her heels clacked against the tile as she took the warm, foil-wrapped bundle from him. "I appreciate you."

He grunted. His stubble scratched against her as she swooped in for a kiss.

"See you later?" she asked.

He nodded. "I'll be there around five. I'm helping the shelter with transport. Mindy's going to be there with you, right?"

"Yes, Mindy and a dozen other workers from the country club. Don't worry. I'm not in any danger."

He raised his eyebrows.

"Well, no more than usual. Thanks for going along with my crazy schemes," she called as she closed the front door behind her. It was go time. She had some disabled pets to save.

Two hours later, Claire and Mindy were hanging a banner above the stage in the country club ballroom.

"Did you check the presales?" Mindy asked as she gripped her corner of the banner. A stapler was clamped between her teeth.

"No," Claire admitted. "I was too afraid."

"Two hundred." Mindy's voice was muffled by the stapler.

Claire's stomach clenched. The country club had set up tables to accommodate 500. Despite all their canvassing, all the flyers and radio spots and social media harassment, it wasn't enough. They were going to be completely humiliated if the room was barely more than a third full. Not to mention the sheer amount of food that would go to waste.

"It's not so bad," Mindy said as she stapled the banner in place. "That's still more than enough to break even without accounting for the auction."

"This is a disaster," Claire muttered. Tears pricked at the corner of her eyes. "We're not here to break even. We're here to save the rescue. We can't save it with two hundred people."

"Marnie did a TV spot this morning, and I'd bet we'll still have some walk-ins who pay the door price." She tossed the stapler to Claire.

Claire stapled her end of the banner with more force than was necessary and stepped off the ladder. The banner mocked her. Differently Abled Pet Talent Show, it read in bold crimson letters. Maybe if some of the animals were adopted tonight, the money from the gala would stretch a little further.

Bang. A door in the corner opened, and Claire screamed and threw the stapler. Was ESA storming the country club?

"Whoopsie," said Stephanie, the head chef for the country club. She sidestepped the stapler and walked over with a plate of hors d'oeuvres. "Care to try?"

Why did everyone in West Haven open doors so violently? Claire popped a crab puff in her mouth. She would never admit it, but Yuffie, the Russian caterer with an attitude problem, made better puffs. Still, if everyone drank enough booze, they would more than suffice.

"Delicious," she said over a mouthful of flaky pastry. "The guests will love them."

Stephanie beamed and left the room.

"Truth?" Mindy asked.

Claire wiggled her hand back and forth, lips pressed into a grim smile. This was not the glitzy, glamorous event she had hoped for. Sure, she only had a week and a half to throw it together. But this was nowhere near the gold standard she had set for Happily Ever Afters.

Mindy nodded. "It'll be okay. Let me make sure the bars are well-stocked," she said in a whisper. "If we liquor these people up enough, they'll be generous with their checkbooks no matter what the apps taste like."

"Good plan." As usual, booze was their only hope. Maybe they should have a drinking game during the talent show. She jotted the idea down on her clipboard and took a surreptitious glance around the ballroom. Mindy had disappeared, and Stephanie the lackluster chef had taken her crab puffs back to the kitchen.

Claire hustled over to her purse and pushed aside a ziplock bag full of alfalfa. Against her better judgment, she had consulted with her stepmother about prosperity magic. Tanya, a practicing Wiccan, had left her laden with herbs.

A dried basil leaf stuck out of her wallet. Though it was supposed to attract money, the only thing it had successfully attracted so far was an overwhelming craving for lasagna. A spray bottle tumbled into her hand. The label read "tincture of alfalfa and chamomile—spray over doorways."

She sighed and bit her lip. Spraying the doorways with this mist wasn't going to make the event more prosperous. If anything, it was probably just going to set off people's allergies.

But it was too late to turn back. The smell of old lady tea crept into the room as she hosed the doorways down with the mist. She sprayed the blackjack, poker, and roulette tables for good measure.

What was next? Another plastic bag crinkled as she removed it. "Aloe—put above doorways." She turned back to the doors. Luckily, the ledge was wide enough to accommodate a few aloe leaves. She sprinkled them and then tossed the bags in the trash.

Now that she had littered the ballroom with hokey magic that would, if anything, probably backfire, it was time to decorate. Glitz and glam with pops of red and black to fit the casino theme. A garment bag slung over a chair caught her eye. Inside was an outfit so outrageous that she would need half a bottle of wine just to put it on.

Several hours later, Claire was hot gluing a scarlet bow on a rather stubborn centerpiece—luckily, it was the last one—when Mindy burst through the doors at the back of the ballroom.

"You're not going to believe this."

Claire glanced at her watch. There was only half an hour 'til the doors were due to open. Maybe a sporting event had been cancelled and some of the patrons had wound up here?

"Well, don't keep me in suspense."

"Just come with me. You have to see it." Mindy grabbed her wrist, and Claire nearly tripped over the hem of her glittering red evening gown as she staggered after her.

Mindy tugged her to the doors in front of the venue. Some guests had arrived and were milling about. Luckily it was a very mild evening, and the predicted rain had never come.

"Okay? So?"

"Look at the back of the lot."

"Is that—"

Mindy jabbed a finger. "*Three* coach buses. That's another two hundred people easily. The assisted living facility ads must have worked."

"Oh, thank god." Claire backed away from the window and leaned against the wall. Her heart beat furiously, but this time it came without the urge to throw up and die. "Can we go through the checklist again?"

"Of course. First, everyone will be funneled toward the bars on either side and encouraged to look at the calendars and the artwork," Mindy said, gesturing to the framed pieces on the walls that had been donated by local artists. "I've enlisted a couple relatives to make slightly misleading statements about the value of some of the portraits."

Claire glowered.

"Don't look at me like that. It's for a good cause. Next, when people are sufficiently toasty from their sneakily strong drinks, they'll be allowed to look over the gambling tables and find their seats. When people are seated, we'll start the talent show and serve dinner."

"Do we really have to put on those ridiculous outfits for the talent show?"

"Hell yes. Sex sells, Claire," Mindy said, poking her with each word. "God has given you two voluptuous gifts. If you're not going to share them with the world to save some innocent dogs, I never knew you at all."

"Fine." Claire crossed her arms over her chest. "And next we'll do the auction?"

Mindy nodded. "Right, we don't want people to blow all their money gambling first."

"Do you think it'll be enough?" Claire turned back to the horde of people outside.

"It'll have to be."

Claire glanced at her phone. "Oh, Bri's here. I better go let her in the back. We can do this, right?"

"Did you see the amount of gold chains on those retirees out there? Everything's going to be fine. We'll buy some time for the rescue, and then we'll absolutely kill it in LA."

"I hope so. By the way, I'm also planning a premiere for Luke's documentary."

Mindy dropped the roll of tape. It bounced on the carpeted floor and disappeared under a welcome table. "You're *what*?"

CHAPTER SIXTEEN

To Do:
- Make that money
- Save the furbabies

"LADIES AND GENTLEMEN," CLAIRE CALLED INTO HER wireless microphone. The stage lights shone down oppressively, disguising everyone past the first row as shapeless blobs. Had she applied enough deodorant that morning? Were the sequins on her ringleader outfit covering up her back sweat?

Her heart jumped in her chest as she stared out at the completely full tables. Miraculously, beyond the two hundred people from the assisted living facility, a last-minute social media post from Brianna had resulted in another hundred attendees. They even had to turn some people away.

"Thank you all for coming tonight. I hope you enjoyed

the art." There was some polite applause. "We're here tonight to save an organization that is very near and dear to my heart, Tender Hearts Animal Rescue. Tender Hearts is a no-kill animal shelter that accepts all animals, not just the healthy ones that are likely to be adopted quickly. This is the shelter I adopted my dog from two years ago. Rosie?"

Claire whistled, and Rosie ran out on stage, reluctantly clad in a top hat and her sparkly ringleader outfit. There was a chorus of *aww* from the audience. Claire gave her a treat, and Luke whistled offstage. Rosie ran back to him and flopped on her back.

"For your entertainment while you enjoy a four-course dinner from the country club's own Chef Stephanie, you're going to meet the animals you're helping to save. Some of them have disabilities, but they are still more than capable of filling your homes with love and joy." She signaled to Mindy, and the house lights dimmed as the curtains opened. A small agility course was revealed. The banner was definitely crooked, but hopefully it added to the whimsy of the talent show.

Mindy burst through the backdoors with Maggie, a three-legged yellow lab. Everyone in the audience turned to look. Mindy could have passed for a Vegas showgirl.

"Please put your hands together for Maggie, a four-year-old lab with three legs and a heart of gold." Mindy gestured to the dog, who panted happily and slobbered in the lap of a local malpractice lawyer.

"Maggie enjoys long, slightly lopsided walks and watching re-runs of baking shows. But don't let this tripod fool you, she has more poise and grace than the New York Ballet Company." After tugging Maggie away from a sociology professor's dinner roll, the pair climbed the steps to the stage. Mindy handed Maggie off to Gloria, co-owner of

Tender Hearts, who had mercifully agreed to change out of her denim overalls for the occasion.

Waiters had begun to descend with salad and bread, but most of the audience wasn't watching as their food arrived.

Gloria let Maggie off her leash and gave her a "stay" command. Gloria moved to the opposite side of the obstacle course and whistled. Maggie dove through the course, rocketing through a small tunnel and leaping between staggered cones. She ran up a ramp and jumped through a hoop before gracefully landing on the other side. She continued to run, gathering speed before clearing a hurdle at the end of the stage. Gloria raised her hands triumphantly, and the audience broke into thunderous applause. The curtains swung shut, and stage hands hurried to move the agility course offstage.

Oh, shit. Claire had been so busy watching Maggie do her course that she had forgotten she was introducing the next dog. She darted into the hallway and jogged to the foyer, squashing her boobs flat as she ran. This was no time to lose an eye. She grabbed the next dog, Brodie, from Sam, and squeezed in a couple deep breaths. The attendees would be looking at the dog, not her. There was no reason to freak out. She should have taken a shot of whiskey before slithering into this ridiculous outfit.

She switched on her wireless microphone and opened the doors. Brodie zoomed inside next to her, hind legs bound up in a wheelchair.

"Next we have Brodie, a red dachshund who comes with his own set of wheels," Claire announced. Her voice boomed back at her from the speakers in the corner of the room. All eyes turned to look at her. Damn it. They were supposed to focus on the dog. There was no way all these probing eyes were going to miss the small ocean of back sweat lurking under her costume.

She caught Nicole's eye as she passed her table, and she pointed to Claire's boobs and gave an enthusiastic thumbs up.

The dachshund shoved his snoot into a woman's purse, and Claire gently tugged him away. "Brodie is just as happy at the lake as he is cuddled under a puddle of blankets on your lap. Be careful if you meet him, because he'll steal your heart. What he lacks in stair-climbing ability, he makes up for with a convenient, portable size and a very special talent."

By some miracle, she had reached the stage without tripping or sweating on someone. Brodie's tongue flopped out as she picked him up and gently placed him onstage, where Gloria took the leash and led him to the center. Three miniature tennis balls hit the ground. Brodie's front legs danced anxiously.

"Wait. Wait," Gloria said, holding her hand up to Brodie. He maintained eye contact. "Okay."

The little dog careened forward and snatched all three tennis balls from the floor. He faced the audience, cheeks and mouth full of balls. The crowd applauded again. Claire escorted Brodie backstage and tucked him back into his designated crate.

Mindy's voice came over the speaker, announcing the arrival of Mittens, a one-eyed Persian cat who was about to jump six feet in the air with the help of a laser pointer.

"I'm not going to lie," someone said in Claire's ear. "I feel ridiculous."

She turned. Brianna stood next to her, looking absurdly beautiful in her costume. She was going to escort the last animal as a surprise for the audience.

"You look beautiful. I really hope we're not about to accidentally sell you into sex trafficking."

Brianna waved her hand. "I'll be fine. Don't you have to go escort a bird?"

"Dammit. You're right." Claire turned and half-jogged to the hallway.

By the time the forks were scraping up the last of the entrée course, Claire's hair hung in damp ringlets down her back and her legs ached from hurrying in heels. Her toes were pinched, her makeup was almost certainly smudged all over the place, and she probably looked like a homeless sewer rat. But if they pulled this off, it would all be worth it.

Mindy and Claire took the stage together. Mindy's brow glistened under the lights, but Claire almost certainly looked like she had just emerged from the deep end of the country club's pool.

"And now, as an extra special treat, please welcome our last rescue animal, escorted by my sister, actress Brianna Hartley."

Brianna threw the doors open in her fishnet stockings and matching ringleader outfit. The audience gasped. Some of them jumped to their feet. Applause broke out, and more people climbed to their feet. She tapped her mic before speaking.

"Thank you, West Haven! Here we have Earl Grey, or Earl for short, an English sheepdog who doesn't let his deafness interfere with daily life. He enjoys lying in front of fireplaces—sir, if you want to keep your fingers unbroken, I recommend that you keep them to yourself."

Brianna paused her monologue to cast a sharp look at a middle-aged man with a shining bald spot and basketball themed tie. He withdrew his hand from her ass and leered at her. Sawyer jumped up from his table and put a hand on the man's shoulder.

Brianna continued her walk—make that strut—with Earl Grey. She climbed the stairs effortlessly and took to the stage as though she had been born there. When she dropped the leash and gave Earl a hand signal, he stayed, panting happily, while she crossed to the middle of the stage and picked a treat from a bowl.

She tossed it toward him, a little too high, and he leapt and snatched it from the air. The audience applauded as Sawyer led the creepy basketball guy from the room. They didn't need his money.

Brianna took another treat and backed up. There was easily ten feet of space between her and Earl. She tossed the treat underhand, and Earl jumped and caught it with ease. He turned in place twice before settling down. Brianna picked a third treat from the bowl and took several more steps back. Could she even throw that far?

Bang. Something metallic clanged backstage.

Claire whipped her head around. The back of her neck prickled. "Do you hear something?" she whispered to Mindy.

As she pulled the curtain back, Brianna shrieked onstage. Peg, a high-energy Doberman who had shown off her rolling-over ability, barreled through the curtain and snatched the treat from the air. She trotted across the stage and stood on her back legs, putting her front paws on Brianna.

"Shit! How did she get out? We need to get her back in the crate."

"Uh, Claire?" Mindy called from backstage.

"What?"

Mindy pointed to the crating area with a shaking finger.

148

A dozen crate doors hung wide open. The only animal still inside was Toots, an overweight chihuahua who wasn't about to let some silly crate door tell him what to do. Claire shut his door and turned to Mindy.

"Oh my god. Get Gloria."

Screams and laughter came from the audience. Claire barreled back onstage. Felix and Archer, two chubby ginger cats, had leapt onto the tables and started eating leftovers. Cracker, an eighteen-year-old African gray parrot, hung from the chandelier. Septimus, a notoriously naughty kitten, was crawling up the curtains on the side of the stage.

Brodie had taken a poo on stage left. Maggie was running through the tables, pausing for a head scratch or offered scrap. Peg had bounded the length of the hall twice, zooming from one corner to the other. She leapt over a table and hurtled into the owner of a local sporting goods store. His chair tipped, which knocked against the table, which sent everything crashing to the floor.

Fuck. They totally weren't getting their security deposit back. Luke chased Peg, but every time he was close to snatching her collar, she would jump away from him and knock into another table.

Hurry, hurry. Shit. Claire whipped the curtain back and dug around in a closet until she found a ladder. She dragged it across the stage and set it up. Septimus was already eight feet off the ground. Her shoes hit the ladder with a *thunk*. Her heart in her throat, she scaled the rungs as quickly as her sequined costume allowed.

Septimus meowed at her as she tugged him gently from the curtain. She clutched him to her chest as she descended. This was a disaster. She needed help. Someone needed to round up these animals. Rosie stood at the bottom of the ladder, one paw on a rung.

"Rosie." Claire made firm eye contact with the corgi. "Go." She pointed to the ruckus unfolding below. This was a problem that only the Fun Police could solve.

Rosie took off like a rocket, barking and nipping at the other dogs' heels. Claire ran backstage with Septimus. Two down, eighteen to go. She scooped up Brodie next and narrowly missed stepping in the steaming present he had left behind.

Audience members had clambered to their feet. Some took videos with their phones while others tried in vain to help. Nicole and Kyle cornered a cat behind one of the bars. Sawyer pulled a bag of dog treats out of his pocket and convinced Maggie to follow him.

Peg appeared onstage. Her stump of a tail was pointed down and her head bowed. She ran from Rosie. Claire held her crate door open, and she crawled inside and sat down.

"Good girl," Claire said, tossing a treat to Rosie. "Keep going." She pointed back out to the audience. Who in the hell would have let all these animals out? The backstage area had been deserted, but there was no security on the doors that led outside. Anyone could have come in.

Her stomach twisted into a knot. Was it insane to think that ESA might have had something to do with this? Did they really have the balls to ruin a charity event? There was time to worry about that later.

Ten minutes later, all the animals were contained in their crates. Mindy had a scratch on her cheek from Felix, who most certainly did *not* want to get back into captivity. Claire had two carpet-burned knees and a sizable bump on her head from chasing after Archer.

The two of them walked back onstage, looking like they had just been through a war. "Well, that was fun." The audience tittered. "How about a little something for our nerves?

A quick round of Fireball for everyone," she called to the waitstaff. It was time to start liquoring the crowd back up, and hopefully the dinner would prevent anyone from projectile vomiting during the event.

When everyone had been served, Claire and Mindy held their shot glasses up to the crowd. "To Tender Hearts." Most of the audience drank their shots. It was time to start the auction.

Three hours later, Claire dumped half a dozen bank bags into the safe in Luke's trunk.

"I can't believe you made that much money," he said, slamming the trunk lid.

"Even all the calendars sold. I have to order more. But really it was mostly thanks to Brianna. I never thought we'd actually get someone to spend $10,000 just to take her to Burger King," Claire mused, fumbling with the buttons on her ringmaster costume. She would rather ride home fully naked than spend another second in this corset.

"I heard the guy talking to Bri. He asked if he could transfer the date with him into her taking his son to the prom."

"That's kind of adorable," she said.

"Claire!" someone called across the parking lot. Gloria jogged toward them.

"I can't thank you enough." She wrapped Claire in a hug. A risky move considering the amount of sweat on her body.

Claire smiled. "It was nothing. I can't believe all the animals were adopted."

"I know. Even that asshole, Toots," Gloria said with a knowing look.

Claire chuckled. "Listen, I know it's not a permanent solution. When I get back from California—"

Gloria waved a hand. "Stop. You've done more than

enough. We'll be fine for another six months. And Sam and I are going to brainstorm. You reminded us that Tender Hearts is worth it. We're not going to give up."

"I'm so glad to hear that." Claire waved as Gloria left.

Luke rubbed her shoulder. "Do you feel better?"

"Honestly? Not really." She climbed into the car. If everything didn't work out perfectly, she would never have the funds to support Tender Hearts. In six months, they could be right back to square one.

"You did something amazing," he said as they pulled out onto the highway. "You saved twelve dogs, seven cats, and a bird."

"Thank you." She squeezed his hand and pulled out her phone. She desperately needed a shower and a stiff drink. In just three days, they would be in California staring down the barrel of the biggest proposal of her entire career. It was going to be flawless. It had to be.

CHAPTER SEVENTEEN

To Do:
- *Grocery list for CA*
- *Does Winston count as a carry-on?*
- *Ship binders*

A ROUGH TONGUE ON HER ELBOW ROUSED CLAIRE FROM SLEEP. Sunlight streamed through the window, and a disgruntled corgi stared back at her. Rosie whined and nudged her. Apparently she had decided it was time for breakfast.

Claire sat up in bed. The dresser Luke had moved in front of the bedroom door was still there, and none of the bedroom windows were cracked. Aha! She hadn't sleep-walked despite the mountain of stress. Who needed medication now, Dr. Goulding?

Out of habit, she picked up her phone. There was an excellent chance half a dozen emails from Brad would litter her inbox.

Her stomach dropped.

"That's weird."

"Huh?" Luke grunted, head under a pillow. Rosie leapt onto the bed and licked his earlobe.

"I have all these voicemails. I thought maybe Brad was trying to get in contact, but none of these are from him. There's one from my landlord for the warehouse. He hasn't called me in years."

He couldn't care less what she did as long as she kept the rent checks coming. She jumped out of bed and stood, playing the one from the landlord on speaker.

"Miss Hartley, this is Mr. Dressler, your landlord. We need you to come down to the warehouse as soon as you can. There's been a fire."

The phone slipped from Claire's fingers. Her knees went weak, and she crashed to the floor. Luke grabbed her arm and spoke to her, but everything was muffled like she was underwater. The edges of her vision went spotty and dark.

"Breathe, Claire. Just breathe." Luke knelt next to her on the carpet. Rosie jumped and licked at her face. Winston whined from his bed in the corner.

She grabbed Luke's hand and stared, hard, into his eyes. "What. The fuck. Did they do?"

"IT'S GONE. EVERYTHING'S GONE." CLAIRE KNELT IN THE ASHES of the warehouse. The acrid stench of melted plastic and charred wood invaded her nostrils. Steam rose from the soggy piles of ash. Despite the West Haven Fire Department's best efforts, the fire had burned so hot and so long that Happily Ever After's headquarters had been taken down to the studs. Several policemen and firemen were investigating the electrical box at the far end of the lot. Luke, Sawyer, and Kyle were with them.

Her heart thumped uncomfortably fast and hard. Tears were on the verge of spilling out, but she wasn't going to give them the satisfaction. This wasn't a fluke electrical fire. She would bet her last dollar an ESA henchman was hightailing it out of West Haven, cackling over a gas can.

Nicole squeezed her hand. "It's just things, Claire."

An easy thing to say for someone whose life was amazing and perfectly on track.

"It wasn't just things. It was everything we had built." Claire rose to her feet and tugged on the corner of a sharp piece of metal. The Eiffel Tower she and Mindy had made for a client's escape room proposal the previous year fell to the concrete floor with a clatter.

"Countless pieces of equipment. Client records. Boxes upon boxes of memories and reusable decorating materials. All gone."

Mindy bent over and tugged something from the ashes. A charred remnant of a shoe broke apart in her hand. "The sparkly shoes," she whispered mournfully. They had been in a display case in the office, a relic from Nicole's proposal. All three girls had a matching pair. They had worn them all together at Nicole's wedding, but now they never would again.

"The binders are at Luke's house, right?" Nicole asked tentatively.

Claire nodded. "Thank god. Luckily we're renting everything for Brad's—oh my god." She clapped a hand to her forehead.

"What?" Mindy asked sharply. Her green eyes narrowed.

"The saddle. From Karen's childhood. It was in the office."

They all turned toward the remains of the small rectangular room that used to be the office. There was nothing left, not even a splinter of wood from their desk. The one-of-a-kind saddle with hand-carved tooling and silver overlay that Brad had dug out of Karen's parents' storage locker was gone.

"Fuck." Mindy's hand fisted in her hair.

"He's going to kill us." Claire's knees buckled. A high-pitched ringing buzzed incessantly in her ears as a scatter of black spots appeared over her vision. "I knew I should have kept it at the house. We're so screwed."

"Hey." Nicole knelt next to her and gripped her arm. "Deep breaths. Come on."

Claire's head spun, and she fought for breath. She had pictures and itemized lists of everything in her inventory, but she never dreamed she would actually have to make an insurance claim on everything her business owned. This kind of loss was incalculable. And how long would it take to replace everything? To find a new space to rent?

There was so much left to plan this year. Luke's documentary premiere alone was going to use half the things in her warehouse. And she had lost something irreplaceable. The panic was rising in her chest again, and the deep breaths she was forcing in weren't helping.

"Do you think it was them? ESA?" Mindy whispered. She and Nicole tugged Claire back to her feet.

"It has to be." Claire kicked a hunk of ash. The toe of her shoe grew warm. "They blew up my car last year. What's to stop them from burning down my warehouse?"

"They'll pay." Mindy bent down and dug through the ash. A moment later, she pulled out the "Happily Ever Afters" sign.

Nicole dusted the sign off, but it was hopelessly singed.

Black soot obscured the words, and the edges were charred from the heat. Claire took it from her and hugged it to her chest. It was too much. The rescue, her family being targeted, Brad's proposal, living in LA, Barney's sentencing. How much was one person supposed to take? How far could she bend before she shattered?

Nicole and Mindy stood on either side of her. They wrapped her in a tight hug. A stiff wind ripped through the skeleton of the warehouse, and ashes spiraled at their feet.

Mindy pulled back and held both of Claire's arms. "Look at me," she ordered.

Claire raised her eyes slowly like a sullen child.

"You are Claire Freakin' Hartley. This is not the end of your story. This is a tiny, cowardly blip that someday we will laugh about when all of ESA is rotting in federal prison."

Claire raised her eyebrows. "You really think law enforcement is going to bring down all of ESA? It's impossible."

"We don't need all of ESA," Mindy said, taking a step back. Her eyes were bright. "A cult without a leader is nothing. If we find the leader, everything else will crumble. That's basically Cult Theory one-oh-one."

Claire sighed. "Who's to say there isn't an equally power-hungry idiot who's second in command? This may never be over. I'm going to have to move abroad." Her Canada plan was looking more attractive by the minute. "Besides, we have no idea who's in charge. The only person we know for sure is involved with ESA is Professor Taylor and he's been missing for months."

Nicole leaned in. "When we're finished here, we're going to stage a Code Purple and spruce up Murder Binder 3.0. We're going to track down the professor, catch whoever's in charge, stomp on his testicles, and then we're going to burn *his* house down."

Claire and Mindy stared at Nicole.

"Sorry, hormones. I stand by what I said, though."

A car rolled into the parking lot behind them. Claire braced herself. Who was it going to be? An insurance claim adjuster? More cops? The press? Someone else who was going to ask questions that she didn't have answers to?

Jack Hartley stepped lightly out of a nondescript black sedan. It must have been a work vehicle. His frown lines were extra pronounced today, but his salt-and-pepper hair was still perfectly molded into place. Between the hair and his well-tailored black suit, James Bond might as well have been walking into their midst.

Claire lifted one hand in a weak greeting.

"I came as soon as I heard. I'm so sorry, Claire."

She shrugged. "I guess this is what happens when you piss off a bunch of serial killers. And have the misfortune of sharing DNA with the head of the task force trying to take them down."

Jack wasn't a hugger, but concern radiated from him as he put one hand on her shoulder. Her stepfather, on the other hand, was the best hugger she knew. When she had a bad day in high school, Roy would hold her close and whisper kind things in Spanish until she felt better.

"I have someone coming down from the Bureau to check out the scene." Jack withdrew his hand and put it in his pocket.

"Thanks," she said. It wouldn't do any good. She needed a nap, a platter of tacos, and a gallon of tequila. But she still had to deal with the insurance company. And triple-check her packing for LA. And close down Luke's house. Now that

ESA had destroyed nearly everything she owned, Brad's proposal was more important than ever. She couldn't delay even by a day. No matter what happened, she was getting on a plane first thing Monday morning.

"I know you're leaving soon, but Tanya's made you some soup. I'll put it in your car before I leave. I'm going to talk to the officers." Jack turned on his polished shoes and set off for the clump of people at the other end of the lot.

"What do vegan Wiccans put in soup?" Mindy whispered loudly.

There was movement at the other end of the lot. Two officers joined her father and headed back toward her.

Claire squared her shoulders as the officers approached. "Let me guess. Arson."

The cops exchanged a glance. "We believe so. We found multiple points of origin and evidence of accelerants. Here's the incident number for your insurance claim."

She took the paper. "Great. Well, luckily, the perpetrators were a secret organization that I'm not allowed to talk about. You can ask this guy." She gestured to her father before turning on her heel. The Happily Ever Afters sign was still clutched under one arm.

"Tacos?" Luke said as he appeared at her elbow. His hand snaked around her back, and he pulled her close.

She nodded and turned to look at the smoldering remnants one more time. Wind stirred the ashes. The warehouse had been like the third member of Happily Ever Afters, graciously hosting every harebrained scheme Claire and Mindy could concoct. They had spent countless hours brainstorming around their polished conference table and wandering the aisles looking for the perfect romantic decor. And now it was all gone.

She turned away, focusing on the warmth of Luke's arm around her. ESA would never take another thing from her. They were going to pay.

CHAPTER EIGHTEEN

To Do:
- Triple check inventory spreadsheet
- Send thank you donuts to fire dept

"Claire. Wake up." Luke's voice cut like a knife.

Her eyes flew open. She was tilted at a curious angle, surrounded by darkness. Wind tugged at her hair. Inexplicably, a steering wheel was clenched in her hands.

"Oh, shit."

Not again. She had just gotten the sleepwalking under control. Now, from the looks of things, she had driven Luke's new golf cart into a ditch.

He removed her hands and slid her across the seat. A slant of moonlight hit him as he climbed behind the wheel. His eyes were bloodshot, brows creased. She bit her lip. This wasn't going to be a fun conversation.

"How did you find me?" she asked.

"I followed the trail of canned ravioli and kitchen knives you left behind." The barely suppressed anger wafted off him like toxic fumes.

"Oh." She fell silent. Something hard was in her bra. She fished it out as Luke reversed out of the ditch and drove them back toward the house.

A Taser and a burrito emerged. She unwrapped the burrito and took a bite. Still good. She offered it to Luke. Maybe a bra burrito would soothe his frazzled nerves. He took the burrito and whipped it into the forest.

"Hey!" She turned around.

"You need to try the medication." His knuckles were white on the steering wheel.

She straightened and faced him. They had had this argument more than once. "I'm not taking Klonopin," she hissed. "I'm going the all-natural route. Soothing sleep routine, meditation, and exercise."

"Oh yeah? And how's that going for you?" Luke reached behind him and dropped a black JanSport onto the seat. Cans and knives were visible through a gap in the zipper. "I'm tired of you ignoring your problems. You're going to hurt yourself. Or someone else."

"I didn't ask for this." She waved a hand at the trees crawling by. "Do you think I want to sleepwalk? To feel so out of control all the time? To have a national network of serial killers burning down my office and blowing up my car? Do you think I want to feel scared all the time?"

"Klonopin would help with your anxiety *and* your sleep-walking. You're being selfish."

Claire's mouth dropped open. It would have hurt less if he had dropkicked her out of the golf cart. "Don't you *dare* accuse me of being selfish. I spend my entire life slaving over details, trying to create beauty for other people. I'm not going to jeopardize my entire career by becoming a drug-addled zombie."

He sighed and wiped a hand over his face. "I don't get it."

"Get what?"

"You would do anything—*anything*—for someone else. But you won't take care of yourself. You can't plan proposals if you're dead, Claire."

"I'll be sure to mention that to the next person who tries to kill me."

She crossed her arms over her chest. Her lip ached where she had bitten it. They rode back to the house in silence. Luke parked the golf cart in the garage and pulled out the key. They both sat, unmoving. Was he about to pick another fight? Her heart couldn't take it.

"I'm sorry for calling you selfish."

Claire unclenched her hands. The comment still stung, but she was tired to the bone. She didn't have it in her to argue. "I'm sorry for stealing the golf cart. For the record, I know this is bad. Maybe the exercise approach isn't sustainable. I'll think about the meds, okay? I just want to do some research before I commit."

His hand rested on her knee. "You're just saying that to placate me, aren't you?"

"No," she said defensively. She would make this decision the way she always (well, usually) made decisions—thoughtfully, and with a binder full of research and a comprehensive pros and cons list. And that could take weeks. Certainly not until after Brad's proposal.

"Come on. Bed." He grabbed her hand and lifted her, draping her over one shoulder. "I'm getting the handcuffs."

"Do what you must."

Hours later, after a medium-okay night of sleep, Claire stood in the kitchen.

"No, Mom, there's no need to come up here." She all but groaned into the phone as she poured another cup of coffee. Opening the refrigerator, she frowned at a container of deli meat and tossed it into the trashcan.

"But, Clairebear, someone *burned down* your office space." Alice's voice was more pinched than usual.

"Yes, but you coming up here would only put you in the path of whatever dangerous idiots are trying to ruin my life. And besides, we leave for LA in the morning so we won't even be here. Stay where you are, please." She picked up the remainder of the gallon of milk and dumped it down the drain.

Alice sighed. "I don't like this, Claire. I'm going to call Brian."

"Don't you dare." The last time Alice had called Brian the PI, Mindy had nearly assaulted him in an alleyway. "I don't need private security. I'm going to the other end of the country. It'll be much harder for them to find me there."

She slammed the refrigerator door and headed to her office, letting her mother yammer on speakerphone. After a quick Google search, several sheets of paper spat out of her printer. She gathered them into a neat pile and three-hole punched them before setting them on top of a binder marked "LA Preparedness."

She glanced down at the list of possible natural disasters on her desk and scratched off "earthquakes." Time for wildfires.

Alice was still talking a mile a minute on the other end of the line as Claire searched.

"Los Angeles is dangerous, Claire. Even if they don't

follow you there, you could get swept up by a tsunami or buried by an earthquake or—"

Claire eyed the corners of the room. Surely her mother hadn't installed security cameras without her noticing. "Mom, everything's going to be fine. It's only a few weeks. I have to go. I need to finish packing."

Alice sighed like Claire had just told her she was permanently relocating to the jungles of Borneo. "Fine. But I'm going to read your cards tonight."

"Please don't. I love you. Bye." She stabbed the "end" button until the call disconnected.

Her gaze fell on the Happily Ever Afters sign that Nicole had rescued from the wreckage. She had abandoned it in the corner of her home office. How was it possible that her whole office was gone? Countless memories, thoughtfully selected linens and decorations. Pictures and thank you notes from clients. Karen's priceless childhood saddle. All gone because of some homicidal assholes. She wouldn't stand for it.

"How'd she take it?" Luke popped into the doorway.

Claire screamed.

"Sorry." He cracked a smile and shifted the messenger bag and backpack he carried to his other hand.

She pressed a hand to her chest and waited for her heart to stop galloping. Rosie jumped up and put her paws on her thighs. Winston whined from his bed at her feet.

"She's threatening to hire a PI again."

"Because that worked out so well last time," Luke observed.

She shrugged. "I think I at least talked her out of coming here. I told her we're leaving tomorrow."

"And we are still leaving tomorrow?" He raised an eyebrow.

"Yes," Claire said firmly. She had waffled back and forth all day, but there was no sense in staying in West Haven just because her building had burned down. "There's nothing I can do from here. I already submitted the insurance claim with itemized inventory photos. It'll take weeks for them to sift through everything, let alone send me a check."

Luke set his bags on the floor and came to stand behind her. Pressing a kiss to her neck, he put his hands on her shoulders and rubbed his thumbs up and down her neck, bobbling her head back and forth.

Their middle-of-the-night argument had been all but forgotten. Her shoulders lowered. Some of the tension that she had been holding onto since she heard the voicemail dissolved. She closed her eyes and turned her attention inward. There was no proposal, no cross-country move. There was only this moment, with her favorite person in the world in the safety of her office. But soon, the crushing weight of reality and a random niggling question that had bothered her all weekend resurfaced.

"Have you thought about kids?" she asked abruptly.

"What?" The warmth disappeared from her neck, and something crashed to the floor. Rosie ran over to inspect.

Claire swiveled her chair to look at Luke. He must have jumped back and knocked her diamond-shaped paperweight over. At least it hadn't broken. Small victories.

"Kids. Do you ever want to have children?"

"I bought a house with five bedrooms. What did you think I was going to put in the other four?"

"Dogs? More screening rooms?" Rosie jumped into her lap, and Claire buried her cheek in the corgi's voluminous fur. The knot in her stomach eased.

"I mean, do you? Want kids?" He took a step away from her and crossed his arms.

"I do. Not for a while. Obviously the business is not in a stable place at the moment, but when things settle down someday—if they ever settle down, anyway—I'd love to be a mother. I just wanted to make sure you were on board in case anything unexpected happened."

"I see," he said, perching on the edge of her filing cabinets. "Have you been poking holes in the condoms?"

She scoffed. "Relax, my biological clock isn't that loud. Sorry, I'm in a weird headspace with everything going on. Do you have everything packed?"

Luke nodded and buried a hand in his already tousled hair. He looked exhausted.

She caught his hand. "Are you okay? I feel like you spend so much time checking in on me and seeing how I'm doing, and we don't always talk about how your day was." A burned-down building was not an excuse to be a bad girlfriend.

"I'm fine. There's just a lot running through my mind too. It'll get better once we get to LA. I'm going to have to work a lot, but I want to make sure we make time for us while we're out there. I want to show you California."

"We're not moving there permanently," Claire said, grabbing her stack of papers and shuffling them into the binder.

"No." He chuckled. "I mean it, though. I know you're going crazy with work. But it's important to me that we spend time together out there too."

She smiled. "I hear you. I'll even let you plan our first date night." She bent forward and kissed him. "Want to help me pack Rosie's suitcase?"

Luke sighed. "Rosie is a dog. She doesn't need a suitcase."

"What if she needs her winter jacket?"

"She has a double coat, and it's Southern California.

Trust me, she doesn't need it. *Or* her galoshes," he said firmly.

Claire threw up her hands. "Fine. They'll need food and toys though, I assume? Or does living in Southern California rid you of that need?"

Luke pulled her from her chair. "Come on, kid. Tomorrow's a big day."

CHAPTER NINETEEN

To Do:
- *Text Charlie when we land*
- *Confirm appt with Brad's assistant*
- *Find safest walking route for dogs*

"SO WHERE DO YOU THINK THE HEAD ASSHOLE LIVES?" MINDY whispered to Claire. She crossed her legs, and her foot banged into Claire's shin. They were stuffed into coach seats. Luke had tried to persuade Claire to join him in first class, but the loan from the bank and inevitable increase in her insurance premium weighed heavily on her mind.

"I'm not sure," Claire said. "Where do they hate women the most?"

"Texas?" Mindy guessed.

Claire shrugged. It seemed plausible. "No hits on Web Detectives yet?"

"I checked this morning, but I'll look again when we land. He can't hide forever."

Claire bit her lip and pulled a binder out of her carry-on, banging her elbow off the window. The woman in the babushka next to them snorted in her sleep.

It had been over a week and they didn't have a single lead on the professor's location. Had he gone to a major metropolitan area, hoping to blend in? Maybe he was threatening indigenous women in Alaska or piloting an airboat in the Everglades. Hours spent scouring his old social media profiles had given them very little. All they had were a few check-ins from the early 2010s—Whole Foods, Dave and Buster's, and an art museum. They couldn't very well stake out every Whole Foods in the nation.

"You're sure Luke doesn't mind me staying with you guys?"

Claire fervently shook her head. "Not at all. It'll be easier to work on the proposal if we're in the same place." Her fancy GPS watch beeped. "Speaking of which...murder break is over. Back to business."

In just a few short hours they would land in Los Angeles, and there would be no avoiding the onslaught of tasks that awaited her. A color-coded list spanning several pages stared back at her. Her stomach clenched. Deep breaths. They had done the impossible before.

"Okay." Mindy flipped her tablet back open. "Luckily I downloaded all of these and made a quick PowerPoint before we got on the plane. We have to talk about the West Coast HEA Affiliate."

The knot in Claire's stomach twisted harder. "Is that what we're calling it?"

Her friend shrugged. "It sounded official."

"Whatever. Show me what we have."

Mindy tapped her screen until a slideshow appeared. "Okay, first candidate. Megan Corcoran. BA in business administration from Berkeley. Currently assisting a tech start-up but looking for something more long term."

"Next," Claire said flatly. "There's no way we can afford someone with a BA from Berkeley."

"Okay, then we have Jenna Sutton. She has a degree in hospitality from Iowa State, recently relocated to California to pursue a career in acting."

"So she can call off all the time to go to auditions? Not a chance. Next."

Mindy set her jaw and flicked to the next candidate. "Heather Clearwater. Bachelor's in hospitality management from Penn State. Relocated to California four years ago to work for a hotel chain. She said she's looking for something with more of a human element."

"Hmmm. Okay, put her in the interview pile. You made sure she's not a serial killer, right?"

Mindy laughed. "Nothing came up on her initial criminal background."

"That means nothing. I'll wait for the federal one to come back, and I will scrutinize her very closely during the interview."

"That won't freak her out at all." Mindy shook her head. "Next there's Alexis Renninger, LA. native. No higher education, but she worked as a production assistant on a lot of reality shows and could probably give us gossip."

Claire leaned forward. "A very important skill. Let's at least interview her."

They flicked through the remainder of the candidates and decided to interview four.

"Great. I'll set up interviews when we land. One more

thing." Mindy closed her tablet and turned to face Claire. "I think I'm going to propose to Sawyer."

Clunk. Claire's backpack hit the floor, startling a snore out of the woman next to them.

"Holy shit, Min," Claire whispered. "When? How?"

"Not for a few months, until everything calms down a little bit. We can start the planning after California."

The words "Are you sure?" were on the tip of Claire's tongue. She clamped her mouth shut. Sawyer had proven time and time again that he was an honest, caring man. Love didn't run on a specific timeline. So what if they hadn't even been together a year? Maybe she could sneakily work their questionnaire into normal conversation. Just to be sure Mindy was really ready. She had boned a wanna-be serial killer in a bar bathroom less than a year ago, after all.

"This is huge. I'm thrilled for you," Claire said, drawing her into a tight hug.

"I know it's crazy. But I've never felt like this before. Normally with guys I can't wait to get some space, but with Sawyer I'm paying for Wi-Fi on a plane in case he wants to tell me what he had for breakfast. Things with him are..."

"Different?" Claire smiled.

"Exactly. He's so down-to-earth. No games, no drama. He's there when I need him and he gives me space when I don't. He just *knows*."

"I've never seen you so smitten," Claire teased, nudging her. "Not even with that lacrosse captain who burped a sonnet for you."

"Ethan." Mindy smiled fondly.

"I'm so glad you're happy. He's a significant improvement from...well, you know." Claire said. Mindy's last boyfriend, Garrett, had turned out to be a member of ESA. He was currently sitting in prison for his role in the attempted kidnapping of Claire's nemesis.

"He'll make an amazing husband," she added.

"He will. Anyway, you want to clock an hour on Brad's proposal, or should we try to squeeze in a nap before we get there?"

Claire yawned. "I vote nap. I keep thinking about Winston and Rosie down there with the luggage. It's breaking my heart. Next time I'm driving cross-country."

"I think that would traumatize them more," Mindy said as she slid on an eye mask.

"You're probably right." Claire closed her eyes and waited for sleep.

CHAPTER TWENTY

To Do:
- *Add Charlie to shit list*
- *Buy sunscreen*
- *Background checks*

"I KNEW WE SHOULD HAVE TAKEN AN UBER," CLAIRE HISSED AS she dragged her suitcase behind her. Rosie trotted at her side, clearly thrilled to be out of the cargo hold. Luke pulled a luggage cart with the dog crates behind him, Winston strapped to his chest.

"Is that Charlie?" He squinted at the tall brunette in platform wedges, white capris, and a coral peplum top. At 5'10", she had clearly inherited her height from Jack. No one would have even guessed that they were sisters.

"It sure is. I'm going to murder her."

Charlie waved enthusiastically and the sign she grasped that read "Welcome home from prison, Claire!" wobbled.

"There she is! Here's your auntie, home from the slammer," Charlie called loudly to the teenage boy next to her. Several people turned to look at them.

"Hope you guys like toilet wine," Claire replied equally loudly. Luke chuckled.

Ryan, Claire's nephew, shook his head and adjusted his earphones. "I told her not to," he said. He reluctantly accepted a hug from Claire and Mindy and a handshake from Luke. Shaggy brown hair hung in his eyes, and it looked like he was due for a shower.

"Charlie," Claire said, drawing her sister into a tight embrace. They hadn't seen each other in person since Thanksgiving. "Cute sign."

"Just wanted to properly welcome you to the City of Angels. Sorry for not making it out for the sentencing," she whispered in Claire's ear. "Rivera Era got caught in another infidelity scandal."

"He's been busy this year," Claire said as she drew back. "Thank you for picking us up."

"No problem. I wouldn't miss a chance to hang out with your live-in boyfriend." Charlie wiggled her eyebrows as she hugged Luke.

Claire shot her a dirty look. "I'm twenty-six. Remind me, what were you doing when you were twenty-six? Oh, that's right, you had a toddler."

"Yeah, yeah. I missed you too. Come here," she said to Mindy. They hugged.

"Are you going to tell us all the hot gossip in the car?" Mindy asked as they broke apart.

"As long as you adhere to the cone of silence," Charlie said, waggling one finger. "I know things about this town that would make your head spin."

"I love it." Mindy followed Charlie to the exit. "Tell me

everything."

"He's one of my most problematic clients," Charlie said quietly. The two of them walked ahead. "Are you familiar with Bitcoin?"

Luke and Claire hung back slightly. He took her hand. "Doing okay?"

She blinked as they stepped into the sunshine. Palm trees waved overhead. The weather was stunning—seventies with a light breeze. How amazing would it be to plan proposals in an area where the weather was almost always the same? Well, as long as nothing was on fire.

"I think so. The crushing reality of Brad's timeline is starting to set in, but nothing I can't handle."

"We'll set up your corner of the office when we get home." He wrapped one arm around her as they descended into the mass of colorful characters roaming outside the airport.

Right. The office. Luke had already briefed her on his California house and, at her request, provided her with a floor plan. It was considerably smaller than his East Coast house and would mean that he, Claire, and Mindy would all share the third bedroom as office space. The chances of them making it three weeks without murdering each other were slim. Luckily, Luke was due to be in the studio for most of their visit.

How had living with Luke for six months made her this bougie? Her old apartment had only one bedroom and was barely the square footage of Luke's kitchen, and she had never felt cramped.

Twenty minutes later, they were hurtling through traffic on an impossible twelve-lane highway. Claire's knuckles ached from gripping the door handle. She glanced over her shoulder. Ryan, squashed in the middle seat, was holding

Winston and looked thoroughly unfazed. Mindy and Luke were on their phones. Did no one else care that they were inches from death on every side?

"I don't know how you drive this every day," she told Charlie and cringed as someone merged into their lane with what looked like half an inch of space between the cars. West Haven certainly had more potholes than LA, but at least there weren't four million people trying to use the road at the same time. She squeezed Rosie so tight that the dog gave her some serious side eye.

"You get used to it." Charlie flipped off someone in another lane. "So, as I was saying, one of my biggest coverups of the year was for Big Z."

Big Z was a forty-something rapper with more money than sense. Claire vividly recalled waving her gangly limbs around to one of his bigger hits at her middle school dances. He demonstrated his lyrical prowess by cramming no fewer than seventy-five mentions of the word "ass" into a single song.

"He rear-ended a school bus while tripping balls on ayahuasca."

Mindy gasped. Her head popped between the driver and passenger seats. "Was anyone hurt?"

"Fortunately, no," Charlie said. "If Ryan had been on that bus, I would have severed Big Z's testicles from his body myself. But anyway, two new cruisers for the LAPD and a brand-new scoreboard for the school district later, the problem took care of itself."

"What a dirtbag." Claire frowned. How often did celebrities buy their way out of trouble in LA? At least the community had gotten something out of his douchebaggery. But she was definitely removing him from her Pump Up playlist.

"I wouldn't have a job if it wasn't for dirtbags," Charlie

muttered, swinging over two lanes of traffic without even blinking.

Luke's hand reached through the gap between the seats and stroked the back of Claire's arm. She pulled out her phone and texted him.

Claire: *We're going to die.*

Luke: *If we die, your sister does NOT get Rosie and Winston.*

At least they agreed on something. After a harrowing forty-five minutes, Charlie pulled to a stop in Luke's drive-way. Claire barely gave the house a glance as she all but dove onto the concrete. She would rather put on a fur bikini and waltz into an ESA meeting with a plate of sliders than get back on the 110. Rosie jumped out next to her and shook vigorously.

"Thanks again for picking us up. Want to come in?" Claire asked as she heaved her suitcase out of the trunk.

"Nah, I gotta get this kid to lacrosse practice," Charlie said, nodding her head toward Ryan, who had been silent the entire car ride. He reluctantly handed Winston to Luke.

"Love you. See you for lunch on Wednesday?"

"Sounds good."

Claire shut the door with a snap and fought the urge to collapse onto the grass with her arms wide open. She had never been so pleased to be out of a car. She had vastly underestimated the traffic situation in LA. Brad's proposal timeline was definitely going to need some fine tuning.

"Okay," Luke said as he fished his keys out of his pocket, "I ordered some groceries, they should be here by eight. I'm getting pizza for dinner."

With any luck, it was the same place he had paid to fly a

pizza boy cross-country to her as an apology. The memory of that crust lived rent-free in her head.

"Backyard is fenced in so Rosie and Winton can play without wandering into traffic," he said as he turned the knob and thrust the door open. "And I have a call out to a security company. They'll be here tomorrow to install an updated system."

His worn jeans hugged his butt as he walked into the house in front of her. It was sexy when he used his bossy, take-charge attitude for good instead of evil.

While his West Haven house was huge and classic and full of hardwood floors and every kind of luxury, this house was smaller, sleek, and modern. The floor was tiled in a herringbone pattern, and all the furniture was black and expensive-looking. A small sitting room stood to the right of the front door, with a staircase disappearing upstairs on the left. A short hallway led to the—again, sleek and modern—kitchen and dining room. A deck led off the kitchen to the backyard, which was indeed fenced in. Another hallway led to a powder room and long, skinny living room.

"Where's the basement? These binders are going to clutter up the office." Claire opened a door in the hallway only to find a closet.

"It's LA. We generally don't do basements. Earthquakes," Luke explained as he opened another door to reveal a water heater. He flipped a handle and closed the door. A rushing sound announced water flowing through the pipes. "Wasn't that in any of your natural disaster research?"

She nudged him.

"Upstairs." He took her suitcase and headed up. Rosie wiggled in her arms, so Claire let her down gently, and she rocketed up the steps past Luke to investigate.

"Our room." He opened the first door on the right and

flung her suitcase inside unceremoniously. Claire cringed. Good thing her laptop wasn't in there. "Mindy's across the hall," he said, opening the door for her and flicking the light switch.

"And here's the office." He ducked, and the string that dangled from the attic access dragged through his hair. He opened a final door, revealing a moderately sized bedroom with a desk and computer monitor. It wasn't what her bougie ass had gotten used to, but it was doable.

"You're going to have to keep the noise down when you're video chatting with Sawyer," Claire teased as Mindy elbowed her way into the office. "These walls look thin." She rapped on one.

It was going to be a tight squeeze with even two of them, but they had been through worse. Before Claire had the warehouse, her one-bedroom apartment had been their office, and they had shared it with her ex-fiancé Jason, the immobile and chronically unemployed lump.

"Oh, good," Mindy said, approaching a bare corkboard fastened to the wall. "We can use this for the new murder board."

"What do you mean new murder board?" Luke growled.

Claire turned to him. "Come on. You can't be surprised. They burned my warehouse down. And they threatened my mom and sisters. That's not going to go unpunished. I'm tired of them messing with my life and my livelihood. We're going to figure out who the cult leader is, and then we're going to—"

"Murder him," Mindy interrupted darkly.

"Right, or, as an alternate plan, we're going to tell the FBI and let them handle it."

Luke shook his head. "Don't get involved. It's not safe."

"When has that ever stopped me before?"

"Maybe one security system isn't going to be enough," Luke said with a sigh.

CHAPTER TWENTY-ONE

To Do:
- *Buy blackout curtains*
- *Emergency preparedness meeting*

"Can you get that?" Luke called with half a piece of toast hanging out of his mouth. "It's probably the security guy."

"Got it." Claire loaded her plate in the dishwasher and picked her notebook off the table. She stifled a yawn and uncapped her pen. Sawyer had provided some questions for them to ask the technician. In her other hand, she clutched her cell phone, ready to call the security company to confirm the identity of whichever technician showed up. She may have temporarily moved 2,500 miles away, but if it didn't stop ESA when she went to Paris last year, a simple cross-country trek wasn't likely to dissuade them either.

She opened the door with a smile, prepared to make

excuses for her identity-confirming behavior, but faltered when it swung wide. Rosie and Winston sat at her feet. Rosie, who normally jumped onto the legs of anyone who visited, remained stationary and growled softly.

"Oh—uh, hi," Claire said, taking in the woman in front of her. She was stunning—easily 5'10", legs for days, yoga booty shorts and a crop top showing off a toned and tanned body. She was carrying a plate with a raised mound covered in tin foil. Who the hell was this mysterious plate-toting woman? Was this how people in California sold drugs? Or got people to join cults? Or worse, pyramid schemes?

The girl's thousand-watt smile slid off her face like tree sap when she saw Claire. "Oh. Sorry, I was looking for Luke."

"He's—uh—" Claire looked behind her. A choking sound came from the kitchen, then footsteps hurried down the hallway, and Luke appeared. A toast crumb clung to his maroon button-down, and Claire brushed it away.

"What are you doing here?" Luke asked flatly.

Claire jabbed him in the ribs. Being rude to strangers was almost never acceptable, especially when the smell of icing was drifting from whatever they were holding.

"I just—uh—I saw lights on last night and figured you had come back. I just wanted to bring this to you and apologize for..." She paused and stared at Rosie and Winston. "How we left things."

Claire bristled. What the fuck did that mean? How they left things? Was this one of Luke's LA girlfriends? She lifted her chin.

And how had she seen lights on? Did she live nearby, or was she actively stalking Luke? Claire drew her shoulders back and stood up straight. She wasn't generally a jealous person, but she would roundhouse kick a cake-making stalker right off the front stoop if the occasion called for it.

A light clatter in the hallway announced Mindy's presence. Luke's jaw clenched.

"Aren't you going to introduce me?" The girl asked, arching one perfectly manicured eyebrow.

"Claire, this is Olivia. My..." Luke trailed off. His face was screwed up in concentration.

"Ex." Olivia extended one hand to Claire.

The bottom dropped out of Claire's stomach. This gorgeous, leggy, ultra in-shape woman was Luke's ex? And he had settled for a girl who could barely even reach the top shelf wines in the liquor store? Oh, boy.

"Nice to meet you, Olivia," Claire said as gracefully as she could manage as they clasped hands.

"So nice to meet you," Olivia said with another smile that didn't reach her sapphire eyes. Her hand was frigid and bony like a salmon.

Claire pulled her hand back and suppressed the urge to shudder. "Well, it looks like you two have some catching up to do. I'll be in the living room getting ready for the meeting." She squeezed Luke's arm and walked back down the hallway.

Mindy joined her. "You're going to let them talk?" she hissed. "Did you look at her?"

Claire ducked behind the corner of the living room and craned her ear toward the foyer. "Obviously I'm going to listen," she said, drawing her finger to her lips. "Shh."

Mindy ducked down next to her.

"Wow, so you replaced me with two girls? That's quite a compliment."

"Why are you really here?" Luke asked gruffly.

"I told you. I felt bad about how we left things. That day can't be the end of our story."

Was it Claire's imagination, or was her voice closer now? Did she let herself into the house? Was she stepping closer to Luke? Over Claire's dead body.

Luke laughed, but it was a hollow sound. "How we left things?" His voice grew quieter. Claire and Mindy leaned farther into the hallway. "You mean when I asked you to marry me and you said you couldn't because you wouldn't leave LA?"

Claire faced Mindy and their mouths both fell open. A hand flew to her chest as hot shockwaves coursed up and down her body. Luke had proposed to someone, and that girl was stupid enough to say no? No wonder he thought proposals were a waste of time and money.

"I was young and stupid," Olivia said. "I didn't know what I wanted. But now I know. When I see you here, in the place where we met, and see this scar—"

Scar? What scar? Luke only had a handful, and she'd better not be talking about the one on his upper thigh.

"It just feels inevitable. You and me," Olivia purred.

Claire's hands clenched into fists at her side. This Booty Bootcamp twat was not going to sink her acrylic claws back into Luke. If Claire could escape a serial killer, she could absolutely headbutt this woman off her property. She straightened up and took a step forward, but Mindy dragged her back into the living room.

"Remember the last time you assaulted a woman?" It had led to a months-long lawsuit that only ended because Claire had saved Wendy's life.

Claire crossed her arms and pressed her ear toward the hallway again.

"Right," Luke said. "And I'm sure the timing of this realization has nothing to do with the fact that I was nominated for an Emmy and I'm about to launch the biggest documentary of my career."

"How dare you?" Olivia sounded indignant, but it felt fake even to Claire. "I came here to apologize. I even made your favorite cake."

Claire straightened again. Luke didn't like cake. It was one of the first things he had told her on their first date after her kidnapping. That was why she had served mini pies at his birthday. Either this bitch didn't know him at all, or she had permanently poisoned him against an entire classification of dessert.

"You're too late, Olivia," he said. "I was an idiot when we dated, end of story. You can take your cake and get out."

"Luke, come on," she said in a sultry voice. "Don't pretend like you can't feel this."

Rosie barked her full-on danger bark, and Olivia screamed.

"Good girl," Luke said. "Seriously, you need to leave."

There was a huff, and the front door slammed. Mindy and Claire rushed deeper into the living room and sat on the couch. Claire picked up her emergency binder and flipped through it to a random page while Mindy grabbed her tablet.

A cabinet door opened in the kitchen, and something heavy landed on the counter. Claire crept down the hallway and peeked around the corner. Luke had a screwdriver in his hand, and he was frowning at one of the cabinets.

"Everything okay?" Claire asked at a barely audible volume. She cringed, bracing for the fallout.

"Can we move the meeting to tonight?" he half growled. "I'm going to fix this and then head in to the studio."

Oof. Luke hadn't angry-fixed anything since Thanksgiving when his semi-estranged brother had followed him around, critiquing all of the legal hazards on Luke's property.

"Of course." As much as she was dying for more details, she wouldn't poke Luke with a ten-foot pole right now.

In the living room, she tossed one of Brad's binders in her purse and left the emergency preparedness one on the coffee table. Luke needed space, that much was clear. There would be time for earthquake safety training later. She had to get ready for their first in-person meeting with Brad anyway. Hopefully there weren't any natural disasters before the end of the day because they hadn't even agreed on a secondary meetup location in case the house was compromised.

She ducked back into the living room and gave Mindy a very knowing look. "Min, you want to head out early and see if we can find some coffee before the meeting?"

Even though it was a ruse, she did desperately need the coffee. Every sound the house made had shaken her out of sleep the night before. Thankfully, it had prevented her from sleepwalking. But she definitely wasn't on her A game this morning, and she needed to be for Brad.

"Sure." Mindy closed her tablet and picked up her purse. "Let me just grab my shoes."

Claire hesitantly approached the kitchen again. "You sure you're okay with us taking the spare car?"

"Yep," Luke said flatly, not even bothering to turn around.

"Okay, thank you." She backed out of the room. Yikes. Olivia had really rattled him. Was it cause for concern? She pushed the thought to the back of her mind and focused on the day ahead.

"Bye, babies," Claire said, bending down to kiss Rosie

and Winston on the nose. "Mommy will be back later, and we'll take a nice walk in our new neighborhood, okay?" And if they happened to find Olivia on their walk, they would chase her into the Pacific Ocean.

Oh, the ocean! They had been in LA for half a day and she still hadn't put her toes in the sand. That needed to be remedied. If Brad left them any spare time, anyway.

Outside the front door, Claire danced three times on the porch to make sure she had locked it.

"I thought you didn't do that anymore." Mindy lowered her sunglasses to stare at her.

"What, the dance?" Claire said, pausing in the middle of a disco point. "I don't. Well, I haven't been. But I think the move and the warehouse and all the stress from work is... making things flare up again."

"Are you sleepwalking again?" Her green eyes burned into Claire's as they stepped down the concrete steps to the short walkway.

"Only a little," Claire said. Those two times Luke caught barely even counted. She hadn't even made it off the property.

"So you are," Mindy said. Her perfectly shaped eyebrows wrinkled.

"It's not a big deal. I'm doing my cardio and meditation." Claire kept her eyes on Luke's second car, a 2000 Porsche 911. It wouldn't be great for hauling proposal stuff, but at least a smaller car would be harder for other vehicles to hit.

"Did you talk to Bernice about it?"

Claire waved one hand. "I will when we get back. I have a session on the books. Don't judge me. By the way, you're driving."

"Obviously." Mindy accepted the keys and slid into the

driver's seat. "By the way, why does Luke keep two cars at a house he doesn't even live in full time?"

Claire patted the dashboard. "This was his dad's favorite car. Luke drove it cross-country when he was discharged from the Navy."

Mindy froze. "And he's okay with us taking it out into the absolute zoo of LA traffic?"

Claire shrugged.

"He must really love you," Mindy mused as she buckled her seatbelt.

Claire smiled. "By the way, I've been meaning to ask. Does Dr. Goulding try to psychoanalyze you at family dinners?"

Luke and Olivia's interaction was still buzzing in her mind, but it was time to discreetly question Mindy about her decision to marry Sawyer. In-laws were a key section of their Ready To Marry questionnaire, so Mindy's response should be telling.

Mindy thought for a moment, then turned the key in the ignition. The engine roared to life, and angry metal music blared from the speaker. "Ugh, let's find something a little happier, shall we?" She twiddled the dial until she found a song by Big Z.

It felt kind of gross to listen to his music after what they had learned, but apparently it didn't bother Mindy.

"Sorry, what did you ask?" Mindy asked as she adjusted the rearview mirror. "Does Bernice psychoanalyze me? Probably. But if she does, she at least keeps her opinions to herself. That lasagna recipe you gave me was a huge hit at dinner two weekends ago."

"Oh good. It's my—well, it's Jack's." Until nine months ago, she had assumed that her legendary family lasagna recipe had come from a friend of her mother's, probably because that was what her mom had always told her. As it turned out, it was her father's signature dish. Alice loathed the man, but let the lasagna live on.

Mindy hummed noncommittally. She wasn't the biggest fan of Jack either.

"Let me just find a coffee place close to the studio. Ah, here's one." Claire pulled up the driving directions and mounted her phone to the built-in holder on the dashboard. "Brad seems like a black coffee kind of guy, don't you think?"

"Probably. Okay, enough small talk," Mindy said as they pulled out of the driveway and went west. "What the fuck is happening with Luke and Olivia?"

Claire slapped both hands on the dash and turned to look at Mindy. "I know! He proposed? No wonder he's such a fucking grump about our business."

"Right? I was ready to stab that bitch myself. She's such a gold digger, you could just tell. He totally called her out."

"I've never once heard him mention her name." Claire crossed her arms and surveyed the palm tree-lined street as though expecting to find the cake-making harlot doing naked jumping jacks on the sidewalk. "What do you think she does for a living?"

"Professional boyfriend stealer?" Mindy guessed, making a left-hand turn at the stop sign.

"If she can afford a house anywhere in Los Angeles, it must be something big."

"Don't internet stalk her," Mindy said, waggling a finger in Claire's direction. "That won't help anything."

"I wasn't going to," Claire said, even though she had been reaching for her phone.

"I know you will. We'll do it together later, after the meeting if Luke's not back."

"I have a feeling he won't be." Claire sighed. The more

stressed out he was, the more deeply he tended to dive into work. "Okay, enough about Olivia. Let's focus. Today is a super important day. We need to make sure Brad's not a serial killer, ensure that his feelings for Karen are genuine, and confirm that he hasn't tried to change anything else last minute."

"If he has, we'll figure it out." Mindy pulled to a stop at a red light.

How many red lights were in this damn town? Would they make it on time for the meeting? Maybe they should skip the coffee run.

"Don't worry," Mindy said as she accelerated through the intersection. "We can handle this. Remember the fake event you threw together in twenty-four hours so we could draw out ESA? The girls in the historical society still talk about that event. I think they're making it a thing again this year."

"Only because the mayor throat-punched an attempted murderer," Claire admitted.

"No way. We can do this. Just imagine what we can do with almost three full weeks. We will absolutely kill Brad's proposal, we'll make a crapload of money, hire someone amazing to handle things on the West Coast, and save the shelter. Oh, and pay back our gigantic business loan."

Claire tightened her seatbelt as Mindy careened onto the freeway. Everything was riding on Brad's proposal. They had no choice but to succeed.

CHAPTER TWENTY-TWO

To Do:
- Buy highlighters
- Check in with a capella group
- Don't stalk Olivia

"SO THE HORSES ARE GOING TO BE WHITE, RIGHT?" BRAD LUX pressed the tips of his fingers together and leaned back in his chair. The sleek leather of his high-backed office chair towered above him, shining in the morning sun. His mahogany desk gleamed with three computer monitors arranged across its surface. A golden nameplate sat on the desk. Even the trashcan was fancy.

Mindy and Claire exchanged a glance. Claire's cheeks ached from the effort of smiling, and her head was full of cotton. The under-eye concealer she had applied this morning had barely made a dent in the bruised half-moons beneath her eyes.

The stress from ESA, the move, and the biggest project of her career was more than enough to send her on a sleepwalking spree. The fear of stumbling unconscious into an ESA trap had kept her tossing and turning for days. And now Brad had spent the entire meeting nitpicking and micromanaging every aspect of the proposal. This was the sixth change he had requested today, and they had two-and-a-half weeks to pull everything together.

Not to mention the fact that they had to conduct interviews and find someone suitable to represent Happily Ever Afters. That alone would have been a monumental task. Interviewing while catering to Brad 24/7 was one of the worst ideas she had ever had. And then there was the fact that Luke had proposed to the neighborhood cake-making hussy but had never so much as broached the subject of marriage with her—

Mindy raised her eyebrows at Claire. It had probably been a full fifteen seconds since Brad had asked his question. *Get it together, Claire.*

Claire straightened her shoulders and made eye contact. "We can request them from the ranch, but I can't promise they'll have two white ones available."

"Even if there's just one." Brad leaned forward and drummed his fingers on his desk, then glanced at his watch. He certainly was fidgety. Barney had been fidgety too. Was he hiding something?

"We'll do our best." Mindy offered him a warm smile.

Brad stopped drumming and leaned forward. His brown eyes burned into Claire's. "It's the least you can do after losing her priceless childhood saddle in your warehouse fire."

Claire's smile slid off her face like toppings falling off a street taco. "And again, I am so sorry about that, Brad. The replica should be done by the end of the week."

"I don't appreciate slip-ups, Claire. And this was a pretty big one." He tapped one thick finger on his desk blotter.

Heat flamed her cheeks. Something inside her that had been strained the entire meeting snapped. "You know we didn't set the fire, right?"

Mindy inhaled sharply and nudged her.

Claire blinked. Her body went numb. What had just come out of her sleep-deprived mouth? Had she just *sassed* their biggest client ever? She gripped the arms of her chair and waited.

Brad looked startled, then laughed. He leaned back in his chair. "You're right. Shit happens. I'll expect an email update as soon as the saddle's done. I want to look it over to make sure it matches the pictures."

"It will," Claire said firmly. "Was there a particular reason why you wanted white horses?"

"Karen had a white horse growing up. Her name was Sadie. I think she'd really like it."

Her heart softened, just a little bit. She made a mental note to talk to the stable. "We'll do everything we can. Was there anything else?" She held her breath. If there was, she was going to leap across the desk and administer a lobotomy.

Brad seemed to debate for a moment, then shook his head. "Let me know what the helicopter company says. I don't love the extra cost, but Luke's right, the traffic downtown can be a real bitch. We don't wanna get stuck."

Claire nodded. Maybe she needed to step it up a little bit since she had just sassed him. "I'll email you as soon as I hear. Thanks for meeting with us today. Your ideas have been very thoughtful and just the right amount of splashy."

Understatement of the century. Changing the Hollywood sign was more than a little splashy. "Karen's going to have an amazing day," she added.

She and Mindy stood. Claire offered her hand to Brad and he shook it enthusiastically. "I hope so. Thanks, girls. We'll check in on Thursday to see where we're at. Same time."

Girls. Ugh.

"Right," Mindy said. "And Claire and I are going to scout the locations today, and then we'll do a run-through a couple times this week to make sure the route is doable."

"Excellent. See you later." Brad had already swiveled his chair back to his bank of computer monitors before Mindy and Claire left the room.

They both exhaled loudly as the office door shut behind them.

"So now we have to find a white horse, swap the appetizers *again*, ask the a cappella group to do a medley instead of the original song, and find a violinist to put in the hedge maze at the Getty," Mindy whispered as she leaned against the door.

"I don't know how we're going to pull this off," Claire whispered back. Dread had settled in her stomach. Was it too much? Had they finally gone too big on a proposal? And out of their comfort zone of West Haven? A rookie mistake.

"That reminds me." Claire straightened and walked over to the reception desk. "Hi," she said with added charm. "Brad told us to schedule another meeting in another few days. I think he said toward the end of the day."

The receptionist blinked at them. Her feet were propped up on the desk, and the glow necklace and neon green tights she wore suggested she had come straight to work from an all-night rave. She couldn't have been more than twenty. Claire hadn't been to a rave in years. Was she getting old?

"Mr. Lux doesn't like meetings at the end of his day," the receptionist drawled in a near-perfect valley girl accent. She blew a strand of pink hair out of her eyes as she typed. "He usually goes to the gym after work. Doesn't like the stress beforehand."

"My mistake. Give us a call when he's ready to schedule," she said, stepping away from the desk with another smile.

A security guard opened a door for them. Outside it was, of course, perfect weather. Claire lifted her face to the sunshine and drank in the Vitamin D. The traffic in LA might have been ten times at stressful as West Haven. But there was something magical about the sun on the West Coast.

Mindy nudged her. "You know he wanted to meet in the morning. Did you have an aneurysm?"

"Oh, I know," Claire said, brushing a dog hair off her blouse. "I just wanted to see what his schedule was like after work. Because we're going to follow him to the gym and make sure he's not a serial killer or creep before we get too deep on this proposal. Can't be too careful."

Mindy shook a finger at her. "You, my best friend, are incredibly wise."

"Thank you." She took a mini bow. "So we'll pick a day to stake out the studio, wait for him to leave, and see where he goes. If he really does go to the gym, we'll sneak in and see if he mistreats anyone there. I refuse to plan a beautiful proposal for another garbage human being."

"I didn't get that vibe from him," Mindy said as they walked toward the parking lot.

"Same," Claire admitted as they passed a gazebo that

was in several of her favorite TV shows. "But I didn't get it from Barney either."

"Good point." Mindy glanced at her phone. "By the way, are you okay?"

Claire crossed her arms. "What do you mean?"

"I've never heard you talk back to a client before. I almost fell off my chair."

She waved it off. "I'm fine. Just tired. New house and all that. I think the sleep deprivation lowered my bullshit-tolerance meter. It won't happen again."

"Sounds like it's time to set up a cot in front of your bedroom door again."

"Don't you dare."

Mindy grunted noncommittally and stared at her phone screen. "Not a single message from Sawyer. It's one o'clock there."

"Doesn't he have a class on Tuesday mornings?"

"Yeah, yeah," Mindy grumbled and tucked the phone away. "So when are you going to talk to Luke about the Olivia situation?"

"I don't know. I feel like he's going to come home late and not want to talk."

"That or he'll be excavating the backyard to install a koi pond," Mindy muttered. Luke's penchant for working on house projects when he was stressed out was endearing. Most of the time.

"She was throwing herself at him, right? I didn't imagine that?"

"Please." Mindy pressed the unlock button. Fifty yards away, the car beeped. "I wouldn't have been surprised if we rounded the corner and she was dry humping him."

Claire snorted. "Want to find somewhere for lunch, send

a couple of emails, and then scout the locations before we head home?"

"Sounds like a plan." Mindy tossed her black hair over one shoulder as she approached the car.

"Hang on," Claire said as they approached.

"Do we have to do the thing?" Mindy groaned.

"I have strict instructions from Jack."

Claire laid a scarf on the ground and dropped to her knees to peer underneath the car. No chloroform-toting stalkers today at least. No rusty nails or other debris hiding behind the tires either. She rose and pressed herself against the backseat window. It was empty. Next, she surveyed the cars on either side of them. Also empty.

"We're good," she said, pulling on the passenger side handle.

"I could have told you that five minutes ago." Mindy climbed into the driver's seat with a dirty look.

Claire glared at her. "I'm sorry, who bought me a GPS watch because I was abducted?"

"Sorry. Thank you for being safe," Mindy said, but she was totally rolling her eyes behind her sunglasses as she reversed out of the parking spot. "I think I'm just hangry. Where do you want to go to lunch?"

"Let me see what's around," Claire said, pulling up an app that listed restaurants nearby. "Oh, this one sounds good. Karma. It has four-and-a-half stars."

"Sounds good," Mindy said as Claire pulled up the directions and mounted her phone to the dash.

When they got there ten minutes later, they frowned at the sign.

"Legalize marinara?" Claire read as she squinted.

"Ten bucks says this is a vegan joint." Mindy pulled into a parking spot.

Claire clicked on the restaurant's website and scrolled. "Damn it. I owe you a ten. Do we eat some tofu or do we go somewhere else?"

"I feel like after that meeting with Brad we deserve a margarita. Mexican?"

"Perfect. Let me look." Claire found another promising sounding restaurant. Mama Casa couldn't be a vegan. Or could she?

They pulled up eight minutes later.

"God damn it." Mindy stabbed a manicured finger at the sign. Kale salad with cilantro avocado balsamic reduction was the advertised special. "We are in Southern California. There's supposed to be great Mexican food here. I want queso, not some hokey-ass kale salad with black beans on it. So help me I will drive to Tijuana if I have to."

Claire closed the app. If she didn't act fast, Mindy would have a hangry meltdown. She Googled instead and found a restaurant that explicitly mentioned carnitas. "Third try's the charm."

Mindy's stomach growled as she pulled back out onto the highway. "If this is another vegan restaurant, I'm dumping you out on the sidewalk and driving back home."

"Luke's house or like...Pennsylvania home?"

Mindy glared at her. Claire hadn't seen her this angry since a twenty-four-hour charity relay in college where the power went out and all the hotdog stands had to shut down.

Thirty minutes and one margarita later, Mindy's mood had improved significantly. "Okay, email to the stables sent," she said through a mouthful of queso.

"Great. I contacted the a cappella leader and asked about the medley. The songs aren't even in the same key and they'll need to rehearse." Claire grabbed a fistful of hair and pushed her half-eaten taco platter out of the way. The stress was messing with her normally voracious appetite. "I might actually murder Brad when this is over."

"Where do we find a violinist? Craigslist?" Mindy asked.

"That sounds like a great way to get Brad and Karen murdered," Claire muttered. "I'll ask Luke. Maybe he knows someone from the studio." She fired off a quick text to him and hoped that he wouldn't be too upset from the morning's events to answer.

"Any word from the insurance company?" Mindy asked hesitantly.

Claire shook her head. "It'll be weeks before we hear anything." A dark cloud settled over her. "I still can't believe they burned the freaking warehouse down. Five years of work, up in flames. Which reminds me, I need to check on the progress of Karen's saddle."

Mindy sighed and crunched on another tortilla chip. Her expression darkened. "We have to bring those fuckers down. Let's do some research tonight after our safety meeting. I'm looking forward to learning about the dangers of pollution."

"Done. Ready to attempt the run-through?" Claire carefully stacked their plates on top of each other.

Mindy nodded. "Business first. Then we squash the assholes."

CHAPTER TWENTY-THREE

To Do:
- *Resist the urge to strangle Brad*
- *Call Mom back*
- *Maybe just a low-level Google search of Olivia*

"Have you heard from Bri?" Mindy asked as they swung into the parking lot of Solar Flare, the restaurant in East Malibu where Brad and Karen had their first date.

"Not today." Claire climbed out of the car and stepped onto the parking lot, which made out of crushed seashells. "She's been doing night shoots for her next movie. It's a drama based on a true crime story."

"Don't try to distract me with true crime," Mindy said as she locked her car door. She was obsessed with the show *Mysterious Murders*. "Aren't you supposed to have lunch with her tomorrow? And Charlie?"

"Charlie doesn't exactly know that it's the three of us."

The only way to get the three Hartley sisters together was to ambush Charlie. Claire stepped up to the fence that lined the parking lot. "Oh, wow."

To their right, a stamped concrete patio littered with tables had flawless ocean views. A steep cliff dropped off not far from the last tables. Weird choice for a restaurant that served alcohol.

"Hell of a place for a first date." Mindy leaned on the fence. Her dark hair shone in the afternoon sun. "So, lunch here at noon."

"The whole patio is reserved for them. Nicole will get some candids while we're here. We'll give them an hour, hour and fifteen at most to eat."

"We should probably have lunch here one day. You know, to make sure that timeline is doable."

Claire nodded and took a deep breath. The salt spray misted her face. She closed her eyes. "You're absolutely right. A business lunch. It would be the most responsible thing to do."

"Okay," Mindy said, turning away from the view. "Next stop. Santa Monica Pier. You have the stopwatch?"

"Just another second." The beach was Claire's favorite place, and she rarely had an opportunity to visit.

Mindy nodded. "Fair enough."

They stood next to each other in silence. The sun beat down above, warming Claire's skin. Waves crashed somewhere below them and a seagull cawed a few yards away. For a moment, she allowed herself to get lost in the present, to enjoy the tickle of salt spray on her face and inhale the earthy spice of basil drifting from the restaurant. Dr. Goulding would have been proud.

"Okay," she said after a minute of silence. "I'm ready." She pulled a stopwatch from her purse. Sure, she could have just used the app on her phone. But this was so much more official.

They climbed back into the car, and Mindy backed out of her parking spot. "And...go!"

Claire hit the stopwatch as they pulled back out onto the Pacific Coast Highway. California may have entirely too many vegan restaurants and more expensive gas than she'd ever seen in her life, but there was no denying it was beautiful.

"This is not an excuse for you to drive like a maniac, by the way." Claire held onto the oh shit bar as Mindy took a turn way too fast.

"I'm not." Mindy shot her a dirty look. "Out of the two people in this car, who owns a vehicle that exploded in the last year?"

"Not because I crashed it off a cliff into the ocean." Claire threw her hands up. "Also, I made a minor addendum to the schedule."

Mindy raised her eyebrows.

"Mandatory three-minute excursion to the beach once we're done. I can't come that close to a new ocean and not put my toes in."

"I'll allow it," Mindy said. They drove in silence for a few minutes.

Claire glanced in the rearview mirror. "That car's been following us for a couple miles."

"It's the Pacific Coast Highway, Claire. Unless they're headed to Tuna Canyon," Mindy said, gesturing at a sign with one hand, "there's literally nowhere else to go."

"I'm sure you're right." Still, she couldn't peel her eyes off the black sedan with tinted windows behind them. Surely lots of people in California had tinted windows. Maybe there was a movie star behind them. Or an FBI agent. Or even a new PI hired by her overbearing mother. It wasn't necessarily a member of ESA.

"Oh yay, we're here," Mindy said, turning off the highway and into a beach parking lot. The pier rose in front of them. Hundreds of people were enjoying the beach, sunbathing, playing Frisbee, even surfing.

Claire glanced in the mirror again. The car was still behind them. Maybe they were just headed to the beach too. She hammered the stop button on the stopwatch. Just short of twenty minutes. Not awful, even with moderate traffic. She made a notation on her clipboard and set it at her feet.

The black sedan disappeared into a back corner of the lot. Claire shook her head and set her eyes on the pier. All the different smells and sounds hit her as soon as she exited the car. People screamed on the nearby roller coaster. The smell of fried fish drifted out of one of the restaurants, mingling with the cloying sweetness of funnel cakes. Dozens of people crisscrossed the pier—families, teenagers, obvious tourists.

The crashing waves drew her eyes, but the back of her neck prickled. If they were being followed, it would be hard to spot a tail on such a crowded boardwalk. She glanced behind her, but there were too many faces to catalog. There were easily a dozen men within ten feet of her, and a tail would probably keep his distance. A place like this must be Sawyer's nightmare.

"What's wrong?" Mindy asked. "You look weird."

"It's probably just me being paranoid, but I feel like we're being followed," Claire said, surveying the pier again. Was that teenage boy looking at them because he wanted to murder them, or just because Mindy was wearing a low-cut top?

"Let's get lost then." Mindy grabbed Claire's hand and

dove into Pacific Park. Children screamed on the nearby rollercoaster. Claire ducked behind a cotton candy cart and watched. Mindy crouched next to her. No one looked in their direction.

"Bathroom," Mindy said. They wound through several rides, dodging strollers and tiny dogs, and sidled into a bathroom.

Mindy dug through her purse until she found a scrap of fabric and a black wig. "Here." She passed them over.

"You went through my suitcase?" Claire frowned. She had tossed half a dozen wigs and disguises in her suitcase before leaving for California. It was impossible to be too careful now that ESA activity had ramped back up.

"I was looking for a phone charger. And then naturally I stole these and shoved them in my purse in case we needed them. I will never doubt your instincts again. Put them on." Mindy pulled another wig out of her purse and swirled her hair into a bun.

Claire stepped into a truly disgusting bathroom stall and hung her purse on the hook. She kept her elbows glued to her sides as she struggled into the hot pink dress that Mindy had offered her. With one look, Claire's late grandmother would have said she could see what Claire had for breakfast. But maybe that was a good thing. She bumped the door open with her foot and stepped back to the sinks. Between the black wig and the bodycon dress, she was unrecognizable.

"Second thing." Mindy turned around, wearing a new top. "Let's split up and meet back at the wheel. If there's someone watching us, they're going to expect there to be two of us. Take ten minutes to make sure we lost them."

"Has Sawyer been giving you lessons?" Claire asked as she adjusted the wig a final time.

"Maybe." Mindy snapped her compact shut. "Okay, you first. Remember, take a meandering route, don't stop to talk to anyone, and scream the code word if someone comes up to you with a chloroform rag. Be. Careful." She punctuated her sentence with a finger jab.

"Platypus. Got it." Claire slung her purse back over her shoulder. "See you at the wheel."

She emerged into the sunlight and slid on a pair of sunglasses. A quick scan of the immediate area didn't reveal any looky-loos. A father and son pulled pieces off a hunk of cotton candy. A toddler screamed at her mother and pointed at an ice cream stand.

She went out the opposite park entrance and kept her head down as she walked. A small clump of people was clustered at the far end of the pier. It would give her a chance to put her back to the ocean and watch all incoming foot traffic. If someone was being shady, she stood a better chance of seeing them from the edge of the pier.

Her Jimmy Choos clattered over the boardwalk. She probably could have picked more low-key footwear for this adventure, but her ballet flats that folded into a bag were in the car.

She rounded the corner of the pier and nearly came screeching to a halt. There, leaning against the railing, was a white male, mid-twenties, arms casually folded. The breath caught in her throat as though someone was squeezing it. There wasn't any reason to suspect him. He was dressed in black from head to toe, which didn't exactly match the attire of the people around him but didn't necessarily make him stick out. He wore sunglasses, but she could feel his eyes on her. Something about him made her skin crawl. Was this guy just a run-of-the-mill creeper, or was this a member of ESA?

Claire's phone beeped, and she risked a glance at it. Was Mindy all right?

Alice: *Are you okay, Clairebear? I just have a bad feeling about this California trip. I said a prayer of protection for you.*

Claire pursed her lips. The last thing she needed was another infamous prediction from her psychic mother.

But still...the base of her spine tingled. Something wasn't right. Claire swung her phone up and pretended to take a selfie. Instead, she snapped a picture of the man on the boardwalk and sent it to Mindy and Luke with the caption "probably nothing, but in case I disappear: bad vibes from this guy."

She walked past the man with her head held high. Every cell in her body screamed for her to turn around. Were those footsteps behind her? Of course it was, there were three hundred other people on this nightmare pier. She quickened her pace, passing men, women, and children, not bothering to search their faces. Her heart rate ticked up like she was jogging a 5k.

She was only twenty yards or so from the railing overlooking the Pacific. At least from there, no one would be able to approach her from behind like a coward. She could get her bearings, decide whether or not she needed to bail on the Ferris wheel, and maybe uppercut a creepy asshole into the Pacific. She pulled her keys from her purse and clutched them between her knuckles. Maybe moving toward the end of the pier that had only one entrance and exit was not the best idea. But it was too late now.

It was foolish to think that moving cross-country would solve anything. At least in West Haven, she had cleared out the ESA sect. Who knew how large the one in California was? There could be a dozen people here right now, waiting to grab her.

Her pulse beat in her eyes as she beelined for the railing. The keys in her hand cut into her fingers because she was holding them too tightly. Her phone beeped again, but she ignored it. If she could just reach the railing, everything would be fine. Everything would be—

Suddenly, something heavy and hard collided with her left side. Claire shrieked like she had been stabbed.

"PLATYPUS," she screamed to the crowd. She tumbled to the ground, falling hard on the planks. A splinter bit into her right palm. Her wig slipped off, exposing her blond tresses to the world.

"Whoa, sorry, dude," someone said. A scarred hand with a wrist guard slipped into view. "I lost control of my board. Did you say platypus?"

She backed away from the offered hand. Sure, it could have been an innocent skateboarder. But it could have just as easily been a murderer in training waiting to drag her into a windowless kidnapping van.

At that moment, Mindy sprinted down the pier hoisting a metal trashcan lid. A security guard trailed behind her.

"I thought you were fucking dead." Mindy chucked the lid onto the boardwalk and pulled Claire into a rib-crushing hug. "Did your thumbs fall off? They must have since you didn't text me back." She pulled away and inspected Claire's hands.

"I'm sorry, I just got bad vibes from that guy—"

Wait. Shit. Where had he gone?

She scanned the boardwalk. A handful of people were still staring at them after Mindy's dramatic trash can release, but none of them were the lurker in the black hoodie.

"Everything okay here?" The bored-looking security

guard with a nightstick and sun-bleached surfer hair popped a chewing gum bubble in their faces.

"I think so. Thank you." Claire scanned the crowd again. No creeper. She blew out a long breath and straightened the hem of her absurd dress. The three-minute beach excursion no longer felt like a safe idea. "We better get on track with checking the route."

Mindy grunted and started back toward the car, her head on a swivel. Claire trailed behind her, probing the crowd.

She couldn't live this way for the rest of her life. ESA wouldn't stop until they were taken down. It was time to topple the first domino—Professor Taylor.

CHAPTER TWENTY-FOUR

To Do:
- Establish a designated disguise bag
- Follow up with helicopter company
- Plan alternate routes for B proposal

WHEN LUKE WALKED INTO THE LIVING ROOM THAT EVENING, Claire was taping a strand of red yarn between a photograph of Dr. William Taylor and a large question mark. The double-sided whiteboard they had bought after visiting Santa Monica was slowly becoming covered by ESA theories. The corkboard in the office hadn't had enough space.

"This doesn't look like a safety meeting." He picked up the almost-empty bottle of cabernet sauvignon on the end table. His gaze shifted to Rosie and Winston, who were wearing matching bandanas that Claire had bought during a mini retail therapy session before they headed home.

"Yeah, we got kind of distracted." Claire set her glass on the table. She rubbed at the marker smudge on her hand.

Was he still in a bad mood? Would he be upset about the ESA board? He seemed more relaxed, and he hadn't dragged his toolbox in with him.

"I see the car is still in one piece." He leaned against the doorframe.

"Despite Los Angeles's best efforts," Mindy said.

"You know you could take the metro," Luke said with eyebrows raised.

"We're not trying to get sold into sex trafficking." Mindy turned back around to face the board.

Claire stood and squeezed his arm as she passed him. In the kitchen, she popped a plate of food in the microwave. Her mind had buzzed with the conversation he'd had with Olivia since she got home. But how would she broach the subject?

Heavy footsteps thudded into the kitchen. She didn't have to turn around to know that Luke had followed her. The microwave beeped, and she yanked the door open.

"I made some pasta." She handed the warm plate over like a peace offering. "I thought some carbs might help after your long day."

"Thank you," Luke said with a kiss. The kitchen chair squeaked as he sat on it. He didn't immediately jump up and dismantle it, so hopefully his stress had leveled out.

"How did everything go at the studio?" Claire lowered herself into the chair across from him.

He wound pasta around his fork. "Honestly, great. The music is excellent, the editing and photography they helped with turned out great. They didn't shit all over my vision at all."

Claire smiled. "So selling your soul to Streamster wasn't the worst decision of your life?"

"Not yet, anyway." He shoved a heavily laden fork into his mouth and groaned appreciatively. "We should be completely finished in two weeks. Then it's just up to Streamster to get it on the release schedule. This is fantastic, by the way."

"Thank you." Claire flushed. She didn't often do the cooking at home, and when she did, she sometimes got distracted with work and burned it.

"How was your day?"

"Mostly good," she said. "Traffic was crazy and I now understand why you shat on my timeline. Brad requested half a dozen changes."

"As a surprise to no one," Luke interjected.

"Right. Oh, and Mindy almost freaked out because we kept accidentally stumbling upon vegan restaurants. But we had some amazing tacos and saw the ocean."

He nodded thoughtfully. "So what was the deal with the guy you sent me the picture of?"

"It was probably nothing," she said, but a lump formed in her throat. "He just gave me bad vibes when I passed him. I was wearing a wig when I saw him, so I don't think he recognized me anyway, even if he was ESA."

"How were you wearing a wig? I thought you stopped carrying those around." It was true. She had stopped carrying disguises shortly after most of the West Haven ESA members had been arrested the previous summer.

"Old habits die hard. Especially when people burn your office down. Speaking of burning things to the ground, are we going to talk about Olivia?"

He sighed and reached across the table for her wineglass, taking a long sip before putting it back. "I'm impressed it's taken you this long to bring it up."

"Come on," she said gently. "You can't blame a girl for having some questions when her boyfriend's ex shows up at our door with a cake and a motive. I saw it in the trash." A waste of cake if you asked her. "Don't you want to just tell me and get it over with? Or do you want me to passive-aggressively hint at it for the next two weeks?"

He folded his arms and leaned back in his chair. "Fine. Olivia lives two blocks down. We met the day I moved in. I pulled up to the house in my dad's Porsche and found a girl twenty yards down the road unconscious in the driver's seat with her car wrapped around a telephone pole. The car caught on fire, and I pulled her out. It's how I got this," he said, tugging his collar to the side and showing off the long, thin scar on his neck.

Aha. Mystery solved.

Claire's mouth dropped open. "That's the best meet-cute I have ever heard. I can't believe it was wasted on your ex." The audacity.

He shrugged. "We dated, things went south, end of story."

"But you asked her to marry you," she said in a reverent tone. "You hate proposals. What happened?"

Luke's mouth hardened into a line. "She turned into a different person. When we met she was sweet, worked in a bakery. She had inherited the house from her grandmother, and she was just trying to make ends meet. When we started dating, I think she got accustomed to my lifestyle and wanted more of that stability for herself. She decided to become an 'influencer' and lost a ton of weight and started promoting herself all over the place. Then she leaked her own sex tape."

Her eyes flew open wide. There was a Luke sex tape out there? She was simultaneously aroused and indignant. That hadn't come up during the light internet stalking she had done before agreeing to work with him for Kyle and Nicole's proposal. How would she explain that one to her mother?

"I'm not in it," he said flatly.

"Oh, wow. I'm sorry." Something wasn't adding up. So Olivia had cheated on him and he still proposed to her? That was some wildly poor decision-making.

"Don't be," he said, shoveling his fork back into his pile of pasta. "I thought we could get past it. I was making plans to move to Pennsylvania, thought for sure she'd come with me and get away from that toxic LA lifestyle. Bought a ring and everything. But I was an idiot. And thank god she didn't say yes. We would have been miserable."

"Just so I'm understanding this correctly," Claire began, pausing to consider her next words. "Your girlfriend cheated on you and released a sex tape, and your first instinct was to...propose to her."

"Love makes you weak. And stupid."

She straightened up like he had slapped her.

"Well, not all the time," he added hurriedly. "Just when you're with the wrong person, I guess." He tore off a hunk of garlic bread and shoved it in his mouth like a caveman.

She pushed her wineglass to him. He drank appreciatively from it.

"No wonder you think what I do is stupid." She pulled a fresh glass from the cabinet and popped the cork on a new bottle. Luke would never propose to her after everything he'd been through. She may have to take a leaf from Mindy's book and propose to him...if they ever got to that point in their relationship. Would they? Would he even say yes? Maybe she needed to run herself through the checklist. They would one hundred percent fail the in-laws section.

"I was pretty jaded when we met," he admitted.

"I understand." She grabbed his free hand and pressed a kiss to it. This was the most personal information Luke had divulged since he told her about his brother pulling his dad off life support. If she overwhelmed him with questions now, he would run away like a startled bunny. It was time to back off.

"Thanks for telling me the truth. We can do the safety meeting when you're done if you want. Or we can just blow it off. You've been through enough today."

He raised one eyebrow. "But what if a fire tornado rips through Burbank and releases all the animals in the LA Zoo?"

"Very funny." What a silly question. Obviously they would utilize Luke's outdoor speakers to play sounds of natural predators to repel whatever wayward lion or howler monkey wandered their way.

Leaving the table, she filled one side of the sink with suds and scrubbed at the pasta pot. Her brain buzzed with the new information Luke had divulged. For a smart guy, he had done some dumb stuff.

She deposited the pasta pot in the drying rack. Luke's presence snuck up behind her, warm and comforting.

"You must think I'm an idiot." He picked up the pot and a towel.

"Nah." She dunked his plate in the suds. "I spent five years of my life with a Cheetos-snarfing donkey. I get it."

Her phone rang, and she glanced at the screen. Alice. They hadn't talked since Claire had arrived in LA. It was time. She answered before she could change her mind.

"Hang on. Hey, Mom. How's Miami?" Claire drained her

wineglass and clamped the phone between her shoulder and ear. The glass landed in the bottom of the sink with a clunk.

"Oh, everything's fine, sweetie. I just wanted to let you know one teensy thing." The bottom dropped out of Claire's stomach. Alice sounded different than she normally did. More hesitant, even tense. Had Roy been attacked by a gator on the golf course?

"What's wrong?" Her voice quavered.

Luke stopped drying and looked at her.

"Everything's fine," Alice repeated, "we just had a small run-in with an attempted intruder."

The edges of her field of vision went dark, and she backed against the counter. Luke put his hand on her shoulder. "What do you mean? Who was it? Was it ESA?"

"Let me talk to her," came her stepdad's voice through the phone. "Claire?" Roy asked.

"Dad? What happened?"

"Your mother saw someone lurking in the azalea bush outside and she hit him over the head with a rolling pin. The police are here now."

"Okay." Claire's breath hissed slowly out of her mouth. There was no need to panic. It could have been any run-of-the-mill creeper. Alice had gained a few overly invested fans from her show, and it was Florida, for god's sake. A meth addict riding a gator had been spotted on her mom's street just the week before. "Was it like an Amazon delivery driver or was it an actual bad guy?"

"Well, he had a bottle of chloroform and a bag of zip ties with him and he was playing a recording of a baby crying, so unless your mother ordered a very specific murder kit, probably a bad guy." Roy always had jokes.

Her breath came in jagged gasps. She gripped the countertop and started her breathing exercise, but the darkness inside was threatening to overwhelm her. "Okay, let me look at some flights, I'll see how soon I can get there. Tomorrow at the latest."

"No, *mija*," Roy said firmly. "There's no need. There's nothing you can do. Your mom's fine. Her aim was great. He still hasn't woken up." An ambulance siren wailed in the background.

Mindy lurked into the kitchen holding Winston.

"I have to call Charlie and Bri," Claire said, taking more deep breaths. "Call me the second there's an update."

"Will do. We love you."

"Love you too." Claire ended the call and stared at the phone in her hand.

"What the hell happened?" Mindy asked.

"My mom clobbered some guy in their garden with a rolling pin." She clicked on Charlie's contact. "It had to have been ESA. They're going after my family. Again. Mindy, call Bri. Tell her to have a neighbor search her apartment inside and out."

Mindy ran into the living room. Rosie jumped up and put her paws on Claire's leg.

"I'm going to check the property." Luke pulled a gun out of the kitchen junk drawer and tucked it in the waistband of his jeans.

"Luke, you're going to shoot your buttcheek—hi, Charlie. Listen, is Bill home? Good. Have him check your house immediately. Someone just tried to abduct Mom."

CHAPTER TWENTY-FIVE

To Do:
- *Call Mom every fifteen minutes*
- *Re-calibrate motion sensors*
- *Email that doggy daycare*

CLAIRE AWOKE WITH A START. WHY WAS IT SO DARK IN HERE? Had the smog of Los Angeles finally completely blacked out the moon? Hang on, was she standing? Oh, boy.

She moved her right elbow and banged into something wooden. Okay, there was a door behind her. At least she was indoors. What was that in her hand? It was heavy and long. She dropped it on the ground. A metallic thud shook the floor. Must be the baseball bat she kept under the bed. And something crumbly was in her other hand. She sniffed cautiously. That was the unmistakable aroma of Mindy's legendary chocolate chip cookies, freshly stress-baked after both sisters had reported their houses were secure. There was no point in wasting it.

Cookie devoured, she slid to the right like she was doing the Cha Cha Slide. *Crash.* Something hit the floor. She screeched and jumped backward. The wall gave way behind her, and she landed flat on her back in the middle of Luke's foyer.

Oof. The impact stunned her lungs. A pinched, shallow breath offered little relief. She glanced up. The folding door to the coat closet stood ajar.

"Claire?" Footsteps thundered down the stairs. Luke, shirtless and panicked-looking, jumped into the foyer. A gun was clutched in his hand, and he swung it from side to side like a cop on TV. "Is someone here? What the hell are you doing? And what are you wearing?"

Claire glanced down. A red, sequined evening gown glittered in the half-light. She had packed it with the intention of wearing it to Bri's premiere. Now it was sure to be covered in six-month-old dust and dirt.

Luke seemed to be staring at her head. She reached up and felt around. Something was stuck to her head. She wrenched back and forth. A spray of bobby pins pinged out of her hair, and a top hat appeared in her hand. A dozen objects slid out and clattered onto the floor. Zip ties.

"Huh." She dropped it onto the herringbone tile. Where in the hell had she found a top hat? That wasn't one of her disguises. "Everything's fine. I think I was just sleepwalking again."

Luke swore. "You need to email Dr. Goulding." His voice was like stone.

"I will. In the morning." She sat up. Her head throbbed. Was it from the wine or falling through a closet door?

At that moment, Mindy charged down the stairs,

hoisting a wooden chair overhead. "If there's someone in this house, I swear I'll ram this entire chair up your ass," she called in a voice much deeper than usual.

"It's fine. There's no one here," Claire said from the floor.

"What are you doing on the floor?" Mindy asked, setting the chair down and helping Claire up.

"Oh, you know. I just thought I'd try to see things from the dog's perspective. Ouch. What is—" She lifted the hem of her cocktail dress. Her Swiss Army Knife was duct taped to the inside of her thigh.

"You're insane," Luke said, disappearing back upstairs with the gun.

"At least my sleepwalking sessions are more tactical now. I had two weapons with me." Three if you counted the cookie.

Mindy sighed and dropped into the chair.

"Sorry for waking you up."

"I couldn't sleep anyway." Mindy drew her legs up, hugging them to her chest. "I can't stop thinking about your mom."

"Me neither," Claire said. "This is so much worse than when it was just Barney. The worst he ever did was break into Luke's house and paw print Rosie. Well, aside from then trying to kill me. Where are the dogs?" She sat bolt upright.

"They're in your room. I already checked."

"Thank god." She really needed to stop leaving them alone. They had passed a doggy daycare business five minutes from the house. If they had sufficient security protocols, she was going to have no choice but to enroll Rosie and Winston.

"Well, since we're up, maybe we should take another

look at the murder board," Mindy suggested. She stood and walked into the living room.

Claire followed her. It was safer than falling asleep again. Anyone who messed with her mom was going to pay the consequences. She would hunt them to the end of the earth...if she could find them.

She picked up her laptop and flopped onto the leather couch. She typed "Epsilon Sigma Alpha" into the search bar. Pages she had perused a thousand times already populated. The top result was a news article about Venor's fraternity getting shut down when all the members were arrested for attempted abduction.

There had to be answers somewhere in this sea of information. Claire opened the spreadsheet Nicole had put together with all the branches of ESA and scrolled down to California. Two colleges in LA listed ESA chapters. She typed them both into the search bar, but all the links were dead ends. ESA had been effectively scrubbed from the internet.

Losing the West Haven chapter must have spooked them enough to send them underground. Where could they go from here? There wasn't any time to visit the abandoned fraternity houses, but maybe they didn't have a choice.

Luke walked into the living room.

"There's a cobweb in your hair," Claire noted.

He brushed it away. "I was checking the attic. Just in case."

"Any bad guys? Or girls. Feminism." Mindy added as an afterthought.

Luke shook his head. "No. What are we doing?"

"Internet stalking ESA," Claire said. "Or trying to. Everything is still pulled down, and the cached links are just news articles about bake sales and highway cleanups."

Mindy looked up from her tablet. "The chapter in Miami went dark too."

Luke sat on the couch next to Claire. He appeared to be deep in thought. "So they went underground when West Haven went under."

"It seems that way. Do you think we could get alumni lists from the universities?" Mindy asked.

Claire shook her head. "I can't imagine they would just give us those. Remember how long it took us to get a freakin' yearbook from Barney's high school? But I'll mention it to Jack. They can't say no to the FBI. I can't believe they haven't looked into it already."

There was silence for a moment. There were ghosts of so many chapters of ESA online. Two dozen at least spread across fifteen states.

"Are we sure that all branches of this frat were really murderers in training?" Claire asked. It seemed insane. How did this many murderous individuals even find each other without raising suspicion?

"How could we know?" Mindy said. "Still, the fact that all these active branches are locking down is very suspicious. They wouldn't do that for no reason."

"You're right." Luke pulled one of his signature tiny notebooks off the end table. He flipped to a new page. "So what do we know about them?"

"They hate powerful women," Claire began. "It seems like they think they're a threat to men in the workplace. Barney said there's only five acceptable careers for women, and they're all stereotypical fields. Maybe I need to go talk to him again."

"No," Luke and Mindy said quickly.

"Let him rot," Mindy followed up.

"Maybe if we could get the answer to his riddle, we could find the next body and then he'd open up about ESA."

"I totally forgot about the stupid riddle," Mindy said, turning back to the board. "What was it again?"

Claire recited it from memory. "She's buried where William Hickory paid the ultimate price."

"But what does that mean? Who's William Hickory?"

"I have no idea. I've Googled it a hundred times," Claire said, shaking her head. "There's no record of a William Hickory living in West Haven or any of the surrounding areas. Hickory is a kind of tree, but there are probably a million hickory trees in Pennsylvania." She leaned back on the couch. No matter what angle they looked at, they hit a dead end. "Maybe we should go back to bed. We're not getting anywhere with this, and we have to attempt another run-through tomorrow."

"Not to mention you're bamboozling Charlie into meeting Bri at lunch tomorrow, right?"

Claire nodded. It was probably going to be a disaster, but with a threat looming on the horizon, they stood a better chance if they stood together. Surely the threat to the family would squash Charlie's temper at being introduced to her half sister.

Claire had barely edged into the hallway when Mindy gasped.

"What is it?" She ran back into the living room, Swiss Army Knife in hand.

Mindy turned to her with wide eyes. "Holy fucking shit."

Claire's stomach twisted. "What? Did you find something?"

Mindy spun her laptop around. "They found him."

Shock froze Claire to the spot. She snapped out of it and

sprinted for the laptop screen. Luke jostled for position. Even Rosie hopped up to look.

Dr. William Taylor, head of the West Haven chapter of ESA and all-around douchebag, glowered from a picture. His hair and mustache had been dyed jet black, but there was no mistaking the ice in those blue eyes.

"Where?" Claire asked breathlessly.

"LA. This was taken outside the Whole Foods on Fairfax."

Luke sighed. Both women turned to look at him.

"What?" Claire asked.

"You're not doing it." He crossed his arms and made steady eye contact.

"Doing what?"

"Another stakeout. Call Jack and tell him. Leave it at that. It's one thing to sit at home and play armchair detective, but these guys are dangerous. Your mom was almost abducted. I'm not going to allow you to put yourself in danger again."

Mindy grimaced and shrank back into the couch.

Claire stood up. "Oh, you're not going to *allow* me? Is this the 1920s? You don't get to tell me what to do. These men are threatening my family, Luke. I don't know how much time we have until they escalate. Something terrible is going to happen. I can feel it, and I'm not going to wait around for the FBI."

"Yes, you are," he shouted.

Claire flinched. Luke took a deep breath. Several seconds passed.

"I'm sorry for raising my voice," he finally said, "but I'm not budging on this. Call Jack and move on."

"Fine," Claire sniped. She left the room and nearly tripped on the end of her glittering red gown. There was no way she was going to let this go. Not when the professor was in the same city. It was time for her to end this, no matter what Luke said.

CHAPTER TWENTY-SIX

To Do:
- *Timed run of whole proposal*
- *New stupid bridle*
- *Mindfulness*

CLAIRE BUSTLED INTO THE RESTAURANT WITH A THOUSAND tasks whirling in her mind. As if it wasn't bad enough that her mother had nearly been abducted, Brad's requests were getting more elaborate by the day. The newest change was a very specific bridle to go with the very specific saddle for the very specific white horse he had already requested.

Mindy had dropped Claire off for lunch with her sisters while she went to a tack shop in East LA. If they didn't have an exact match, they would be up all night distressing and staining a bridle to Brad's exact standards. She could appreciate detail-oriented people. But this was getting insane. She fired off a text to Mindy.

Claire: *Think we could shut off his internet for the next two and a half weeks?*

"Claire!" someone called. She glanced up. Brianna was waving at her—at least she assumed it was Bri. Her half sister was difficult to recognize due to her paparazzi outfit—baseball cap, oversized sunglasses, and baggy sweater.

"Hey, Bri," she said, trying to push the proposal out of her mind so she could be present in this moment. Her therapist would be proud. "How's the movie coming?"

"Not bad so far. The director's kind of a dick, but that's par for the course out here." Bri took a sip of white wine.

A server stopped by the table as Claire settled into her seat and she ordered two drinks.

"Tell me more about the story," she said to Bri.

As Brianna chatted, Claire glanced around the restaurant. The odds of her spotting Professor Taylor at a restaurant were slim. But since he was the only known link between her and the mystery of ESA, she would hunt that useless mustache to the ends of the earth. Or at least the end of LA.

Her phone buzzed and a text from Alice lit up the screen confirming she was, in fact, still alive. The knot in her stomach relaxed a little. The perpetrator had regained consciousness but had refused to answer any questions. Miami PD was still investigating, but it seemed like the case was going nowhere. Alice's responses were getting shorter and snippier, almost as if she was annoyed at her daughter for doing the same thing she had done for Claire's entire adult life.

Charlie hadn't arrived yet, but they would know the second she did. A glass of red wine and a whiskey sour appeared at Claire's elbow. She slid the whiskey sour to the third place setting. A little liquid courage for her, and a peace offering for Charlie. It was sure to be a disaster no matter what, but hopefully her careful planning would pay off. The restaurant was two blocks from Charlie's office and it was inside only, so neither a commute nor her allergies should aggravate the circumstances.

"And then—spoiler alert—it turns out her stepbrother was the bad guy the whole time," Brianna finished with a flourish.

"Holy shit," Claire said, taking a sip of her wine. "That's quite the story."

"I know. I think it'll do medium-well during awards season. They could have sprung for a bigger name for the stepbrother, but my co-lead is very handsome." She punctuated the sentence with a hand flourish.

"What the hell?" Uh oh, Charlie was here.

Charlie had stopped in her tracks five feet from the table. "What is *she* doing here?" She was never one to mince words. Claire had spent a lot of her childhood apologizing for her big sister's mouth.

"Charlie," Claire said slowly. She pushed her chair back and stepped forward like she was approaching a hungry tiger. "I thought it was time you met our sister, Brianna."

Charlie's lips hardened into a thin line, and she crossed her arms so severely one of the seams in her blazer popped. Not a good sign. Claire handed her the whiskey sour. Charlie released one of her arms from the straightjacket-like hold to sip at it.

Brianna stood and removed her sunglasses. She held one hand out. "Hi, Charlie. I'm Bri. I've heard so much about your work in town. You're a legend at the actors guild."

Charlie took a half step forward and reached out her

hand. Brianna winced as they shook. It was going to be a long lunch.

"Sit, sit." Claire ushered them back to the table. She signaled to the waiter to bring another round. If Brianna's sunny personality and alcohol couldn't loosen Charlie's vise grip on her hatred for all things Jack-related, nothing could.

"How's work going today?" Claire said pointedly to Charlie.

"It's a slow day," Charlie said, pausing what appeared to be a head-to-toe assessment of Brianna. "Just a run-of-the-mill pregnancy coverup and another DUI. But you'd know all about those, wouldn't you? Boyfriend crash into any Denny's lately?" she sniped at Bri.

"Charlie," Claire warned.

"It's okay." Bri grabbed a roll from the bread basket. She crossed one leg underneath her and stabbed her knife into the butter. "That was a weird time in my life. Have you ever dated someone who just has this bizarre hold on you? Like you know that he's an idiot, but for some reason you just can't cut that cord?"

Claire, who had spent way too many years of her young life with Jason, nodded and shuddered.

Charlie removed her sunglasses and tucked them in her purse. She folded her arms again. "So why haven't you ever reached out to us? Before Jack got shot?"

Bri leaned back in her chair. Half a roll lay abandoned on her plate. "To be honest, I didn't know you existed. I knew Dad had been married before, but I didn't find out that I had half sisters until Dad got involved with your case, Claire. I was really upset at first, to have this whole family out there that I didn't know about. I couldn't believe he kept it from me."

Claire glanced at Charlie. Her eyes didn't give anything away. "I see. And after you found out?"

It was like watching an innocent child get interrogated by the principal.

"I didn't even know if you guys would speak to me," Bri admitted. "He abandoned your family to start a new one. Who would want to start a relationship with a living, breathing reminder of that?"

"Exactly. Why would we?" Charlie said coldly.

"Hey," Claire scolded. "Don't be a dick. It's not Bri's fault. She didn't ask for any of this."

"You don't remember what it was like, Claire." Charlie turned and pointed at her. "When Dad left, you were only six. I was six*teen*. Mom couldn't afford the rent and utilities by herself, so I had to get two part-time jobs and go to school. And drive you everywhere, babysit while Mom worked triple shifts at SaveShop."

Brianna sank lower in her chair. Maybe Claire should have talked to Charlie in private first.

"I remember," Claire said slowly. "I also remember you leaving the second you could. You left for college and moved across the country. Then it was just me and Mom until Roy showed up."

"I was tired of being a second parent," Charlie admitted. "I didn't want that responsibility, but I had no choice."

Claire took a deep breath. "I'm sorry you had to do all that. I completely understand why you're furious at Jack, and I respect your decision not to have a relationship with him. But that doesn't mean you can take all that out on Brianna."

Charlie exhaled, and her shoulders dropped a millimeter. She uncrossed her arms and picked up her menu. "I suppose you're right. If the situations were reversed, I would be mad at me for being an asshole. But this does *not*"—she dropped the menu to point at Claire—"mean that I will be okay with any more sneak attacks like Thanksgiving. And today."

Charlie had spent all of Thanksgiving hiding in Luke's basement with Roy, Ryan, and a big glass of wine.

"Never again." Claire crossed her heart. "So I have some drama." Perhaps some gossip would take the wind out of Charlie's sails.

Bri's eyes widened. "Go on."

"I found out yesterday that Luke proposed to someone before he met me."

Charlie choked on her whiskey sour. "He *what*? Mr. Anti-Romance?"

Claire dove into the Olivia saga until their food arrived.

"Wow," Charlie said as she speared a bit of salmon on her fork, clearly more relaxed than she had been ten minutes prior.

"No wonder he thinks proposals are stupid," Charlie and Brianna said at the same time.

Claire smiled and took a bite of her twenty dollar arugula and endive salad. It tasted like someone had pulled unwashed produce directly from a field and drizzled the world's tiniest hint of olive oil over it. But she would eat grass clippings from a lawn mower bag if it meant Charlie and Bri actually made some progress.

Her heart grew in her chest. They started as strangers, and now they were three sisters, semi-reluctantly bonding over gossip. They weren't best friends yet, but things were moving in the right direction. Her dream of having an intact, bicoastal family could still become a reality.

"Charlie, there was something else I wanted to ask you."

Charlie harrumphed. "What, does Jack need a kidney now? Because he can go fuck himself."

"No," Claire said quickly. She lowered her voice. "It's about ESA."

"Ugh." Charlie tossed back what remained of her drink. Brianna leaned in.

"Things are ramping up. You know Mom was almost attacked yesterday. I'm very nervous for both of you. Especially you, Bri. You don't have a husband and a nephew who has spent most of his life playing first-person shooter games at home to watch over you."

"We'll be fine." Charlie waved one hand. "I get like thirty death threats a year in my line of work. Bri probably gets even more."

"Bri's already being targeted by ESA," Claire hissed back. "She's already had a note and the flowers. These assholes are serious, and they're dangerous. You know what they tried to do to me twice already. You need to be careful. I'm serious. Don't go anywhere alone, especially after dark. I emailed you both some safety tips I got from Sawyer."

"I think you're overreacting," Charlie said. "So they sent some flowers and they know where I live. Who cares? Anyone with a computer can figure out where I live."

"We're Jack's children. These people have a score to settle with us. This is serious, Charlie. Promise me you'll start being more careful." They didn't seem to be grasping the magnitude of the problem.

"Relax, Claire. I'll read your safety tips."

Bri reached across the table and squeezed Claire's hand. "Dad's been on me anyway about hiring security. I have some interviews lined up. A body double from that huge guy on *America's Next Top Backup Dancer* applied."

Claire breathed a sigh of relief. "Thank god. Please find someone as soon as humanly possible, or I'm going to make you move in with me. Do not test me."

"So you said you wanted to ask me something?" Charlie interrupted. "You said you had a question and then you just lectured us for ten minutes."

Claire slapped herself on the forehead. "Right, sorry. I got caught up. Charlie, is there anyone you can think of in Hollywood who might be in ESA? A known misogynist with outdated views on women in the workforce?"

Charlie snorted so loudly that a couple at a nearby table looked over. "If you want a list of all the misogynists in Hollywood, we'll be here for a decade at least."

"No one?" Claire pressed.

Charlie shook her head. "No one specific. I'll do some digging in my old files though. Ask around. See what I can come up with."

"Thank you," Claire said, leaning back in her chair. Her sad, expensive salad was gone and she was still hungry. "Last night, someone posted a sighting of Professor Taylor on Mindy's murder blog. He's here, in LA. Jack says the FBI is working on tracking him down, but with all the red tape they have to cut through I'm worried that something catastrophic will happen long before they find him."

"Thanks for the doom and gloom." Charlie raised her eyebrows and dropped her fork. "I promise I'll text you as soon as I think of someone."

Claire leaned forward. "Good. I think the leader is here too."

Brianna drained her ice water. "What makes you say that?"

"West Haven getting shut down spooked them. They're closing ranks, pulling down all the information on the branches from the internet. It can't be a coincidence that Dr. Taylor came here. I'd bet anything the higher-ups are here. Maybe even Hollywood elite." She glanced around the restaurant, half-expecting to see a B-lister in a Greek letter T-shirt.

Charlie leaned forward and stared her down. "Don't go snooping, Claire. Leave it to the professionals."

"I won't." Claire crossed her arms. She was totally going to. A plan was already half-formed.

Claire's phone beeped—Mindy was outside.

Claire's stomach clenched. Lunch had already gone longer than she intended—to be honest, she had fully expected Charlie to storm out and refuse to eat at all. She needed to get back to Brad and billable hours. The proposal was crawling closer by the second.

"Guys, I have to get going." Claire dug cash out of her wallet and tossed it on the table. "Thank you so much for having lunch with me. I hope we can do it again before I leave."

"Yeah, we'll do it," Charlie said begrudgingly, standing to hug her. "I'm going to stay for a few more minutes."

"Me too," Brianna said, also hugging Claire. "So, Charlie," Bri continued as Claire walked away, "you're probably burned out from Hollywood bullshit, but I wanted to invite you and Bill and Ryan to my upcoming premiere."

Claire hurried outside. Even with the mounting stress of Brad's proposal and an increasingly ballsy ESA, her heart was lighter than it had been an hour ago. Things were falling into place. Her sisters were finally on speaking terms. In less than two-and-a-half weeks, Brad's proposal would be over, and it would be so beautiful and romantic and over-the-top that they'd be showered in big budget requests.

Happily Ever Afters would be a bicoastal business (well,

as soon as they hired someone to help,) and they could return to West Haven in time to save Tender Hearts permanently. So what if there was a legion of serial killers after her? She would find them and stomp out every last one of them. Nothing could stop the power of true love.

CHAPTER TWENTY-SEVEN

To Do:
- *Buy Luke's favorite kombucha*
- *Research LA parking laws—wtf?*
- *Find the professor*

"So the florist had amazing news." Mindy paused to straighten her wig in the car's rearview mirror. "We are going to hit the very small window for peonies. They can do a mixture of blush and red for the arch at the proposal site. They'll also throw in some cream for the table at the restaurant if we tag them on social media."

"Perfect. One less thing for Brad to complain about." Claire pressed a pair of binoculars to her sunglasses and leaned forward. They sat in the parking lot of a CVS, eyes glued to the entrance of the Whole Foods on Fairfax. Even though she had explicitly promised Luke not to get involved, ESA had almost kidnapped her mother. The chances of her staying out of it were less than zero.

In the twenty-four hours since her lunch with Brianna and Charlie, there had been no new developments with ESA. No threatening notes, no flowers. But it was only a matter of time, especially since their attempt to abduct Alice had been unsuccessful.

Jack's current wife, Tanya, had been assigned her own cop. She was making use of the extra house guest by enlisting him to help her propagate succulents.

A strand of fake red hair fell across her view, and Claire blew on it until it moved. Two dozen people had come and gone from the store, but none of them were Professor Taylor.

"We're never going to find him. What if he's Googling himself and saw the Web Detectives post?"

"It is a long shot," Nicole said. She was FaceTiming them from her studio. "Wait, is that a mustache? Zoom me in!"

Claire and Mindy practically plastered themselves against the windshield. Claire held her breath. Straw fedora, jet-black mustache. Could it be? A gust of wind blew his hat off. The man was bald, and a Nine Inch Nails tattoo took up most of the real estate on his head. Unless the professor had found a new, all-consuming appreciation for heavy metal, it couldn't be him.

"Damn it." Mindy pounded the dashboard.

"What? It's not him?" Nicole's voice came from the phone.

They both leaned back in their seats. "No, just some other fedora-wearing dingus," Mindy said.

"Damn it. All right, I have to go. I have a family shoot and if I don't eat an entire loaf of bread beforehand, I might throw up on a toddler."

"Love you, Coli," Claire and Mindy said together. They blew her a kiss, and the video cut out.

"So much for our lunch hour stakeout," Claire said. She balled up their food wrappers and tossed them into the car trash can she had insisted Luke install.

Her phone rang, and she jumped. It was Luke.

"Hey," she said. "I'm with Mindy and you're on speaker. What's up?"

"Just leaving the farmers' market. They had baby carrots for Winston."

God, even the words "baby carrots" were sexy when they were said in that gravelly voice.

"Awesome. Thank you for doing that. How did the lunch go?"

"It was good. They wanted to talk about securing some of my future projects."

"Luke, that's huge!"

"I know. I wish you had been there for it."

Shit. She cringed. Luke had asked her to come to lunch with him, but she had been so consumed with proposal drama and the need to seek out information on ESA that she had turned him down.

"I'm really sorry. I promise I'll be at the next one. I'm glad they could see past that grumbly exterior to the soft, squishy genius inside you."

Luke grunted. "So you had a good lunch then?"

"Mmhmm. We just finished up and are about to leave for the ranch."

"I didn't know CVS served lunch."

"What?"

Something banged on her window. Claire screamed and dropped her phone. The Taser was halfway out of her purse before she registered the fact that the person outside her window was a rather pissed-off Luke.

She sheepishly rolled the window down. "What are you doing here?" Did he have access to her phone's GPS too?

"The farmers' market is literally across the street." He pointed at a large, glowing sign that read "The Original Farmers' Market."

"Oh."

His brows were drawn together. "So, just to be clear, you can make time to do lunch with your sisters, but when I ask you to go to lunch, you'd rather sit in the parking lot of a CVS and eat gas station wraps."

Oof.

"I'm so sorry. We were—"

"I know what you were doing." He pointed at the Whole Foods. "We talked about this. In fact, I remember expressly forbidding you to do this."

"I'm not alone. Mindy's here. And Nicole was on FaceTime."

"You could be with an entire team of Navy SEALs and I still wouldn't want you dangling yourself in front of them like a piece of meat. We're not done talking about this." He shook a finger at the car, then turned and strode off down the street.

"Love you," Claire called out the window. She rolled it back up. "Oh boy. He's mad."

"I think we've eclipsed mad and gone straight to fuming. You should have gone to lunch. This was a total bust."

"I know. But now that I know he's here somewhere, I just need to find him." Claire typed the address for the ranch into her phone. She would make it up to Luke later. Skipping lunch had been shitty. She needed to do better. "Think we can stop for ingredients for apology pie on the way back?"

"I think you better," Mindy said.

"Okay, let's get going. It's going to take us either twenty minutes or two hours to get to the ranch."

Mindy backed the car out of the spot and sped toward the hills. As they drove, Claire checked the doggy daycare app. With everything going on, leaving the dogs home alone was no longer an option. They had enrolled Winston and Rosie in a twenty-four-hour daycare the day before, and Rosie had been so exhausted she had to be physically carried out to the backyard to go pee before bed. The app had a live camera available at all times. Both dogs were safe and sound. Rumor had it that Rihanna's dog attended the same facility.

Thirty minutes later, they rolled into a dusty parking lot. Claire and Mindy stepped out into the sunshine.

"It's a beautiful day!" Mindy stretched her arms out and twirled in the light.

"Are you just saying that because you're going to see Sawyer this weekend?"

"Maybe." Mindy booped Claire on the nose. "Riding boots?"

"Right." Claire popped the trunk and pawed through half a dozen garment bags before finding the right one. She slid on a pair of socks and her rarely used equestrian boots.

"Ready?" Mindy brushed a bit of dirt off her jodhpurs.

Claire glanced over her own outfit and tossed her French braid over one shoulder. She may have copied her equestrian outfit from an American Girl doll. "Ready. The website said the ranch is about a quarter of a mile up that way. It's too narrow to drive."

"That's fine. I could use the steps."

Claire locked the car and nodded. After a quick bout of hula dancing, they were on their way. Sweat pooled on her lower back by the time they reached the check-in area of the ranch. This hunt coat was *not* breathable. A flannel-and-denim clad woman greeted them inside.

"You must be Rita. It's so nice to finally meet in person." Claire extended a hand to the woman. The woman reached over and returned the handshake with a strong grip. She couldn't have been more than five foot two, and there was a gold tooth where her incisor should be. "This is the saddle I told you about."

Claire handed over a shopping bag containing the saddle they had picked up that morning. A pang hit her. It wasn't the original. She had lost something irreplaceable. Would Karen be able to tell?

Rita whistled through her teeth. "Well, goll-dang. That's a beautiful saddle."

"And it'll fit the horse okay?" Claire knew nothing about horses.

"I don't see why not," Rita said, rubbing the saddle with the end of her sleeve. "You wanna ride Sugar today?"

"Sure," Claire said. She had never ridden a horse before, unless she counted the pony at a classmate's tenth birthday party. If she could handle the quick jaunt on Sugar, there was no reason to think that Karen, an accomplished equestrian, would fair any differently.

Twenty minutes later, they trotted down yet another dirt path at a fair speed. Sugar had not been impressed with Claire's attempts to get in the saddle, but she seemed to have forgiven her. Mindy had ambled onto Rhone, a majestic brown thoroughbred, as if she did this every day. They captured a quick selfie as the horses plodded down the path.

It was peaceful out here in the hills, far away from the

hustle and bustle of downtown. Aside from the arid beauty of the hillside though, the ride was exceptionally boring. Visually, there was nothing to look at but patches of dirt and scrubby little plants. This wouldn't do for the country's most romantic and over-the-top proposal. This wouldn't do at all.

"Scenery kind of sucks, no?" Mindy whispered.

Claire nodded fervently. "Some adjustments are definitely needed." But what would be appropriate? Lanterns? Floral wreaths?

They rounded a bend. The back of her neck prickled. She turned abruptly and peered over her shoulder. No one was behind them. The path ahead was clear as well. So why couldn't she shake the feeling that she was being watched?

Her gaze probed the hills as Rita chatted about the history of the ranch. Something down the hill flashed, like sun hitting glass. Her heart leapt into her throat. As hard as she looked, nothing jumped out of the arid terrain. Was someone down there watching them? Was that the sun flashing across the scope of a rifle? Or was it just an influencer with a malfunctioning ring light?

Mindy nudged her. "What's up? You're on high alert." She looked over her shoulder.

Claire patted her cross-body purse. Her Taser, at least, had not fallen out during her attempts to get on the horse. "Just a weird feeling. It's probably nothing."

Mindy puffed herself up like a cat, staring all around them with a glare that would intimidate even the scariest misogynist.

Claire's shoulders hunched and the reins went limp in her numb hands. They were here. Even if they weren't watching right now, ESA was in the city. What were they planning? How much time did she have before they made their move? And who would they hurt in the meantime?

Her vision darkened at the corners. Sugar's ears flicked. Everything seemed far away. Her breath hitched. Numbness tingled up and down her arms.

Mindy leaned forward and peered at her. "Hey. Take a breath. Do you need to stop?"

Claire shook her head. She was not about to give ESA the satisfaction of a dramatic reaction. What did Dr. Goulding say she should do? Deep breaths, mindfulness, find a focus object. This was just a panic attack, and she wasn't dying. She swung her head left to right, fighting the tunnel vision. A scrubby tree stood at a fork in the path.

If she had to plan a proposal at that exact spot, what would she do? If it was winter, dress it up like a shabby Christmas tree for sure. Stage some fake plants. A gingham blanket and a classic picnic basket. Maybe even a yurt.

By the time they reached the end of the trail where the picnic was scheduled to take place, the imaginary proposal she was planning had distracted her long enough to allow the panic to recede. Her limbs still shook, but at least she could function.

Claire and Mindy hopped down from their horses, and Claire's knees nearly buckled. Mindy steadied her, concern written across her face.

"I'm fine, seriously." It was almost true. "Let's go over the checklist."

They spent twenty minutes drawing a diagram of exactly where everything would be stationed. Claire took dozens of pictures and sent them to Nicole to help plan her shots. The Hollywood sign stood tall on the hillside above them. Claire wasn't an expert in photography, but even her untrained eye could imagine the airlifted Marry Me letters shining bright in the sunset. It would be beautiful. Now she needed to address the ride.

"So, Rita," Claire said on the way back down. "I was wondering if you might allow me to make a couple of enhancements to the trail."

"What kind of enhancements?" Rita called over her shoulder.

"I'm thinking some fairy lights to mark the path and maybe a framed and backlit picture of our couple every hundred yards or so."

"Honey, for an extra hundred bucks, you can throw all the crap you want out here long as you pick it up after," Rita said.

Well, that was a relief. Now she just needed to talk to Brad about the extra cost, choose some pictures, and spend the weekend scrounging up supplies. Easy. She and Luke were supposed to have a day date on Saturday, but surely he'd be okay with making a few pit stops.

"One more thing. It's kind of silly."

"Oh?" Rita looked over her shoulder and raised one eyebrow.

As much as it pained her to admit, something was telling her walking back to their car alone right now would be a very dangerous idea. "Are there any men working at the ranch today? Maybe a couple who might not mind walking us back to our car? My mom worries," she hastily explained. Hopefully if she had reinforcements, ESA wouldn't do whatever it was they were planning.

"Sure thing. Hank and Brycen will see you the whole way. Hank's a bit of a talker, though, just to warn ya."

"Thank you so much."

Thirty minutes later, Claire and Mindy trudged back to their car, kicking up dust the entire way. Hank, a bow-legged man wearing overalls with more dirt than denim, regaled them with story after story. Brycen, almost as if to compensate, didn't say a word the entire time.

"So one time," Hank said, pausing to sling a rifle over one shoulder. "Me and the wife were in Italy, right? On a bus tour, the whole thing. One morning she was mad at me because I didn't want to wear the collared shirt she had picked out, so she sat ten rows ahead of me on the bus. Frankly, I didn't mind as I enjoyed the peace and quiet. Now we stopped at a gas station in Naples. Everyone got their snacks and piled back on. I took a nap and woke up when we arrived in Rome. Got off the bus, looked around, she was nowhere to be found."

Mindy gasped. "You left her in Naples?"

"I sure did. This was way back before cell phones too, so we had a helluva time meeting back up. Doesn't help that neither of us spoke a lick of Italian."

"That's quite the story," Claire said. She would have murdered Luke if he had left her behind in Paris.

"I still don't think she's quite forgiven me. This you?" He lifted his chin in the direction of the black Porsche. They had finally reached the parking lot.

"That's us. Thank you so much, Hank. And Brycen. I felt a lot safer with you two."

"Can't be too careful out here, miss. Never know what you're gonna see. Those wild pigs are becomin' a real problem."

Great. Another topic to add to the safety meeting.

Claire paused with her hand on the driver's side door. She hadn't done her vehicle safety check. As she knelt, the dirt clung to her hands. She wrinkled her nose and glanced under the car.

"You all right, miss? You lose an earring or somethin'?" Hank called.

"Just taking a look. I've had some trouble with—"

Something caught her eye. There, behind her passenger side tire, was a shining, two-inch-long screw. She froze, paralyzed. The screw wasn't laying on its side, accidentally discarded by a maintenance truck. It was standing straight up, directly behind the tire, ready to puncture it. Breath caught in her lungs, and she choked back a scream.

She stood so quickly that she staggered, dizzy for a moment, then reached into her purse and pulled out her pepper spray.

"Claire? What the hell is going on?" Mindy ducked down and looked under the car. She gasped. "Motherfuckers."

Claire inched around the car, keeping her back to it as she surveyed the area. Arid hills rose around her, showing nothing but short, scrubby plants. A dense patch of trees stood on the hillside between her and the ranch. Her knuckles went white as she clenched the pepper spray.

Hank and Brycen whirled around, each staring into the distance.

"Should we call the police?"

"I don't know. And tell them what, I found a screw behind my tire? Maybe we should just go." Nothing moved on the hillside except for the bushes stirred by breeze, but she couldn't shake the sensation of eyes on her.

"I don't like this," Claire muttered.

A shadow moved in the patch of trees that separated them from the ranch. She pointed a shaking finger.

Hank whipped his rifle up, but didn't release the safety. "Damn tweakers," he muttered. "*Hey*! You are trespassing on private property. I'm going to give you to the count of five to clear out of here. You hear? One...two..."

Just then, a man dressed all in black sprinted from the

tree line and crossed over the road. Claire screamed. Hank lifted his rifle in the air. The man flinched and turned toward them, face as pale as the moon. He made menacing eye contact for a split second before disappearing over the crest of the hill.

Brycen took off after him, footsteps thudding heavily in his work boots.

Hank sighed and slung his rifle back over his shoulder. "I swear we get a new troublemaker every day. What do they think we have up here, a meth lab?"

Claire's stomach shriveled. That was no run-of-the-mill tweaker. That was ESA.

Her hands shook, and she clenched them into fists. Her feet propelled her across the lot to the place between trees where she had spotted the shadow. There, lying in the dirt, was a pile of zip ties, a brown glass bottle, and a filthy rag. She backed away, nearly stumbling down the incline.

"Mindy?"

Her friend appeared next to her. She inhaled sharply. "I've got it." Mindy dialed a number on her phone and held it to her ear. "Hi, we're going to need an officer at Twilight Ranch. We need to report a suspected abduction attempt. White male, midtwenties, super pale." Mindy walked off to the other end of the lot.

Claire glanced around her, but the overwhelming feeling of being watched was gone.

If even one thing had gone differently today—if Mindy hadn't wanted to go along, or if Hank and Brycen hadn't been at work, she would be dead. Tortured by a bunch of woman-hating hooligans. She was tired of being harassed and intimidated. It was time to do something about it. She dialed Luke's number, a plan already forming in her mind.

CHAPTER TWENTY-EIGHT

To Do:
- Ask sketch artist for copy?
- Prep interview questions
- Hack into Brad's Pinterest and lock him out?

"YOU'RE NOT GOING INSIDE." THE LIGHTS FROM THE dashboard cast a blue glow over Luke's stoic face. His jaw clenched.

A mere eight hours had passed since the incident at the ranch. Although Brycen had pursued the man to make sure he left ranch property, the attempted assailant had escaped into a dark sedan with the license plate removed. The zip ties and chloroform had been confiscated by the police, and Claire and Mindy had been taken to the station to provide statements.

Claire didn't have time for this nonsense. Brad had emailed four times while they dealt with the fallout.

Although she was more exhausted than she could remember being in her entire life, she couldn't rest. After a rather heated discussion, Luke had reluctantly agreed that it was better to strike while ESA least expected it. And so they had impulsively jumped into the car and traveled to the nearest abandoned ESA frat house at the San Fernando University campus.

Streetlights glowed overhead, accenting the Greek letters Epsilon Sigma Alpha that were fixed over the porch on a building down the street. The windows were dark, and everything was still. There was no telling what lay beyond that front door. Would they find clues, or would they be up to their elbows in discarded beer cans and crunchy Kleenexes?

Claire slammed the glove box closed and adjusted the black latex gloves she had just donned—perhaps the first time in modern history that the compartment had been used for its intended purpose.

"Respectfully, this is a Code Purple. And as the Safety Czar for the group, my attendance is mandatory."

"You know you just made up all these rules, right?" He stared dubiously at her.

This man was going to be the death of her. She laid a hand on his arm. "First of all, how dare you. And second, I know this makes you uncomfortable. But I'll be safer inside with you two than out here by myself."

He sighed. "Fine."

"What do you think? Purple or red?" Mindy stuck her head into the gap between the front seats and swapped between two wigs.

"Red," Luke and Claire said together. Mindy slapped the purple one on Claire's head.

"Is this really necessary?"

"What, you don't think ESA has cameras monitoring their abandoned frat houses just in case? Wigs are mandatory. For you too." She tossed a short, black bob at Luke.

He grumbled and put it on. They made quite the trio.

It wasn't Claire's finest plan. There was no time to make a binder or dig for blueprints. They had barely found time to get the lay of the land via Google Maps. But, using a complex system of garters and headbands, she had managed to affix four different Tasers to her body.

"I wish we were there with you." Nicole's voice said. She, Kyle, and Sawyer were crammed into the same frame on Mindy's phone.

"For the record, I do not support this," Sawyer said. Kyle nodded and crossed his arms.

Claire tugged the wig down over her gargantuan bun. "This is the least dangerous thing we've done all day. ESA's gone. The worst thing we might come up against is a group of wily cockroaches."

"I thought we decided the frat brothers had left the building?" Mindy asked.

"Ha!" Claire and Mindy high-fived. Luke didn't seem to appreciate the joke.

Mindy popped an earbud in. The audio from her phone cut out. "Ready?"

"Let's get the bastards." Claire flung her car door open and stepped out into the night.

The streetlights buzzed overhead. Music bumped from a different frat house down the block. A group of three girls in crop tops opened the door and stepped inside, but otherwise everything was silent.

Claire glanced over her shoulder and scanned the dark street. There was no sensation of being watched, but that didn't mean anything. ESA had been ready to take her today, even with Mindy in tow. It was impossible to say if they had been followed. Was there a creep in a car watching them right now? She suppressed a shudder and turned back to the task at hand.

Claire and Mindy had both traded in their heels for sneakers. Luke looked over his shoulder every few seconds, short black bob lining the edge of his chiseled jaw. Was her manic pixie dream boyfriend expecting ESA to reach out and grab Claire at any second? They hadn't talked much about what had happened, but it was clear that it was weighing on him. During their brief stop at home, Luke had applied WD-40 to the garage door and sanded down a chair leg.

They approached the building. It seemed to yawn at them, windows an abyss. Claire's stomach clenched. Measured breaths whooshed through her nostrils. She pulled out her phone and checked the live camera at the doggy daycare. Rosie chomped on a bone while Winston was curled up beside her. They, at least, were fine.

As she went to exit the app, she paused. Doggy daycare. It was a relatively new concept. There weren't any in the greater West Haven area. Would Sam and Gloria be interested in the idea? It would require a different license, but it could add a permanent revenue stream. She quickly typed the idea into a note and pocketed her phone. If ESA wasn't brought down, nothing and no one in her life was safe. If they burned down the shelter, she would never forgive herself.

She rolled her shoulders back and set her eyes on the house. When they had infiltrated the ESA frat at Venor, they had utilized the university's underground tunnel system. Unfortunately, due to California's penchant for shaking the crap out of its residents, there were no tunnels under this frat house. They were going to have to resort to good old-fashioned breaking and entering.

Grass crunched underfoot as they stepped off the sidewalk and skirted around the edge of the house. They followed a six-foot privacy fence to the backyard and flanked the backdoor. A small yard with a scorched fire pit sat before them. The concrete path dead-ended at a shed. A beer pong table that looked virtually untouched was askew next to it.

"Let me get the kit." She rummaged in her purse and handed a small lock picking set to Luke.

"Here goes nothing." Luke, a lifelong student, had spent a long weekend the previous summer learning how to pick locks. He snapped a pair of gloves on and crammed a tension wrench and rake into the keyhole.

Claire stepped around him and pressed herself against the window. Moonlight streaked across a suspiciously clean kitchen. No sign of life inside.

Mindy stepped into the shadows and pointed the phone up at the rafters of the house.

"Any cameras?" Claire hissed.

Mindy listened intently for a moment, then shook her head. "Sawyer says he doesn't see anything obvious."

"Tell him to keep looking. I don't trust them." She shuffled to the edge of the building and peeked around the corner. A car drove by but didn't slow down.

"Got it." There was a click, and the door swung open.

Claire stepped back to the door and took Luke by both arms. "You are a sexy genius." She kissed him, then dragged him inside. Mindy followed.

The door closed behind them with an unnerving *thunk*. The inside of the house was dark and completely silent. For a frat house, it was almost suspiciously nice. Hardwood floors stretched back to a cushy-looking living room with leather sofas. The kitchen they stood in was full of gleaming stainless steel appliances. Maybe the university had hired a cleaning crew after ESA had disbanded. There was no way a bunch of twenty-year-old dudes lived like this. Where were the cartoon penises and dented walls? There wasn't even a single broken bifold door or overflowing trash can.

"Where do we start? Bedrooms?" Claire leaned forward and glanced into the dining room as though she was rooted to the spot. Was there anything worse than the prospect of digging through a bunch of frat boy's bedrooms? Hopefully the quart of hand sanitizer she had packed would be enough.

Mindy panned her camera around the room. "Sawyer says don't forget the floorboards."

"Great. I'm sure we won't find any weird sex things at all."

A brief survey of the first floor revealed little. Paintings hung in the hallway. A couple of bags of rice were left in the pantry. There were shadows on the wall where what looked like plaques had once hung. No doubt they had had ESA brothers' names on them and were removed in case anyone came snooping.

"Welp, that explains all the paintings," Mindy said. She held up her phone. "They're Gauguin prints. He was a misogynist who 'married' multiple underage girls."

Claire pursed her lips. "Yeah, that seems right." She slapped the nearest painting off the wall. Glass crunched underfoot as she moved past.

"What the hell was that?" Luke's head popped out of a room.

"Just shattering the patriarchy. What's this?"

Her shoes clacked over the living room floorboards as

she approached a set of French doors. She gripped the handles and turned. Locked. Luke arrived next to her and wrenched at the doors. They didn't budge.

He grunted. "Let's do the bedrooms first and circle back."

The wooden stairs creaked as they made their way to the second floor. Numbness tingled up and down Claire's arms. Everything about this house was unnerving. She had been in a fair number of frat houses during her tenure at Venor, and none of them had looked like this. The almost military-like cleanliness was creepy. Headlights flashed past the windows, and her breath caught in her chest. The last thing she needed was to be caught breaking and entering by the group of people trying to murder her. Or worse, the cops. She paused on the last step, but the lights moved on.

More ghosts of plaques long since removed lined the walls. Could they have forgotten one somewhere? Maybe somewhere in this house was the name of an ESA brother. It would be a start.

"I'll take this one. You take that one." Bossy Luke was back. He was probably still mad about the attempted kidnapping incident from earlier.

Claire and Mindy made a face at each other and disappeared into the bedroom Luke had indicated. A nondescript room appeared in the beams from their phone flashlights. A bare mattress sat on a wooden frame. Thick maroon curtains hung from the windows. Mindy immediately began opening dresser drawers. Claire headed for the desk. There was nothing—no discarded paper, no writing utensils. It was like no one had ever lived there.

After ten minutes of jamming her metal nail file into floorboards, Claire jumped when Luke stepped into the room.

"Nothing?"

He shook his head.

"Nothing here either." Mindy said. She stood and dusted her gloved hands off. "I did find a dried out Cheeto under the desk, but I don't think that helps."

Claire reached out a hand, and Luke pulled her to her feet. They searched the remaining bedrooms together, but there was nothing. Not even a discarded sock. All evidence of the ESA brothers had been erased. How many of them had lived here, plotting evil things? Where were they now?

"I guess the mysterious locked room is our last shot. Come on." Claire led the way down the stairs to the locked French doors. Was this all going to be a bust? There were other abandoned ESA chapters in town, but they didn't have time to search them all.

Luke stood next to her and pulled his lock picking kit out. Thirty seconds later, the doors popped open. He shined his flashlight into the room.

"Oh, hell." His voice echoed off the walls. Floor-to-ceiling velvet drapes lined the room. A two-foot-tall golden statue with a massive erection stood on a pedestal in the very center.

"We meet again, Priapus," Claire growled. Barney had very thoughtfully carved Priapus's symbol into her neck when he had abducted her. It had largely faded, but the memory would always sting.

"*Ha!*" Claire roundhouse kicked the statue. It fell onto the carpet with a thump. A golden penis rolled out from underneath it.

"Shit." She clutched at her ankle. It burned like the statue had been made out of lava. Not her finest moment.

"Sawyer says 'good form.' Are you okay?" Mindy stared at her over the edge of her phone.

"I'm fine." Tension was welling in her belly again. She took a pained breath and swiveled. A bulletin board was tacked to one wall. Holes riddled the surface, but no scrap of evidence had been left behind.

What did they use this creepy-ass room for? And why had they stripped the house of everything but left this stupid statue behind? She was drawn to it like a magnet. She dropped to her knees and picked it up. It was heavier than it looked. There was a hole where the penis had popped off. A glint of white caught her eye. Was there something inside?

Her heart raced. She shook the statue. A shuffling sound came from inside.

"Guys. I think I found something."

Mindy popped out from behind one of the velvet curtains. She sneezed and dropped her phone. Luke stormed over, expression broody and unreadable.

"There's something inside. If I can just—" She twisted the base in her hands. It unscrewed and popped off. A tube of paper slid into her gloved hand.

"Holy shit." Luke and Mindy crowded around her. Claire held her breath and unfurled the paper. Two things emerged—a flyer of some sort and what appeared to be a handwritten list of topics.

She spread them on the floor and glanced over them. Unfortunately, the handwritten list didn't have names—just weird topics.

"The Dangers of Women in the Workplace, Reclaiming Your Sacred Masculinity, Women and the 'Five Acceptables.' What the hell is this about?" Luke's voice was sharp. One hand curled protectively over the small of Claire's back.

Her breath caught in her chest. "The flyer. Do you see this?"

"Men's Rights Conference. Los Angeles. May thirteenth," he read.

Shockwaves coursed through her body. "Guys, this is it. Our chance to catch ESA."

"You mean the FBI's chance to catch ESA," he corrected. His grip on her tightened.

"Right, the FBI. Shit. I better call Jack."

Mindy carefully tucked the flyer and paper into a ziplock bag as Claire dialed Jack's number.

Tingles ran up and down her arms. For the first time in days, there was a tiny glimmer of hope. Maybe things would work out after all—ESA would be remanded into custody and she could finally go back to her busy and beautiful life of being a proposal planner.

"What's wrong?" Jack's voice was sharp.

"We're at the ESA house at San Fernando University."

Jack swore. "What are you doing there? We already swept that house."

"You did?" She made a face at Luke and Mindy. "Well, then your guys did a shitty job. We found something."

There was a pause on the other end. "What is it?"

"A flyer. For a men's rights conference in Los Angeles. Two weeks from now."

Jack sighed. There was another pause. "We're aware of the conference."

"And the fact that we found a flyer for it in an ESA house is not at all suspicious to you? Come on, this one is a no-brainer. ESA's going to be there."

"We're going to handle it, Claire. Now please get out of there before you get arrested for breaking and entering."

The call disconnected.

"He hung up on me. Did you hear that? He basically told

me to shut up. I didn't even have a chance to tell him about the handwritten note—"

"He just wants you to stay out of it," Luke said. "Come on, let's go. You have a therapy appointment first thing in the morning."

"I do?"

"You do now. In case you forgot, you were almost abducted today." Luke tucked his phone into his jeans.

Her stomach tightened. Breaking into the ESA house had been a wonderful distraction from the events of that afternoon. Now she was going to have to speak to Dr. Goulding and hash through everything. Was she even ready to talk about it?

Claire allowed him to steer her out of the house and back into the car. ESA was in the FBI's hands now. Probably.

CHAPTER TWENTY-NINE

To Do:
- *Research Men's Rights Conference*
- *Grill Jack*
- *Check in with Bri*

WHEN HER ALARM WENT OFF AT FIVE A.M. ON SATURDAY, Claire rolled out of bed like a ninja and crouched on the floor. She peeked over the edge of the down comforter. Luke was still sleeping, brows furrowed like he was lecturing someone. He probably was. Rosie raised her head, but apparently was too sleepy to follow her mom out the door.

Claire stepped silently down the stairs and quickly changed into the outfit she had laid out the night before. After two painfully lengthy meetings on Thursday and Friday, Brad had decided he needed another and it couldn't wait. Happily Ever Afters had never followed a Monday-Friday workweek, but this was getting ridiculous. Mindy had done the smart thing and flown back to West Haven for the weekend, so Claire was going to the meeting alone.

She was supposed to be spending the day with Luke. He had planned a day date to show her all his favorite places in the city. But now it would have to wait until this infernal meeting was over. Brad insisted it would be quick, so there was no reason to believe it wouldn't be. Surely he had some rich people stuff to do on Saturday—golfing, maybe? Or an underground fight club?

She set a pot of coffee to brew and pulled out one of Luke's tiny notebooks—he had a literal drawer full in his kitchen. The pen scratched across the paper as she scrawled a quick note explaining her absence. Would he be upset when he found her gone? Probably. But her whole future was riding on this proposal. It had to be done.

Luke-

I HAVE NOT BEEN ABDUCTED. Quick meeting with Brad. Be back soon.

xoxo

Besides, he had forced her into a therapy session *twice*. She had not been mentally ready to unpack what had happened at the ranch, and her session with Dr. Goulding had ended in a panic attack. He had no room to argue about boundaries.

She triple-checked that all the doors and windows were locked before hustling outside to the car. The sky blushed pink, but the sun still hovered below the horizon. Car keys were threaded through her fingers as she tiptoed across the lawn. ESA could be anywhere. Spying through a hole in a neighbor's fence, lurking in a parked car. There would barely be time to inhale the sharp, sweet scent of chloroform before she was incapacitated. It had happened before. She quickened her pace and ran through her vehicle security check at double time.

Her heart pounded as she threw herself into the driver's seat. She clutched a hand to her chest and fought for measured breaths. She smelled the stupid black licorice air freshener (Luke had the worst taste,) listened to the hum of the engine. There was only so much she could do to ground herself in reality in this tiny, ineffective car. The Porsche was sorely lacking in hauling capacity. She could barely fit a breath mint in the backseat let alone a set of professional grade speakers.

After a minute, her heart rate slowed. Her fingers cracked as she pulled them off the steering wheel and flexed. There was no need to lose her damn mind every time a shadow crossed her path. If ESA was run predominantly by frat boys, there was a zero percent chance that they were up at five thirty in the morning on a Saturday.

She needed to refocus and get to work. In two short weeks, the proposal would be in motion. Once Brad's project was over and the shelter was effectively saved, she could breathe again. Well, if ESA didn't manage to murder her in the interim.

She backed slowly out of the driveway and turned down the street toward the studio. Burbank was quiet this early on a Saturday. A couple of elderly neighbors puttered around in their gardens, watering flowers and reaching for their morning papers. She waved to Mr. Nesbit, a kind neighbor with an adorable golden retriever named Hank. He had left a bag of produce on their front porch the day before.

But what the hell was this? She almost stomped on the brakes.

Olivia stood outside a modest two-story brick house. She

unfurled a yoga mat on her patch of front lawn that was more dirt than grass. Her neon yellow sports bra made Claire's eyes water as she drove by. A complicated-looking ring light with a cellphone harness stood ready in the grass.

Her knuckles tightened on the steering wheel. As much as she wanted to, she wouldn't flash a middle finger at the attempted homewrecker. With her luck, it would end up on TikTok and her reputation would be even more brutally destroyed.

Thirty harrowing minutes later, Claire pulled into the studio and locked her doors. Despite its best efforts, Los Angeles traffic had not managed to claim her life. She did a quick bout of two-stepping and triple-checked her purse for Brad's master binder. It had a fresh new tab devoted solely to trail decoration. Since her own stash was torched, she had spent the remainder of her Friday getting quotes from rental companies in the area. Hopefully Brad wouldn't have any additional outlandish requests. They were running out of time.

Claire hustled into the studio. There was minimal staff here today, and they waved her back without bothering to check her ID. She knocked hesitantly on Brad's door.

"Come in," he said. "Ah, Claire. Thank you for meeting with me."

Claire slid a coffee across the imposing mahogany desk. "It's no trouble. So, two weeks out from the big day. How are you feeling?"

Brad stood and faced away from her. He sipped his coffee for a moment and stared out the window like a Bond villain. Her stomach clenched. Was he about to make some dramatic proclamation that he wasn't ready for marriage after all? If so, she was going to torch the entire studio.

"I feel great. I only wish we didn't have to wait another

two weeks. My head just buzzes with ideas on how it can be bigger, better. But I know there's only so much we can accomplish in a single day. Maybe I should have planned a proposal week." He chuckled.

Claire's smile froze. If he was about to propose that they stretch these events out over the course of a week, she was going to lose her shit.

"I think one beautiful day exactly as you have planned it will be perfect," she said diplomatically. "You can always take a vacation afterwards to celebrate."

"Now there's an idea." Brad pulled out his readers and scribbled something on a sticky note. "How's Luke doing, by the way? He's okay with me dragging you away from home so often?"

Claire smiled. "He knows how important this is."

"How's his next documentary coming?"

"Almost done," she said. "Streamster's been instrumental in completing the finishing touches. He was able to shorten his timeline by almost six months with their help."

"Luke Islestorm, sellout. Never thought I'd see the day."

She narrowed her eyes. No one talked shit about her boyfriend's life work, even if he was paying her a crapload of money. "Luke's still in complete creative control. He's just added some resources, that's all. But anyway, what did you want to talk about today?"

Brad pulled out a folder of his own and flipped it open. Printed copies of their emails were hole punched and grouped neatly inside. His binder skills definitely needed work though. There wasn't a sheet protector or a tab in sight.

"Let's talk about my vision for the trail ride." Brad leaned forward and shoved his folder at her. A lighting scheme complete with oscillating spotlights and LED color-changing string lights stared back at her. Great. It was going to be borderline impossible to acquire and install all the materials before the proposal.

They dove into conversation about the trail. Claire cursed herself for even bringing it up. It would be a sunset ride, wouldn't the natural beauty of the hillside have been enough? The patchy grass and stunted trees stood out in her mind like a sore thumb though. It was annoying, but this was the right way to do a proposal of this magnitude.

She glanced at her watch. An hour had passed since they had started the meeting. Surely Rosie had gotten Luke up by now. Her phone was in her bag, and she wasn't about to check it while she was with a client. Hopefully the coffee she had brewed would improve Luke's mood.

Next, Brad wanted a complete financial update. Claire pursed her lips as she wiggled her laptop out of her bag and pulled up the shared spreadsheet that Mindy had been updating religiously. She scrolled down to the bottom so Brad could see the final tally. He leaned back in his chair and nodded.

"Now does that include the quote for the upgrades to the trail?"

"Not until we decide on exactly what you want. It'll be probably an extra couple hundred to a thousand, depending on how much you want."

"What about fireworks?" Brad said thoughtfully.

She shook her head. "Rita at the ranch explicitly said no fireworks. It would spook the horses, risk injuring someone, and getting the permit would be nearly impossible. You don't want Karen to get hurt on proposal day."

"No, you're probably right. I just wish there was something else, some final element we could add for real pizzazz."

Apparently flying in fifty-foot-tall self-lit letters wasn't pizzazz-y enough for Brad.

"You know, I really think we have enough." She peeked at her watch again. Another hour had gone by. Luke was definitely going to be pissed. "You don't want to overwhelm Karen with too much. All that matters to her is the question. Have you been working on your speech?"

"As a matter of fact, I have." He ducked his head and slid open a desk drawer, then pulled out another folder containing several handwritten and stapled documents. He dropped them on the desk. Damn it to hell. Why couldn't she shut her mouth? "I have several different versions. Can I try them out on you?"

"Of course." She gritted her teeth. This would never end.

Brad read six different versions of his proposal speech over the course of the next ninety minutes. With Claire's help, he narrowed it down to three versions.

"I really like the way you incorporated the story of how you met in this version." She pointed to the speech she had marked with a yellow highlighter. "I think if you combine that with the anecdote about your first date at Alcatraz and your cross-country Christmas road trip from year four, you'll really highlight all the beautiful things you love about Karen. That's a powerful proposal right there."

"Do you really think so? Because I was kind of partial to the story in this version where we—"

Bang.

Brad's office door flew open.

Instinctively, Claire stood and kicked her chair toward the door before tucking and rolling. Shit, her pepper spray was in her purse, and she had kicked her purse at the intruder. Her instincts needed some work. She grabbed a book off Brad's shelf and hoisted it like a Frisbee.

A scream was caught in her throat. Was it ESA? Had they grown tired of their cat-and-mouse game and stormed the studio?

But no. It wasn't a chloroform-toting lackey staring at her from the doorway. It was a very grumpy Luke.

"Sorry, Brad, Claire has another meeting," he said. He crossed the office in two steps and pulled Claire up from the floor. Her world inverted as he tossed her over his shoulder like a rag doll. "She'll email you later." He stopped for a brief wave before slamming the office door behind him.

"Luke! What the hell? I was right in the middle of a meeting." The blood was rushing to her head, which did nothing for her mood. She kicked her legs, but he held her in a vise grip.

"We have a date planned," he said simply.

"I know that, that's why I planned the meeting so early."

"It's been five hours," he snapped. "I texted you three times."

Claire's hands balled into fists. "You know how important this proposal is to me. And you know we only have two weeks left to get everything perfect. If I can't pull this off, the West Coast branch of Happily Ever Afters will be dead. It'll be almost impossible for me to support the shelter. Failure is not an option, Luke. The stakes are too high."

A glass door swung open, and then they were back in the blinding sunshine. He set her down on her feet and stared at her, eyes stormy.

"You always think your work is more important than mine." She sniped before he could say anything. "I would never pull you out of a meeting with a client."

"That's not true. And there's more to life than work."

Her face burned as she ripped her purse out of his hand and flung it over her shoulder. She opened her mouth, but

Luke put up a hand to stop her. He cupped her cheek in his hand and stared into her eyes.

"You're using work as a distraction. That's your thing. But if you keep going at this pace, you're going to kill yourself with stress. You need to make time in your life for other things. You've barely slept in days. I wake up six times a night expecting to find you rollerblading on the 405 with a burger from In-N-Out."

Okay, so maybe she hadn't considered the impact her stress had on him. Her face still burned, but it wasn't from anger.

"And stop worrying so much. If something goes wrong, we'll face it together. If you go bankrupt, we'll deal with it. If the shelter goes under, we'll adopt all the dogs and make our own. If ESA kidnaps you while you're out at a top secret meeting at six in the morning, I'll burn their headquarters down and save you myself. You're not alone in this world. You have me, even when you're being kind of an asshole. Do you understand?"

Claire's lip quivered. She put her arms out, and he pulled her in.

"Also, stop fucking going places alone. We talked about this."

"Mmph," she mumbled into the crook of his arm. Enveloped by his arms and the steady thrum of his heartbeat, the ever-present storm in her mind quieted. But just a little.

CHAPTER THIRTY

To Do:
- *Follow-up email to B*
- *Practice mindfulness*
- *Quote on LED rentals*

"I CAN'T BELIEVE HOW BAD YOU ARE AT BOWLING," LUKE teased as they traipsed across the parking lot of Kingpin Bowling Alley.

"Hey!" Claire reached over and shoved him. He bounced off a rusty pickup truck. "I'm good at a lot of things. Sticking my fingers in dirty holes and hurling a ten-pound ball at some pins doesn't happen to be one of them."

"But you were like, sensationally bad. That might have been the worst game I've ever seen. I think they wanted to put you on the wall."

"Good thing you got tons of footage of it." She glared at him. He had barely put his camera down all day, from their trip to Griffith Observatory to Olvera Street to the bowling alley.

"I'm just documenting our trip."

"Document this." She flashed her middle finger at him.

He cracked a smile and turned the camera off. "One more stop, then I promise I'll let you get back to work."

"All right." Claire slid into the passenger seat. As nice as this date day had been, Brad's proposal hovered incessantly in the back of her mind like her own personal black cloud. There was so much to do. She still hadn't heard back from two of the light vendors and—

"Shit." The seatbelt snapped back. She popped the door open and dropped to her knees.

Luke's face appeared on the other side of the undercarriage. His smile faded. "Get in. I'll do it."

"I appreciate you." She sat back in her seat and took thirty seconds to check her emails. Aha, one of the other vendors had come in lower and said she could pick up the supplies tomorrow. One thing could be crossed off the mile-long checklist.

Luke, apparently satisfied that the car was not booby-trapped, dropped heavily into his seat. He reached into his pocket and pulled out a black silk eye mask.

"What's this for?"

"I don't want you to see where I'm taking you. I don't want you to be able to find it alone."

"Okay," Claire said slowly. "Are you planning to murder me when we get there?"

It would really suck if Luke had been in ESA all along. The longest of long cons.

"No. But you'll see."

As they pulled out of the parking spot, she started the timer on her watch. Just in case. Then she slipped the eye mask over her head. Luke turned some music on. Driving in Los Angeles was even more disorienting when she couldn't see anything.

She found his leg in the dark. "Hey. I really appreciate you planning all of this. I know you have a lot going on—and let's be honest, just dating me is a full-time job right now between the security concerns and my stress levels. Thank you for taking me on a date. I'm sorry I've been such a stressy nightmare. When this is all over, I'm going to make it up to you."

He squeezed her hand. "I get it. I've been known to get intense about my projects too."

"Hmm. What is it you do for a living, again?"

Luke booped her on the nose and they fell into silence.

They made a left, then a right, then went straight for at least ten minutes. Finally, they turned left again. The car crunched over gravel. They pulled to a stop. Were they in a parking lot or some rural road where he planned to dispose of her body and go back to his previous life with sex-tape-star Olivia?

Claire clicked the button to turn her stopwatch off and made a mental note of the direction they went when they left the bowling alley. With that information and the time distance, she was certain she could find it again if she had to. Jack would be proud.

"All right," Luke said. "You can take it off."

The blindfold slid off. She was immediately assaulted by brightly colored flashing lights.

"Luke. What is this place?"

"This," he said, sweeping his arm wide, "is food truck central."

She opened her door and stepped out into the parking lot. There was a hint of sea breeze in the air, and a dozen tantalizing smells were all tangled together. The chipotle spice of a taco blended with the velvety sweetness of an alcoholic whoopee pie. Smothered French fries stood a few stands away. Specialty grilled cheese was to their right. Soft pretzels. Margarita trucks. Dear god, she was in heaven.

She grabbed his wrist. "This is the most beautiful place I have ever seen," she whispered.

He tucked something in her hand, and she glanced down. She was clutching a handful of crumpled twenty-dollar bills.

"Go." He pointed to the cluster of trucks.

She didn't need to be told twice. She ran off without a backward glance.

"So why didn't you want me to be able to find this place on my own?" She grilled him twenty minutes later at a picnic table covered in food.

"Are you kidding me? If you knew where this was, you would sleepwalk to it every night."

"You have a point," she said around a mouthful of pretzel. It was almost as good as the Amish pretzels from the farmers' market back home. "Thank you for this."

"For what?"

There was a smudge of mustard on his cheek. She reached over and wiped it off.

"Today. For pulling me out of that meeting and reassuring me that I'm not going to end up a homeless failure."

He patted her hand. "A failure, maybe. But not a homeless one."

She glared at him. If this wasn't the most perfect carnitas taco she'd ever eaten, she definitely would have thrown it in his smug face.

An hour later, Claire groaned as they entered the foyer.

"I'm never eating again. And I need to do like two hours of cardio to make up for that."

"Stay here. I'm going to check the house."

"There wasn't anything on the cameras," she reminded him, but off he went. She sighed and set her purse on the table in the foyer. The dogs, thoroughly exhausted from doggy daycare, immediately flopped on the floor and refused to get up.

Screw it, she was going upstairs. She was sure to have another half dozen emails from Brad. The wooden stairs creaked as she tiptoed up them. She reached the office and opened her laptop. Only three emails from Brad, one from the insurance company asking for clarification on an inventory item, and one from Mindy setting up interviews for their candidates.

Claire dove into her work, answering emails, updating quotes, and streamlining the Proposal Day schedule for the millionth time. An hour later, sixteen different sticky notes had been added to the "follow up" column of her wall. She was in the middle of writing a seventeenth when the doorbell rang.

She jumped away from her desk like it had turned into a snake. Who could it be? Mindy was back in Pennsylvania. Bri was shooting in the desert. Charlie was at one of Ryan's video game tournaments in San Francisco. She tucked Winston into her arms like a football and backed against the wall.

"I got it. Stay with the dogs," Luke ordered from downstairs.

Claire pulled her phone out and connected to their video doorbell. It was hard to tell because the figure wore a baseball cap and baggy clothes, but it looked like a woman.

If it was Olivia again, she was going to track down a torch and pitchfork.

"Hey, Bri," Luke said at the front door. "Everything okay?" He stepped back to let her inside.

Claire shut the app and ran down the steps into the foyer. "Hey!" She pulled her half sister into a hug. "I thought you were filming this weekend."

Brianna shook her head. She looked sullen and glum, not like the technicolor beam of pure sunlight she usually was. "There were dust storms in the desert. It was a bust."

"What's wrong?" Claire's danger senses were tingling.

"I just didn't want to be alone tonight. Do you think I could stay with you guys?"

"Of course you can," Luke said. "What happened?"

She pulled a Tupperware container out of her boho handbag and handed it to Claire. "Thank you. I made croissants."

Brianna was an emotional baker. This couldn't be good.

"I got a note and some more flowers." She reached into the pocket of her oversized sweatshirt and pulled out a crumpled piece of paper.

"Cancel the film or you'll be sorry," Claire read.

"It was shoved underneath my front door. After what happened to your mom and you, I didn't feel safe being alone."

"You still don't have a bodyguard?" Luke asked.

Brianna shook her head. "I did some second interviews, but there's so many creeps out there. And before you ask, no, I don't need help. You have enough going on."

"I'm so sorry." Claire drew her sister in for another hug and led her to the living room.

"I'm going to open a bottle of wine," Luke announced and left the room.

"I'm sorry for bothering you. I know you have your own shit going on. I just feel so...helpless." Brianna flopped onto the couch. Rosie jumped into her lap and licked her earlobes.

Claire's brain leapt into problem-solving mode. Brianna could move in with her and Luke, they'd turn the dining room into a bedroom, run background checks on the prospective body guards. She opened her mouth to speak, then stopped. All of this was likely to be a major imposition to Luke. She was no longer a single woman forging her own path in this world. They were a team, and she needed to clear it with him first.

"I'll be right back."

In the kitchen, Luke drove a corkscrew into a bottle of red.

Claire pulled glasses from the cabinet and sidled up next to him. "I almost impulsively did something, but I thought I should ask you first."

He raised his eyes. "This is new."

"I know. I'm trying." She lowered her voice. "What would you think about Brianna moving in with us? At least until she gets a bodyguard? It's too dangerous for her to be alone."

The cork slid out with a *pop*. Luke poured wine into three glasses. His brows knit together in concentration. "Let's do it."

"Really?" She had already made a mental list of half a dozen sexual favors to offer.

"Yes. She's family."

Heat crept into her cheeks. She swooped in and kissed him. "Thank you."

They collected the wineglasses and carried them to the living room.

"So," Claire said, handing a glass to her sister, "we have a proposition."

Brianna shook her head. "No."

Luke frowned. "What do you mean, no?"

She tapped a finger on her glass. "I know what you're going to offer, and it's so sweet of you. But I'm not going to bring more danger to your door. They want both of us." She gestured between herself and Claire. "If I moved in here with you, they would just toss a flashbang through the window and take us both."

Claire cleared her throat. "I love you, but that logic is bullshit. What's to stop them from doing that right now? Or any day for that matter?"

Bri pursed her lips. "I really appreciate what you're trying to do. But when I'm not filming, I need my space. I'll schedule another round of security interviews tomorrow. I promise."

Claire huffed. So there was a bit of stubborn old Jack in Brianna after all. She couldn't very well force her sister to move in with them, especially since they were leaving again in a few weeks. But Brianna was the only one in their family with no live-in partner. Even in her fancy gated community, she was in danger at all times.

"I wish there was something we could do," Brianna said quietly. "About ESA and everything. I know Dad says they're working on it, but it really doesn't feel like progress."

Claire sat next to her and drew her legs up into her chest. She would leave Brianna's living situation alone. For now. But she was definitely going to demand hourly proof of life texts. "I'm going to take a wild guess that Jack hasn't shared the news with you."

"What news?"

"We kind of broke into an ESA house and found a clue."

Her eyes came alive. "Tell me everything."

Claire explained their discovery and pulled up the document where she had compiled information on the conference.

"So I told Jack everything. And all he said was they're 'aware' of the conference. Isn't that bullshit?"

"I'm sure they're planning to plant some agents there." Brianna stared pensively at Rosie, as if the secrets of the universe were wound between the fibers of her double coat.

"It's not good enough." Luke set his glass down hard on an end table. The table wobbled.

Claire stared blankly back at him. "What do you mean? The wine? I love an Australian cab."

He shook his head. "No. The FBI response. I've been thinking about it, and I decided I'm going to the convention."

Brianna and Claire exchanged a glance. Claire's stomach twisted at the thought of him in danger. Luke had been team "leave it to the FBI" for months. What was with the sudden change of heart?

He stood and bent down to put a hand on the table. It wobbled again. "I'm tired of these assholes messing with people I care about. The FBI hasn't done anything to protect either one of you, and I'm not going to keep waiting around for them to track them all down. I'm going undercover, and I'm going to that convention."

Claire shook her head. "No, you're not. Are you kidding me? They'll recognize you in an instant, and then they'll abduct you just to torture me."

He scoffed. In seconds, he had taken everything off the end table and flipped it upside down. "No, they won't."

"Then I'm coming undercover with you," she blurted.

"No, you're not," he said flatly. "No offense, but no one could mistake you for a man." He glanced at her chest.

"I'm going too," Brianna proclaimed.

"No, you're not," Luke and Claire said in unison.

"You're too recognizable. Besides, you'll probably be shooting," Claire said.

"Shit. Right. Work. Can you at least FaceTime me during? I'm a little offended that I wasn't included in the Code Purple at the ESA house." Brianna took a sip from the glass that Luke offered and grimaced. "Sorry, still getting used to dry wines."

"Yes, of course we will." Claire looked at Luke, who was examining the legs on the end table. The idea of rubbing elbows with ESA made her nauseated, but she couldn't put the safety of her family in the FBI's hands. Claire made steady eye contact with him. She raised her eyebrows.

He sighed. "Go ahead."

She sprinted off to the upstairs office and returned moments later with a fresh binder. She scrawled "Douchebag Convention" on a piece of paper and slid it behind the cover. "So let's talk about this plan."

CHAPTER THIRTY-ONE

To Do:
- *Laminate douchebag plan*
- *Check extended forecast*
- *Google Food Truck Central*

"Get down," Claire hissed. "We don't want him to see us."

In light of the threats against Claire's family, she and Mindy had decided to follow through with their plan to stalk Brad. They couldn't be too careful. Barney had become her client to get closer to her. What if Brad had done the same thing?

Mindy slouched in the driver's seat. The platinum blond wig she wore was slightly askew, but surely Brad wouldn't notice from across the parking lot. She started the ignition.

Brad stared at his phone as he unlocked his fire-red Lamborghini and climbed in without hesitation. He didn't duck under his car to check for pointy objects that would puncture his tires. He didn't cast a cursory glance in the back seat. There could have been ten homicidal clowns stacked on top of each other back there and he didn't even bat an eye. Typical man.

"Do we know where his gym is?" Claire asked.

Mindy shook her head. "We'll have to hope we don't lose him."

"In Los Angeles. During rush hour. On a Monday."

Mindy huffed. "I tried. The secretary wouldn't tell me anything. How's your mom? And Bri?"

"Mom told me she's fine and if I didn't stop texting her she's going to mute me for two days. The guy from her garden's still not talking. And Bri is shooting again this week. The studio's assigning her extra security."

Brad's Lambo purred to life, and he slid smoothly out of his parking spot. Mindy followed, leaving a few car lengths between them.

"So it's okay for Alice to harass you fifty times a day about your personal safety habits, but when the shoe's on the other foot she loses her mind."

Claire nodded darkly. "Like I don't have enough to panic about. Now I have to worry ESA will send someone slightly more capable after her and she'll be too stubborn to tell me about it."

"You should hire a PI." Mindy followed Brad as he took a right out of the studio lot.

"I should." Claire slapped the dashboard. She pulled out her phone and almost searched for private investigators in Miami but stopped. "But I can't really afford it right now. Not with the rescue and the loan repayment schedule. Everything's tied up until after Brad's proposal."

"Are you sure saving the rescue needs to be your sole

responsibility?" Mindy glanced at her as they paused at a red light. "You've done a lot for them already. You got all of the animals adopted and gave them another six months to stay afloat."

"That was the alcohol," Claire said, waving one hand. "If you put a bunch of drunk people in a room with adorable animals, they're going to be adopted. It's basic science. Besides, the rescue's taken in three more dogs just since we've been in LA. It's never empty for long. But I'm going to have a chat with them when we get back. I don't know if they'll go for it, but I think they should open up a doggy daycare. That would bring a steady stream of income in and take some of the pressure off. I might have already put together a rough business plan for them."

Mindy nodded. "Um, that's genius. Where did you find the time to do that?"

"I didn't sleep much this weekend," Claire said carefully. The four cups of coffee coursing through her veins were all that were keeping her going. Sleepwalking in LA was not something she could risk right now.

"Color me shocked. I admire your philanthropic spirit. So now that things are pretty much all nailed down for Brad's proposal, can we talk about the interviews we lined up?"

"Sure." Claire's insides twisted. The thought of adding another team member was about as appetizing as the vegan meatballs she had had for lunch. But it was all part of the plan. Maybe they would find someone incredible.

She pulled up an email on her phone. Another bold-print item on her To Do list. "The federal background checks came back today on all four interviewees. Everyone's clean. Well, one had a public urination charge, but it was on her twenty-first birthday."

"That doesn't count," Mindy said.

"Exactly." She brought up Mindy's PowerPoint again and flipped through to their four chosen candidates. Heather Clearwater, a Pennsylvania girl turned California girl. She seemed promising, and she had even included a video cover sheet. Ashley Dresham and her five years of event coordinating experience for recording studios also intrigued her.

"Are you concerned about Ashley's image?" Mindy asked, glancing at the phone in Claire's hand. In all the pictures they tracked down on social media, Ashley had committed strongly to a goth aesthetic.

"Not really. The dark and broody vibe is totally working for her. And just because she dresses differently than we do doesn't mean she's any less professional or committed to true love. Don't judge a book by its cover and all that."

Mindy nodded. "Oh, he's turning! Wow, he really is going to a gym."

Claire breathed a sigh of relief. Thank god he wasn't pulling into a motel to be whipped by his mistress or leading a meeting full of misogynists. Unless the mistress worked at the gym. Hmm.

"I'm following him in." Claire unbuckled her seatbelt and waited with her hand on the door. Brad emerged from his Lamborghini, talking on his phone. He was completely unaware. Did he even lock his car door? Anyone with a phone could Google how to hot-wire his car and snatch it before he ever noticed.

While Mindy locked the car, Claire moonwalked twice before hustling to the entrance of the gym. She wouldn't make the same mistake as Brad. Not that anyone would want to steal a twenty-year-old Porsche when there was a red Lamborghini and a dozen other exotic cars parked outside this upscale gym.

"Hi! How can I help you?" The girl at the check-in desk swept her cornrows over one shoulder and flashed a blindingly white smile. A romance book with a tattered cover was splayed page-down on her desk.

"Hi, uh, two day passes, please," Claire said.

"Sure thing. It's sixty per person," the girl said. "Cash or credit?"

Oof. Her bank account couldn't handle much more of this West Coast price gouging.

"Think we can expense this?" Claire wondered as she handed over her credit card.

"We might as well actually work out while we're here," Mindy whispered back to her. "Oh, he's headed into the locker room."

They took their passes and dillydallied in the hallways outside the changing rooms, pretending to stretch against the wall. Minutes later, instead of the classic middle-aged-man workout combo of too-short shorts, New Balance sneakers, and a shirt from an obscure 5K that happened at least a decade ago, Brad walked out clad in suit pants and a button-down shirt.

Claire exchanged a glance with Mindy. Why would Brad wear a button down to work out in the gym? *Was* he meeting a mistress? Wordlessly, they followed him down the hallway. They passed several doors on either side, occasionally marked by words like "trapeze" or "death metal yoga."

Brad ducked into an unmarked one and closed the door behind him.

"What do we do?" Mindy hissed.

"Listen, I guess?" Claire craned her neck. "I don't see any vents we can crawl in."

Mindy ducked low and pressed her ear to the crack. Claire leaned over her and listened hard against the door.

"Welcome, Brad. Are you ready to begin?" a sultry female voice cooed. What fresh hell was this?

"Yes, Topaz. It's good to see you again."

"Very well. Touch me, Brad. Here," the voice commanded. "Closer."

Claire's mouth dropped open. Was this gym a front for a brothel? Her stomach dropped into her butt. She truly thought Brad had been the real deal. Sure, he was annoying and he changed his mind sixteen times a day. But she had been utterly convinced of his love for Karen. He glowed when he talked about her.

What were they doing now? Was that a passionate murmur? She leaned even harder into the door. Maybe it was all a misunderstanding. Maybe—

"Oh, hang on, I forgot my speakers," the female voice said. There were two footsteps that sounded like high heels ringing on tile. Suddenly, the door moved.

"Oh shi—"

Claire and Mindy pitched forward and tumbled straight into the room. Mindy's elbow crashed into her ribs as Claire rolled to avoid the legs of the mysterious woman.

"Claire? Mindy?" Shit. That was Brad's voice, and he didn't sound pleased to see them.

Something itchy was on Claire's hand. She glanced down. The ginger wig must have slipped off when she catapulted into the room.

"Oh, hey, Brad. What are you doing here?" Mindy called from the floor. Her neck was on Claire's ankle.

"I'm taking dancing lessons to surprise Karen," Brad said. "What are you doing here?"

He sounded pissed.

"We were—uh—" Mindy stammered.

"Spying on you," Claire confessed. "To make sure you

weren't a cheater or a crime lord or a serial killer." Brad was a reasonable man. Honesty was the best policy. Surely he would understand.

"I'll leave you to chat," Topaz said. She sashayed out of the room in a sparkly gold cocktail dress. She must have been at least sixty.

Brad went red from the center of his bulbous nose to the tips of his sticky-out ears. "Never once in all my years has someone I've hired treated me with this level of distrust."

Well, shit. This was not going as expected. She should have lied and told him she was there to do hot yoga. In a wig.

"Brad, I'm so sorry." She pulled her foot out from under Mindy's neck and stood. Her elbow stung. "You have to understand, what I went through with Barney has really impacted my ability to trust people. I just had to be sure that you were a good guy."

"Did I give you any reason to believe that I'm not a good guy?" He raised his eyebrows and crossed his arms. Power emanated from him. In this moment, it was easy to see what a force of nature he must be in a conference room.

"No, not at all," she said with her hands held out. "But I've thought that before and almost lost my life. I didn't mean to offend you. For the sake of the business and for me as a human being, I can't lead another woman into the arms of a murderer. That day is going to haunt me for the rest of my life. You understand, don't you?"

"I don't, Claire. Luke knows me. You trust him. He trusts me. Why is that not enough for you? Why do you have to sneak around and spy on me? Is this how you treat people? You know, other planners reached out to me, but I said no. I wanted a Claire Hartley original."

"I'm so sorry, I—"

Brad lifted one hand, and Claire clammed up.

"I need to think," he said. "I don't know if I can work with someone who treats their clients like they're guilty. You work for me, remember? For now, anyway." He sighed and turned away from them, ran a hand through what hair he had left. A second later he turned back, looking slightly more composed. "Come to the office tomorrow morning. We'll discuss if I'm still using your services then."

Claire bit her lip. Fuckity fuck fuck. She had finally done it. She had let her paranoia and obsession with safety destroy a relationship with a client.

"We understand," Mindy said, gripping Claire's arm and steering her out of the room.

The fluorescent lights in the hallway wobbled through the tears that stung Claire's eyes. She wasn't going to cry. Not here, not in this stupid overpriced gym where people paid a small fortune to throw tires around. Not because of some guy named *Brad*.

They stepped out into the early evening—perfect weather, of course. Reality hurtled out of the sky like a meteor. She had just paid $120 to destroy her relationship with a client.

"I screwed up, Min." She stared at a scatter of cotton candy clouds and blinked her tears away.

Mindy patted Claire on the back. "We both screwed up. I thought we were doing Karen a favor. How can you know two people are really in love unless you know they're not two-faced, lying, cheating assholes? It's part of our process. Why is he so upset about it if he doesn't have something to hide?"

Claire's breath hitched. After an incredibly long Sunday, everything had finally been perfect. Every vendor confirmed, every piece of décor acquired. It was the longest, most frustrating proposal she had ever arranged. It was going to be stunning, the shining jewel on the crown of her career. And now it might be gone forever.

"Not everyone's a bad guy, Min. I don't know when I started feeling like that. I didn't stalk Tyler to make sure he wasn't pretending to have mobility issues. I didn't follow Aaron home to make sure there weren't dead bodies hung on meat hooks next to Jane's paintings in their storage shed. And Brad's right. Luke trusts him. Why don't I trust him?"

"It's okay. We can find another client."

She whirled around. "Another client? This was supposed to be our inaugural West Coast proposal. Everything is hanging on this. If Brad doesn't keep us on, the shelter is screwed. The business is screwed. We're screwed. The amount of money lost in deposits alone—"

Her vision was going dark. She kicked the tire of Luke's car, then groaned and got on her knees. After a few deep breaths, her vision stopped swimming. Nothing sharp behind the tires. She stood and peered into the back seat. Rinse, repeat.

"And we have nothing to fall back on because ESA burned our fricken warehouse down. It's going to take months to replace everything, and we'll have to outsource everything—linens, décor, greenery, sound equipment, lighting—and it'll be so much more expensive."

She sat on the ground and wrapped her arms around herself. "I've ruined everything. I pissed off the wrong person and my car was blown up. My mother was almost abducted. An international mob of hitmen are trying to kill me. All because I friend-zoned Barney almost a decade ago and my deadbeat biological father was tasked with taking them down. Now Brad will write something awful on Yelp, we'll lose all our clients, we won't be able to pay the loan back, we'll go bankrupt, and Luke will leave me and I'll have to move back in with you. Oh, and let's not forget I'll be sending a bunch of innocent dogs to their death."

"Claire," Mindy said calmly. She put a hand on Claire's shoulder. "Just breathe, okay? Even if Brad does fire us, it's not the end of the world. Actually, if he does fire us, I'm going to burn *his* office down. If he can't understand why you take extra steps to make sure your clients are good people, he's not the kind of client we want anyway."

"Right." She wrenched the car door so hard that it squealed. "I won't say 'fuck that guy' just yet because he has a point, but if he fires us, I will unleash holy hell on this town."

"And I'll be right there with you." Mindy turned the car on and shifted into gear. "We won't be allowed back here ever again."

"Stupid LA with your stupid *kale* and your stupid *avocados*. There's more to life than vegetables and TikTok!" Claire shouted out the window at a group of AirPod-wearing hooligans with beanies and slumped shoulders.

Her phone buzzed. She glanced at it. Five texts and two missed calls from Luke.

"Oh, shit." She bit her lip and lifted the phone to her ear. It rang.

"What?" Mindy glanced over at her as they pulled out of the gym parking lot.

"I forgot Luke was making dinner. And now he's not answering." Claire typed out a hasty apology text and tucked the device back in her purse. It was almost seven, and Luke had specifically told her dinner was at six. He was not going to be happy.

CHAPTER THIRTY-TWO

To Do:
- *Don't panic*
- *Breathe*
- *Craft the world's most moving apology*

DIM CANDLELIGHT WAS VISIBLE THROUGH THE FRONT DOOR when they arrived at Luke's house. Claire slid her key in the lock and turned the knob. At least he hadn't locked her out. Almost all the lights were off on the first floor. Mindy rushed upstairs, leaving Claire to confront Luke alone. Traitor.

Stress swirled around her like a toxic tornado. If Brad fired her, she would have wasted months. Months that she could have spent taking on clients in West Haven. The West Coast branch would be dead. She wouldn't be able to join Luke in LA when he traveled and see her sisters. She would be tethered to West Haven, slamming in as many clients as she could to make up for the revenue lost from Brad's proposal.

Her hands shook as she unloaded her purse and removed her shoes. Rosie catapulted herself out of the family room and skittered to a stop in front of her. Winston attempted to follow and crashed into the closet door.

Claire kissed both dogs on the head and tiptoed down the hallway toward the kitchen. Only the light above the sink was on. Luke stood at the sink. He was wearing her favorite button-down, a surprising change from his usual black T-shirt. On the kitchen table, candles had burned down almost to the studs. Empty plates and glasses gleamed on the table. Gray and white striped placemats she didn't recognize nestled under the dinnerware.

"Hey, I'm really sorry." She put a hand on Luke's shoulder, but he didn't turn around. "Luke?" Was he catatonic?

"Brad called me." His answer was short, clipped, like the act of speaking out loud was personally inconveniencing him.

"Ah," she said lamely. "Did he mention the thing?"

"You mean the thing where you stalked an innocent man and accused him of having an affair?"

She drew herself up, indignant. "All I said was we were checking to make sure he *wasn't* having an affair. Or murdering someone. Why would he take that personally if he didn't have something to hide?"

"And was he? Hiding something?" Luke spun around. His dreamy green eyes were harder, darker, more moss than sea.

"Well, no. Not that we know of."

"Exactly. He called me, wondering why I recommended someone who actively stalks their clients."

Claire crossed her arms over her chest. "Can you blame me?"

He raised his eyebrows. "Yes."

"Excuse me?" This conversation was not going how she thought it would.

Luke pulled steaks out of the fridge and ripped the plastic off like it had stolen his dog. "Do you want me to sugarcoat it, or do you want me to tell you the truth?"

She took a deep breath. If she wasn't careful, she was going to spew a giant volcano of crazy all over him. "Truth."

He sat the steaks on a cutting board and pulled out a meat mallet. "You disrespected him. And in turn, you disrespected me."

Her mouth dropped open. What did Brad have anything to do with Luke? It's not like she had asked Luke to drive the getaway car.

"I'm not sure if you remember this," she said slowly, "but I recently helped a hotel tycoon serial killer propose to his innocent teacher girlfriend. Brad is a high-profile, middle-aged Hollywood executive dating a hospital administrator. I have a moral responsibility to my clients to make sure that I'm not repeating history. I ruined Victoria's life by not seeing the signs." Everything spilled out without her realizing it. Was that why she didn't trust Brad? In so many ways, he was like Barney. More money than sense. Powerful, intimidating, opinionated.

Luke smashed the mallet into the steak. His eyes cut over to her. "Victoria was the one who agreed to marry him. They lived together and she didn't even see the signs. You need to stop using Barney as an excuse to not trust people. Especially people that I personally recommend you to."

She paused. Something wasn't connecting here. "So you're upset because I made you look bad to Brad?"

"No," he growled, hitting the meat with more force than was necessary.

She wasn't about to critique a man holding a mallet, but the steaks would be the width of a piece of paper before long.

"I'm upset because you're questioning my judgment," he added.

"Oh," she said. She put a hand on his. The mallet came to rest. "I'm sorry. I didn't mean to make you feel like I don't trust your judgment. You know I do. I listened to your very valid concerns about transportation for Brad's proposal. I even let you pick the tile replacement for the bathroom, and you were so right. Marble would have been a terrible choice in a multiple dog household."

Stubble covered Luke's rugged cheekbones. He scrubbed a hand over his face. His eyes were hooded. "Respect is important. And respect and trust are tied up together. You need to do better."

His words slapped her like a prizefighter. "*I* need to do better?" She took a step back. Her insides burned. This was the last thing she needed when she was on the verge of getting fired.

"My mother was almost kidnapped, Luke. People are threatening my family. Forgive me if I'm having a hard time trusting strangers at the moment. And by the way, light stalking and surveillance have always been part of our process at Happily Ever Afters. Do you know how many cheaters and people who were mean to waitstaff and other red flags we uncovered as a result of our efforts? It's one of the reasons why we were so successful."

Were. The past tense slipped out unintentionally. Why did it hit so hard? It was like every project that happened before Barney was sitting neatly in a golden filing cabinet marked "Before." Every proposal that had come since, no matter how romantic, had had just a slight tinge to it, a note of apprehension and uncertainty.

"You can't go based off surface interactions when you're helping someone pledge their undying love. Did you ever have dinner with Brad? Hang out at a bar? Game night? Anything not in a business setting?"

"Not exactly," Luke said. "But he's a good guy. I know he is. And you should trust my word."

She turned away from him. He wasn't being rational. Was he really upset about Brad, or was this something else?

She whipped back around and crossed her arms. "Do you want me to sugarcoat this next part, or do you want the truth?"

"Truth."

"You're being a bit of an asshole," she half shouted. Winston snorted and looked up from his bed. Half of his tongue poked out the side of his mouth. "Why?"

"Brad is a friend and—"

"This isn't really about Brad," she interrupted. "Tell me what's going on."

The mallet hit the cutting board with a clang. He put both hands on the island and leaned toward her. "I asked you for one thing. Be home for dinner at six, so we can spend some time together. Just the two of us. And you forgot. Do you know how it makes me feel when you prioritize spying on your clients over having dinner with me?"

Claire deflated like a balloon. With all the Brad drama, she had almost forgotten about the missed dinner. This was just the latest in an unfortunate series of putting Luke on the back burner. If he was an hour late for a dinner *she* had slaved over, she would have been pissed.

"You're right. I messed up. I'm sorry."

He turned his back to her and washed his hands methodically in the sink. Was he about to pick up his tool belt and start building a treehouse? He dried off with a dish towel and took a deep breath.

"Lately, I've been feeling like an afterthought. We said we were going to make time to be together while we're out here, and every time I try, it's like pulling teeth. Do you not want to spend time with me?"

Oof. She was going to have a ton of material to take to her next therapy session. Was there a limit on the number of topics? Maybe she should make a PowerPoint. If she forced Luke to sit down and take a quiz right now, she could almost guarantee his love language was quality time. And she hadn't been giving him any of it.

She laid a hand on his, gentle as a bird landing on a branch. "Luke, I love spending time with you. You're my big, grumpy, opinionated bear. You plan the best date nights. I'm sorry that I haven't been as available lately. I think I've really been letting the stress get to me. You know you're more important to me than any of this—" She flapped one hand toward the six binders sitting on the kitchen table. "And I'm going to try harder to show it."

Luke's hand slid out from under hers. Oh, no. Had she said the wrong thing? Would he disappear to blow off some steam? Maybe he *was* going to build that tree house.

He caught her wrist and pulled her into him. His arms surrounded her. Warmth engulfed her, followed closely by the scent of clean linen and rosemary. She melted like an ice sculpture in July.

He pressed his lips to her hair. "It'll be okay."

"But what if he fires me?" Her voice was muffled.

His arms tightened around her. "You'll be fine. We'll be fine. There's always a way."

She nodded, then pulled back. He swiped a finger underneath her eyes. His expression was cloudy, but he wasn't yelling at her anymore. Her phone vibrated in her pocket. Her hand twitched, but she stayed where she was. Even if that was Brad texting her with a preemptive decision, it wasn't worth looking. If she messed this up, she could lose much more than her business.

"Can I help with dinner?" she asked.

Luke put the mallet in the sink full of soapy water. "That depends, are you planning to stick around or are you going to go spy on someone else?"

"Ha-ha." She elbowed him and picked up an onion. Anything to distract from her imminent firing.

CHAPTER THIRTY-THREE

To Do:
- *Grovel*
- *Research bankruptcy*
- *Be a better girlfriend*

"You look like you haven't slept in a year," Mindy said as she pulled the car out of the driveway.

Claire yawned and flipped the mirror down. Her new under-eye concealer was being tested to its limits today. Since there was nothing she could do about the Brad situation, she had spent most of the night working on the plan for the men's rights conference. Thirty minutes of sleep was better than nothing, wasn't it?

"It's probably a good thing I didn't sleep much last night. There is so much stress in my body right now I probably would have just ended up sleepwalking to a vegan restaurant and arming myself with English cucumbers. Shit!" She slapped her forehead.

"What?" Mindy shot her some side eye as she turned left down a residential street. The park they passed needed a fresh coat of paint on the playground and some grass seed, but the walking path was lovely.

"I forgot the gift basket. I was so worried about my apology note that I forgot the good stuff." She had raided Luke's liquor cabinet after he had gone back to bed and found an unopened bottle of Mount Gay Rum. She tucked it in a basket she had found underneath one of Luke's cabinets along with emergency snacks she had brought from Pennsylvania—beef jerky, Middleswarth chips, and Herlocher's Dipping Mustard.

Mindy shook her head and swung the car into the parking lot between a holistic yoga studio and a turquoise building with a sign that read "Psychic Readings by Clementine." It was a good thing they had left with plenty of time. "As excited as I am to hear your plan about the conference, you need to sleep. Remember last year when you drove a car five miles while sleepwalking? Avoiding sleep altogether is just going to make it worse. Remind me to install a padlock on your door when we get home."

Claire shrugged. "I just couldn't sleep. With everything up in the air and the conference. And then there's this fact that I ruined everything and doomed our business and the shelter and my relationship and—"

Mindy reached over and touched Claire's face. Then she smacked it lightly, keeping her eyes on the road. "Stop it."

Claire touched the cheek Mindy had slapped. "Stop what? Feeling things?"

"No, thinking that everything is doomed. We're not doomed. You're just stressed. We'll turn on the charm and

Brad will keep us on. We're going to throw the biggest, splashiest, most romantic proposal anyone has ever seen. And we're going to stake out that convention, find Professor Taylor, and follow him wherever he goes. Then we're going to kick ESA's ass for burning down our office, hire an amazing person to help run things out here, and go home and get back to normal."

Normal. Could things ever really be normal?

"I hope so. Also, don't you think it was kind of dumb to schedule this interview right after our meeting with Brad? What if he fires us? We can't hire someone if our West Coast dreams are dead."

Mindy shook her head. "We don't need Brad. We are scrappy and resourceful. If he fires us, we'll find an even bigger Hollywood figure and rub it in his stupid face. You know I slipped into D. Nasty's Instagram DMs offering our services. He's been dating Krystal Blake for almost two years."

"Who or what is D. Nasty?"

"Come on, you've heard his songs. *Slam Dunk Your Ass, Beat Booty, Nic Cage's Wooden Leg...*"

As Mindy turned back toward Luke's house, something caught Claire's eye. What the hell was she looking at?

"Mindy?"

"And another thing—" Mindy plowed on. Claire slapped at her arm and pointed. "What?"

"Is somebody climbing our drainpipe?"

The engine whined and the car lurched forward. "Not today, Satan." Mindy hunched up against the steering wheel as they sped down the residential street. Claire gripped the oh shit handle.

Her heart was in her throat. Was it ESA? Were they going after Luke? Her hand wrapped around her Taser. It was hard to tell from this distance, but there was definitely a fluorescent pink blob that was out of place.

"Is that—" Mindy squinted.

"Tell me it's not—" Could it really be?

"Olivia," they both muttered as Mindy whipped the car into the driveway. But she didn't stop there. She drove the car straight into the yard, directly below where the mysterious figure was climbing the drainpipe to the second floor.

Olivia, clad in bubblegum pink lingerie and matching high heels, put one foot on the roof of the porch.

Claire threw her car door open and jumped outside. Her skin prickled like a thousand needles were jabbing her. "Can I help you?"

"Oh no, I'm fine. Just locked myself out of my boyfriend's house. So embarrassing," Olivia called without even looking back.

"You mean my boyfriend?" Claire's hands clenched into fists at her side.

"Don't punch her, please. We can't afford another lawsuit," Mindy whispered.

It might be worth another lawsuit to bitch slap Olivia. Claire relaxed her hands and took a deep, steadying breath like Dr. Goulding had taught her. She counted to ten. "I need you to get off the roof, Olivia. If you don't, we're going to have to call the police." That should be a fun story to explain to the officers.

The front door opened, and a shirtless Luke shot out into the yard. "What the hell are you doing? Why are you parked in the middle of the yard?"

Claire and Mindy gestured wordlessly to Olivia, who had successfully climbed the inclined porch roof and was now attempting to slide Luke's bedroom window open.

"Olivia, what the fuck?" he boomed. "Get down."

Ooh, angry Luke. Claire's toes curled in her pumps. Sure, last night he had been grumpy and hurt. But it was extremely rare for angry Luke to come out. Thank god it wasn't directed at her.

"You didn't give me a choice," Olivia said. Tears sparkled in her eyes. "You didn't respond to my cake or my letters."

Letters? What letters?

"That's because I threw them out without opening them."

"Things could be good again, Luke." Olivia got down on her knees. This bitch was for sure going to fall off the roof.

Claire glanced at her watch. They were still early, but if this didn't come to a head soon she'd have to leave. Not even an ex-girlfriend on the roof trumped this appointment with Brad.

"You're trespassing," Luke said, a note of danger in his voice. "If you're not off this roof in thirty seconds, I'm going to call the police."

"But I told my parents we're engaged!" Olivia wailed like a scolded toddler. She was sitting on her butt now.

"Why would you tell them that?"

"You asked me!"

"That was a year and a half ago."

"And now I'm saying yes!"

Luke planted his hand over his face. He looked back at Claire. "Can you call the police?"

"Of course," Olivia said, pulling a phone from her rhinestone-studded bra. "You want me to get these girls off the lawn?"

"Oh my god." Claire brushed past Luke and entered the house. "Rosie?" There was a skittering in the hallway, and the dog barreled straight into Claire as though she hadn't seen her in a year.

"Hi, sweet girl. Okay, Mommy needs your help. Can you come with me? Up." She pointed at the stairs.

Rosie rocketed up the stairs and spun around on the landing, apparently thrilled by their new game. Claire followed and bumped open the door to the master bedroom. She unlocked the window closest to Olivia and flung it open. She turned to her furry best friend and ripped the flat sheet off the bed. She wrapped the bottom of it around Rosie's belly twice and knotted it tightly.

"Rosie? Up!" Claire ordered, pointing to the windowsill. Rosie sat below the windowsill and scooted back and forth several times before gaining enough momentum. She parkoured up the wall and onto the sill and stepped out onto the roof. Claire gripped the edge of the sheet.

Olivia screamed.

"A dog! Get it out of here." She stood, took a step backward, and her ankle wobbled.

"*You* get out of here," the three humans who weren't trespassing said in unison.

Rosie, oblivious to the hubbub, seemed delighted to discover a new friend on the roof. She stepped toward Olivia, eliciting more shrieks from her. Neighbors were starting to gather on the sidewalk.

"Need me to call the fire department, Luke?" Mr. Nesbit called. Hank the golden retriever panted happily at his side.

"I think we've got it handled," Luke's disembodied voice said.

Claire glanced at her watch again. Okay, they were down to ten extra minutes. Their coffee run was already toast. This harpy needed to get off the roof *stat*. She added more slack to Rosie's bed sheet line, and the corgi happily lurched toward the uninvited guest.

"Get away from me," Olivia ordered with one finger held out to the dog. "Stay!"

Claire had never been so glad that she had never successfully taught Rosie to stay.

"I'm warning you, get that dog away from—AHHH!" Olivia's foot slipped off the edge of the roof, and she disappeared. Luckily, it was barely an eight-foot drop to the ground, and from the sounds of it, she had landed on the clump of maiden grass in the flower bed.

"Rosie, you want some cheese?" Claire called. Rosie wasn't a fan of the command "come" either, but she definitely knew what "cheese" meant.

Rosie hopped back in through the window without incident, and Claire unwound the sheet and kissed her between the eyes. What a good dog. What she wouldn't give to topple into that bed and just sleep for a couple hours with her furry companion. But there wasn't time for that. There was an ex-girlfriend to finish evicting, some cheese to dispense, and a business relationship to save.

CHAPTER THIRTY-FOUR

To Do:
- *Stare into the void*
- *Order some bird-repelling spikes for the roof?*
- *Get my job back*

"Okay, what are we going to say?" Mindy said quietly to Claire as they took a seat on two plastic chairs shaped like hands. While Brad's office was decorated like a supervillain's lair, his waiting room was decidedly more eclectic. The cellophane crinkled loudly on the gift basket as Claire set it on the carpeted floor.

"That I was deluded because of my past trauma. I'm in therapy and I'm working on it." LA people *loved* mental health. "Wait, what's your excuse?" Claire glared at Mindy.

"You're the boss. I just follow orders." Mindy shrugged to proclaim her innocence.

"Great, thanks for that." Claire leaned back in her seat.

Her stomach was in knots. Was this sleep deprivation or nerves? It was impossible to tell.

The office door swung open behind them, and they both flinched. "Ladies?" Brad said in his raspy voice.

They jumped up and hustled into the office. Claire gripped the gift basket so tightly that the wood bent under her hand.

"For you," Claire said, handing over the gift basket and a calligraphed apology note.

"That wasn't necessary—wait, are these Middleswarth chips?"

Claire and Mindy nodded.

Brad tore open the cellophane and pulled out the bag. "I haven't had these since my last trip back east." He opened the bag and popped a chip in his mouth. "Mm, barbecue. My favorite."

"We just wanted to apologize," Claire said in a rush. She wasn't normally afraid of public speaking, but Brad held the future of their business in his hands. "What we did was incredibly unprofessional," she continued. "Working with Barney really messed me up, and I'm having a hard time trusting people. I'm in therapy for it, but some of the coping mechanisms I developed during that time are still here. Such as spying on clients to make sure they're not cheating on their significant others or killing people or secretly running a drug ring."

Brad put up a hand to stop her. "I'm familiar with your history. I didn't want to work with you because you know Luke, or because I felt bad because of your damaged past. I agreed to work with you because you do good work. You're a professional, like me, and I thought you were committed to your job. But I was wrong. I don't like to be wrong, Claire."

Her nails bit into the palms of her hands. She opened

her mouth, but no sound came out. Next to her, Mindy squeezed her purse, and her rage was plainly written on her face.

He leaned forward and put the tips of his fingers together. "I've decided to go without a planner. Most of the big stuff is already in place. I'm sure my receptionist can handle the rest." Light glinted off a gold pinky ring as he tapped a binder on his desk.

Here it was. The worst thing that could have happened. If the floor had opened up into a black hole and sucked her in, she would have welcomed it. Images flashed through her mind—disabled dogs rounded up and swept into a van. A hard look in Luke's eye as he set her suitcase on the front porch. The stuffy guest bedroom at her mom's house in Florida. This was the first domino in her personal apocalypse. Everything was going to come crashing down.

Claire gripped the arms of her chair so hard that the wood creaked. A rage she had never known was bubbling inside her. How *dare* he? She had sacrificed so much for this project—her sanity, sleep, countless date nights, family dinners. And now he was going to take credit for everything she slaved over for months and *fire her* days before she pulled off the crowning achievement of her career? Not today. Not ever.

She rose to her feet like a volcano bursting from the earth and reached across his desk to snatch the gift basket back. Brad didn't deserve it. The Middleswarth bag crinkled as she yanked it away from him, sending a spray of chips across the carpet. Good.

A thousand words flowed through her mind, threatening to come tumbling out in an unintelligible scream of rage. She could flip his stupid mahogany desk over. Or smash his tacky art prints. Her fingers twitched, like they might start hurling things of their own accord. She paused, mouth pursed. The inside of her cheek throbbed from her teeth clamping down.

The last time she had lost control of her anger and punched someone, they had almost taken her business from her. And Brad had far more resources than Wendy. She needed to get out of here before she fed Brad through his industrial-sized paper shredder.

"Good luck to you, Brad. Coming?" she asked Mindy.

Mindy stood with a testicle-shriveling glare. She reached out one elegantly manicured hand and slapped the pencil holder off Brad's desk. Highlighters and fancy pens rolled out of sight. She linked arms with Claire, and they walked out of the office together.

Claire resisted the urge to pick up one of Brad's stupid hand-shaped chairs and punt it through a window. His assistant's desk was unoccupied, a half-finished matcha latte sitting next to the unlocked computer.

Claire glanced around, but none of the other people at their cubicles were paying attention. She slid behind the desk and glanced at the computer screen. Brad's schedule. Tingles ran up and down her spine as she clicked through the rest of the week. Perfect. In two days, Brad was meeting Rita at the ranch. She tucked this information in the back of her mind and backed away from the desk.

Instead of relief, the California sun brought panic as they burst through the double doors. Everything they had worked so hard for had been eviscerated. Spots appeared in Claire's vision and her ears rang as if Brad had dismissed them with a giant gong.

"Mindy?"

"Hmm?" Had Mindy sprinted to the end of a tunnel? Her voice was so far away.

"Is there an unscheduled solar eclipse happening, or am I about to pass out?"

"Whoa." Mindy caught Claire's arm and guided her to a bench, then pushed her head down between her knees.

Slowly, the spots receded from her vision. But nothing abated the panic. "They're going to die. All those dogs. We have interviews and vendors to cancel and now we need a Plan B and—I just—I really didn't think he'd fire us."

Mindy's shoulders slumped. She plunged her hand into the open bag of chips and popped one in her mouth. Why was she so nonchalant? Normally a betrayal of this magnitude led to her threatening to drive a vehicle through someone's home.

Claire jumped up, and a new wave of dizziness almost took her to the ground. She whirled around, heart thudding against her chest like a drum line. "What are we going to do? We have to cancel the interview. Do you have Ashley's phone number?" Her synapses were already firing, half-formed plans spiraling out like a spider's web.

Mindy rolled the top of the bag of chips down and put it back in the basket. She took a deep breath and rolled her shoulders back. "I say we do the interviews anyway."

Claire spluttered. It was an insane suggestion. "Why? We have no clients. There's no money to pay a new person."

Mindy waved a hand. "We have the loan. And we weren't planning to utilize this person during Brad's proposal anyway. We'll get more California clients, Claire. We kind of have to, because our entire stock of items in West Haven were burned to a crisp. You said yourself it's going to take months to get everything replaced. We'd have to charge West Haven clients way more if we had to rent everything again, and then we run the risk of only being able to plan proposals for rich douchebags. And you're going to be out here anyway for Bri's premiere and Luke finishing up his doc. We have nothing to lose. We might as well find some replacement clients out here while we're waiting for the insurance company. Maybe a B-list celebrity or an influencer like I mentioned earlier. Someone who can get the word out."

Claire stared at her. "Why the hell are you so calm? We just lost our biggest client ever."

Mindy shrugged. "Don't get me wrong. I'm angry and I think Brad's a self-righteous douchebag. But I'm not worried about it. You know why?"

"Because you have carbon monoxide poisoning from Luke's guest room?"

"No. Because you're Claire Freakin' Hartley. And we're Happily Ever Freakin' Afters. We've been through so much worse. This—" she pointed at the studio—"isn't the end."

Claire slumped. It sure felt like the end.

"An interview doesn't necessarily mean we need to make an offer. But we might be surprised. Not to mention an LA native would be better equipped to find the best local spots and know the reputable companies to deal with. No matter what way you look at it, we still need someone else."

Claire collapsed on the bench again. "But how will we even attract any clients?"

Mindy snorted. "I guarantee if I go through the email right now we'll have a dozen requests from LA alone. And I'll ramp up our location-based social media campaign."

Claire was silent. All that work. The ranch, the Hollywood sign, Santa Monica, the Getty, the friggen New Jersey ice cream. Hours upon hours of painstaking planning and micromanaging from Brad. And now they were starting over with nothing to show for it.

Mindy dropped down into her eye level and grabbed

her hand. "Hey. I meant what I said. This is *not* the end. Screw Brad." She jabbed a finger at his office window. "Sure, we might have to do a half dozen smaller proposals to make up for the lost revenue on his, but we have faced worse odds. We can do it. It's just one interview since Heather and Jenna can't meet until next week. Let's meet Ashley and then we'll go home and eat pizza and be a little bit sad."

Claire rose again, numb. Mindy might as well have been speaking Portuguese. How could she concentrate on interviews when they had just lost their biggest client ever?

"Onward and upward. Let's go." Mindy grabbed her hand and tugged her toward the car.

Claire's limbs were like jelly as they trudged through the parking lot. The failed apology basket weighed her down like an anchor. Brad's steely gaze was burned into her brain as if he had taken a brand to her. Surely he didn't mean it.

Maybe she hadn't apologized hard enough. Should she have brought a different rum?

"Hey." Mindy nudged her. "You're fixating. There's nothing we could have done to change his mind. You want to check the car for murderers? That usually makes you feel better."

Claire took a deep breath and performed her vehicle safety check. It was time to compartmentalize. They needed a new plan. She pulled her interview binder out and grasped it like a lifeline.

"Alternate nostril breathing?" Mindy suggested as she flopped into the driver's seat. "We have plenty of time."

It couldn't hurt. They both plugged one nostril and took deep, steadying breaths, then switched sides. The storm inside her subsided just enough to refocus. Was this really wise? An interview when they had no clients? She was so upset that at this point she welcomed the chance to think about something else. Anything else.

The interview binder might as well have weighed a thousand pounds. She flipped through the pages unseeingly, willing it to distract her. Line by line, she re-read Ashley's resume. *Focus, Claire.* Don't think about Brad.

The weight of what they were about to do settled in her chest. Dread and anxiety swirled around her insides like a black hole.

"Why am I so nervous?" Claire stared at the sheet protector that enclosed Ashley's resume. A breakdown of her social media profiles and a list of potential red flags followed. "I shouldn't be nervous. We're the ones doing the interviewing."

Mindy flopped into the driver's seat. "It's a big deal. We've never added a permanent staff member before." She swept her dark hair over her shoulder and started the car. "Let alone one that would be running things pretty independently three thousand miles away from our home office."

Ah, yes. Their home office which was currently a pile of ashes. "What if they don't like us? We can't even offer health insurance yet. Who wants to work for someplace that can't even offer them a comprehensive benefits package?"

"They wouldn't have applied if they weren't interested," Mindy said as she pulled out into the parking lot. "And they'll buy their own health insurance just like we do."

Without announcing their intent, both of them lifted a hand and flashed a middle finger at Brad's office building.

"Should we have a code word in case the interview is going really poorly?" Claire asked. "So we don't waste our time?"

"Should we just go classic 'platypus'?" Mindy suggested.

Claire nodded. It wasn't going to be easy to work into

conversation, but they'd find a way. Alice had suggested the safe word long before Claire had been kidnapped. It hadn't really helped yet, but it had stuck.

"Okay, I'll give the company spiel and an overview of our services," Claire said, running down her checklist. "And you can ask the first question."

A tiny sliver of hope slid into the mire of her mind. Maybe Ashley would be exactly what their crew needed. She might even come up with a plan to save everything.

"Sounds good," Mindy said. "I asked Sawyer's mom for tips, so she forwarded some stuff about body language and traits of narcissists."

"Great. How is Sawyer doing?" Maybe running Mindy through the pre-marital questionnaire would distract her from the fact that her life had just imploded.

"Good. Missing me too, he says." She sighed wistfully. "This weekend can't come soon enough. Oh, I guess I can leave sooner now since we got fired. Maybe we can move Heather's interview up and I could check for flights on—"

"Have you guys thought about kids?" Claire interrupted. "It's been on my mind since Nicole told us." Okay, that wasn't super subtle.

"Kids?" Mindy arched a dark eyebrow. "I'm only twenty-seven."

Claire tried to look nonchalant. "But you've talked about them? With Sawyer? Since you're planning on getting engaged, I mean."

The car rolled to a stop at a red light, and Mindy turned to look at Claire. Her mouth was hanging open, and she looked like Claire had just gravely insulted her mother. "Stop it. Right fucking now."

"Stop what?" Whoops. She should have given Mindy more credit.

"You're questionnaire-ing me." Mindy slid her sunglasses down her nose. Her green eyes burned into Claire's with laser intensity.

"I don't know what you're talking about."

"Admit it. You think we're moving too fast. That's why you've been asking me about his mom and our plans for the future. Was your next question going to be about finances? Division of household chores?"

"No." A total lie. "I was just curious. With everything happening with Kyle and Nicole. Luke and I talked about kids the other day."

Mindy pushed her sunglasses back up and drove forward. "You can say whatever you want, but I know what you're trying to do. And frankly, I'm insulted. You know Sawyer's a good guy. He saved your life. How else do you want him to prove himself?"

"I know he's a good guy!" She should have kept her mouth shut. Mindy was an adult, and she could make her own decisions. Maybe Claire really did need to sleep—she seemed to be losing control of her inner monologue. "I just want to make sure you're ready. Marriage is a big commitment."

"You don't think I know that?" Mindy's voice had reached an octave only dogs could hear. This was bad. She hadn't seen her this mad since Claire had tagged the ESA house at Venor while sleepwalking.

Great, now she had pissed off her best friend too. She needed to dial down the meddling. "I'm sorry. You know I love you. I just wanted to be sure that you're both ready for this. Do you really feel like you've gotten past what Gavin did to you?"

Gavin, Mindy's boyfriend the previous spring and summer, had turned out to be in ESA. She had punched him in the face during the fake event they had thrown to save Wendy.

Mindy squared her shoulders and the car continued down the highway. "I appreciate your concern," she said carefully. "And I'm sorry for snapping. I think I'm just hungry. And maybe a little stressed since we got fired. But I don't think I need to remind you that we work for the same company and have the same feelings about love and marriage. Have you ever heard me even mention marriage with any of my exes?"

It was a good point. For someone whose career revolved around planning proposals, Mindy herself had never expressed interest in getting married, even to her serious suitors.

"You're right. I'm sorry. I'll stop grilling you. I understand if you want to make Nicole your matron of honor."

"Nicole will be responsible for an entire human being at that point. She'll have enough to worry about. The job is yours. As long as you stop questionnaire-ing me."

"I promise." Claire crossed her heart. "Oh, is that the place?"

A turquoise building with a bright orange sign that read Espresso Yourself stood to their right.

"Yes. You're sure I can get *real* cream here? Not some-thing that was squeezed out of an almond?" Mindy asked as they parked. She wrinkled her nose.

"Positive," Claire said, getting out of the car. She pulled a lint roller from her purse and quickly ran it over her blouse and pencil skirt. The amount of animal hair in their home seemed to have increased five-fold since Winston came home. "The reviews online specifically mentioned animal milk, which is apparently what milk is now called."

"LA is just the worst," Mindy muttered.

Claire almost smiled. "Okay, you go pick a table and I'll grab us some muffins and lattes. Do you think I should get one for her too? Is that too presumptuous?"

Mindy shrugged. "Do it."

When they finally emerged from the café an hour and a half later, the afternoon sun shone oppressively overhead.

"Well, we're not hiring her," Mindy said as the door swung shut behind them. "I don't think she'd ever stop talking long enough to figure out what a client actually wants."

"I didn't see her take a breath for ten minutes straight when she was describing her work history. Or blink. She's a medical marvel," Claire said, shaking her head.

"I don't like to say unkind things," Mindy began. Claire snorted. "But I think I would rather hire Luke's crazy, drain-pipe-climbing ex-girlfriend to work for us."

Claire collapsed in the passenger seat and hugged the binder to her chest. "Don't even speak her name. I fully expect her to try to sue Luke even though she was the one trespassing on his property."

"At least we have the security cam footage," Mindy said, reversing out of her parking spot. "It won't hold up in court."

"Thank god. So one interviewee was a huge flop already. And we only have three more scheduled. What if they all suck?"

The tiny sliver of hope she had been carrying was effectively extinguished. What a fucking *day*. Everything was trash. She shouldn't have been surprised after how the morning had started. Clearly the universe was punishing her for something.

Mindy shook her head. "They can't all suck. Ashley was an anomaly."

"I've never seen such a chatty goth," Claire marveled. "Can we stop at the liquor store?"

"Obviously," Mindy said. She was already headed toward the nearest one. "Maybe check on your mom before we start drinking, though?"

"She's still screening my calls." Claire rolled her eyes as she picked up the phone. It was already ringing.

CHAPTER THIRTY-FIVE

To Do:
- *Leave dog poop in Brad's car?*
- *Figure out how to start over*

"Why are the garage walls vibrating?" Luke's voice rang out, louder than usual over the whining guitar of an emo song. "And why is Winston wearing a rainbow wig?"

Claire whirled around, a chocolate chip cookie clutched in her right hand. A half-empty bottle of cabernet sauvignon dangled from the other one. The world was swimming, but at least she wasn't having a panic attack. Alcohol to the rescue.

"Wouldn't you like to know?"

"I would. That's why I asked." He pulled the wig off Winston and set it on the couch. If he noticed the eyebrows they had drawn on Rosie with eyeliner, he didn't say anything.

The bottle hit the end table with a clunk. She picked up a hot pink party hat. "Put on your hat, fancy boy. It's a pity party." She wrestled the hat onto his head. The elastic slapped against his Adam's apple, but he didn't even wince.

"Luuuuuuke!" Mindy continued bopping to the beat, hair gathered into a top bun and stunner shades hiding her green eyes. Her cheeks ballooned with cheeseballs. Orange dust particles settled over one of Sawyer's shirts, which draped down to her knees. She took a swig out of a bottle of rosé.

The anxiety Claire had carefully been ignoring all day had reached a fever pitch the second she came home and saw Brad's binders sitting on the kitchen table. Self-medicating with wine and cookies was not as effective as she had hoped. They had been fired. *Fired.* All because she couldn't trust her client. Where could they go from here?

Claire poked Luke in the chest. "Lemme tell you what happened. You know the thing I was worried about? The whole Brad-might-fire-me thing? Guess what happened. I'll give you three guesses."

Luke narrowed his eyes. "He didn't."

"Bingo." She booped him on the nose, then stared at the ceiling. The tears she had been fighting back with early 2000s pop punk music were threatening to leak out. She picked up the wine bottle again. "I don't know what I did to piss off the big guy upstairs, but it must have been a doozy."

Mindy whirled around like she had just been struck by a great idea. "We should set his house on fire."

"No," Luke and Claire said together. The last thing she needed was to be arrested for arson.

Mindy went back to dancing, and Luke turned to Claire. He cupped her face in his hand and brushed a calloused thumb down her jawline. "I'm sorry."

She shrugged and took another swig out of the bottle. "It's okay. It's only my entire career. Down the toilet. All because I spied on a middle-aged man doing the cha-cha. And now his receptionist is taking over and she'll either drive it into the ground or take credit for all my ideas. This is fine. Everything's fine." A giggle escaped. It didn't even sound real.

"We could burn the saddle," Mindy whispered loudly. She pointed to the corner, where the saddle they had painstakingly distressed to match Karen's childhood one rested.

"Does leather burn?" Luke asked.

"It does if you have enough gas." Mindy slid her stunner shades down and wiggled her eyebrows.

Claire considered it for a millisecond. It would be freeing. "Nah, we'll probably need to sell it."

Mindy pouted. "You guys are no fun. I'm going to go pack." She disappeared down the hallway. It had taken all of fifteen seconds after arriving home for her to book an earlier flight to West Haven.

Claire yawned. Even her bones were tired. The twenty-minute catnap she'd had the night before clearly hadn't helped.

Luke took a step closer. "Hey. It's going to be okay." So serious for a man wearing a hot pink party hat.

She stared up at him. "I think you'll find the kennel full of three-legged dogs in Pennsylvania begs to differ."

He took her by each arm. His touch was like fire, but she was drowning.

"No, they won't."

She raised an eyebrow. "No? You don't think they'll mind being brutally murdered?"

"They won't be. Don't get mad at me."

She crossed her arms. "Why would I be mad at you? Did you make out with Olivia after I left?"

"No. I made a donation to the shelter."

Her eyes narrowed. "How much?"

"Enough to get them through a year. Plenty of time for you to find your next big thing."

She turned away from him and buried her hands in her hair. Relief warred with rage. The shelter was her responsibility to save. Not Luke's. "So you knew I would get fired. You didn't believe in me."

"I believe in you. But I also believe Brad has a mega ego and can be pretty impulsive. I just didn't want you to have another thing to worry about."

Claire sniffed and stiffly uncrossed her arms. Luke pulled her into a hug and stroked her hair. "Thank you," she said, muffled against his chest. He had bought her some time.

He moved back and looked her in the eyes. "I know it doesn't feel like it right now, but everything's going to be okay."

"It's not going to be okay. My warehouse is gone, Luke. My biggest client dumped me. I have a gigantic loan that I now have no way to pay. Our interview was a disaster, so now we don't have anyone to help us look for more California clients, which we desperately need to help replace the lost income from Brad. Oh, and let's not forget that ESA won't leave me alone." They had been quiet since the parking lot incident. That couldn't be good. She shelved it to worry about later.

"Right," Luke said. "That reminds me. Since Mindy's leaving after your interviews are done, you're not allowed to leave the house without me. It's not safe."

Claire grunted. She had no intention of following that rule.

His eyes searched hers. His strong arms pulled her back in, and she burrowed into the clean scent of his T-shirt. "We've faced worse odds. You're not alone. You'll find new clients. And now you don't need to answer the phone at three a.m. when Brad's calling you with an idea."

Claire sighed. One of Brad's binders sat on the coffee table, taunting her. He had easily been her most aggravating and opinionated client. But she had created something beautiful. And now Karen wasn't going to get her perfect moment. The proposal was way too complicated for someone with no background in event planning. Claire could barely handle all the moving pieces and she had an assistant and capable team. What chance did Brad's receptionist stand?

"Look at me." Luke pushed her back, firmly gripping her arms again. "Who are you?"

She frowned. "Did you have a stroke?"

He shook her gently. The cabernet sloshed in the bottle. "You're Claire Freaking Hartley. Say it."

She squirmed. "I don't want to."

It didn't feel true today. Claire Freaking Hartley wouldn't have gotten fired by her biggest client. She wasn't sure who she was anymore.

His green eyes burned. "Say it. Tell me who you are."

"A failure. A wildly irresponsible, wine-drunk idiot who couldn't plan her way out of a cardboard box."

His grip tightened. "Stop. Say it."

He wasn't going to stop. "Claire Freaking Hartley," she mumbled.

His head tilted. "I can't hear you."

"Claire Freaking Hartley," she said, a bit louder.

He raised his eyebrows. "One more time."

The wine bottle hit the floor. She pulled her rainbow party hat off and slingshotted it at a framed poster of the movie *Goodfellas*.

"*I'm Claire Freaking Hartley,*" she shouted over a drum solo.

His mouth twisted up into a half-smile. Her own mouth curved in response, acting completely independently from the mental freakout she was having. And yet, maybe it was still true. Maybe she was still Claire Freaking Hartley. She wasn't going to let one overly-sensitive, gold-pinky-ring-wearing control freak ruin her life. She had escaped a serial killer, for god's sake. Surely she could find a way around this financial pickle.

Luke kissed her forehead. "That's right. Now put your pants on, we're going out."

She had been inching toward the whiteboard, eager to put a plan to save the business into motion. "But—"

He shook his head. "Later. Let's go."

So bossy today. She found a pair of jean shorts in a basket of laundry she had yet to put away.

"Where are we going?" she asked as he steered her out the front door and down the steps.

"You'll see." Typical Luke.

They got into the car. Thankfully, there were zero ex girl-friends climbing the drainpipe. Luke flipped through songs on his phone until he found Claire's favorite metal song. Her body thrummed with the double bass. Bar by bar, her anxiety quieted.

The sun hung low on the horizon. Neon lights flashed by. Luke's thumb brushed small circles over her knee. She wound one arm through his and, for once, focused her attention on the city instead of her phone. They passed a

Thai place, and the intoxicating smell of drunken noodles stirred her appetite.

"Is there food where we're going?" The chocolate chip cookie had been delicious, but it was definitely lacking protein.

Luke nodded, keeping his eyes on the road. Maybe they were going back to food truck central.

"How was your day?" She hadn't even asked.

"Less dramatic than yours."

She bumped his shoulder. "Come on. Tell me something. I could use the distraction."

He glanced at her. "Are we seriously not going to talk about what happened this morning?"

This morning? What was he talking about? Oh, right. His ex-girlfriend trespassed while clad in lingerie and a plastic smile. How polite of him to remind her.

"What, the Olivia thing?" Claire scoffed. "I'm over it. I've lived and lost a thousand dreams since she fell from the roof like an oversized bird of prey wearing Victoria's Secret. She is at the very bottom of my ever-growing list of problems."

It was true. She hadn't even bothered to check Olivia's Instagram for her inevitable sob story. "You would tell me if I had something to worry about, right?" she asked.

Luke frowned. "What are you talking about?"

She folded her hands in her lap. It was like the alcohol had evaporated from her system. "A year and a half ago, you wanted to spend the rest of your life with her. And this morning, she climbed your drainpipe."

He sighed and seemed to be thinking hard. "I was in a weird place after my dad died. I came home when my enlistment was up, drove across the country so I didn't have to see my brother."

Claire bit her lip. Luke's brother, George, had pulled

their father off life support before Luke could get home from Afghanistan. She had forced the two to hang out during a painfully awkward dinner party that culminated in her incapacitating George and forcing him to leave. But things had seemed marginally better at Thanksgiving.

"I did some night classes and bartended while I started my first project," he continued. "Anyway, Olivia was simple, safe. At first, anyway. Then with all the influencer bullshit, she got addicted to drama. That was our entire relationship, day and night. Accusing me of cheating, picking fights, trying to make me jealous, turning my friends against me."

And then he had proposed. Not that Claire could judge —she had spent nearly one-eighth of her life with a sentient, Doritos-dusted beanbag with gamer's thumb.

"That sounds exhausting," she said carefully.

"It was. So no, you don't have anything to worry about. Here we are." He pulled into a parking lot.

"Where are we?" She sat up and looked around. A yellow sign several yards away read Will Rogers State Beach.

"Oh! The beach." She had been so tied up with Brad's proposal that she had never even managed to put her toes in the Pacific.

The sea breeze hit her the second she opened her car door. Salt spray misted her face. Not even the tantalizing smell of the cheesesteak food truck in the parking lot could have derailed her from her first Pacific sunset. She kicked off her shoes and tossed them in her purse. Luke's hand found hers, and they trudged barefoot through the sand to the edge of the water.

A trail of light skimmed across the waves, leading to the setting sun. Cotton candy clouds stood like sentries, guarding the view of the stars that, in West Haven at least, would have peeked out.

A few young families and a handful of elderly couples strolled the beach, but when she turned to look at Luke, they might as well have been the only two people on the planet.

He was still here, even in the aftermath of her greatest career failure. He hadn't yelled at her or left her to go to poker night like Jason would have. He had built her back up, stepped in to take care of what she couldn't do alone, and pulled her out of her self-pitying nose dive. It was a level of security she had never known. Warmth and gratitude flooded her.

"Here," Luke said.

Claire glanced down. He held a Tiffany-blue sticky note with the Happily Ever Afters logo at the top. *Brad* was scrawled in Claire's handwriting, followed by his phone number.

"Found it in my car. Thought you could symbolically toss it into the ocean. I know you love to burn stuff, but"— he paused, gesturing around him—"there's pretty much always a burn ban."

"Damn gender reveals." She started to crumple the note, then stopped. "What if a turtle eats it?"

He raised one eyebrow. "You know as well as I do that you only use biodegradable sticky notes."

He wasn't wrong. Brad's name stared back at her, a stark reminder of the hell that was the last twenty-four hours. She pursed her lips and squashed the paper into a tight ball. Frigid water tickled her toes as she stepped to the edge of the shore. Her arm stretched back like she was about to release a javelin. With all her strength, she flung the note.

It immediately blew back on the breeze and bonked into her nose. With a frustrated grunt, she plucked the note from the ground. Was it her imagination, or had Luke taken a step away? She threw the note again, harder this time. It landed on the damp sand behind her.

Her hands balled into fists at her side, and she looked up at the cloud canopy. Why was she being punished? Stalked, abducted, harassed, psychologically scarred, fired, and now she couldn't even throw a stupid piece of paper into the stupid ocean?

As if on cue, lights turned on down the beach. It must have been about half a mile away. What was it? Her stomach clenched, and she squinted. She would recognize that wheel anywhere. The second stop from Brad's proposal—the Santa Monica Pier. It jutted out from the beach, mocking her with its colorful lights and theme park screams.

Her purse hit the sand with a muted thump. She took a step into the water. The cold curled her toes. She waded deeper, shredding the note into tiny pieces as she walked. Waves lapped at her knees. The cool tendrils of the Pacific snaked around her, soaking the hem of her shorts.

The intrusive thoughts she'd been fighting crept back in as she methodically shredded the note. She had worked so hard. It wasn't supposed to end like this. Was it even possible to overcome a setback like this? Could this be the end of Happily Ever Afters? Was Brad posting a scathing Yelp review right now? It just. Wasn't. Fair.

A wave crashed directly on her. Her knees buckled like they were made of cardboard, and sand bit into her palms. Water surged past. Now her shirt was soaked. A strong hand tugged on her arm, but she jerked it back.

"No. I'm doing this." She clambered back to her feet. She turned sideways as the next wave slapped at her, sending a spray into the air. Deeper she staggered until the water was up to her chin. She opened her hand. Tiffany-blue confetti scattered into the sea, calmer here behind the breaking waves. The paper drifted away. Finally.

She stood for a moment, allowing the ocean to buffet her back and forth. She kicked off the sandy floor and stretched onto her back. The colors of the sunset drifted away, bleeding into the inky blackness of night. For just a moment, she allowed herself to simply be still.

CHAPTER THIRTY-SIX

To Do:
- *Buy more wine*
- *Check inbox for CA proposal requests*
- *Ask Alice to make Brad voodoo doll?*

"MA'AM, DROP THE MACHETE. DO IT NOW."

Claire opened her eyes. Bright beams of light hit her directly in the pupils, and she grimaced. Red and blue lights flashed off granite tombstones that stuck out of the ground like teeth.

What the hell was going on? The last thing she remembered was tumbling into bed with an empty bottle of wine.

"I repeat. Put the peacock and the machete down." The voice was coming from a bullhorn.

She glanced down. A bird with bright blue feathers bobbed its head inquisitively from the crook of her left arm. Crumbs littered her shirt. Moonlight glinted off the machete

Luke had used to clear some of the weeds in the backyard. It thumped onto the grass.

The bird, apparently startled by the noise, thrashed its neck and backed out of her arms. It hit the ground soundlessly and strutted off down a narrow bridge, tail feathers streaming behind. Water stretched around her. Fountains tinkled pleasantly. Where the hell was she? She stepped back and bumped against something hard. Luke was going to be so pissed. This is what she got for falling asleep.

She swung her head around as the lights approached. An imposing marble mausoleum with a bronze door stood behind her. Her elbow stung where it had bounced off one of the columns.

"Get down on your knees!" The voice behind the flashlight yelled. She had really done it now.

She dropped to her knees and put her hands behind her head. It was harder than it should have been to stretch her arms up. As the flashlights approached, she took stock of her outfit. Half the time, her nighttime wandering outfit didn't include pants. She didn't seem to be wearing them now, but it was difficult to tell because she was one hundred percent dressed as a human-sized hotdog.

The top of the wiener fabric stretched snugly over her head, and a drizzle of ketchup and mustard ran down her torso. Apparently Luke had frequented some Hollywood Halloween parties. And now she was sleepwalking with a machete in the middle of a cemetery. In Los Angeles. Dressed as a hotdog. After Luke had expressly forbidden her from leaving the house alone because a group of serial killers was stalking her. All-around great choices.

"You have the right to remain silent," one of the cops recited. Her ears rang like he was still shouting through the bullhorn. He droned through the rest of the Miranda Rights. Was he speaking underwater?

Claire fought for breath as her vision darkened. Her heart beat so fast it was almost painful. "You're arresting me? For what?" Was it illegal to dress as a hotdog in Los Angeles? Was this a vegan police force?

"Ma'am, you were trespassing and carrying a dangerous weapon."

God damn it, Sleepwalking Claire. She had skipped her cardio and meditation exercise before bed, and now she was paying the consequence.

Her limbs shook. The short, sharp breaths she was able to steal burned her lungs. "I-I have a sleepwalking disorder. Let me call my therapist, she can explain it to you."

The cop scoffed. "Yeah, yeah. We've heard it all before." He slapped a pair of handcuffs on her. "Let's go."

They tugged her to her feet. She tripped over an unseen rock, and they all but dragged her down the short bridge.

It was really happening. She was being arrested. Just when she thought things couldn't possibly get any worse. She never should have come to this stupid city.

Rage and panic clashed inside her like two seas meeting. When the cop finally successfully stuffed her into the back of his cruiser, the grate between her and the front seat almost broke her. Here she was, in the back of a cop car, while hundreds of members of ESA roamed the streets looking for innocent women to kill. It wasn't fair.

The panic attack was winning. Hot tears streamed down her face while her body trembled like a leaf in a hurricane. She couldn't take it anymore. Stabbed. Fired. Arrested. Even if Brad hadn't fired her, her reputation would never survive this. How much lower could she sink?

The ride to the police station passed in a blur. She

couldn't do alternate nostril breathing due to the handcuffs, but she forced herself to take deep breaths. By the time they screeched to a halt under the fluorescent lights of the parking lot, the attack had subsided, but things still looked equally as bleak.

Latex gloves snapped in the din as a female officer prepared to search her. A custody sergeant inside the building took the only things she was carrying—her GPS watch and a pair of leftover breadsticks she had duct taped to her biceps. The machete had already been bagged as evidence.

It was like she was watching all of this taking place from outside her body. The sensation of her ink-covered thumb rolling across the ledger. The flash of a camera illuminating every flaw on her face. Luke's address tumbled out of her mouth as they badgered her—where did she live? What was her birth date? Why wasn't she carrying her driver's license?

The bars of the holding cell pressed into her back when the door slammed shut behind her. So this was what rock bottom looked like. A half dozen other women sat on benches inside, twirling their hair around their fingers. They all turned to watch her enter. One of the women leaned forward and stared at her with dead eyes. Pockmarks littered her skin.

"Don't I get a phone call?" Claire called after the cop.

"Soon," he said.

She cast a glance around the room and backed into the corner. This wasn't good. It was too hard to sit in her hotdog costume, but she didn't want to turn her back to these women either. Who knew what they were capable of? Maybe she should act more menacing. This hotdog costume wasn't thick enough to stop a shiv someone had whittled out of Jolly Ranchers.

There was no need to be intimidated by these women. She had escaped serial killers more than once. A holding cell in LA county jail was nothing. She squared her shoulders and slowly looked at each of the women. She made eye contact with the pockmarked girl until she averted her gaze. Ha. Now that she had established dominance, she needed to figure out how the hell she was going to get out of this mess.

The clock on the wall ticked incessantly. It was one in the morning. Who would she call even when she had the chance? It was too late to call Luke, and Kyle was probably in bed. Maybe they'd let her leave a voicemail? But what happened then? She would just stay in jail?

Somewhere, a faucet dripped. The sound was louder than it should have been, magnified by the steel and concrete. Her heart galloped again. Was trespassing a misdemeanor? Or worse, a felony? There was no way she could run a proposal planning business with a criminal record. Her stomach twisted. Every time she thought things couldn't possibly get worse, the universe dropped another shitstorm on her.

Luke was going to be so pissed. Unconscious Claire had clearly figured out a way to bypass all the anti-sleepwalking safeguards he had added to the house. Had he already noticed that she was missing?

By the time a cop led her to a phone, two more women had joined them in the holding cell. It smelled like urine and stale cigarette smoke. She really had to pee, but she was not about to do it on a metal toilet bowl while half a dozen women watched her struggle out of a hotdog costume.

The dial tone droned. The phone was heavy in her hand. Who could she call? Who would be the least ashamed of her? There was only one choice, and the very thought was enough to make her stomach churn.

CHAPTER THIRTY-SEVEN

To Do:
- Pray
- Ask Tanya about herbs for luck

A COP WITH PERMANENT FROWN LINES APPROACHED THE holding cell. All the women looked up expectantly. With any luck, they'd take the woman in a denim jumpsuit who had started chewing her toenails.

"Hartley," the cop said flatly. His voice was like sandpaper. "You're free to go."

Claire jumped up. She had only just figured out how to sit in the hotdog costume. "I'm—I'm not being charged?" The top of her costume scraped against the cell door.

The cop's brown eyes hardened. He slammed the door behind her. "Your father's here to pick you up." He handed her two evidence bags. The breadsticks were squashed and unappetizing. A length of rainbow duct tape was coiled next to them. How kind they were to return them.

They ushered her into the main lobby. Jack and Luke stood stiffly next to each other like the worst buddy cop duo of all time. Luke closed the distance between them in two steps and roughly yanked her into a hug. She just managed to catch a whiff of his deodorant before he pulled back and held her at arm's length.

"What the hell were you thinking?" he asked. His entire body was rigid, his mouth a hard slash.

She stared at him blankly. "I was thinking nothing. I was literally unconscious. You think I went to a cemetery dressed as a hotdog to feed a wild peacock on purpose?"

He released her and put both hands on his head. His fingers twisted in his disheveled hair. Maybe he was searching for words. "You need to call your therapist."

"But—"

"No." His voice had more finality than the bang of a gavel. "The second we get home, you're going to call her. And you're starting that medication."

"I'm sorry. You're right." Things had really gotten out of hand now. She cast a glance behind her. Were they really letting her go? She had thought that calling in her FBI agent father would at least get the rest of her due process moving, but she didn't expect them to actually drop the charges. Just how important *was* Jack?

"Let's get out of here." If she had to spend another second in this overly harsh lighting with these hardened criminals, she was going to lose it. Again.

"Thank you, Jack," she said as soon as they were outside and she could finally breathe again.

Jack tucked his phone in his pocket. Even though it was

the middle of the night, he was dressed in a suit and tie. Did he sleep in one?

"The judge owed me a favor." An appropriately mysterious answer.

What kind of thank-you gift did you give to an absent biological father who may have missed your college graduation but had reappeared in time to save your life and reputation all in less than a year? An Edible Arrangement?

"Well. I appreciate it." She smoothed a lock of hair away and crossed her arms as best as she could over the wiener suit. "I hope you didn't fly in for me." She didn't know what time it was, but there was no way he had booked a flight that quickly.

Jack shook his head. "I was already here. Chasing down a lead." He turned on his heel and took a step. He paused and looked back around. "You need to be more careful, Claire. They're still out there."

She squared her shoulders. "I am aware. I'm already dialing my therapist." She wasn't, since her phone was presumably plugged in at home. But it seemed to satisfy Jack.

"We're not telling my mom," Claire said as she climbed into the passenger side of Luke's car. The top of the costume rubbed against the roof. If it wasn't a sure-fire way to add an indecent exposure charge, she would have ripped it right off.

The thought of her mother made her stomach twist. Alice had only just started answering Claire's calls again. There hadn't been any more abduction attempts, and the man in custody refused to talk. Still, the danger lingered. Would they come for Alice again? Or Claire? Had Charlie installed that security camera Claire had sent her? And what about Brianna?

Speaking of abductions, why had ESA gone quiet? Were

they just toying with her? She would have bet her last dollar they had a hand in the ordeal at the gala. But there hadn't been a note or threat in weeks. Maybe they had shifted focus. She gripped the handrail. And how had they missed so many viable opportunities to capture her? Even when she presumably rode the L Line quite alone and unconscious while dressed as something that people couldn't agree on was a sandwich. What the hell were they waiting for?

Streetlights flashed by as they drove home in silence. The blackness of night was retreating, replaced by a burst of crimson on the horizon. Luke's hands were both squarely on the wheel. Normally he held her hand while driving. There wasn't even insane LA traffic to blame. In fact, he hadn't said a word since they got in the car. Maybe he had finally had enough of her. And who could blame him?

He had said only hours before that his relationship with Olivia was terrible because of the drama. Was that really worse than dating Claire? Since they'd gotten together, she had been a near nonstop stream of drama. Between the multiple attempted murders, the sleepwalking, and her borderline obsession with her career, she'd been a hot, unavailable mess. Maybe he deserved better.

Her stomach growled, and she placed a hand over it as if to muffle it. Those old breadsticks didn't sound as unappetizing any longer.

Luke put on his turn signal and swung into a Starbucks. He ordered them both coffee and breakfast sandwiches. At least he was talking to the barista. Minutes later, he pulled into the driveway. Claire unbuckled her seatbelt, but he didn't move.

"Are you coming?" She plucked the coffee from the cup carrier.

Luke shook his head. His eyes were cold. "I need to head

in early. Can I trust you not to leave the house while I'm gone?"

The iced coffee sweated in her hand. As tempting as it was to make a joke about being under house arrest, she simply nodded.

"Good. Arm the alarm and call your therapist." The tires screeched as he reversed out of the driveway. He didn't look back as he drove away.

As his taillights disappeared, she blew out a deep breath. She had successfully pissed off the love of her life. There was no more putting it off—time to call Dr. Goulding and get a handle on this sleepwalking business.

Rosie and Winston swarmed her the second she opened the door. They followed her up the stairs, where she flopped dramatically on the bed. Stupid body refusing to stay in bed. All she wanted was sleep. Why did her subconscious insist on these nighttime wanderings? With a few recent exceptions, the meditation and cardio routine Dr. Goulding had recommended had been at least semi-successful for weeks. But then her warehouse had burned down, and it all went to shit.

The empty wine bottle stared judgmentally at her from the nightstand. She could definitely stand to cut back on the booze. Maybe she could try that first. There was no need to bother her therapist. It was barely eight a.m. on the East Coast. She probably hadn't even had her coffee yet. A nap—with a more elaborate door barricade, handcuffs, and safety restraints—was what Claire really needed. And then she was going to wake up, pick a new proposal to take on, do some ESA research, and throw together a date night for Luke.

It was time to adjust her priorities.

CHAPTER THIRTY-EIGHT

To Do:
- *Thank you note for Jack*
- *Prep for Heather interview*
- *Google Men's Rights again*

"BLOT." MINDY HANDED CLAIRE A TISSUE.

Claire dabbed lightly at her mouth and threw it in the trash.

"Perfect. You're ready." Mindy unplugged a curling iron and wound the cord around the handle.

"I really hope this helps." Claire stood and stared at her reflection in the bathroom mirror. Her normally unruly hair had been tamed and curled. She looked more pinup girl than proposal planner with her red lipstick and false eyelashes. A black negligee lurked beneath the silk robe she wore.

"This will totally help him forget that you sleepwalked as a hotdog and got arrested last night. Okay, I'm leaving."

Luke had thoughtfully made the choice to let Mindy sleep during the hubbub the night before. She slung her purse over her shoulder and twisted the doorknob. "Good luck. I'll text before I come home so you can at least throw some pants on."

"Fine." Claire sighed, but she smiled.

Mindy left, and Claire ran around the downstairs a final time, adding finishing touches and corralling the dogs into the dining room that they never used.

She blew a long breath out and flapped her hands. Her stomach was a tangle of nerves. Would this be enough to help Luke forgive her? The timer on the oven went off, and she pulled out a tray.

The door to the garage opened, and Claire whirled, muffins in hand.

"Hey," Luke said flatly, bumping the door shut with his hip. His jaw was set, like he was ready for a fight. She hadn't heard from him since he had peeled out of the driveway, but at least he was speaking to her again. "Something smells good."

"I made some muffins. We're having a Sorry-for-Sleepwalking Date Night."

"A date night?" His mouth twitched at the side.

She nodded. "I owe you. You can lose the shirt but keep the pants. For now."

"Fair enough." He set his briefcase down in the hallway and tugged his shirt off. "Where's Mindy?"

"Out. For a while. She went to look for the perfect gift for Sawyer."

Luke nodded. "Tell me about your day."

"Later. First, the date." Claire pulled him down the hallway and into the living room.

"Shit. A blanket fort?" A genuine smile cracked the grumpy marble facade of his face. Maybe a day at the studio had helped him forget how mad he should be.

"It is. And I had to install some serious updates, but we're going to play *Murder Melee 3*." Claire had destroyed Luke the first time they had played together in a blanket fort in her apartment. It had been months since they had time for video games. Maybe this time in the spirit of reconciliation she would let him win.

Maybe.

"I see." Luke cradled the back of her head in his hand and pushed her up against the wall. Her toes curled, and her heart stuttered. "Is this robe hiding another date night surprise?" He trailed a finger down the silky length of the seam and paused at the knot at her waist.

This was going way better than expected. "It might be," she said breathlessly.

In the blink of an eye, he had scooped her up so she was straddling him. He pinned her against the wall and undid the knot on her robe with one hand. It fell open to reveal the black lace negligee she had been saving for a special occasion.

His sea green eyes raked over every inch of her body as his hand cupped her. He dipped his head to her neck and feasted ravenously on the exposed stretch of skin.

A moan escaped her lips as she raked her nails down his back. Legs dropping to the floor, she swapped their positions. They had spent so much of the past year swept up in her drama. Tonight was about him.

Pressing him to the wall with one hand, she knelt in front of him. Her knees wobbled uncomfortably on the hardwood floor, but she barely noticed. Her hand trailed down the familiar topography of his torso—seriously, how was a girl supposed to concentrate with abs like these right in front of her?

She unbuckled his belt and tossed it aside. The zipper slid down easily, and the pants puddled around his ankles. She freed him from his boxers and took him eagerly, greedily into her mouth.

His hand fisted in her hair. He looked down through long lashes and locked eyes with her. She was going to make him feel the way he made her feel. Safe. Loved. Cherished. Desired. *This* was what was important. As long as they had each other, she had all she needed. It was about time she showed it.

"Come here," Luke grunted a minute later, grabbing her by the hand. He pulled her up to him and kissed her, gripping her like he would never let go.

She melted into him and the stress slipped away from her shoulders. There would be all kinds of problems to confront tomorrow. But now, in this moment, it was just the two of them.

He picked her up again, carried her across the threshold into the living room, and flung open the blanket that covered the entrance.

"Oh, be careful," Claire said. "There's—"

It was too late. A cardboard box crumpled beneath her lower back. Luke had tossed her gently into the fort and directly onto a pizza box. The smell of marinara was stronger than it had been a moment ago.

"Uh oh." She rolled onto her belly.

Luke burst out laughing.

"What? What is it?" She sat up on her knees and twisted. The cardboard was mangled. Red sauce was splattered across one of the blankets a solid four feet above them and, from the feel of it, down her back. Well, shit. So much for her sexy negligee and apology date night. Was there anything she couldn't ruin?

"Damn it." She sat down in the blanket fort. "I'm sorry. This was supposed to be special."

"Oh, it's definitely special," Luke said, barely concealing a grin. He extended his hand to her, and she took it. "Come on."

"Where are we going?"

He pulled her to her feet and led her down the hallway.

"The shower." Then he scooped her up and flew up the stairs. He didn't seem to mind that his hand was directly in the marinara danger zone. Maybe the black negligee wasn't wasted after all.

"I love you like this," Luke said. His head was propped in his hand, and he stretched the length of the blanket fort.

Claire paused midway through a slightly mangled bite of pizza. "Like what? A failure with pizza sauce in my butt crack?"

"No." He leaned forward and pressed another kiss to her neck.

Her once perfectly curled hair hung down her bare back in wet ringlets, and all her makeup had been washed away during a very interesting shower. She hadn't bothered to glance in the mirror, but she probably looked like a busty Marilyn Manson who had just run a 5k in the desert.

"Relaxed. Happy. Natural." He brushed a finger beneath her eyelid. A smudge of something black rubbed off.

Claire smiled. "I spent a lot of time on that makeup, you know."

"Oh, sure. And don't get me wrong, you scorched the pants right off me. But you don't need it."

She dabbed her mouth with a napkin and leaned forward. Her lips pressed to his. It might have been slightly garlicky, but it filled her with warmth.

The tension that had been between them since the missed dinner had trickled away. Here, in a blanket fort with no cell phones, no laptops, and no distractions, it felt like the day he had swept her around the ballroom while they were practicing for Nicole's proposal—heat, excitement, and an indescribable feeling of being home. In just over a year's time, Luke had transformed from a grumpy, arrogant film-maker who criticized her every step to a grumpy, arrogant film maker who made harnesses for blind dogs and had created a home with Claire. They had faced family secrets, mothers who wanted to strangle each other, and crazy stalker exes who climbed drain pipes or started dating their arch nemeses. While this latest setback had been a pretty devastating one, at least they had each other.

"Tell me about your day," she said, breaking apart and shoving the pizza box at him. "I want to hear everything."

CHAPTER THIRTY-NINE

To Do:
- Plan another date night. Maybe a series?
- Meeting with Mindy to narrow down applicants

"SEE YOU LATER?" LUKE GRABBED CLAIRE AROUND THE WAIST and pulled her in tight.

Her toes curled, and warmth spread between her legs. She snuggled deeper. His clean linen scent mingled with the coffee wafting in from the kitchen. He pulled back, but she gripped tighter. His calm, steady presence was the glue that was holding her together. As soon as he left, she would have no choice but to confront her new reality.

How was she going to rebuild? Since coming to Los Angeles, she had been threatened, fired, and *arrested*. This whole trip had been a giant mistake. Thankfully, Brad hadn't posted anything nasty on the internet yet. Maybe he would forget? Or wait until after the proposal?

The proposal she had given months of her life to. Planning, dream-boarding, calling, scheduling, emailing, bending over backward, and catering to every whim. Seventy-hour work weeks. Missed dinners with Luke and friends. And now it was all for nothing.

"Hey." Luke put a hand on her cheek. His eyes locked onto hers, stormy and gray today. He pressed a kiss to the tender spot on her wrist where heavy duty BDSM handcuffs had bound her to the headboard the night before. "Everything's going to be okay."

She exhaled a long, slow breath. "Things can only get better, right?"

A grim smile formed. "I love you. Don't leave the house, okay? Not unless Charlie or Bri is with you. And keep the security system armed." He gestured to the new keypad on the wall.

Claire nodded, but her insides twisted. Today was Brad's meeting with the ranch. Going there to spy on him was a stupid, dangerous idea. What would she gain from it other than more unbridled rage? It was stupid to chase after lost dreams, but she could at least do more research on ESA. The sleepwalking, the sabotage —none of it would stop until they were brought to their knees.

"I love you." She tugged Luke close once more and kissed him. Their tongues danced, heat rushed to her face, and she had half a mind to pull him back upstairs.

"You're killing me. I gotta go. Bye." There was regret in his eyes as he kissed her on the cheek and left.

She twisted the sash of her robe in her hands as he hustled down the front steps. The sun slanted across the yard and illuminated him in a golden glow. His chest muscles rippled as he opened his car door. Butterflies danced in her belly. God, he was gorgeous. He waved and shot her a half-smile as he reversed out of the driveway.

In his absence, the house was too quiet. Mindy had left in a cab earlier, bound for the airport. Rosie sat at attention at the backdoor, fixated on the squirrel that was trying to climb the bird feeder. Winston was next to her even though he couldn't see anything.

Taking one final glance at the front door, Claire hustled into the kitchen and pulled out a paper map of Hollywood Mindy had picked up during a star tour. She spread it open on the kitchen table and dragged her laptop over. An email appeared from Mindy with a breakdown of five potential Los Angeles clients. Her flight must have had Wi-Fi.

Claire's hand hovered over the mouse. They needed to pick some new couples, figure out next steps. But ESA was sabotaging her at every turn. What if they moved on to targeting her clients? Anyone she associated with could be in danger. She minimized the email and opened her web browser.

A dozen tabs stood open, each leading to a different news article. A handful of women had gone missing in Los Angeles County over the course of the last six months. Was it ESA, or was it some other lowlife? Maybe if she visited the locations where they disappeared, she could spot something that would lead her to them. It was probably crazy, but she had to start somewhere.

She glanced down at her list of names and typed them one by one into the search bar. As she read through social media accounts and, in some cases, Wikipedia pages, their lives unfolded before her. Several of the women seemed like classic ESA victims. A couple of executives, a winner of the Great American Barbecue, even a state senator.

A chill ran down her spine. All these high-profile women, and there was barely a blip on the news. Every single day women were at risk. Sitting by and letting these assholes continue to run amok was not an option. She had to do something.

She parsed the articles until she found the last known locations of the victims. Robin Turbot, the CEO of a chain of local health food stores, had disappeared from her gym on Hollywood Boulevard. She marked the location with a red X and perused the next article. Kyla Rivers, the owner of the Los Angeles Sparks, had gone to the bathroom at a club on Santa Monica Boulevard and never returned. Trebek Open Space had been the site of the disappearance of Letisha Humboldt, a tech CEO.

They were all over the place—Hollywood, Laurel Canyon, Universal City. She marked a dozen spots and stared at the map.

Were the places significant? Why hadn't any of the women been found? Where was ESA operating from? There were so many questions. Someone very important had to be at the top. But Los Angeles was full of important people.

On a whim, Claire took a pencil and drew lines between the sites of the disappearances. At least half of the lines intersected over the Hollywood Hills. Her stomach clenched. Was this where ESA's hideout was? She was no expert on LA, but she was fairly certain that the Hills were littered with celebrities and influential people. She couldn't explain it, but something in her gut told her there were answers there.

She slammed her laptop shut, then immediately reopened it and calculated the distance between the Hills and the ranch. Twenty or thirty minutes. Not that she was going to do anything about it. Brad deserved to fail on his own. There were higher stakes.

She crossed the room and twitched the curtain aside. Luke was long gone, and the black Porsche was just sitting there. He would be furious if she left, especially after he just forbade her from doing exactly that. But the mystery beckoned. Until ESA was brought down, nothing and no one was safe. It was time to act.

An hour later, Claire crawled through the winding streets of the Hollywood Hills. With any luck, she would look like any other touristy rubbernecker trying to catch a glimpse of George Clooney taking out his recycling.

Her phone beeped, and she jumped. Her heart hammered in her chest. Had Luke discovered that she left the house?

But no, it was only Mindy following up on her email.

"Sorry. ESA research. Video chat this afternoon?" she dictated to her car. The message was sent, and Mindy confirmed.

She passed yet another gated driveway leading to a mega mansion. Ugh. She was wasting so much time. She should have researched who lived in the Hills, which residents had a history of misogyny. It was probably a long list, but better than going in blind. The only thing she was catching was severe home envy.

Frustration grew as she crawled the streets. Gates and sun-drenched, Tuscan-inspired houses flanked her on each side, but there was no way of telling if anyone beyond those gates was in ESA. What was she expecting to stumble across? A giant penis fountain in the front yard? A basement full of female CEOs?

Her phone beeped again. She pulled over and put on her hazard lights. This time it was an alert from her calendar—she needed to leave now if she was going to spy on Brad and his assistant at the ranch. Her hands hesitated on the wheel. Luke was already going to be upset if he found out that she left the house to go amateur sleuthing. But he would be furious if he found out she risked her safety to spy on a former client.

And yet, she had to know. Was her vision going to be destroyed, or was his receptionist secretly an event planning wizard? It was bound to be a disaster. And then what if he wanted Claire to come back? Her fingers twitched on the wheel. She counted the clicking of the flashers until she got to thirty. There was only one answer. She was going to that ranch.

Thirty harrowing minutes of honking horns and BMWs refusing to use their turn signals later, she rolled into the parking lot and kicked up a cloud of dust. There was Brad's obnoxious Ferrari parked as close as he could get to the front of the lot. She glanced around, but the rest of the lot was empty.

Claire slid on a pair of tennis shoes and locked the car behind her. She would only watch for a few minutes—just long enough to make sure everything was falling apart without her—and then she would head straight home and pick the dogs up from daycare. Maybe she'd even make Luke a guilt dinner. He loved her stepdad's empanadas.

Gravel crunched behind her. She whirled around and immediately plunged her hand into her purse as her heart hammered in her throat. A stun gun nestled in her hand, she scanned the parking lot. What had she heard? Was it a human? ESA?

A mama deer and two fawns stepped out from behind her car. Their doe eyes stared blankly at her. Claire blew out a long, slow breath. Apparently East Coast and West Coast deer both enjoyed popping up at the worst possible time. Electrified venison was not on the menu this evening. She sheathed her stun gun and began the quarter-mile hike to the ranch.

Brad's voice hit her like nails on a chalkboard as she slunk up the hill. She darted off the path and hid behind a bush. Concealed by shrubbery, she peered through the branches.

Brad's assistant, who had added rainbow bangs since Claire had last seen her, clutched a clipboard.

"What do you mean you didn't bring the pictures?" He stared down at her.

"I thought you wanted to wait until we got the ivory frames in—you said the off-white wasn't right."

Ha. So Brad was still micromanaging every minute aspect of the project. For once, it was nice that it wasn't her problem.

He wiped a hand over his face and stared up at the midday sun. "Goldie, how do you expect me to visualize everything if we don't bring the necessary materials? I expect better from you."

Goldie straightened up. "Mr. Windsor, I'm not an event planner. This is not in my job description." She pointed at a horse who was taking a dump.

"It's called 'all other duties as needed,' kiddo," he said grimly. "I know you can do it. You do a great job with my schedule."

"Whatever. I'll put it on the list. What else?"

Claire listened for another twenty minutes while Brad's requests grew increasingly absurd. A sheen of sweat had appeared over Goldie's brow. The first item on her To Do list was obtaining a new saddle for Karen. There was no way they'd get it done in time. Brad was going to have to buy the existing one from Happily Ever Afters. Ha.

Her watch beeped. Shit. It was time to head home so she could beat Luke back. After one last look at the stressed-out receptionist, she slunk back around the corner and stole down the hill. Her heart was lighter than it had been since she had been fired. A breeze lifted the ends of her hair as she half-skipped down the narrow gravel road. It was a beautiful, sunny day. For once, someone who had wronged her was facing the consequences of their actions. It wouldn't be long before Brad realized Goldie couldn't cut it. He would probably call at any minute. Maybe she should turn her phone on silent, make him sweat for a few hours.

"See?" she said to a chipmunk that darted across the path. "I went on a whole outing by myself and didn't get abducted." ESA had better things to do than mess with her in the middle of the day on a Thursday. Most of them were probably either frat boys or grown-up frat boys who were now chronically constipated middle managers with nine-to-five jobs. They couldn't keep tabs on her all the time. There was no reason for Luke to forbid her from going out alone.

Luke's protectiveness had once been hot. Lately it was just irritating. She stretched her arms out at her sides and lifted her face to the sunshine. God, it was good to be free. No overbearing boyfriend probing every corner, no FBI dad checking her flip-flops for tracking devices. Even though LA traffic was unbearable, she was grateful for the crush of people that allowed her to be, for once, anonymous.

Something on the dirt road caught her foot, and she nearly fell ass-over-end to the parking lot.

"Son of a bitch." She kicked a rock and sent it flying into a thicket of trees. Somewhere in the dense clump of vegetation, a twig snapped.

Her sneakers halted on the dusty trail. Was it her imagination, or did a shadow just dart behind that tree? Goosebumps spread up and down her arms. She expelled a long, slow breath, but nothing stopped her galloping heartbeat.

Would they really try the same thing twice? Another abduction attempt at the ranch? There was no way. They wouldn't even know she was here unless they had followed her all day. She was being paranoid.

Her eyes probed the space between the trees. The branches swayed, but they could have been moving for any number of reasons. A light breeze, a small earthquake. Maybe a really energetic group rain dance.

She resumed her walk and slid her sunglasses down onto her nose, peering fervently out of the corner of her eye on her way to the car. The keys clinked as she withdrew them from the cavern of her purse and threaded them through her knuckles.

There wasn't any sign of movement from the thicket. She was almost to the car. Even if there was someone hiding back there, they wouldn't be able to stop her once she got to her vehicle. She quickened her pace and breathed a sigh of relief when she touched the warm metal of her door handle. The leather seats burned her legs as she slid into the driver's seat and buckled her seatbelt.

Shit. She hadn't checked the undercarriage. Jack would be furious. But he didn't have to know. She turned the car on and threw it into reverse. Whatever may or may not have been hiding in the trees was about to eat her dust.

As she reversed out of her parking spot, she cocked her head. Was the car suddenly leaning? And what was that sound? She shifted into drive. *Thump thump thump.* The speed of the thumping increased.

Son of a bitch. Of all the times to get a flat. Was it a coincidence, or was it ESA?

She threw the car into park. Casting a cursory glance around the still empty parking lot, she stepped out of the car. Yep, there it was. A huge nail protruded from her now flat tire.

A strangled yell escaped her throat as she kicked it. She needed to get back to Luke's for what was sure to be a sound lashing. Now she was going to have to rely on the memory of the one time Roy had showed her how to change a tire when she was a shiny-faced sixteen-year-old.

"I can do this. I went to college," Claire said as she opened the trunk. If she could ace her sociology final, she could absolutely change a tire. She pulled up the floormat. Where there should have been a tire, there was a crumpled energy drink can. What the hell, Luke? Now what?

Something moved behind her. She whirled around, grabbing the nearest object—a travel umbrella. What was that? Her shoulders tensed and her heart thudded in her ears. It had sounded like pebbles crunching underfoot.

"Who's there?" she called out, gruffer than usual. Her voice sounded unfamiliar to her own ears. One hand slid into her purse, and she searched past a spare dog leash, pack of sticky notes, and a dozen assorted pens until her fingers rested on the stun gun.

"If you're after money, you're going to be sorely disappointed," she called out to the empty parking lot. There was silence. She shut the useless trunk and put her back to the car.

"If you're in ESA, I'll be able to hear you coming because of your tiny, tiny balls clanging together like a Newton's Cradle." She took a step to the side. The vaguely threatening tree line was still, but she couldn't shake the feeling that there were eyes on her. All she had to do was get in the car and lock the door. Then she could call AAA. Or maybe she should run back to the ranch?

She took another step to the side and pivoted. Maybe it was all her imagination. But something inside was screaming at her to call the police.

Her phone was halfway out of her bag when she almost collided with a man leaning against her driver's side door.

CHAPTER FORTY

To Do:
- Panic

"*No!*" THE WORD RIPPED ITSELF FROM HER THROAT. IT WAS happening again. They had found her, tracked her like an animal. Luke was right to tell her to stay home. Was she going to die? Panic shot through her veins like ice.

Instinctively, she threw her purse at the man's head. He caught it by the strap and lowered it onto her hood. Her phone tumbled onto the dirt parking lot, and he grabbed it before she could even take a step forward.

Oh hell. She had just thrown every weapon in her arsenal at this stranger. Great job, idiot. Way to not panic.

"Hello, Claire. We've been waiting for you," the man said.

She was silent as she scanned every direction for assistance. Calculations bloomed in her brain like drops of blood. She could run back to the ranch, but he was clearly faster than her. She would never make it. What choice did that leave her?

"*Help*," she screamed. "*Fire!*" Surely one of the four million Angelenos would hear her. She repeated her cry for help. It reverberated off the hills, but there was no answering call.

The man glanced behind him, cocked his head. His arms were casually crossed in front of his scrawny chest, his posture relaxed. Why wasn't he worried? What did he know that she didn't?

"No one's going to come save you, Claire. We're in the middle of nowhere. Tweedle Dee and Tweedle Dum won't hear you this time. They're dealing with an incident." He gestured up the hill, where a plume of smoke was rising.

Numbness shot through her arms and nausea rose in a wave. Every cell in her body was screaming, screaming, screaming. *Get out.*

The man stood up straight. He took a step closer to her. Then another. She stepped back. What were her options?

"You're a hard girl to pin down. But you're going to come with me now." His eyes were blacker than night.

Her blood chilled. Never go to a second location. Her mom had drilled that into her ever since she was a child. If she left this parking lot, she was going to die. They would probably never find her body. Rosie would never know what happened to her. Luke would hunt them down and get himself killed in the process.

Snap out of it. What did she need to do? She had already stupidly thrown every potential weapon she had at him. She had no phone, no Taser or mace. On the off chance she made it out of this encounter alive, she needed to memorize his face. Keep him talking. Buy herself some time. The fire department would have to respond to the fire up the hill, wouldn't they? They would drive straight past them.

"That's not going to happen," she said, surprised at the lack of tremor in her voice. Her hand shook, and she clenched it into a fist. Could she incapacitate him and get her phone back? "You're going to get the fuck away from my car and leave this place, or my FBI agent father will personally make sure you go to prison for the rest of your cowardly life."

"Oh, we know all about your dad. Bit of a dick." The man took another step toward her. He was short, maybe 5'7". Skin pale as skim milk. His feet, clad in black sneakers, were too big for his body. Dark, greasy hair was matted to his head. His ears were too small, his nose too red. A toothpick rolled around in his mouth, and a flash of gold peeped from his gumline. A scar slashed through his left eyebrow.

She took a step back. He moved toward her. They marched around the car in a bizarre, waltz-like cadence, each of them keeping their eyes on the other. Maybe she could kick him in the balls and then make a run for it.

Without consulting her, her body hurled itself toward the mouth of the lot. She sprinted, arms pumping at her sides. The gate to the ranch was only fifteen feet away. If she could just get close to enough to call for help, she stood a chance of—

Something plowed into the side of her head. Pain hit her like a lightning bolt. She cried out as she sprawled, crashing to the dirt lot. She flipped onto her back. He crouched over her, and she aimed a kick at his face. The crunch of bone split the air, and blood poured from the man's nose. Great. Blood all over her sneakers. But that wouldn't matter if she was dead.

She threw another kick at his chest and toppled him to

the ground. A cloud of dust rose from the lane. Blood dripped onto the earth as she rolled onto her side and clambered to her feet. She lunged forward, but he caught her ankle, and she tumbled again onto the rocks. They bit into her skin, and her head stung from the impact.

He was already on her, his knee pressed heavily into her back. She writhed like an angry cat, summoning every ounce of strength. This wasn't going to be how she died.

"*Help*," she called out again. Her desperate screams echoed back at her. He was so heavy. He dragged her hands behind her back. Something cool and thin threaded her wrists. Oh, hell. He had zip-tied her. She kicked her legs, but her thumps to his back went unnoticed.

She shut her eyes and concentrated. Maybe her psychic mother could hear her somehow. She pictured Alice in her mind.

Help. Ranch. Help. Ranch. She repeated the words over and over again as the man tightened her bonds. *Come on, Mom.*

Suddenly, the man lifted her off the ground and tossed her over one shoulder. What he lacked in height, he certainly made up for in strength. He smelled like body odor and the cloying, sweet smell of a citrus energy drink that her ex Jason had been obsessed with for months.

She wiggled and wriggled with everything she had left, calling for help the whole way. Couldn't Brad and Goldie hear her?

Apparently unfazed by her best impression of a fish out of water, the man only held her harder. He carried her across the parking lot and a short way down the road. A nondescript white car sat under the shade of a tree. At least a bird had had the good manners to take a dump on the trunk lid.

"Help!" she yelled one final time before he dropped her into the trunk. Her last view of the world was a greasy, annoyed-looking man who hadn't even remembered to zip his fly.

God, it was hot in here. Panic was setting in. She was all but dead. What could she do? *Think, Claire.* Alice had gone over trunk abductions with her before. Sawyer had mentioned it in lessons too.

The car growled to life beneath her. Gravel crunched under the tires. This was it.

CHAPTER FORTY-ONE

To Do:
- Survive

IT WAS PITCH BLACK IN THE TRUNK, AND CLAIRE'S HANDS WERE still bound behind her back. Country music wailed from the front seat. She rolled her eyes. There was no way Conway Twitty was going to be the background music of her untimely death.

Oh, a left turn. So far that made two rights and a left. The drive was smoother now. They had to be on a highway. She was running out of time. There was no knowing what was at the end of this road. ESA made people disappear. Would she be tortured? Raped? No one knew where she was. No one even knew to look for her. If she somehow managed to survive, Luke would undoubtedly kill her.

Okay, this was Los Angeles. There were cars and people everywhere. All she needed was to kick the taillights out and wave at the cars behind them. Abduction 101. The drivers call the police, creepy dude gets pulled over, boom. Home in time for dinner. She could do this.

But there was a snag in her plan. Her hands were bound tightly behind her back. How was she supposed to yank up the corner of the carpet covering the taillights with no hands? She rolled onto her side and braced herself. The plastic bit into her wrists as she strained against the zip tie. It didn't budge. She tried again, harder this time, but didn't gain a centimeter. She was trapped.

She went limp even as her breath went ragged, coming in hitches.

Death had been in the back of her mind since the Barney incident. Prior to her first abduction, she had assumed that, like most people, she would live a long and plentiful life and die of old age surrounded by a crowd of loving grandchildren. If she died young, surely it would have been from doing something heroic, like saving dogs from a burning building or jumping in front of a bullet. She had never imagined that death would almost come in a dimly lit parking garage at the hands of a knife-wielding serial killer. Nothing could have prepared for her to face death again less than a year later.

Was this the end? Claire Hartley, dead at twenty-seven. Murdered by misogynists. She would never get married. Rosie and Winston would be orphans. She would never meet Nicole's baby. She would never again hug Luke so tight that he almost threw up.

Against her will, a tear slid down her cheek.

"No." She bit down hard on her bottom lip. She would not give this idiot the satisfaction of making her cry. "Focus, Claire," she scolded herself. Dr. Goulding's instructions came back to her. "Count to ten."

She counted, breathing deeply to slow her rapid heartbeat. She should have just agreed to take the stupid anxiety medication. Now was not the time for a panic attack. Slowly, painfully, the trembling subsided. Her heart eased to a slightly more normal pace, and the all-encompassing feeling of doom inched away.

She was not helpless. If she could bring her hands to her front, she would have options—punch out the taillight, break into the back seat, punch this asshole in his stupid, greasy face. She had done more complicated poses in yoga class.

The car hit a bump, and her head smacked off the carpet. At least when Barney had kidnapped her, she had been unconscious for her trunk ride. The smell of stale fast food wafted in from the back seat. Her stomach clenched.

She planted her feet and thrust her hips toward the lid of the trunk. Shit. This was never going to work. There wasn't enough room to maneuver.

The panic crept back in. *Think, Claire. Think.* There was always a solution. She wiggled and scooched until her elbow banged something metallic. She reached one hand out and felt the curved, metallic tip of a shovel. A dozen feelings hit her at the same time. Surely she could use this shovel to escape her bonds. But a shovel meant her captor meant to do some digging—probably six feet of digging, if she had to guess.

Her captor was now singing along, painfully out of tune. This idiot was not going to take her life. She flipped over and backed up until her bound hands reached the tip of the shovel. Plastic sawed against metal as she worked her wrists back and forth over and over again. Her arms burned. Her face ground against the scratchy carpet.

There was a light snap, and her wrists sprung apart.

They smarted like they had been burned. Claire flipped and wriggled toward the tail light. Her head brushed against something—a latch! Of course. Most trunks these days had a latch to open the back seat. Her fingers curled into a tight fist, and she pulled. The smallest click was barely audible over the country music droning from the driver's seat. The seat nearest her collapsed. The music grew louder, but her captor didn't notice over the drone of the radio.

Now what? Did she hit him with the shovel and try to incapacitate him? If he lost control of the car, she could hurt someone else. A tractor trailer rolled by the left window. The car bumped smoothly down the road. They were definitely on a highway. She stuck her head an inch into the back seat.

Aha! Flopped unceremoniously next to a greasy bag of Burger King was her purse. The tip of her mint-colored cell phone case stood out. She snatched the phone and retreated back into the trunk, pulling the back seat half closed behind her.

Her hands shook as she dialed 911.

"911, what is your emergency?" a calm female voice asked.

"I was abducted from Twilight Ranch approximately twenty minutes ago and placed in the trunk of a car. We were going south when we left the ranch, but now I'm not sure which direction we're going," Claire whispered into the phone.

"Okay, ma'am. Do you know your abductor?"

"Not him specifically, but it's kind of a complicated situation. I put away a serial killer in Pennsylvania and I'm here on business and some of his friends are mad at me and—"

"Okay, okay. We are working on tracking your location now. Is the car moving?"

"Yes."

"Can you safely exit the vehicle?" The operator's voice was careful now, more measured.

Claire glanced out the window. Telephone poles flashed by. "Not at this speed."

"Ma'am, we have your location. I am dispatching officers to you right away. Does he know you have your phone?"

Claire peeped through the hole into the back seat. Her attacker was slapping his hand on the steering wheel in time to the music. "No."

"Just hang tight, honey. Officers should be there in just a few minutes. Now I want you to stay on the line with me and tell me if anything changes. What's your name?"

As Claire rattled off her name and Luke's home address, her mind spiraled. Would he stop for officers? Would he simply kill her before they could pull him over? Would he hurt the cops too? If he was anything like Barney, he was capable of unimaginable horrors.

A click came from the front seat, and the rhythmic ticking of a turn signal sounded. *Shit*. They were turning off the highway. That must mean they were approaching whatever horrible, twisted place they were headed to.

"We're turning," Claire hissed into the phone. "I have to do something."

"Ma'am, I must advise you to stay calm and do nothing unless you are in imminent danger. The police will be arriving soon."

Imminent danger? Did being zip-tied and tossed in a trunk not count as imminent danger? Bullshit. The last time Claire had involved the police, a team of frat boys had nearly murdered her archnemesis. There wasn't any time to waste. She snaked one arm into the backseat and shoved her hand into her purse. Her fingers closed around the cool metal of a can of mace.

The car shifted. Her head popped up. Bridge struts flashed past the window. She raised her head just high enough to get a visual. They were in the exit lane—and who knew what lay beyond. Armed with the mace in one hand, she slithered into the back seat.

"Ma'am?" The operator called faintly from her phone. Claire tossed the phone into her purse. She leaned forward. For an abductor, this man was incredibly unobservant.

"Are we there yet?" She whispered in his ear before unloading the entire can of mace.

Shit. That was a mistake. The cloud of pepper spray engulfed her, burning her eyes and lungs.

Her captor swore and jerked the wheel. The car smashed into something and tilted into the air like the Titanic before it sank. Suddenly, there was a feeling of weightlessness. The nose of the car tipped down. Through her streaming eyes, a graffitied support structure was barely visible sticking out of some water. Was that a cartoon penis? Seriously, universe?

Oh, god. They were going to crash. Would the water be deep enough for her to survive? She would still die, but at least not at the hands of a bunch of sociopath frat boys. Luke was going to be so angry.

Splash. The car hit the river with ten times the force of the log flume rides Claire had loved in her youth. Untethered, she slammed into the back of the front seat, still coughing and sputtering from the cloud of pepper spray.

"Oh my god, I'm going to die." Her idiot captor cried in exaggerated, short gasps, like someone being chainsawed in a horror movie. He fought with his seatbelt, eyes streaming and red. He coughed violently as he pulled on the door handle. Good.

The car bobbled in the river. Water poured in from the door cracks and hood. They were sinking. Great.

Okay, what were the rules of escaping a sinking car? She had definitely watched a *MythBusters* episode on this. She closed her eyes, gasping through the burn of the pepper in her lungs.

"Wait until the car sinks, then open the door," she whispered to herself. Could that really be right? Something about equalizing pressure. If she was wrong, she was going to drown in the Los Angeles river. It wasn't even a real river, with lush banks full of wildflowers and ducks. Solid slabs of concrete funneled the river downstream.

The water line was halfway up the windows now. The shoreline shrank behind a wall of muddy water. Apprehension grew. Would she really survive this? Even if she made it out of the car, could she swim to the shore?

Water poured into the vehicle. Her feet and ankles were soaked. The smell of mud and vegetation instantly transported her back to the Jet Ski proposal she had coordinated in a river back home. But there would be no tuxedo-wetsuit-wearing groom coming to her rescue today.

The man ripped furiously at his seatbelt.

"Ma'am?" The voice from her purse was louder now. The operator must have been practically shouting.

"Sorry, sorry," Claire choked out over the burn in her esophagus. "I pepper sprayed him and the car crashed into the river."

There was a sigh on the other end of the phone. She faintly heard the operator requesting the fire department and water rescue.

"Claire, what I need you to do is—"

"This is your fault!" The man lashed out with his right hand. It clipped Claire across the face, and her phone tumbled into the murky water.

She searched frantically through the water, which was now up to her waist. By the time her waterlogged phone emerged from the depths, it was dead. Her only link to the outside world was gone. She was trapped in a fast-sinking car with a homicidal maniac.

"My fault?" She coughed as the water reached her elbows. "You're the one who kidnapped me!"

"You deserve much worse than a watery grave," the man hissed. He blinked almost constantly in the rearview mirror, but there was no mistaking the malice in his eyes.

"Oh, fuck you." She slung her soggy purse across her shoulder and tossed her dead phone inside. Nothing a bowl of rice couldn't fix. Assuming she lived.

Her captor wrenched his seatbelt back and forth, vinyl scraping against plastic, but it didn't budge. For once, karma was delivering justice.

Where was it? She dug around in her now-muddy purse. Tablet. Breath mints. Sticky notes. Dog treats. Aha! The combination flashlight/seatbelt cutter/window breaker Alice had given her four years ago. Her entire life now rested in the hands of a product she had never intended to review on Amazon, much less use in an emergency.

The water brushed her chin and goosebumps scattered up and down her arms. Sunlight dappled on the water as the muddy river crept ever higher up the windshield. She turned the flashlight on and clipped it to her purse. Her chin tipped to the ceiling, and she took slow, measured breaths. Her limbs trembled. Adrenaline surged in her veins. At least the burn was subsiding from her eyes.

Her captor was now openly hyperventilating and crying in his seat. The crash must have damaged his buckle.

Claire paused, hand on her emergency tool. Could she let him die? Would she watch another human being drown in front of her? If anyone deserved to die, it was this idiot. Wouldn't one less murderer in the world be a good thing?

The last of the daylight slipped out of view as the car sank below water level. This was it. The water crept up the man's chin, covered his mouth. His eyes opened wide, pleading with her in the rearview mirror.

She clutched the tool, frozen to the spot. The plastic pressed into her hand. She had seconds to make this decision.

Did he have a family? Would a cop knock on his mother's door to tell her that her son was dead? And someone could have saved him but chose not to?

"Fuck." Claire floated between the front seats. The water was almost to the ceiling. She took a deep breath and plunged beneath the flood, feeling around blindly until she located his lap belt. Everything was muffled.

She aimed the blade and sawed. Seconds passed. Was it working? She opened her eyes, but all she could see was muddy water and the faint glow of her flashlight.

She had waited too long. Now she was going to drown right alongside this idiot. She sawed again, harder and faster. Seconds crept by. Something gave. The man thrashed and flung the severed belt aside. Claire swam to the back seat and felt around until she located the handle. Her captor was on his own now.

She yanked on the latch until the door opened, drifting on its hinges. She kicked off the sideboard and surged into the river. Her lungs screamed for air.

Something caught her ankle, and she gasped. Bubbles of

the breath that burned in her lungs drifted in front of her, rushing to the surface. Particles of mud swirled around rays of sun. She kicked. Her heel connected with something, and the weight around her ankle left. She kicked violently, surging toward the surface.

Her head broke through, and she gasped, sucking down the smog-polluted air like it was a glass of chilled rosé on a sultry summer evening. The river current dragged at her as she took breath after breath, dizzy with relief. Oxygen rushed into her lungs, invigorating her. She bobbled in the water, floating like an overdressed cork. Time to reassess.

Sirens wailed above her. The traffic on the bridge had stopped. The guard rail above was warped as if it had melted in the sun. A beady-eyed blue heron lurked beneath the bridge.

She wasn't a great swimmer. Never had been. But she sure as hell wasn't about to drown in a dirty concrete river in Los Angeles. Not after everything she had faced. Stubbornly driving one arm into the water and then the other, she swam to the bank.

Her waterlogged sneakers squelched as she climbed to her feet. There was a one hundred percent chance that she looked like a drowned sewer rat. Her phone and tablet were surely fried. But by some miracle, she was alive.

Where was he? The thought hit her like a lightning bolt. Cops and firefighters swarmed down the sides of the bridge. She whirled around. It was difficult to make out at this distance, but she could swear a pair of wet footprints went up the opposite bank and disappeared. Son of a bitch.

CHAPTER FORTY-TWO

To Do:
- *Apologize to Luke*
- *Call Dr. Goulding*

"I'm confused. Do you want to die? Is that why you keep doing this?" Luke paced across the living room.

Claire sighed. Her clothes still smelled like river water, and she had spent hours in the police station. This had undoubtedly been the worst week of her life—fired, arrested, abducted. Even worse than the time Barney had tried to kill her, or when Jason cheated on her with Wendy. She was at rock bottom. And now her one true love was shouting at her.

"No, I just—"

"I'm not done," he interrupted. "Do you have any idea what it's like to come out of a meeting expecting to celebrate with your girlfriend and then instead find out that she took advantage of my absence by sneaking away—"

"To work—" she clarified.

He jabbed a finger at her. "Brad fired you. This wasn't work."

Ouch. It would have hurt less if he had slapped her in the face. But he wasn't done.

"You went to spy on him to see how badly he was messing things up. And you snuck away when you know full well there's an entire team of homicidal maniacs trying to kill you. And when I specifically told you not to leave the house alone."

She waved her hands. "I'm sorry that I'm unemployed and don't feel like waiting around all day for you to get out of your meeting."

"It went great, by the way. Thanks for asking." His beat-up high tops screeched against the hardwood. She would never get used to the business casual dress code in LA.

She bit her lip. She hadn't even asked about the meeting. Not okay. "Tell me mo—"

"I'm not done." He whirled on her again. His normally styled hair was sticking up like he had driven home in a convertible. "It's disrespectful to me, to Mindy, to your mom—"

"Oh god. My mom. You didn't tell her, did you?"

"Of course I told her. She's furious."

Claire swore. It was a good thing her waterlogged phone was dead because Alice would surely be blowing it up. If she hadn't already called the National Guard and arranged for Claire to join the Witness Protection Program.

"This isn't just about you." Shadows hung beneath his eyes. He had aged a decade since that morning. "It's about me. And Nicole and Mindy and the dogs." He pointed to the corner, where Winston was lying upside down in yet another new dog bed. Rosie rested next to him, snoot on his belly.

"We need you. And we need you to start taking this seriously. You're being selfish. I know you want to pretend like everything's normal and you can just run off and do whatever you want, but that's not our reality. A stranger incapacitated you and threw you in a fucking trunk today. You could have died. You're in danger, Claire. All the time."

"*I know*." She jumped to her feet, hands balled into tight fists. The bubbles of rage had grown the longer Luke talked. "I know I'm in danger. Trust me, no one ever lets me forget it. 'Don't go to the grocery store, Claire, someone might jump out of the green bean pyramid and chloroform you,'" she mimicked in a near-perfect impression of Alice.

Luke's eyes smoldered. She frowned.

"I'm sorry, okay?" She folded her arms across her chest. As much as she hated to admit it, she could really use a hug right now.

"Sorry's not good enough." His voice was quiet now. There was so much in his sea green eyes—hurt, exhaustion, worry. "You know, even when you're here, you're not here."

"What's that supposed to mean?" Was this Air All Your Grievances with Claire Day?

"You're so obsessed with work that—"

She laughed. "Me? Obsessed with work? Coming from the guy who locks his office down and refuses to talk to anyone while working on a project?"

"You have no boundaries with your clients. It's killing you right now, isn't it? Wondering if Brad is trying to call, begging you to work for him again. So he can call you every four minutes trying to change the color of a horse or the shape of a firework or—"

"Well, you don't have to worry about that anymore, since as you so kindly pointed out, he fired me." This wasn't the tearful reunion with her boyfriend that she had imagined. She had known he would be mad, but this was another level —a hurtful one.

They both stared at each other.

Luke rolled his shoulders back and cracked his neck. "I've hired a private security team," he said quietly. "They should be here any minute."

This shit again. "Luke, I don't need private security. Remember I had a PI and police detail the first time I got abducted."

"You do need them. Because I won't be here."

A ball of lead dropped into her stomach. "What do you mean?"

"I'm going to stay at a hotel. I can't keep watching you do this. I can't be in love with someone who doesn't care if she lives or dies."

The weight of his words hit her like a Mack truck. What was he saying?

"Luke, please—"

"It's done, Claire. I'll talk to you in a few days." He turned and left the room without looking back.

The room echoed with his absence.

She collapsed onto the couch. This couldn't be happening. Her entire world was crumbling beneath her. She was losing count of the number of times douchey frat boys had tried to kill her. Her biggest client had fired her. And Luke had just effectively dumped her. Where could she go from here?

Dog tags jingled. Rosie jumped onto the couch next to her and shoved her head under Claire's arm. She sighed like she had been the one with the long day.

Her throat still burned from the pepper spray. Claire reached for her glass of water, but her fingers were trembling too hard.

Smash. Water splashed her feet. Glass shards glistened on the floor.

Perfect. Just perfect. She dropped to her knees and picked up the shards, cradling them in her palm. A creeping sense of doom was setting in.

"Stay," she said to Rosie and Winston. She'd run the vacuum cleaner over the hardwood floors to suck up the tiny fragments.

The edges of her vision blurred as she tossed the glass into the garbage can. One of the shards sliced across her finger.

"Ouch."

A well of crimson rose, dribbling down her finger onto the floor. She gripped the sink and breathed forcefully through her nose, willing her galloping heart to settle. Her hands shook.

There was a clatter behind her. Something wheeled across the tiles in the entryway. So he really was leaving. The wheels paused for a moment, and she lifted her head. A sliver of moon peered back at her through the kitchen window.

Would he change his mind? The front door opened, then slammed shut. The silence in the house was palpable.

She was alone.

The weight of the day hit her all at once. Tears she had been holding back for weeks dribbled messily down her cheeks. Her chest heaved, and she bit her tongue to fight back the sobs that threatened to erupt. Blood dripped into the sink, swirling with water and disappearing down the drain.

How much more was she expected to take? Her knees gave out, and she slid down the cabinet until she sprawled on the floor.

The pitter-patter of paws announced Rosie and Winston's entrance. Rosie laid her snoot on Claire's trembling thigh and whined. Winston plowed into the kitchen island before curling up at Claire's side.

She had almost died today. And it was partially her fault. Why didn't she just wait? What had she even gained from today? Sure, Brad's proposal was falling apart. It was what she had hoped for. But that didn't give her the satisfaction she thought it would.

The only "win" was unmasking another member of ESA. Her eyes closed. In fact, she would never forget that face. The cold eyes, the humorless smile. Contempt oozing from every pore. Hooked nose. Greasy, matted hair. Eyes blacker than coal.

Her heartbeat sped up to a full gallop, and pain flared across her chest. Was she having a heart attack on top of everything?

"Count to ten," she instructed herself sternly. She counted, taking deep breaths. "I am not dying." The chest pain begged to differ. Maybe she should call Dr. Goulding.

Oh, wait, that was right. She couldn't call Dr. Goulding. She couldn't call anyone, actually. Her waterlogged phone was sitting in a bowl of rice on the counter.

Forcing breaths in and out, she climbed to her feet. Her laptop sat on the island. She connected to the Wi-Fi and made a video call.

Dr. Goulding answered, bags under her eyes. "Claire? Everything all right?"

Claire took a deep breath and pressed a hand to her chest. "Do you have a minute? I need your help."

CHAPTER FORTY-THREE

To Do:
- *Keep breathing*
- *Instacart some ice cream*

A KNOCK AT THE FRONT DOOR DRAGGED CLAIRE FROM HER sleep prison. The dogs went wild. Rosie leapt off the couch and sprinted for the foyer. Claire pried her eyes open and stared accusingly at the ceiling. Her neck ached from sleeping on Luke's Sylvester Stallone pillow. It smelled like him. Luke, that is. Not Sylvester Stallone.

She had fallen asleep on the couch, but at least her makeshift sweatshirt handcuffs had prevented her from sleepwalking. The floorboards creaked as she rose to her feet. A shower of crumbs rained down her front. A box of Triscuits lay discarded on the floor.

What fresh hell awaited her today? Maybe she'd be accidentally guillotined, or the government would come claim eminent domain over the house. She trudged to the front door and peered through the peephole.

Sunlight streamed down, glinting in her sister Charlie's hair. Claire pulled the door open.

With a pizza box perched on one shoulder, Charlie tapped one foot on the porch and craned her neck, casting a sweeping glance over the front yard. A black Toyota with a SoCal Security sticker stood at the curb. Mr. Nesbit, the neighbor with the golden retriever, was watering his hydrangeas. Several inches of pasty flesh were visible above his knees. Those were some short shorts.

"Hey," Claire said simply.

"Hey," Charlie echoed. She handed over a crinkly pharmacy bag and pursed her lips. Her eyebrows were drawn together.

"You promised no lectures." Claire turned away from the door and made for the kitchen.

Charlie sighed and followed her. "I had to show my driver's license to the guy out there. I half expected him to ask for my DNA."

Claire declined to comment. The security person stationed outside had introduced himself via her video doorbell the previous evening after Luke's departure. The security team's presence at the curb was a blatant reminder of the fact that she had driven away the only man she had ever truly loved. All because she just couldn't get it together.

Charlie's espadrilles tapped the herringbone floor. Apparently she hadn't received the unwritten "shoes off in the house" memo. "Did you try your phone?"

"Not yet." Claire eyed the bowl of rice. As long as her phone was out of commission, there was no need for her to engage with the sure-to-be-endless barrage of texts and emails.

"Try it. We'll get you another one if it's dead. Can't have you phone-less with a squad of hitmen after you." Charlie was never one to mince words.

"Yes, Mom," Claire grumbled.

"So," Charlie said as Claire withdrew an orange bottle from the paper bag.

Claire braced herself. She had only texted Charlie because she didn't have it in her to go to the pharmacy and pick up these stupid anti-anxiety meds for herself. The thought of going outside and facing the world made her stomach twist.

"I Googled the name of your medication," Charlie said tentatively. How uncharacteristic.

Claire raised an eyebrow.

"Sounds like something you should have been on for a long time. Things must be pretty bad if you're finally agreeing to take them." Charlie sat the pizza on the island between them like a peace offering. Rosie danced on her tiptoes, aiming her snoot in the direction of the pie.

Silence stretched. The orange bottle was a grenade in her hand. If she opened this idiotic, fluorescent orange cylinder, it was over. She was admitting that she had a problem. One that couldn't be fixed by alternate nostril breathing or sun salutations. A panic disorder, Dr. Goulding had said.

"I messed up," Claire said. "Brad fired me and I just... went a little crazy."

Charlie set her purse on the counter and swung her long legs onto a bar stool. "Tell me what happened."

Claire slumped into a chair next to her sister and told her the whole story in intimate detail, from spying on Brad to the abduction to Luke leaving.

"I think this is my rock bottom." Claire ran a finger over

the red mark on her wrist. The police had cut off her zip ties, but she still felt their burn. "I don't think it can get any worse. Can it?" She looked to the ceiling, half expecting to see a meteor hurtling toward the house.

"Things are pretty shitty, I'll give you that." Charlie's eyes were bloodshot. She had traded in her standard tailored pantsuit for a pair of white capris and a rumpled button-up blouse. There was a stain on one shoulder. She leaned back in her chair and folded her hands in her lap. "I'm not going to boss you around and tell you what to do, because I think you already know what you need to do." She glanced pointedly at the prescription bottle.

Claire grunted and popped the top off the bottle. She chased one of the round white pills with a swallow of water. There. She had done it. She paused, waiting for some monumental shift in her worldview, but there was nothing.

Charlie stood and slung her purse back over her shoulder. "Come on."

"Come on where?" Claire was in no state to go into public. Her mass of curls had globbed into an untrimmed bush perched on her head. Her leggings had an ice cream stain on them.

Charlie glanced at her watch. "You have ten minutes to make yourself presentable. We're going out."

Claire crossed her arms. Had Charlie literally not just said she wasn't going to boss Claire around? That promise had barely lasted five seconds. "I don't really feel like leaving the house right now. I was abducted less than twenty-four hours ago, you know."

Charlie plunged one hand into the mound of rice and pulled out Claire's phone. Her baby blue eyes cut like lightning. "We're Hartleys, Claire. Hartleys don't hide from the world and pout."

What if she wanted to hide from the world and pout? Hadn't she earned that? If ever there was a day to hide under a blanket, it was today. But it would be too much effort to keep refusing Charlie. One way or another, Charlie always got what she wanted.

Claire let out an exasperated sigh and stomped through the kitchen and up the stairs. By the time she came back downstairs, Charlie had cleaned the kitchen, taken out the dogs, and, from the looks of it, alphabetized her spice rack. Apparently she was going to have to wait for pizza.

"Well? Where are we going?" Claire asked as she shut the door behind her and ushered the dogs down the front steps.

"Please." Charlie darted across the lawn and rapped on the window of the black sedan. The window rolled down, and she exchanged a few words. The engine fired up.

Claire slammed the car door and slumped in Charlie's passenger seat. Rosie shook in the backseat, sending a cloud of fur over the interior of the Lexus.

A field trip was the last thing she needed. If she wasn't going to be allowed to pout, she needed to figure out her next steps. Did she go home and move her things out of Luke's house? Where would she go? Mindy was living in Claire's old apartment. Oh god, was she going to have to move to Florida and live with her mom? Alice would certainly love that. She shuddered.

"What?" Charlie asked. The car roared to life, and a finance podcast droned from the speakers.

Claire twiddled the dial. "Am I going to have to move in with Mom?"

Charlie cringed. She swung out of the driveway and headed east. "Let's not worry about that right now. We're going to give Luke a couple days to cool off and change his mind."

"And if he doesn't?" Her voice was barely more than a whisper.

"Then fuck him." Charlie slid her sunglasses over her eyes.

Easy to say for someone who had married their college sweetheart and never regretted a single day. A lead ball the size of an eggplant lurked in Claire's stomach. Not even the determinedly cheery California sun could lift her mood. She wasn't ready to start all over again. She had done it after leaving Jason, and it had nearly destroyed her. The vision of her engagement ring pinging off Jason's nose was still fresh in her mind.

She stared at the bare spot on her left ring finger. If she was being honest with herself, she thought that in a year or two she and Luke would be engaged. As much as they drove each other crazy, she couldn't imagine a life without waking up to his stupid, smug face every morning.

And now she would be forced to. And this time, she wouldn't have her friends at her beck and call whenever she needed a pick-me-up. Charlie and Bri would be in California. Nicole didn't need Claire's drama while she was growing a tiny human. And Mindy was attached to Sawyer like a fleshy backpack. Claire was on her own.

Her phone blipped. Her breath caught in her chest. Messages streamed through, and her phone vibrated continuously as Charlie dropped the dogs off at daycare. Claire flipped through them, but none of them were from Luke. There must have been thirty from her mother alone. Her lead eggplant constricted, and she dropped her phone into her purse.

"Phone works," Claire announced as Charlie climbed back inside.

"Good. Guess who apparently stopped by daycare earlier today looking for the dogs?"

Panic gripped Claire's chest. Who was it? ESA?

"Sorry," Charlie said quickly. "It was Luke. Not a bad guy."

Claire's fingers shook as they curled around the grab handle over her door. It was like a faucet inside her had been switched off. The grief vanished, replaced almost instantly with white hot rage. Her lips pursed so hard she could practically feel the fine lines etching themselves into her face.

"Was he trying to take the dogs from me? He has the audacity to dump me after I've been abducted, and then he's going to take my babies? So help me, I will fly them home to Pennsylvania and he will never see them again. Go back." Claire pointed at the daycare center behind them. "I need to revoke his visitation rights."

Charlie ignored her and merged onto the highway. How she did it without screaming and panicking, Claire would never know.

"I love this energy," Charlie said, "but he wasn't trying to take the dogs. He brought them treats and just asked if he could see them."

Claire made a mental note to track down his car at the studio and fill his backseat with their poo. Maybe even a bee hive. That would teach him.

"He left me," she said. "He doesn't get to be a part of their lives. Can he sue me for joint custody?" If this went to court, she would lose the dogs on top of everything. She couldn't afford to hire a lawyer, and Kyle was sure to take Luke's side.

Charlie cast a glance in Claire's direction. "You're spiraling. He's not going to take your dogs, and he'd never take you to court."

"Whatever." Claire crossed her arms and stared out the window. This morning had been a rollercoaster of emotions. "Are you going to tell me where the hell we're going? I have things to do, you know."

"Do you?" Charlie looked at her over the rim of her oversized sunglasses. "I thought you were funemployed."

"Do you want me to jump out of this car?" Claire put a hand on the latch.

"Stop being a drama queen. We're almost there."

As dire as her business and romantic life were, a new itch had been working its way under her skin. As Charlie had not-so-kindly pointed out, for the first time in years, Claire had a stretch of free time. A deep dive into ESA beckoned. They had taken everything from her, and she was going to make them pay.

"Where the hell are we?" Her thoughts of revenge came to a halt when Charlie parked outside a building with metal siding. A chain-link fence with barbed wire stood behind the business.

"Bash Bar," Charlie said, pointing to the sign. "Did you lose your ability to read?"

Claire shot her a dirty look. "What is this place?"

"I do lunch here once a week," Charlie said, twisting her curls into a knot at the back of her head. "I hope you put deodorant on today."

Claire sniffed her armpit, then shrugged. Who cared? She had no clients, no boyfriend. She didn't know anyone in this city besides Mr. Nesbit and the guys at the pizza place. And Brad, of course, who was effectively dead to her.

"Come on." Charlie opened the front door.

Brilliant paint colors assaulted Claire's eyeballs. Comic book style murals with callouts lined one wall. A bar stood to their left, a handful of patrons wearing safety goggles, white suits, and holding cocktails. A sledgehammer stood next to a redhead. A metal baseball bat rested across a man's lap.

Claire's spine tingled. What was this place? She ran a hand over the stained oak bar.

"Hey, Charlie. The usual?" The bartender, a bearded stud in an open flannel shirt, asked.

"Not today." She glanced above the bar, where a series of signature cocktails were written in chalk. "We're going to have two Ex-Boyfriends."

The bartender nodded and picked up a cocktail shaker.

"So, did you bring me here to kill me?" Claire nodded at the patrons with weapons.

"Tempting, but no. This is a rage room." Charlie grabbed two sheets from a stack of papers on the bar and slid one to Claire.

"Oh, wow." She should have known. One had opened up in West Haven the week before they left for California. "What's this?"

"A waiver. Don't worry. I only get cut once every couple of weeks."

"Great," Claire said. Just what she needed. She signed the waiver and pushed it away from her without bothering to read it. Who cared what she had just signed away? Did she really need two kidneys?

Ten minutes later, Charlie pushed two drinks at Claire. "Hurry up. Our time slot is in five minutes."

Claire set a golf club and tire iron on the empty stool next to her. The white safety suit was itchy against her skin, and the goggles pressed into her forehead. She took the drinks without comment and downed one in a few gulps. They were definitely strong. She probably should have checked to see if her new medication could be mixed with alcohol. Oh well.

Warmth spread to her fingertips, and she slouched in her stool. Things weren't so bad. It was a beautiful, sunny day. She had all of her limbs. Her dogs were safe. Sure, she had been almost murdered a shocking number of times. Frat boys had blown up her car and burned down her business. Luke had dumped her. She had been fired from the biggest project of her career. Her ex-boyfriend had had to bail out the animal shelter she was supposed to be saving. She was failing on every level—personally, professionally, romantically.

Okay, never mind. Things were still awful. She downed the second drink for good measure, then followed Charlie across the room to a set of double doors. A man led them down a narrow hallway. They passed small rooms full of broken electronics. He held open one of the doors, and Claire entered.

A row of kitschy little girl figurines smiled eerily at her in a row on the floor. A stack of decorative plates stood next to them. Shards of glass glittered in every corner.

She took a step back and bumped into Charlie. She jumped.

"Okay," Charlie said, taking Claire by the shoulders. "I want you to take a moment and think about how unfair everything is."

"That implies that I ever took a break from thinking about how unfair everything is. It's a twenty-four-seven pity party right now." Claire drove the head of the golf club into the plywood floor.

"Just humor me. Conjure up all those feelings you've been failing miserably at hiding."

"This is why I love you, Charlie. You're so warm and nurturing."

"Shut up." Charlie squeezed her arm and left the room.

Claire stood in the center of the room. Plywood covered the side walls. Concrete blocks made up the back wall. Gleaming breakables were waiting to be destroyed. Eyes closed, she took a deep breath. Feelings, right. God, they were the worst. The last thing she wanted was to dredge up all her feelings. She didn't have time for the weary baggage of emotions.

Luke's face surfaced in her mind, sporting a cheeky half-smile the way he did when she talked about a proposal and he was about to point out something wrong with her logic.

No—she couldn't think about him. It was too painful. Think of something else.

Brad's punchable face swam up next. Her fingers tightened around the golf club. She had given him everything—all her free time, her very best ideas. Countless dates postponed or missed because he had a last-minute change. She had fought with the city of Los Angeles, called in every favor she was owed. And where did it get her? Fired. Disgraced.

As unwelcome as a cockroach in a deli, her abductor's face appeared next. Her breath stilled. Who the hell was he? Would he ever be brought to justice? Why was it that ESA had a million chapters and were probably responsible for hundreds of disappearances, and the FBI couldn't manage to find a single one of their members? Was she supposed to do everything? Why was she planning proposals, confronting murderers, kidnapping her nemesis to prevent her from being killed, and tracking down the members of this terror group all by herself? Why couldn't everyone just leave her the fuck alone?

"AHHHHH!" Claire swung the golf club back and brought it down smoothly, the way her stepdad Roy had taught her. She opened her eyes in time to see one of the creepy little girl figures shatter into a thousand pieces against the concrete wall.

Oh, that felt good. She tossed the golf club to the side and picked up another figurine.

"Burn in *hell*," she shouted. The figurine flew across the room. Shards pinged off the wall.

Her hands shook at her sides. Something was happening inside her. Everything she had been shoving down since Barney's abduction was rumbling to the surface. Fragments of memories went zinging past—the day her father left, waking up in the parking garage, Luke pulling that damn tandem bike into a proposal, Wendy winning Planner of the Year.

An unintelligible roar escaped her throat. She picked up the metal baseball bat and attacked the first thing she saw— an industrial copier. Expletive after expletive poured out as she beat the hell out of the stupid equipment. Pieces of plastic went flying. The screen cracked like an egg. Dents littered the sides. Still, she couldn't stop.

Her arms burned with the effort. She dropped the bat and picked up the stack of plates. That knot and whirl on the plywood side wall sure looked like Luke's face. She aimed the first plate. One by one they exploded against the wooden imitation of Luke.

How dare he? After everything she had been through? And everything they had been through together? How could he leave her now, when she needed him more than ever? She loved him, and he had left her. She should never have abandoned her sex embargo and let him into her heart. Men only led to trouble.

Claire whirled, searching the floor. She was ankle-deep in debris, but there was nothing left to break. Her chest heaved. Sweat streamed into her eyes. She marched over to the door and ripped it open.

"You," she boomed, startling a man in the hallway. "Get me more stuff to break. Please," she added as an afterthought. There was no need to be rude just because she was having a breakthrough.

"Yes, ma'am."

CHAPTER FORTY-FOUR

To Do:
- *Take the stupid meds*
- *Drink more water*

THE HOUSE WAS EMPTY AND SILENT EXCEPT FOR THE TIP-TAP of dog toenails. Charlie had left to pick up Ryan for lacrosse practice. Claire went through the first floor, systematically snapping all the curtains shut. The skin on her wrist still burned where zip ties had held her captive barely twenty-four hours ago. If Luke were here, he would undoubtedly have some top secret Navy salve for treating it.

But she was alone. Exhausted and raw, like a freshly peeled potato.

In the living room, she dragged her laptop close and flicked on the TV, then perused the list of recorded shows. Why did Luke insist on recording every episode of *The Sopranos*? She mashed the delete button until they were all gone. Finally, Alice's TV show appeared. Maybe a little bit of psychic nonsense was just what she needed.

Her mother droned about a departed parakeet reaching out from the great beyond as Claire opened her web browser. She resisted the urge to check Luke's Instagram and instead opened a new document. Short of begging on her hands and knees, there wasn't anything she could do about Luke or her career at the moment. She was done being victimized, threatened, harassed, abducted. Screw them all. She was going to that convention. Luke wasn't going to be around to stop her.

A knock at the door peeled her eyes away from the computer. A prickle of fear tingled her spine. But surely the security staff wouldn't have allowed a stranger to approach the front door. Easing herself off the couch, she opened the doorbell app on her phone. Brianna. She breathed a sigh of relief and trudged to the front door.

"Did Charlie send you to check on me?" Claire said as a way of greeting.

"No, no. I'm here of my own accord." Brianna shoved a Tupperware container at her and drew her into a tight hug. Coconut shampoo and spearmint gum lingered in the air. She drew back and took Claire by both arms. "Are you okay?"

Claire raised one eyebrow.

"I mean, all things considered." Brianna nudged Claire inside and shut the door behind them. Rosie and Winston surrounded Brianna, sniffing and demanding pets.

Claire hesitated, fully prepared to put on a brave face and insist that everything was fine, that tomorrow would be better, there were great things in store. But she wasn't sure of any of that anymore. Her lip quivered, but she straightened her shoulders and took a deep breath.

"It sucks. All of it. But at least I'm not dead."

Brianna bit her lip and gave her another hug. Cupcakes jostled in the container as she took it back from Claire and stepped lightly down the hall to the kitchen. She tossed her tote-sized purse and a reusable shopping bag on the kitchen island and started piling vegetables and more Tupperware containers into Claire's fridge.

"Bri, you didn't have to do any of that." Claire's shoulders slumped. It was unclear if it was the rage room or the crushing weight of her failure, but either way she was utterly exhausted.

Brianna turned around, head of lettuce in one hand and container of salmon fillets in the other. "I know you don't like to ask for help. Or even admit to yourself that you need it. So instead, I, your overbearing half sister, am here to inconvenience you with company and food. We're having salmon and spinach salad for dinner. I had a feeling you might need some protein and, you know, vitamins."

"Thank you. Truly. I'm grateful to not be alone tonight."

"Good. Now where is your washer and dryer? I want to do your sheets so you have a nice, clean bed to sleep in tonight." For a twenty-one-year-old, Brianna was almost suspiciously thoughtful. That had certainly come from Tanya.

Claire showed Brianna where everything was, then retired to the living room. She had a video chat scheduled with Mindy. It was time to figure out their next steps. She couldn't keep holding out hope that Brad would call and beg her to come back. He was dead to her. It was time to move forward.

Claire rubbed at her temples. The Ex-Boyfriends on an empty stomach had been great for her rage but weren't so great for adulting. She took a swig of water and opened her laptop.

"Hey," she said when Mindy answered the call. Mindy and Nicole had sent a barrage of texts and phone calls after the abduction, but Claire had only sent a few updates in response. She had a sneaking suspicion that Charlie had been intervening for her since the flood of questions had slowed to an ebb.

Mindy's hair was a veritable rat's nest, and her face was red. Somewhere in the room, there was the sound of a zipper being zipped. At least someone was having a successful relationship. "Hey, yourself. How are you?"

Claire held up the okay sign. "Awesome. Really good. About to write a self-help book on how to be super well-adjusted and successful."

Mindy pursed her lips. "All right, Sarcasm Queen. I have a feeling you don't want to talk about emotions right now. Can I show you our options?"

Claire nodded, relieved to think of anything but the trauma of the past two days, and Mindy screen-shared details on six different couples. Three couples from West Haven and three from Los Angeles had passed the initial questionnaire.

"So," Mindy concluded. "Though it would be annoying to get scuba-certified, I really think we could do something amazing at the Scranton Aquarium for Todd and Leslie. And we wouldn't have to worry about the cost of renting items since we wouldn't have had anything we need for this one anyway."

"I love that," Claire mumbled, only half-focused as her mind spiraled with ideas. "Greenlight the stalking phase for Todd and Leslie. I'll get in touch with the manager at the aquarium in the meantime."

"What do you want to do about our California couples?" Mindy asked.

Claire sat back on the couch and tucked her feet under her. The thought of choosing another couple to be her first California proposal tugged at her heartstrings. This wasn't the way it was supposed to be. She shook away the haunting image of a sunset proposal with the glow of the Hollywood sign in the background and refocused. Her failure with Brad didn't mean she couldn't still create something beautiful.

"Well, I love Darius and Nick. But the logistics might be tricky. I kind of doubt the U.S. Figure Skating organization will be cool with me effectively hijacking one of their events."

Mindy tapped a pen against her lips. "You never know until you ask."

"True. And if all else fails, we can still rent it out, stage a fake exhibition, plant family members in the audience, and score an amazing musical guest."

"There's my girl." Mindy slapped her desk. "Glad to see you're feeling better."

She wasn't, really. But it helped to have something else to focus on.

"If you reach out to the couples, I'll start the dream boards, and we'll go over our ideas in a couple days. Sound good?"

Mindy nodded. "Have you heard from Luke?"

An icepick jabbed Claire's heart. "No."

Mindy crossed her arms. Her face grew sullen, more drawn. "If you want me to hit him with my car, just give the word."

"I'll keep you on speed dial," Claire said with a smile that she didn't feel.

"Love you. Text me."

Claire nodded and disconnected. She leaned back on the couch and pressed her palms over her eyes. The smell of pan-seared salmon wafted in from the kitchen, and her stomach growled.

Luke had assumed the responsibility of cooking while Claire handled Brad's case. He was surprisingly competent in the kitchen, but then he seemed to excel at everything he did. It was incredibly annoying. Her fingers tensed. His absence was like a bruise.

How could he have done this? Sure, she had "disobeyed" him. But he wasn't her boss. They weren't married. He couldn't just tell her she wasn't allowed to leave the house alone. It wasn't the 1850s. She didn't need a chaperone.

Her heart beat uncomfortably fast. In spite of his douchebaggery, she missed him. The scrape of his calloused hands over her body as he tended to her near-constant stream of various wounds. That stupid scar on his neck from pulling Olivia out of a burning car. His rarely flashed thousand-watt smile. The grumpy, protective superiority. He was flawed, but he was hers. Or at least he had been before she got herself abducted. Again.

"Appetizer?"

Claire shrieked and opened her eyes. Brianna stood in front of her with an apron, offering a cheese plate.

"Sorry. Cheese?"

Claire took a slice of gouda to calm her nerves. "How do you walk so silently? Did you go to charm school?"

Brianna grimaced. "Force of habit. My mom always told me I would 'startle the fairies' if I stomped around."

Claire nodded. "Yeah, that sounds about right." She stood and stretched. If she didn't put the thoughts of Luke behind her now, she would spiral even more. "So after dinner, I might need your help with something."

"Anything." Bri's green eyes sparkled with interest. "What is it?"

"I've decided I'm going to infiltrate the men's rights convention."

Brianna shook her head. "Luke's not going to like that."

"Well, he's not here to stop me, is he?" Claire smiled grimly.

"Good point."

"I really think Professor Taylor is going to be there. If he is, I can follow him, find out where he's staying, and tell Jack."

"He's also not going to like this." Her half sister popped a piece of cheese in her mouth.

"We're not going to tell him."

Brianna nodded but frowned. "Screw it. Filming's going to wrap right before this. Let's get these idiots."

Claire sat back. She had anticipated a lot more protesting and convincing. Nicole and Mindy almost never agreed to go along with a first draft of a plan. "Thank you," she said after a pause.

Bri reached over and grabbed Claire's hand. "We're going to catch the bastard who did this to you." Her thumb brushed over the raw flesh where the zip tie had bound Claire's hands.

She winced. "Thanks, Bri. We can't keep waiting for Jack. I'm tired of being a sitting duck, of waiting for a phone call saying they've taken my mom or you or Charlie. All of this bullshit is going to end. I'm going to that convention, and I'm going to rip ESA down brick by brick."

She jumped up from the couch even though the event in question wasn't for another week.

"Now, I've already pulled up the blueprints for the hotel. There's a service entrance I can use to—"

"Hold on." Brianna stood and picked up the cheese plate. "Dinner first, then plotting."

"But the blueprints—"

"They'll still be there when you've had some actual nutrients. Now scoot." Bri gestured down the hallway, a dare in her eye.

Claire grumbled, but for once she listened to her sister. She all but inhaled her (admittedly delicious) dinner and returned to the living room. She plugged her computer into a projector Luke had installed.

"Hang on. I think I'm going to need a drink. Can I get you one?" Brianna asked as she saw the first of seventy PowerPoint slides.

Claire shook her head. During the post-rage-room session Charlie had bullied her into, Dr. Goulding had prescribed another medication—a sleeping pill. Mixing with alcohol was definitely not recommended. Her liver, at least, could stop being mad at her.

"I will take a cupcake, though."

Brianna disappeared and reappeared with a glass of wine and two cupcakes. She handed one to Claire. "All right. I'm ready."

"Are you sure? Because there's no turning back now. And we can't tell Jack. If he finds out, he's going to be very angry." Claire took one frosting-covered finger and pointed to the title slide, which she had just updated to read "Claire and Bri Take Down the Patriarchy" in WordArt.

Brianna squared her shoulders. "Let's do it."

CHAPTER FORTY-FIVE

To Do:
- *Sephora gift cards for Bri and Charlie*
- *Figure out how to put life back together*

RAISED VOICES JOLTED CLAIRE AWAKE THE NEXT MORNING. Her eyes snapped open, and without stopping to think she rolled out of bed and onto the floor. The designated under-the-bed baseball bat was cool to the touch as she withdrew it.

She barely even paused to register that she had not sleepwalked.

"What's going on?" Brianna's head popped up from a cot on the floor. She flung her sheets off.

"Voices," Claire said. She rose and snapped the curtains open. If a member of ESA was out there trying to kill her private security guy, she was going to have to fight him in Luke's Navy sweatshirt and corgi-print panties.

The bottom dropped out of her stomach. Oh, hell. There she was. Alice Alejo, dressed in a hot pink track suit and arguing loudly with the security officer. Claire dropped the baseball bat and ran down the stairs two at a time. Brianna and the dogs chased after her. She missed one step and fell, spectacularly crashing down the stairs and banging her elbows off every ninety-degree angle in sight. She crumpled in a heap at the bottom and moaned.

"Are you okay?" Brianna rushed to her side.

"I'm fine." Every part of her body already hurt from being abducted and nearly drowned. What was a few more bumps? She clambered to her feet and thrust the door open.

"Mom, what are you doing?" Claire stood in the morning sun, corgi underwear and all.

"There, see? She called me Mom. Honestly." Alice slung her purse back over her shoulder and stomped across the grass. Was that the flash of a Taser being tucked into Alice's bag? The man in the SoCal Security polo raised his eyebrows at Claire, and she nodded. He got back in the car.

"Darling, what are you wearing?" Alice's carry-on hit the porch with a thump and her arms snaked around Claire in a suffocating hug.

"Pajamas," Claire said defensively.

"Not that, though I do wish you'd put on pants before you open the door. On your face."

"Huh?" She ran a hand over her face. Apparently her new anti-sleepwalking medication had been so effective that she had fallen asleep before she could remove the false mustache Brianna had glued onto her the night before. Their efforts to disguise her as a man had been surprisingly successful, and it hadn't exactly raised her self-confidence.

"Ah, well. That's—"

"You don't have to tell me." Alice pulled back and took Claire by both arms, shaking her a little. Tears had welled up in her mother's eyes. "I can't believe you got abducted *again*. Where was your Taser? Why didn't you call the police?"

Claire's shoulders slumped. Her fifty-five-year-old mother had managed to incapacitate her attacker with nothing but a rolling pin. Claire had been in one of the most populated cities in the world with a litany of weapons at her disposal and self-defense training, and she had still almost died. How embarrassing.

"Come in, Mom." The door creaked open behind her.

Alice was momentarily distracted by Rosie's delirious joy at seeing her grandmother. Bri passed Claire a pair of shorts on her way into the kitchen, and Claire scrambled into them.

This was not going to be good. Alice wasn't exactly adept at de-escalating crises. If anything, she was only going to stir up more trouble—probably in the form of yet another PI. And a well-paid new PI was sure to tattle on Claire if she infiltrated a men's rights conference.

Brianna appeared from the kitchen, two steaming mugs of coffee in hand.

"Good morning, ladies," she said, far too chipper for the chaos that had just unfolded.

"Brianna! How are you?" Alice swooped in for another strangle hug. Claire mouthed a thank you over Alice's shoulder, and Brianna smiled.

Claire glanced at the front door behind her. One hand hesitated on the knob. She could totally run away before Alice noticed. Alice turned around and shook her head. Holy shit. Had she taken up telepathy now? Claire sighed and trudged into the kitchen.

After an hour of chatting about her new project, Bri left to meet with her trainer.

Then the ranting began. Eggs jiggled in a frying pan on the stove as Alice paced in the kitchen.

"I can't believe the police haven't been more proactive. They know about your history. Surely your father has spoken to them. And now Luke has had to hire private security just to keep you—"

She must have noticed the grimace Claire made at the mention of Luke's name.

"Where is Luke, sweetheart? Working already?"

Claire slid the pan off the burner and took a deep breath. She addressed the spatula. "He left. Pretty much right after I was abducted. He said he couldn't be with someone who didn't care if she lived or died."

There was a small gasp behind her. Claire turned to find Alice's enormous sky-blue eyes watering cinematically. "He didn't."

She offered a flat smile. "It's okay. I think I was just too much for him. It's better to know now than in five years, right? Besides, he spent the last month bossing me around. Telling me I can't leave the house by myself. I'm not a child." Despite the casual nature of her words, thousands of daggers pierced her insides. She had opened her heart again, and look where it got her. Maybe she really was meant to be alone—a starry-eyed spinster creating happily ever afters for everyone but herself.

Alice collapsed into a chair at the kitchen table. She seemed lost in thought. "It's not like him to just leave. He must have been really upset."

Claire wrenched the refrigerator door open. She needed to focus on something else, or she was going to lose it. The fancy kombucha Luke had requested sat on the bottom shelf, mocking her. She yanked the glass bottle out of the fridge and twisted the top off. The scent of vinegar was strong in the air as it swirled down the drain.

Words bubbled up on their own. "I still can't believe he said that to me. You know? That I don't care if I live or die. Who is so casual about their existence? Of *course* I don't want to die. I just want things to go back to normal. I'm tired of being hunted like an animal. I'm tired of waiting to see what twisted way ESA is going to try to ruin my life next. I'm tired of putting everyone around me in danger all the time." She slammed the bottle down on the counter and whirled around. "They're threatening Brianna and Charlie. And they almost took you from me."

"Sweetheart, put the knife down." Alice's hand closed over her wrist.

She had picked up the chef's knife without even noticing.

Claire dropped the knife and sank into another mom hug. Patchouli and vanilla infiltrated her nose as Alice squeezed her tight. She had come perilously close to losing the strongest woman she knew. Alice had spent Claire's formative years lecturing her endlessly on personal safety. Without her mother, she wouldn't have been able to slip her bonds that night in the parking garage. The emergency tool wouldn't have been in her purse. Her mother had prepared her for the worst, and she had survived because of it.

"You'll never lose me, darling." Alice whispered. "And I don't think you've lost Luke either, for what it's worth."

Claire withdrew and went back to the pan. She couldn't think about Luke right now.

Alice hovered behind her. "Sweetheart, you're tough. Like me. I know you didn't have the best childhood, and I'm sorry about that," she said.

Oh boy, an impromptu therapy session. Had she not suffered enough? If she didn't head it off now, they'd both spend the entire day weeping and eating ice cream out of the container.

"Mom, that's—"

Alice put a hand on her cheek. She smiled, but there were tears in her eyes. "I fell to pieces when your dad left. You and Charlie held things together. I relied on you both too much, I know I did. You were such a sweet girl, even then. Making sure the bills were paid and making grocery lists. You're used to having to be tough. And I think in some ways that's served you well. You have grown into a miraculous woman. You are kind, fierce, loyal, independent, silly, beautiful, all the best things a person could be."

Claire bit her lip. Crying was not on the agenda for the day, but the tears were welling up of their own accord. Damn it, Mom.

Alice's hands cradled hers, cool and soft. "You've been through so much, Clairebear. You've been hurt, in more ways and by more people than most of us will ever experience."

Now her lip was quivering. Deep breaths.

Alice squeezed her hands and continued. "I know you hate that he was trying to tell you what to do. But imagine you were him. Wouldn't you want him to do everything he could to be safe when you weren't physically with him? He told you to stay home because he can't protect you while he's gone."

Claire opened her mouth, ready to protest that she didn't need anyone to protect her. Alice silenced her with a stern look.

"But you left anyway," she continued, "knowing full well that there's a group of crazed idiots out there hell-bent on killing you, and look what happened. You keep putting yourself in danger for no reason. He loves you, sweetheart. It's no wonder he's upset."

Claire frowned and pulled her hands away to cross her arms. Even if her mom was right, it was no reason to just leave.

Alice tucked a curl behind Claire's ear. "He just wants you to take this seriously. To be safe. To value your own life. To think about him, and all the other people who love you. You mean so much to so many. Especially your mama."

She booped Claire on the nose. "Relationships take work, sweetie. You have to be willing to make concessions for each other. And I know part of you is afraid to give up your independence. To feel like you're accountable to someone. To fully open your heart again after what Jason did to you. But Luke is *not* Jason. I don't want to see you throw away the great love of your life because you're too proud to look at things from his perspective. You need to know when it's time to apologize if you want to make this work. So why don't you do what you can to make it right?"

Claire sniffed and rubbed at her fake mustache. Her mother had an annoying ability to put a complicated situation simply. "Do you guys have a group chat going or something? You're not supposed to take his side."

"I'm not, darling. You're right—he shouldn't have left. But I understand why he did, and I think you do too."

"Well," Claire said, sitting up and wiping a finger underneath her eyes. "There's nothing I can do about it now. He's gone."

Alice nudged her. "You know that's not true. You, my sweet girl, have an unparalleled talent for creating beautiful moments. Why don't you do what you were born to do and create one for him?"

Claire dragged the sleeve of Luke's sweatshirt over her face. The fake mustache caught the fabric and ripped itself off. The tears were out in full force now. She pressed a hand to the raw spot and looked at her mother.

"But what if he doesn't come back?"

Alice squared her shoulders and took Claire by both arms. "Then he's an idiot, and you're finally going to move to Florida with me."

Claire laughed in spite of herself. "That is *not* happening."

"Oh, come on, just think of the proposals. Beautiful sunshine, sandy beaches."

"I'm sorry, didn't I read that a Miami wedding was interrupted last week when a gator attended the ceremony and death rolled with the aisle runner?"

"Stop deflecting, sweetie. Go get one of your binders."

"Yeah, yeah," Claire said as she left the kitchen.

Anxiety rippled through her. Luke had been almost unrecognizable when he left. Stoic, cold, the spitting image of his notoriously icicle-like mother, Rachel. He had left, mere hours after she had been abducted. Did she really owe him a big romantic gesture?

A picture in the hallway caught her eye. She stopped and ran a finger over a pooka shell glued to the frame. She and Luke were pressed together, his fingers caught in her windswept hair. A cotton candy sunset colored the sky behind them. A pang of regret gripped her stomach. Could she spend the next sixty years of her life without him? Watch as he fell in love again, married someone who wasn't constantly being abducted? Had beautiful, grumpy, suspiciously in-shape children with an Olivia clone?

Ideas were creeping in, but her stomach was still in a vise. Alice was right. She had been foolish, dangerous. If

Luke was in her position and he had run off alone, she would be furious. And even before that, she had allowed herself to be so engulfed in Brad's circus that she had forgotten to prioritize her relationship. All Luke had asked was to spend some time together in his second home. He wanted to show her what he loved about Los Angeles, and she barely made a spare minute to give him that. It had all been for nothing.

Even if he didn't want to get back together, she owed him an apology. Her hands shook as she pulled a fresh binder out of the closet in the hallway. Would he understand, or was she about to put herself out there just to have her heart stomped on?

CHAPTER FORTY-SIX

To Do:
- Win him back
- Soundproof Mindy's room?

"THANKS FOR NOT TAKING IT PERSONALLY." CLAIRE LIFTED ONE end of a projector screen and handed it to Jeff, her private security officer of the day.

Long shadows intruded into Luke's backyard. There was a slight chill in the air, and a breeze tugged at the hem of her bright red cocktail dress. She stoked the small flames in the stone fire pit.

Jeff shrugged. "I can understand why you'd want someone you already know to look after you." A handgun holstered on Jeff's hip clashed with the tuxedo and bright red cummerbund he wore. "Besides, this is better than sitting in a car holding my piss for eight hours."

Claire glanced at her watch. Finally, after an exhausting

twenty-four hours during which she had saged the entire house twice, Alice had flown home to make the next taping of her show.

Sawyer and Mindy were due to land any minute. Their arrival accomplished two things: first, Sawyer would serve as a 24/7, live-in bodyguard. And second, Mindy and Claire were going to give California one last shot by taking on Darius and Nick as clients. Their final West Coast representative interview was taking place tomorrow, and if Heather Clearwater wasn't their girl, it was back to the drawing board. And if Luke didn't want to reconcile, she would be apartment hunting as well. The future of her entire personal and professional life hinged on these next few days.

Would moving Sawyer in be enough to show Luke she was taking the threats against her seriously? And would firing the security team be enough to drag him back to the house? She had been too nervous to outright ask him to talk. Her heart couldn't take another rejection. If firing SoCal Security didn't summon Luke, she was going to be forced to set a bush on fire.

"Does that look straight?" Jeff asked from the ladder.

"It's perfect. Thank you."

She glanced around the yard. Any time she left the house, the hair on the back of her neck prickled. Was it paranoia, or was it ESA? Any one of these houses could hide a member of ESA, and there was nothing she could do about it.

Jeff stepped heavily down the rungs and waited while Claire pressed a button on her trusty projector—one of the few things that survived the warehouse fire since it had been at Luke's house. Her laptop hummed, and the title menu of Luke's favorite movie, *The Departed*, appeared onscreen. It was a little violent and depressing for her, but Luke could spend hours discussing every shot.

Rosie ran underneath the screen and sniffed it suspiciously. Winston trailed not far behind. Both wore doggie tuxedos.

"Well, shit. He's mad for sure," Jeff said, looking up from his phone. "He says not to go anywhere and that he'll be here in twenty minutes."

"Perfect. Thank you. Do you need time to tune?" Jeff's true passion, which he had told Claire about the previous day when she brought him some of Alice's empanadas, was music.

He nodded and disappeared into a corner of the yard. Claire whirled around and re-checked everything for the fifth time. Edison bulbs stretched over a pair of Adirondack chairs. It wasn't her finest work, but she no longer had a warehouse full of elegant props or generous wiggle room in her budget.

Her apology was intimate and cozy, but would it be good enough? Was it even a small step toward bridging the gaping hole between her and Luke?

Her phone buzzed, and her heart jumped. Was he calling to curse her out? She glanced at the screen. Brad's name flashed impatiently. What the hell?

Her thumb hesitated over the button. She didn't owe him anything. He had mercilessly fired her, humiliated her, made her question her entire life's work. She sent the call to voicemail and set her phone on the picnic table. Suck it, Brad.

Someone knocked on the fence. Jeff jumped up, hand on his gun. He approached the gate and demanded that someone show their ID.

"It's just pizza, man," called the voice of the teenager from the restaurant down the street.

"He's fine, Jeff." She edged around Jeff's suspicious stance and handed over a generous tip. "Thanks, Nate. How was your geometry test?"

"Nailed it. Got an A-," the teen said with a smug smile. Braces peeped through.

Claire offered a high five and took the pie. "You're killing it."

"Flash cards. Who knew?"

Claire and the seventy-two blank index cards she always carried in her purse knew. She waved as the teen retreated to his beat-up Volvo. The tantalizing aroma of marinara wafted toward her as she carefully arranged the pizza box on the gingham cloth draped over the picnic table. She lifted the lid and exposed the pizza. It was a near exact replica of the apology Luke had sent her the previous spring —a pepperoni corgi, but this time with a bonus tiny cluster of pepperoni that looked like Winston.

She touched one hand to the recently unplugged crockpot that sat next to it. It was still warm, and full of chili. But not ordinary chili. This was Luke's dad's famous recipe, apparently made for many game days in his youth. George had reluctantly handed over the recipe the night before. But would it be enough?

Her phone vibrated. Someone was pulling into the driveway. Shit, he was here.

She climbed up the stairs to the deck and took a second to compose herself. Her stomach rippled with nausea. She was *not* going to cry. Shouting at him for leaving was also going to have to be off limits. They were going to talk this out like adults, and then maybe, if she was lucky, he would agree to come home.

She pulled the front door open, and he paused with his hand in midair. A pang of longing hit her, and she almost rushed into his arms. He was in a tux, hair slicked back. *Damn it.* She must have interrupted something important. A studio party, maybe? That wasn't likely to put him in a great mood.

His eyes were stormy, brows drawn together.

"What the hell are you doing, firing the security team?"

Her hands shook, and she hid them behind her back. Fighting for control over her voice, she spoke. "I hired someone better."

Good. She hadn't cried or screamed.

"I did hours of research, checked references. These guys are the best." He stabbed a finger at the SoCal Security car on the curb. "If this is about money—"

Claire held up a hand. Her temper was threatening to flare. "It's not about money. Mindy and Sawyer are moving in with me until I go back to Pennsylvania."

"You—what?"

"I'm trying to take things seriously. It doesn't get much more serious than paying a security professional to live with you. I hope you don't mind. It should just be for a couple weeks while I figure out what to do next."

He visibly deflated. "That...sounds like a good idea."

Silence stretched between them. Crickets chirped, and a car door down the street slammed.

"You look like you're about to pull off a diamond heist," she observed, then bit her tongue. Dr. Goulding had scolded her about her use of humor to deflect her feelings during their last call.

"Yeah, well, Harry Winston had too many anyway." Luke stared at the floor and fiddled with the cuff links in his sleeves—his father's.

"Do you have a second to talk?" Her heart staggered. Yikes. This was like standing in a middle school hallway asking Robbie Yoder to go to the Sadie Hawkins dance all over again.

His eyes snapped up to meet hers. He nodded. She stepped back to let him inside, and the sleeve of his jacket brushed against her. Electricity crackled between them. God, she had missed him.

"I'm surprised you haven't completely remodeled." He walked into the foyer, and his eyes immediately zeroed in on the barely visible orange pill bottles on the kitchen island. He turned back to her and glanced up and down, as though expecting to find a gaping head wound or staph infection. The curiosity was clearly killing him, but he didn't ask.

"It crossed my mind, but I figured you had enough to be upset about."

Luke frowned but didn't answer. The glimmer of flames must have caught his eye because he crossed to the door that led to the deck.

"Having a party?" He looked over his shoulder. His jawline was even more defined in the flickering half-light. Bags hung under his eyes.

"Kind of. Will you come with me?" Ugh. Even her voice was hesitant. What had happened to resourceful, don't-need-a-man Claire? Luke's douchey entrance into her life had turned her into a puddle of dreamy codependent goo.

"Just for a minute. There's a party I have to get back to."

The doorknob was cold in her hand. Her heart fell. Any other Sunday night he would have wrapped up work in time to watch a baking show with her and the dogs in bed. She shouldn't have counted on him being a creature of habit. That's what she got for trying to live in the moment.

All she could do was word-vomit her feelings as quickly

as possible and hope that he listened. Should be a fun evening.

Claire made eye contact with Jeff through the pane of glass. She nodded, and violin music drifted across the yard.

Luke squinted and stepped out onto the deck. "Is that Jeff?"

"He's a very accomplished violinist." She shut the door behind them. "Did you know he was wait-listed for Juilliard?"

Luke cracked a smile, but it vanished immediately. Just then, Rosie and Winston rocketed up the stairs and all but tackled Luke. He dropped to his knees and folded them into his arms, then they all collapsed on the deck in a cuddle puddle. Rosie licked his ears furiously, and Winston crawled inside his jacket.

"They missed you," she said. "So did I."

His eyes shifted from the cloud of fur drifting off Rosie. His penetrating gaze cut her to the core, turning her legs to jelly. The night was cool, but her cheeks burned. Something about him transformed her into a stupid schoolgirl. She had never felt this way about anyone before, and she might have lost him forever.

He dusted his pants off and stood, Winston and his makeshift halo tucked under his arm. "Is that *The Departed*?"

"Yeah. I didn't realize you'd be in the middle of something. I'll just take it down." She reached for the corner of the projector screen, but Luke caught her hand. A rush of adrenaline hit at his touch. She couldn't see her reflection, but she was almost certainly glowing like she had just climbed out of a vat of radioactive waste.

"Leave it. You wanted to talk?"

She nodded and took a deep breath. Where were her

damn notecards? She should have reviewed them before he got here. Her mind was as blank as a fresh Word document.

"Can I say something first?" Luke put Winston down and walked over to the picnic table. He sat and leaned forward, elbows on his knees. It might as well have been the cover of *GQ*.

"Okay." She followed and perched on the bench across from him. The wood was probably going to snag the fabric of her cocktail dress. Was he going to yell at her some more? Tell her to move out now instead of later? She deserved some yelling, but her heart could only take so much. It was a good thing she had taken her meds earlier.

"I'm sorry," he said.

She blinked. "For what?"

"For leaving you. Right after you were abducted. I was just upset and so worried about you that I just...lost it. It was really shitty, and I'm sorry."

Oh, thank god. The shoulders that had been hunched up near her ears all night dropped back to their natural spot. As much as she deserved it, she wasn't sure she could have handled another fight about how irresponsible she was.

"No, I'm sorry." She reached across the picnic table. Her hand shook as she laid it on top of his. "I knew I shouldn't have gone out alone. It's so hard for me to just sit here and do nothing. They've taken so much from me and put everyone I love in danger. I know that's not an excuse. You were right. It's not just about me anymore. There are other people in my life who care about what happens to me, and I need to be more careful. If you were gallivanting around while someone tried to murder you, I would be furious. I underestimated them. It won't happen again."

Luke ran a hand through his hair and shook his head. "I

was too harsh. You were in such a vulnerable place—barely three hours after getting abducted—and I just fucking *left*."

Her phone vibrated, clattering on the wood. Brad was calling again. Luke's eyes lowered, hardened a bit at the corners when he saw the screen.

Claire picked up her phone and threw it over her shoulder. Something smacked against the vinyl siding of the house and clattered onto the cement. For once, she didn't care if it was broken. Eat a dick, Brad.

She bit her lip and continued. "That part did suck. But I think your leaving actually helped me. Maybe."

He tore his eyes away from the possibly destroyed phone and raised his eyebrows. He looked different—lighter, almost amused. "What do you mean?"

Jeff's violin sang in the background. The Edison bulbs swayed in the breeze. She shivered and crossed her arms over her chest. The thoughts she had scribbled on flash cards were evading her. Ugh, feelings.

"You get a whole new perspective when you hit rock bottom." She avoided his gaze, preferring instead to talk to a crack in the concrete. "I finally listened to Dr. Goulding and started anti-anxiety meds. And benzos for the sleepwalking. I can't really tell if they're helping yet, but it's a start. I worked through some feelings with Charlie. We should really go to Bash Bar together sometime, by the way. It'll do wonders for your stress. And then I called in a serious favor from Sawyer. It'll give us both some peace and let me figure out how to start over."

She squared her shoulders.

Luke's calloused hand closed over hers. "You don't have to start over."

She met his eyes. They were soft.

"Does this mean you'll come home?" Her voice was barely more than a whisper.

"My bag was already in the trunk." He stood and picked her up before she knew what was happening.

Her heart stuttered, and her cheeks burned. It was like being held by lightning. "What about your party?"

"Screw the party." He lifted her into the air and twirled her. Her cocktail dress got caught in the wake, spinning around her in a velvety cloud of red. She raised her arms to the sky. The stars blurred overhead like their magical evening in Paris. Violin music bled into the night.

He lowered her, slowly, deliciously until she was pressed against his chest. They simply looked at each other for a moment, locked in a tangle of arms. Finally, for the first time since her abduction, she was home.

CHAPTER FORTY-SEVEN

To Do:
- *Welcome papers for Darius and Nick*
- *Triple check Heather's criminal background*
- *Check in with Gloria and Sam*

VIBRATIONS FROM CLAIRE'S PHONE RATTLED THE SPOON IN HER empty cereal bowl. The morning sun slanted through the window, revealing every speck of dust she had missed during yesterday's cleaning binge. She glanced at the screen. Brad again. Not today, Satan. Five days separated him from the big proposal. He must have finally realized it was all too much for one person. Good.

She shoved her phone across the table and went back to the binder in front of her. Quotes from West Haven caterers were neatly encased in sheet protectors. Now that Luke wasn't imminently throwing her out on her butt, it was time to buckle down on the planning for his premiere.

"You sure you don't want to get that?" Luke glanced over his steaming cup of coffee. The microwave beeped, and he stood up.

Rosie sighed under the table. Even she knew it was a bad idea. Winston briefly lifted his head, then set it back on Claire's lap.

She stroked him behind the ears. "Why would I want to talk to the client who ruthlessly fired me? Besides, I'm busy planning your screening."

A steaming bowl of chili hit the table with a *thunk*. Cumin and cilantro overwhelmed her nostrils.

"You're having chili for breakfast?"

"Yeah, I never got to have any last night. Anyway, it's okay if you want to answer it. The proposal is what, five days out? He's probably desperate."

In spite of the potential Brad drama, the bowl drew her eyes. Would he be able to tell it was his dad's recipe?

He put a steaming spoonful in his mouth, chewed for a second, and cocked his head to the side. "Hang on. Is this...?"

Claire nodded. A smile crept over her face.

"How did you get the recipe?" He took another bite and closed his eyes.

"George. He wasn't super eager to give it to me, but I can be pretty persuasive."

He reached across the table and pulled her out of her seat and into his lap. "I love you. Thank you."

She snaked her arms around his neck and kissed him. Was it Luke or the hint of chili powder that warmed her from the inside?

The phone vibrated again. She didn't need to look at the screen to guess who it was. Could Brad *be* more of a cockblock?

She pulled back and glanced at the binder propped next to the coffeemaker. The first of Brad's six proposal binders. She hadn't had the heart to throw it away. Some of her best ideas were in that binder. But following Brad down his increasingly elaborate rabbit hole had almost cost Claire her relationship. It wasn't worth it.

Creaking upstairs drew both their eyes upward. A jetlagged Mindy and Sawyer hadn't gotten out of bed yet, but at least their bicoastal lovemaking hadn't caused them to plummet through the ceiling. It was going to be a long couple of weeks.

"I love you too. And that's why I'm not going to let this" —she gestured vaguely at the phone, searching for the right words—"overbearing, finnicky dingus come between us."

Even though he had apologized for them, Luke's words were still cemented in her heart. Even when she was home, she wasn't really there. That needed to change. There would be other ways to create her California empire and save the rescue for good. She didn't need Brad.

"Celebrating your documentary is more important," she added firmly. She frowned at the binder. Planning this screening would be so much easier if ESA hadn't burned down her warehouse. Her lights, tablecloths, and faux floral arrangements had all been burned to a crisp.

He nudged her. "I know how hard you worked on this. Even I'm impressed at the scope of things. You could try setting some boundaries. You know, for once."

She shot him a dirty look.

"Strict business hours except for the day preceding a proposal," he suggested. "Saying no to bringing an ice cream cone 2,800 miles. A limit to the number of times you can change your mind."

Silence.

He nudged her. "What about Karen? Doesn't she deserve the proposal of her dreams? A Claire Hartley original?"

Shit. In her commitment to eschew Brad until the end of time, she had forgotten all about Karen. Kind, level-headed Karen.

"Why are you pushing me to do this?"

Luke gently tugged on one of her curls. "Because I know you'll regret it if you don't. I don't want to be the reason why you don't follow your dreams."

Her phone vibrated again. They both looked at it. Brad's picture lit up the screen. Something deep inside pulled at her.

"Fine," she said, snatching the phone. "But if you dump me over my work ethic, I'm keeping both dogs."

She left the kitchen and wandered into the hallway. Her shoulders squared, she answered the phone. "Yes?"

"Thank god. Claire, you gotta help me." Brad's voice was urgent.

"With what?" She had never spoken to a client with this tone of voice. She might as well have been speaking to an uninvited snake in her garden.

"The proposal. My receptionist can't handle it. She quit today."

Quit planning the proposal or quit her whole-ass job? Apparently Claire wasn't the only one who had had enough of Brad.

"Hmm. That's unfortunate," she said. "That's why we always recommend hiring a professional, especially with an event of this scale."

Brad sighed. "What will it take for you to come back?"

Claire glanced at her watch. "A meeting. Two hours from now. Your office."

"I have a golf—"

"Two hours from now, or no dice. There are new rules. If you can't abide by them, I'm not going to take you on as a client." Her voice shook at the end, but she waited, silent. Her heart galloped.

"I'll see you in two hours." The phone disconnected.

Claire half-ran back into the kitchen. She picked up a broom and banged it into the ceiling. She and Mindy now needed to cram two weeks' worth of work into five days. It was going to be chaos.

There was a thwack behind her. She turned. Luke was piling Brad's other five binders onto the kitchen island. He pushed her prescription bottle across the island at her and raised his eyebrows.

"Yeah, yeah," she said, popping the top and swallowing one of the pills. "Thank you." She kissed him on the cheek and ran upstairs. The biggest project of her career was back on. Maybe all wasn't lost.

"So, boundaries," Mindy said as they rushed across the parking lot two hours later.

"Yes. Very important. Strict business hours, extra charges for last-minute changes."

"This is new for us," Mindy observed. "So you're not going to answer Brad's three a.m. calls anymore?"

"No," Claire said firmly, brushing a dog hair from her blazer. "No calls before eight or after six, except for proposal days and the day before."

Mindy grabbed her hand. "I love boundaries."

Claire smiled. As much as it pained her to admit it, maybe Luke had been right. There was no way they'd be able to keep up with the intense client catering they had been performing for Brad. It wasn't sustainable, especially not at their base fee. Happily Ever Afters's wild standards had affected Mindy too. But she had never once complained.

"You're the best, you know that?" Claire said, pulling her friend in for a side hug. "Our company would not be what it is without you."

"Stop, you're making me blush." Mindy shoved Claire, and she almost bounced off a parking sign. "Well, this certainly sets the stakes a little higher for Heather's interview this afternoon."

Shit. In light of Brad's proposal potentially being back on, Claire had completely forgotten about the interview.

"It'll be okay," Mindy said, gripping Claire's arm like she was teetering on a ledge. "She seems so promising, and if she wants to work with us, it'll give us an extra pair of hands this week. And she could help with Darius and Nick's proposal."

They had reached the doors of the studio offices. Claire opened her mouth, then clamped it shut. "One thing at a time," she said and thrust open the double doors.

Sure, her heart was skipping like children playing hopscotch and she had an immediate urge to start leafing back through Heather's criminal background check. But that was going to have to wait.

Brad's secretary wasn't there. His door was ajar. Claire and Mindy looked at each other. Mindy adjusted a strand of Claire's hair, then nodded.

Claire ignored the urge to kick the doors open, opting instead to knock twice before entering.

Brad looked up. His hair stuck up like he had jammed a fork in an electrical socket. Purple bags hung under his eyes. "Watch your step," he muttered.

A potted plant was tipped over in the corner. What must

have once been a vase was now a sparkling pile of shards on the carpet. A painting on the far wall was crooked. Was that a dent in the drywall? All signs pointed to a pissed-off Goldie.

"So," Claire said, pulling a stack of stapled papers out of her manila folder. "Thank you for your interest in Happily Ever Afters." She slapped the papers on his desk. At least that had remained unscathed.

"This is an updated contract," she continued. "You'll notice there are several changes, including an inconvenience fee for the short window, and updates to our business hours."

Brad flipped to the last page and scribbled his signature without looking at the document. "I'll do whatever you want. I just need you to fix this."

"Great," Claire said, sliding the packet into her folder. "Let's talk."

An hour passed while they hammered out the details.

"All right." Claire handed a copy of her notes to Mindy as they walked away from Brad's office building. The sun beat down overhead, but a breeze wicked away the sweat on Claire's forehead. "I'll do everything from the helicopter company to the ranch. You confirm with the restaurant and the caterers."

"Done," Mindy said as she pulled out her phone.

Claire took a deep breath and looked up at the sky. "I don't know if I have it in me to jump back in with Brad. But it's only five more days. And it's all for Karen."

"For Karen." Mindy offered a fist bump, and Claire accepted.

"What time is Heather's interview again?"

Mindy glanced at her watch. "Two o'clock. We're meeting at a café in the valley."

"Working lunch?"

"Let's do it."

CHAPTER FORTY-EIGHT

To Do:
- Don't panic
- Do what you were born to do

"SO HOW DO WE TELL HER THAT 'ALL OTHER DUTIES AS assigned' might sometimes involve busting a serial killer ring?" Mindy flipped down the mirror in the car and adjusted her lipstick.

"I think that's more of an after-she-passes-the-probationary-period kind of revelation," Claire said, rifling through her purse. She pulled out her interview binder. "I really hope this is the one. She's our last option since Megan took another job and Jenna dropped everything to be in a Pledge commercial."

Mindy shook her head. "If it's meant to be, it will be."

"You're very zen for someone who has a life-altering deadline this week," Claire said.

"Well, I did just come back from a mini sexcation," Mindy said, flipping the mirror shut and opening her car door.

"Right. Please remember our rafters can only take so much." Claire shook her head and climbed out. She opened the door to the coffee shop and was about to approach the counter when someone in the corner caught her eye.

Heather Clearwater, the Pennsylvania-girl-turned-LA-hospitality-manager, waved at them from the corner table. Three coffees and an assortment of pastries sat in front of her.

"Holy shit, she beat us here," Claire muttered to Mindy as she waved back. They walked over together.

Heather stood and offered her hand. "You must be Claire and Mindy. It's so nice to meet you in person." She was dressed in a silk blouse and ascot with a pencil skirt, and her red hair was slicked back into a bun. Her teeth were a dazzling white, and Claire would have stolen the shoes off her feet if she thought they would fit. There was something familiar about her, but Claire couldn't quite place it.

"Love your shoes," Claire said, settling into a chair.

"Thank you! I took a guess and went with iced coffees." Heather gestured to the cups on the table. "I'm happy to get you something else though."

"Iced coffee is great." Mindy pulled her tablet out and set it up. "Thanks."

Claire smiled. Punctual, professional, and went out of her way to get refreshments. Could this be their person? The vise grip around her throat loosened by an inch.

"So, if you're ready, we'll start by telling you a little bit about what we do," she said.

Heather took a sip of her coffee and folded her hands together on the table. She leaned forward and nodded.

She gave Claire her undivided attention, occasionally interjecting a "wow" or "amazing" as Claire explained the business. She maintained eye contact, but not in a creepy way.

"Mindy can show you a couple examples of what we've done in the past."

Mindy swiveled her tablet around, ready to hit play on one of the videos Luke had filmed for them.

"Oh, you don't have to if you'd rather save the time. I've watched every single one of your proposal videos. And your interviews. Marnie's actually my aunt."

"Marnie's your aunt?" No wonder Heather looked familiar. Claire sat back in her chair. Marnie, from the local Pennsylvania talk show *Marnie in the Morning*, had featured Claire as a guest twice. "It's a small world."

Heather laughed. How had she applied her lipstick so perfectly? There wasn't a single smudge. "It really is," she said. "But like I said, I'm very familiar with your work. The patriotic proposal you did with Tyler and Ericka was my favorite." She clutched one hand to her heart. "Well, that one and the one for your best friend, of course."

Claire beamed. Heather had actually done her research.

"Well, thank you." Claire shredded a napkin in her lap. This was going too well. There must be a catch. "We do it because we love it, and because we believe in true love. It's kind of nonnegotiable if you want to work with us," she added with a smile.

"So I guess we can move on to the questions, then," Mindy said. Claire passed her a piece of paper. "What made you apply for the job?"

"Oh, here," Heather said. She leaned down to pull two laminated sheets of paper from her purse and slid them across the table. They were resumes, expertly formatted and concise. She pulled out a small binder next and sat it on the table.

"Honestly, ever since you started making the proposal videos, I couldn't stop watching them. What you do is so beautiful," Heather said, leaning in. "In the hotel business, we get a little taste of making dreams come true—pulling off the perfect corporate event or wedding reception, some-times hosting dignitaries from different countries. But nothing we do is quite like this." She gestured to the still on the screen, where a tearful Cassie hugged Steve in his tuxedo wetsuit.

Claire nodded. Mindy nudged her under the table.

"What's your idea of a perfect proposal?" Claire asked, scribbling a few notes under the previous question.

"Well, if you're talking about a proposal for someone else, it depends entirely on their interests, personality, and their love story. I think everything should be as unique to the couple as possible. Some people don't want a giant public display, for example."

Claire nodded and made a note on her question sheet. They grilled Heather over the course of the next forty minutes. In every category that mattered, she had a great response. She even had her own ideas for proposals, neatly tabbed in a binder and organized by interest.

"Sidebar?" Mindy asked Claire after their last question.

"We'll be right back," Claire said.

They walked to the other side of the coffee shop and stood in the window.

"So we'd be crazy not to hire her, right?" Claire asked.

"She's amazing," Mindy agreed. "She was even okay with the salary and no health benefits. But I feel like we have to play it at least a little cool."

Claire nodded. "What if we ask her to shadow us for

Brad's proposal? See how she reacts under pressure? And then make a formal offer."

"I love it. Let's do this." The two girls turned around as one unit.

For the first time in weeks, there was a tiny glimmer of hope. Maybe her California dream wasn't dead. Was Happily Ever Afters really about to be a bicoastal business?

"Heather," Claire said calmly, folding her hands on the table. "We were wondering if you'd be interested in shadowing us for a proposal we're doing on Saturday. It's the biggest, splashiest one we've ever done, and it would be a great chance for you to get a real feel for it and make sure it's something you're serious about."

Heather nodded enthusiastically. "I'd love to. I do want to be straightforward with you, though."

Shit. There was the other shoe hurtling out of the sky. What now?

"I had an interview with another event planning company, and they said I should expect an offer by the end of the week. And please don't get me wrong, I'm very interested in working for Happily Ever Afters. I just wanted to be honest with you and let you know that you're not the only company I'm waiting to hear from."

Claire's happy bubble popped like someone had sprinted full force at her with a needle.

"We understand. Thank you for being up front with us. If anything changes for you before Friday, please let us know." Mindy handed her a business card. "Otherwise we'll email you to meet up for the proposal."

They shook hands, and Heather left the coffee shop.

"Do you think she was bluffing?" Mindy wondered out loud.

Claire shook her head. "Of course she's in demand. Look at her." She pointed out the window.

Heather was helping an elderly woman cross the street next to the coffee shop. "She's perfect," Claire added.

"Damn it, you're right. Should we have just made the offer?"

Claire shrugged. "If it's meant to be, it will be. I have a feeling we'll win her over. Planning proposals has to be way more interesting work than whatever other event planning company she's working with."

"I hope you're right. We should get going. We have about eight hundred hours of work to do before Saturday."

CHAPTER FORTY-NINE

To Do:
- Check in with a capella group
- Touch base with helicopter and limo company
- Remember to take meds

"Can you move that just like half an inch to the left?" Claire stood ten feet back from the table at Solar Flare. She squinted and craned her neck.

It was here. After five days of frantically re-confirming all the details and a dozen run-throughs, it was finally happening. The biggest proposal day of their entire career. In just half an hour, Brad and Karen would sit down at the restaurant and set into motion the biggest project Happily Ever Afters had ever undertaken. All they could do was wait. And fuss with details, of course.

"Here?" Mindy moved the vase of peonies.

"Yes. Now sit at the table." Claire ordered. She squeezed

her side. Running back and forth had given her a side stitch. California had played havoc with her cardio schedule.

Mindy sat obediently.

"Coli?" Claire glanced over her shoulder. Nicole was checking something on her camera. "What do you think, two inches off the stems? I want to be sure we don't cover her face."

Nicole, who had arrived the night before and was finally starting to feel better, checked it through the viewfinder of her camera. "Definitely. Maybe even two-and-a-half inches."

"Two and a half," Luke called from the corner of the restaurant despite the fact that no one had asked him. His tripod was somewhat successfully disguised behind a large topiary on the back deck. He swiveled his camera and peered into it.

Luke would film at the restaurant and then head straight for the Getty Gardens. Carlos, a friend Luke knew from the studio, was going to meet Claire at the Santa Monica Pier to film the second stop. They would then both meet up at the ranch to get different angles on the proposal. Luke had insisted two cameras was plenty. If he was wrong, she might murder him.

The door opened, and Sawyer stepped inside. "All clear," he reported. Every five minutes, he left the building and swept the perimeter. He had spent the last five days tailing them from proposal stop to proposal stop and fussing over the security system Luke had installed.

ESA had once again been suspiciously quiet in the wake of her abduction. A detective from the LAPD had called yesterday to say that her abductor had been driving a stolen car. Another dead end.

Were they intimidated now that there were two men in the house, or were they closing ranks to plan something even more heinous? The convention was tomorrow. But she couldn't think about that yet. Not until Karen got her perfect moment.

"This is so exciting," Heather whispered to Claire. She had shown up that morning to volunteer her time and hadn't made any comments about the other organization offering her a position. If nothing else, she would be an extra pair of hands for the day. "So many moving parts. How do you keep track of it all?"

"Lots and lots of practice," Claire said with a smile. "And, of course, the master timeline," she said, flipping open her Day-Of binder to show Heather a color-coded and time-stamped sheet.

"Isn't that them?" Heather gestured out the window to a middle-aged couple getting out of a limo.

Brad didn't look nervous at all. Against all odds, he had mostly respected Claire's new business hours. Although a flood of emails had come in after hours, he had never once called. He was beaming as Karen took his arm. She was resplendent in a red cocktail dress and matching lipstick. A confident stride in kitten heels showed off her shapely legs. A jeweled comb gathered her hair to one side. The camera was going to love her.

"Shit, hide!" Claire said. "They're here," she whisper-shouted to the rest of the crew. There was a minor stampede as they all triple-checked everything was perfect before ducking into the restaurant. Luke remained outside, concealed by the topiary. The rest of the party hid behind the wall that separated the bathrooms from the restaurant as Karen and Brad made their way to the table. The restaurant wasn't busy yet since it was early, but the handful of patrons who were there shot confused looks at the mass of people hiding.

As soon as the couple sat down, Nicole jumped into action. She pulled out a telescopic lens and leaned into the window with one leg resting on the booth. She clicked away as Claire noted the start time on her master timeline. Karen and Brad had arrived five minutes early. He was many things, but at least he was punctual.

Her phone vibrated with a text from Carlos—he was set up at Santa Monica Pier and ready for their arrival. The a cappella group had also arrived and was running through their warm-ups. Things were exactly on track so far. Perfect. It was going to be the most beautiful day. Claire danced on the spot and bent to scratch Rosie behind the ears before remembering that she and Winston were at doggy daycare. Unless ESA and/or Olivia had broken in and stolen them. Maybe she should take a quick peek on the daycare app.

Olivia had been quiet since the roof incident. As far as she knew, anyway. Claire had made it a policy to never go through a boyfriend's phone. If he left her for that sports bra full of pissed off bees, that was on him.

Satisfied that the dogs had not been kidnapped, Claire fired off a message to Carlos to ask about the lighting and leafed through her binder. Appetizers and wine had arrived at the table. They were still well within the time limit.

"Videography, how are we doing?" Claire asked into her headset.

"Fine," Luke's voice muttered. "I wish I had free range over the angle, but it could be worse. She looks stunning in this light."

"Doesn't she?" Nicole said dreamily over her headset. She had moved to another corner of the restaurant for more pictures. Had Claire not sternly forbade her from scaling the roof in her condition, Nicole certainly would have ambled up there for a better angle.

Thirty minutes passed, and the last of the entrées were disappearing from their plates. It was time to move on to the second stop. Claire made a note on the master timeline and flipped her binder shut. She was about to step out from behind the wall when a nervous-looking man in a chauffeur's hat appeared.

"Yes?" She asked.

"Miss Hartley. I have some bad news."

Fuck. A stone settled in Claire's gut. Everything had been going so well. What would it be—flat tire? Bird poop? Some idiot had parked them in? Their crew was definitely big enough to roll a car away if needed.

"What is it?" She gripped the clipboard so tight that a bone cracked in her wrist. It sounded like a gunshot.

"We can't take the planned route to Santa Monica."

A jolt of panic clenched her stomach. "Why not?" There weren't any mudslides in the forecast. It hadn't even rained for six weeks. As far as she knew, there weren't any wildfires either.

"There's been a bomb threat on the 1. We'll have to take the long way around, and that will add a considerable amount of time to the trip depending on traffic."

"No can do," Heather said. A live traffic map of Los Angeles was pulled up on her phone. "Topanga Canyon's gridlocked. Everyone must be diverting to Route 27."

Claire's heart hammered in her ears. Okay, this was bad. But it could be worse. She had planned for this. She pulled out her phone and dialed the number for the helicopter company.

After a brief, frazzled conversation, Claire flung her phone into her bag and took a deep, steadying breath. The helicopter company wasn't allowed to fly over bomb threat zones. They were shit out of luck.

What was she going to do? Bargain with the police to let them through? Find whoever issued the bomb threat and take a baseball bat to their testicles?

She couldn't think in this dimly lit restaurant. She needed the sunshine, the sea breeze. There was a solution. There had to be, or Brad would probably dismember her piece by piece.

Claire walked out the front door. The chauffeur followed lamely behind her. Her eyes swept over the highway behind the restaurant as she tried to fight the molten wave of panic that threatened to suffocate her. There must have been a roadblock set up down the highway. Cars were already pulling to a stop just a few hundred yards from the restaurant. Soon they would be backed all the way up to Solar Flare. They needed to get out now.

She pulled out her phone and searched the route between Solar Flare and the pier. The bomb threat was located on a small state beach exactly halfway. Who called a bomb threat on a beach, anyway?

There was a route that wound up into the hillside and bypassed the affected section of highway. If she could find a way to slip onto that road, she just might save the whole thing.

Then she saw it. A bright red bicycle rickshaw. The owner was standing at the edge of the road, dawdling and staring at his phone. In a second, her decision was made.

"Excuse me, sir," Claire said, striding across the parking lot. "I'll give you five hundred dollars if you let me drive your rickshaw to Santa Monica."

The owner swung around and stared at her, open-mouthed.

She pulled an envelope out of her purse and leafed out five hundred-dollar bills from an envelope marked "Emergency Bribes." Today would mark the first time she had ever needed to use the envelope.

"You got it, bro." The man swung his dreadlocks over his shoulder and climbed off the bike. "You know it's like eight miles to Santa Monica though, right?"

She handed him a business card. "It doesn't matter. I'll leave it chained to one of the bike racks right by the pier, okay? You call me if you can't find it later. Thank you so much. You—" she barked at the chauffeur. "You stand right by this and make sure no one steals it until I come back with the couple. When I leave, you are going to take whatever alternate route you can find to Santa Monica. Understood?"

"Yes ma'am," the chauffeur said. He stared at the bike as if expecting it to disappear on its own.

Claire stormed back toward the restaurant. They hadn't even made it through the first stop of the proposal before disaster struck. This wasn't a sign, was it? Maybe she should have stayed in West Haven.

She stepped back inside to relay instructions to Mindy and the rest of the crew.

"You're going to pedal two people eight miles? Are you sure?"

"Remember that spin class we used to take? We did like fifteen miles in a forty-five-minute class. I can do this." She hadn't been tugging two extra people during said spin class, but this was practically a matter of life and death.

"I need you, Heather, Sawyer, and Coli to get in the car and take the alternate route. The second photographer is already down at the pier, so we'll have something even if it doesn't have Coli's magic touch. I need you to leave now because traffic is almost backed up to the restaurant."

"Got it." Heather threw her backpack over her shoulder. "Good luck, Claire."

"That goes for you too, Luke," Claire called over the headset. "Get out now."

Claire glanced out the window. Brad had finished and was standing to put his jacket on. It was go time.

"Mr. Lux," she said, bustling out the backdoor with a smile that she hoped looked natural.

Brad's eyes bugged out. Claire wasn't supposed to interact directly with the couple until everything was over. "There's been a small change of plans. Hi, you must be Karen. I'm with the event planning company," Claire said, reaching out to shake Karen's offered hand. "There's been a road closure between here and your next stop. We've had to arrange alternate transportation. If you're ready, you can follow me."

Brad's smile looked rather strained as he put his hand on the small of Karen's back. The couple followed Claire through the restaurant to the parking lot.

She nodded at the chauffeur, and he took off to the limo. Luke waved as he pulled out of the parking lot and turned left. With any luck, he'd find a way to the Getty. Mindy's car was already gone. That left the rickshaw.

"Please forgive the informality," Claire said, "but you'll be taking an open-air rickshaw down the coast with beautiful views."

Brad's face immediately reddened. He looked ready to protest, but Karen spoke up.

"Oh, I've always wanted to do one of these rickshaws! Did you plan this?" Karen nudged Brad. Her voice was throaty and a little raspier than Claire expected.

"Gotta have a Plan C," Brad said with a strained smile.

"Climb on in," Claire said, gesturing to the two seats at the back. She settled at the wheel. She could do this. It would be just like one super intense spin class, that was all.

When this was all over and they were back at Luke's tonight, she'd celebrate with a massive burger and fries from that place down the street.

The couple sat, and suddenly the pedicab felt much weightier. She pushed her feet on the pedals. It was startlingly heavy, but it did move.

She pulled a romantic playlist up on her phone and chucked it into the cup holder so the sound would amplify behind her. Straining with all her might, she inched the rickshaw forward. As it gained momentum, it became slightly less terrible.

She set her GPS on her watch to keep track of the miles so she could monitor their progress as she pedaled with everything she had, dragging them ever closer to Santa Monica. Despite the views Claire had promised, they had to get past a long stretch of small homes and businesses. They passed tiny parking lot after tiny parking lot. They hit the traffic jam and rolled onto the shoulder. One of the wheels slipped off into the gravel, but she persisted.

One mile went by. The sun seemed to be laughing at her from its lofty position. Sweat formed behind her neck. Her lungs burned. Her side stitch had gotten worse. Had someone stabbed her with a chef's knife while she wasn't looking?

"This is so romantic," Karen said behind them.

In spite of the sweat dribbling into her eye, Claire smiled. Things weren't ruined. Not yet, anyway.

The line of cars stretched and wound over the serpentine highway. Two miles. Not that much time had passed. They were barely behind schedule at all. Finally, the long row of homes and businesses ended. The shoulder was even more narrow here, but at least the cars weren't moving. The sun sparkled off the ocean. It was almost blinding.

Claire pedaled on, ignoring the intermittent honks from other drivers.

Three miles. They passed more homes, more businesses. Her thighs were screaming. Four miles. A public beach crawled by on their right. The road they needed to deviate onto would be coming up soon.

"Inceville," Claire muttered under her breath as she finally took a left turn onto Sunset Boulevard. Thank god it was still open. Just a hundred yards or so down the highway, the traffic ended and the blockade began.

Sunset Boulevard was obnoxiously windy and far hillier than the highway had been. Nevertheless, she pushed on. Her legs wept. By the time she made it back to the highway, every part of her was drenched in sweat. The bridge of her nose was dry and tight. She was definitely sunburned. She needed electrolytes. Or a hospital.

It had been forty-five minutes since they had left the restaurant. The detour had wasted a big chunk of time, but the quartet was still booked for another hour and fifteen minutes. It was still possible. There was no way in hell she was going to be outdone by a stupid bomb threat and an unscheduled pedicab. All she had to do was get them there.

Breath burned in her lungs like fire as she slammed her legs against the pedals, urging it forward ever faster. Her side stitch was getting worse, but they were getting close now. They passed another beach, then a park. Finally, just ahead, the top of the Ferris Wheel rose majestically from the ocean. Thank friggen goodness.

Ten painful minutes later, they pulled up at the pier.

"Mr. Lux, would you like to take it from here?" There wasn't a response. She glanced behind her. Both of them were sound asleep, mouths hanging open. He couldn't have been too mad, then.

Claire stood and got off the bike. Her knees nearly buckled as she gently shook him awake. "We're here. Sorry about the cart, there was a bomb threat."

"I heard. Thanks for getting us here." He blinked and wiped the sleep from his eyes.

"Head for the wheel," she whispered as he gently shook his soon-to-be bride. They were going to have to skip the Skee-Ball portion if they wanted to get to the Getty in any kind of reasonable timeframe.

Once Brad and Karen had exited the rickshaw, Claire nearly cried in relief. She had done it. Nothing could stop true love—not a bomb threat, not a roadblock, not even a town with a stupid number of people in it. Surely the rest of the proposal would go smoothly.

CHAPTER FIFTY

To Do:
- *Drink a five gallon bucket of Gatorade*
- *Murder whoever set that bomb threat*
- *Pray that Brad doesn't have a pig farm to feed me to*

WITH THE RICKSHAW SECURED TO A BIKE RACK, CLAIRE hustled down the pier as efficiently as she could on legs made of meat jelly. She ducked into Pacific Park and dashed through the rides. The pain in her side was finally subsiding as she bobbed and weaved around screaming toddlers, harried-looking parents, and mountains of cotton candy. Casting a glance behind her, she found that Brad and Karen had stopped to stand on the pier. Karen pointed at something on the horizon. Was she going to have to scoop them back up on the rickshaw and hand-deliver them to the wheel? The timeline was already skewed.

Squaring her shoulders and counting to ten, she turned her back to them and approached the wheel. There was the bucket truck, cordoned off by a set of cones. The a cappella quartet sat in the shade of a French fry stand, tugging at their collars and fanning themselves.

Claire ran to the ride operator and pulled up a picture of the couple on her phone. He acknowledged with a curt nod. The smell of hot oil coated her nostrils as she ran to the fry stand.

"They're here. Get ready," Claire said as she approached the group. Carlos, the cameraman, was already pointed toward the couple. Tabitha, the second photographer, appeared to be getting a close-up of a seagull. And Gisele, their drone operator who would be capturing the footage from the top of the wheel, was smoking.

"Are you okay?" one of the singers asked. There were armpit stains under his seersucker button-down. Hopefully Tabitha could edit them out.

"I just biked eight miles while carrying two people. I've had better days." Claire drew her emergency deodorant out of her purse and reapplied. At least she wouldn't have to do any more cardio tonight. She unscrewed the cap from her metal water bottle and guzzled from it. "Oh, here they come. Places, everyone!"

Claire ducked behind a "this tall to ride" sign. Brad and Karen stepped up to the ticket taker and climbed aboard one of the cars. A second later, the wheel started to rotate. Thank god. They were behind schedule, but at least now they were on the right track.

She pulled her phone out and dialed Mindy. "Hey, where are you guys? Have you heard from the limo driver?"

"We're pulling up to Santa Monica now. Heather showed

me a back route and suggested the same thing to the limo so hopefully it won't be long. Did you make it?"

Claire breathed a sigh of relief. Thank god Heather had come along today. If she went to work for another company after all this, it wouldn't be easy to replace her.

"Yes. I can't breathe and I'm dying, but we made it. I'm going to check with Luke and make sure he made it to the Getty. We should finish up at the wheel here in ten to fifteen minutes. Do you have any ibuprofen in your purse? I left mine in the car."

"I have ibuprofen and Gatorade. I got you."

"Thanks. Love you," Claire said and hung up the phone. She dialed Luke next.

"What?" he said gruffly.

"Luke, it's a proposal day. Please try to be a professional."

He cleared his throat. "Hello, Miss Hartley. How can I assuage your concerns today?"

She rolled her eyes. "I was just checking to see if you made it to the Getty. Dick."

"What was it you were saying about being professional? Yes, I'm here." There was a shuffling sound on the other end of the line. "Just setting up now. Ice cream guy is here. The cones look good."

"Thank you for checking. They're on the wheel now. I'll text you when we leave. I'm just waiting on the limo."

"Claire?"

"Yeah?"

"Just breathe. It's going to be okay."

Easy to say for someone who hadn't just biked a million miles while hauling a good three hundred pounds behind them. "Whatever you say. See you soon." She hung up without waiting for a response.

"Here," a familiar voice said. A bottle of Gatorade and an ibuprofen appeared at her side.

"You're a lifesaver." Claire hugged Mindy. She had never been so glad to be reunited with her team. "Heather, thanks so much for navigating. I promise things aren't usually quite this crazy on proposal day."

Heather smiled. She looked cool and unbothered, hair drawn back into a ponytail. "It's hard to control things in a city of this size. You never know when someone is going to threaten to bomb the beach for no apparent reason."

A mechanical groaning came from behind them. Claire turned. One singer's straw hat poked another in the eye as they jostled for position in the cramped quarters, but it was perfect. Exactly as Brad had requested, down to the last pinstriped bowtie.

The sun glared from overhead, another cloudless California day. As the a cappella group rose, a melodic hum surrounded them. They launched into their first song as they reached the peak. In spite of the gallon of sweat in her underwear and the various aches and pains in her body, Claire's romantic heart grew in her chest. It really was beautiful.

Then she snapped back to reality and made a note on her time sheet. A drone buzzed by her and zipped to the top of the wheel. She pulled a pair of binoculars from her bag and pressed them to her face. It was hard to tell from this angle, but the couple looked happy. Karen said something excitedly and shoved Brad.

"I'm going to call the limo driver and see where he's at." She tucked the binoculars away.

"Don't bother." Mindy pointed over Claire's shoulder. "He just pulled in."

"Good." Claire laid a hand over her heart.

Maybe the universe had punished them enough for one day with the bomb threat. Maybe from now on it would be smooth sailing. Unless ESA had something to do with their misfortunes. There was no proof, of course. But why wouldn't they try to retaliate after Claire had thwarted an abduction attempt? And what better way to retaliate than destroy the biggest proposal of her career? For all she knew, this could have all been another elaborate training exercise like the ones orchestrated by the East Coast ESA.

The a cappella group launched into their third and final song. A small crowd had gathered around the base of the truck. Onlookers smiled and filmed the spectacle.

She tapped Mindy on the shoulder. "Can I have the car keys? I would really love to sit in the air conditioning for a couple minutes while I touch base with the Getty and the ranch."

Mindy handed them over, and Claire traipsed to the parking lot. Remembering Sawyer's self-defense instructions, she pulled her hair out of its ponytail and scanned the parking lot. Getting abducted or stabbed again on the day of Brad's proposal was *not* going to happen. Thankfully the parking lot was devoid of creeps, and there was no vehicle sabotage to be found.

She sank into the back seat and called her contacts.

By the time Mindy, Heather, Nicole, and Sawyer had hustled back to the car, Claire had confirmed final details with the remaining stops. The Getty had been apprised of their expected arrival time, the helicopter company was on standby to airlift the letters onto the hill, and the ranch was ready with two white horses.

"Everything go all right?" Claire asked. She emptied the Gatorade bottle and tossed it into her purse to recycle later.

"Perfect. The bucket truck didn't get stuck. I know you

were worried about that," Mindy teased. "They're getting in the limo now. I asked him to wait for five minutes so we could get there first and check on everything."

"You're a goddess." Claire made a note on her time sheet.

Mindy pulled out of the parking lot and began the slow trek to the Getty. It was a tight squeeze with all five of them. Heather had heroically opted for the middle seat between Claire and Sawyer.

"I would take a left here and go through Brentwood instead." Heather pointed at the approaching red light. "They're bound to get stuck in some traffic on the freeway."

Mindy obliged and followed Heather's directions. To their great relief, Heather navigated them around the traffic snarl. They arrived at the Getty less than twenty-five minutes later, which Heather declared was a new Saturday record.

"Just the gardens and the ranch separate us from the start of Brad and Karen's happily ever after," Claire said to the girls as the four of them climbed out of the car. Now that the great transportation crisis had passed, the warm glow that came with proposals had crept back in.

"The gardens were a great choice," Heather said as they walked through the arrival plaza and past a large fountain. People were crawling all over the place, but the staff had assured Claire that the gardens would be closed.

After spotting the manager, they were escorted through a door to the gardens. Mindy and Heather stayed at the entrance, hidden from view, so they could cue everyone outside. Sawyer crept around the perimeter, peaking beneath benches and sweeping the area. A bored-looking teenager in a Candy's Creamery shirt stood a short distance away on the patio, a cooler dangling from his hand.

Claire barely had time to admire the bougainvillea arbor

and zigzagging pathway before she found Luke. The sun was creeping lower in the sky, elongating the shadows. But there was still easily three hours to sunset. There was time, even if Brad dillydallied like he had at the pier.

Jeff, her private-security-guy-turned-concert-violinist, tuned his violin across the azalea maze. He paused to wave.

A breathtaking view of the city was visible beyond the gardens. Even the smog seemed to be cooperating. Proposal magic at its best.

She slunk down the path and stood next to Luke.

"All good?" She asked.

"Yeah." He pulled back from the camera to look at her. "And you? Dragging two people eight miles can't have been easy."

Claire shrugged. "I'll let you know tomorrow when my body is sure to be irrevocably broken."

Luke smiled and turned back to his camera. His hand snaked out and pinched her butt. She swatted him and moved back toward the entrance.

A trio appeared suddenly on the patio. Mindy flashed a square of red construction paper. Nicole ducked her head behind her camera and crept through the zigzagging pathway.

"That's the sign!" Claire announced as the bored teenager handed over two perfect ice cream cones.

Luke pressed his eye to the viewfinder. Jeff dragged his bow across the strings, sending sweet music sprawling across the gardens. Karen laughed at something Brad said. They ate their ice cream cones in a leisurely manner. Karen, an amateur horticulturist, pointed excitedly at the flowers.

Claire glanced at her watch. They were still on time, but all their cushion time had been used in the transportation snafu. How long did it take Brad to eat a damn ice cream cone?

Finally, the couple reached the azalea maze. Karen turned to Brad. He extended his hand, and she took it just as the violinist transitioned into a cover of a country song—soon to be their first dance at the wedding.

The jeweled comb in her hair sparkled as they danced. It was almost too perfect. Luke picked up his tripod and circled the gardens slowly. Karen seemed to notice, and Brad must have said something reassuring, because Karen giggled and waved at the camera.

Claire ducked behind the foliage and raced up the walkway. It was time to head to the ranch. The ending was so close she could almost taste it.

"Let's go," she hissed at Mindy and Heather. Heather dabbed a tissue under her eyes. Mindy sniffed, and she handed her one too.

The three of them exited the Getty as quickly as they had arrived. They needed to beat the couple to the ranch to make sure everything was perfect, and this would be their longest stretch of travel yet. If someone in their path called in another aimless bomb threat or plowed their car through an In-N-Out, she was going to set something on fire.

A tense thirty minutes passed as Claire checked traffic cams and Heather described points of interest along their route. She was an expert at de-escalating tension. Finally, they pulled into the same parking lot where Claire had been abducted just over a week before. Dread settled on her like a stifling blanket, but there was no time to fixate on her trauma. She dug a little white tablet out of the prescription bottle in her purse. Dr. Goulding said she could take an extra dose of meds on extra stressful days. Surely this counted.

A line of expensive-looking cars were parked next to them, presumably belonging to Karen and Brad's family and friends. Her phone dinged, and she glanced at it.

"Letters are in position! Oooh, I'm so excited." She danced on the spot even though her anxiety flared like a wildfire. The magic moment was so close. Every painful aspect of this proposal would be worth it when Karen entered the clearing.

"I can't believe you actually changed the Hollywood sign," Heather said. "I didn't even know that was possible."

"With Happily Ever Afters, anything is possible," Mindy parroted from their website.

"I didn't realize how literally you meant it," Heather replied.

"Let's go, we have to get in position." Claire half-jogged up the dusty dirt road leading to the ranch, fighting the urge to look behind her every step of the way.

CHAPTER FIFTY-ONE

To Do:
- *Thank you cards for vendors*
- *Check on Bri, Mom, and Charlie. Air tags?*
- *Buy new meat thermometer*

"It's so much better with the fairy lights," Claire commented as she bounced on the horse's back behind Mindy.

"It was a good call. The landscape is so dreary out here." Mindy gestured at the dusty path. "Oh, I love that one."

A picture of Brad and Karen waving from the bow of a ship was strung on a tree and surrounded by a halo of string lights.

"Isn't it great? They're such a photogenic couple," Claire said. They were almost to the finish line. The happy ending was in sight. It would be perfect. It had to be.

The horse walked into the clearing, and Claire's heart soared. White linen tablecloths were laid over the candlelit picnic tables. A pair of uniformed butlers stood at attention next to the serving tent. The tantalizing smell of roasted duck and sweet potatoes—Karen's favorite—permeated the air. A dozen family members crowded around the tables, laughing and telling stories while clutching glasses of wine. Even Brad's grandchildren, a three-year-old pair of twins in adorable matching dresses, were glued to their tablets and behaving.

The Hollywood sign was now covered by a row of identical letters that read "Marry Me?" They rose dramatically up the slope behind the picnic tables, thrown into sharp relief against the pink-streaked sky. The noise of the city was left behind. Assuming the couple arrived in the next five minutes as scheduled, the view would be nothing short of spectacular.

A ranch hand took their horses and helped them dismount. Claire ran over to inspect the proposal spot. An arbor covered in an explosion of blush and red peonies was propped against the hillside. A half-circle of string lights surrounded it, exactly as Brad had wanted. It was a miracle —the letters were in place, nothing was on fire, everything looked perfect. He may have been an unrelenting nuisance for the entire duration of their business relationship, but the man had taste.

Mindy and Heather went to speak to the caterers, checklists in hand. They chattered about serving times over the headset. Luke was in position to film the couple's arrival. Nicole crouched in a patch of weeds, seemingly trying to get a perfect angle with the arbor and the sign in the background.

The clip-clop of horses announced the couple's impending arrival. Claire's heart fluttered. The HEA team scattered to their designated hiding spots. She slid partway down an embankment so she was mostly out of view. Leaning against a tree for support, she pulled her binoculars back out.

Brad and Karen rounded a corner and came to the clearing. Karen's mouth dropped open, and she clutched a hand to her heart. "Oh, Brad. It's so beautiful. Oh my gosh!"

Their family members waved merrily from the picnic tables. The ranch hand helped Karen down first and put her horse in the stable with the others. Brad dismounted next. He glanced at the sunset and then at the spot where he knew Claire was hiding. He flashed her a thumbs up. She breathed a sigh of relief. Apparently he had forgiven her for the detour earlier.

Karen started to head for her family, but Brad took her hand and guided her to the arbor.

Claire pursed her lips. She generally preferred to keep rings safe for her clients until the moment of the proposal. Brad, however, had insisted on carrying his ring. He had sworn up and down that he would remember it, but there was no guarantee.

Brad kneeled in a circle of lights, and tears formed in Karen's eyes. Nicole got in position and clicked away. Another photographer circled, taking shots from different angles. Luke and the second cameraman filmed from separate vantage points.

The back of Claire's neck prickled as Brad knelt. Something was wrong. She cast a glance over the scene, but everything was perfectly in place. So what was it? Her phone buzzed, and she glanced at it. A text from her mom.

Alice: *Everything okay, Clairebear? Something feels off tonight.*
Love you xoxo

Shivers ran down Claire's spine. The hair stood up on her arms. She surveyed the area while Brad launched into his proposal speech. The caterers poured glasses of champagne. With the exception of the twins, who were still clutching their tablets as if their lives depended on them, the family members were watching Brad with tears in their eyes. No one was choking or suffering a medical emergency. So what the hell was it? The danger was so clear to her that she could almost taste it.

"Mindy?" Claire hissed into the headset.

"What? You're interrupting the speech," Mindy hissed into the headset.

"Something's wrong. Do you see anything off?"

Mindy rotated in a full circle next to the tent. "Everything's fine, Claire. What are you talking about?"

The horses rustled in their stalls. One of them snorted and pawed at the ground. Something was going on. Were they on an active volcano? Was there an earthquake coming? She hadn't prepared for being on a hillside in the earthquake. What if there was a landslide? *Shit shit shit.*

Something low to the ground slinked around the edge of the clearing. Her heart leapt into her throat. Her hands clenched into fists at her side. Was it a person? ESA? Or an animal of some sort? Hank *had* mentioned feral pigs. How dangerous were they?

"Mindy, I see something. I'm going to investigate."

Mindy glanced in her direction. She shook her head fervently, but Claire had no choice. Brad was still speaking. As long as she moved quietly, she shouldn't disturb anything. She picked her way across the inclined slope downhill from the clearing. She skirted the edge of the site and headed back toward the trailhead. Every cell in her body screamed at her as goosebumps trailed up and down her arms. She dug around in her purse and pulled out her pepper spray.

Brad's voice was still audible, but quieter now. He was a boisterous talker, which at least helped cover the noise of her tramping through the dirt. Maybe she had imagined seeing something slinking along the clearing. It was sunset. The light could have played tricks on her eyes.

She tripped and caught herself on the rocky embankment. Her hand stung, but there was no time to check for blood. If there was something that could impact this perfect moment, it needed to be dealt with immediately. She crossed the trailhead and peeked around the cluster of trees. Her heart jolted.

There, a mere ten yards from the arbor where Brad was proposing, was a full-grown mountain lion.

Claire froze. The cat's massive head shifted and locked eyes with her. Her mind spun. Primal fear gripped her entire body. What was that around its neck? Was that...a red bow? The edges of her vision went dark. Adrenaline punched through her veins.

Brad and Karen were in danger. If they were mauled to death by a mountain lion seconds after getting engaged, Claire would never forgive herself. That would be the exact opposite of a Happily Ever After. The lion needed to be dealt with. Her mind raced. She had done a whole segment on mountain lions during their safety meeting.

"There's a mountain lion," she whispered into the comms. "Brad's four o'clock."

"A what?" Mindy whisper-shouted. She beelined for a ranch hand.

Luke's head popped up from behind the camera. He locked eyes with Claire. The mountain lion took a step toward her. A twig cracked under one of its massive feet. His shoulders rippled with pure predator strength.

Her heart was in her throat. "Make yourself big," she muttered to herself. "Shout and make noise and wave your arms. If that doesn't work, throw things at its feet."

She pulled her metal water bottle out of her purse and located a nice-sized rock on the slope next to her.

Cheers and applause broke out. Brad must have finished his five-page proposal.

"Mindy, I need you to lead a very loud rendition of 'Jolly Good Fellow.' Right now," Claire said firmly.

"What?"

"For he's a jolly good fellow," a strong female voice boomed out, but it wasn't Mindy's. Between the trees, Claire spotted Heather singing. She took directions immediately without asking questions. Another good sign.

The family members glanced around, confused, but joined in. Claire leapt on the opportunity. She put her arms out at her side and shouted.

"Get out of here, you big furry asshole!" she yelled at the mountain lion while banging her water bottle against a rock.

The lion flinched and hunched down. The sliver of pupil narrowed. Oh no. Shouting wasn't working. She needed to escalate.

"Don't approach it, don't crouch, don't turn your back," she muttered to herself. Without taking her eyes off the animal, she clapped her hands and yelled at it again. It took one step back but didn't retreat.

Why the hell was it wearing a bow? This wasn't an accident. Was it ESA? How was that even possible? Did they have evil zookeepers on their staff?

She plunged her hand into her purse. The next step was to throw things in its direction in the hopes of scaring it away. She tucked her water bottle away in case she needed to use it as a club and pulled out the first thing she touched —a tin of breath mints.

Claire wasn't gifted in the hand-eye coordination department. She flung the tin like a Frisbee. It landed a foot away from the cat. He slunk back another step but didn't leave. She clapped her hands and yelled again. The group was still singing. Only seconds had passed, but it felt like a lifetime.

Next she threw a hairbrush. It landed just inches from its feet, and it jumped back. Her stomach twisted and heaved. Her vision was starting to go dark at the edges. This was no time to have a panic attack. It was fight or flight, and the only choice was to kick some furry ass.

A bottle of Tylenol joined the hairbrush. The cat barely flinched. She put one hand on the bejeweled binder cover. Brad's proposal was over. It was okay to throw it. Just one of them. She hefted the binder out of her purse and threw it with all her might. It landed directly in front of the cat with a huge *thump*.

The animal hissed and turned. For one heart-stopping moment, it made direct eye contact with Claire over its broad shoulder. Then it ran away, down the trail toward the ranch.

Claire leaned against a tree to catch her breath. A hand fell on her shoulder, and she leapt what felt like thirty feet in the air.

Luke looked at her with concern in his eyes. "Easy. You okay?"

Claire frowned. "No."

Luke scanned her from head to toe. A ranch hand went flying past them down the trail.

"Did it swipe at you?" He turned her around as if expecting to see a gaping wound somewhere.

"No. I don't care about the cat."

"Okay," he said slowly. "Then what's wrong?"

"I missed the 'yes.'"

CHAPTER FIFTY-TWO

To Do:
- *Send congratulations card to B&K*
- *Google William Hickory one more time*
- *Touch base with Darius*

"I AM TELLING YOU, ESA SENT THAT FRICKEN MOUNTAIN lion." Claire heaved her purse into the foyer. It fell over, and a thick envelope spilled out.

It was after midnight. After several hours of picking up trail decorations and making sure every vendor had been tipped appropriately, she was beyond ready to throw her useless body into bed. But there was still work to be done.

"What's that?" Luke let Rosie off her leash, and she scampered over to the envelope and sat on it.

Claire released Winston, and he sniffed his way across the floor. "Cash tip. Apparently Brad has forgiven me for the salsa dancing snafu."

Luke grunted. "You're sure it had a bow around its neck? The light wasn't great, and cats are spotted in the hills regularly."

"You think I hallucinated a mountain lion wearing a bow?" She cocked an eyebrow.

"That's not what I'm saying. Bed?"

She scoffed. "We have so much work to do. The convention is tomorrow—today? I don't know what time it is."

"Haven't we earned like a two-minute break?"

She gave him a serious look. "You can go to sleep. But I need to prepare. This is our best chance to catch them. To end this. To tear it down from the inside."

He sighed and swiveled his backpack around to the front. His camera bag emerged from within. "Let me lock this up and I'll sound the alert on a brunch Code Purple."

She gripped his arm. "I have never loved you more."

Hours later, early morning sunlight streamed through the kitchen windows. The smell of French roast coffee warmed the room.

It wasn't a true Code Purple since Nicole and Kyle were at the airport, but they would have to do what they could with who was left.

"Okay, so we need to nail down roles," Claire said, a half-eaten scone on a plate in front of her.

Brianna leaned in. "I'm going in."

"No, you're not," Luke and Claire said together.

"You're way too recognizable," he added.

Brianna straightened. "Excuse me, but out of everyone here, I am the most equipped to blend in. Hollywood is lousy with misogynistic douchebags. I'm surrounded by them all day long."

Claire shook her head. "Not happening. Besides, we need your expertise with makeup for the disguises."

Luke looked at Claire. "I don't know why you're being so bossy. You're not going in either."

"The hell I'm not."

"No offense, but you're the least masculine person I know. They're not going to have to look any further than the two kegs strapped to your chest. Plus, I'm not letting you put yourself in danger again."

She glared at him. "First of all, Brianna and I worked out a very sophisticated plastic wrap method. And second, no one in ESA would suspect that I'd infiltrate their meeting. It's probably the safest place I could be."

Luke took a long sip of coffee. "I'm going to lose this argument, aren't I?"

"Definitely," Mindy said from her perch on Sawyer's lap. "Besides, Claire has some kind of sixth sense for bad guys. She spotted that one on the pier from a mile away."

"Exactly. Now Bri, Mindy, and Sawyer, we need you guys watching the exits. The street view of the hotel showed at least four, so just split up and do what you can."

"Why don't I get to come inside?" Sawyer asked.

"Because we need your surveillance expertise on the outside if one of them leaves. Also, you kind of stand out too much," she said, waving a hand at his boat-sized feet.

He frowned. "Fine."

"Anyway," Claire said, turning to Luke, "we need to go over their beliefs or you're going to stick out like a sore thumb."

"I know how to be a misogynistic asshole," Luke said defensively.

"Of course you do, sweetie," Claire said. "But you need to know men's rights movement platforms if you're going to blend in."

"All right. Lay it on me." He finished his coffee and moved it to the side. Its spot on the table was quickly claimed by one of his thousands of tiny notebooks.

There was a whole binder on their beliefs, but she didn't bother to open it. She knew the diatribe by heart. "First. Circumcision."

Luke raised his eyebrows. Mindy looked intrigued.

"They believe that circumcision is genital mutilation and should be outlawed," Claire explained.

"Huh," Luke said. He stared at the ceiling. "I never thought of it that way."

"Second. This one is a little messy because different groups believe different things, but they're anti-feminist."

"Where did you get all this information from?" Brianna chimed in.

"The internet is a very scary place," Claire responded. "It's how they organize without judgment. I may have infiltrated some forums while things were...bad."

"What exactly do you mean, anti-feminist?" Brianna scooted her chair closer to the table.

"Some of them think women have unfair opportunities, like higher rates of admittance to higher education programs. Others think they're leeches on society who are dependent on men to exist."

Mindy scowled. Sawyer patted her arm reassuringly.

"There's a lot of other stuff too," Claire said. "Higher rates of suicide, less likely to be awarded primary custody of children in a divorce, paternity fraud, female-on-male violence. Just read the handout, okay? And study the picture of the professor. He's going to be there. I can feel it."

She slid the binder across the table to him.

"Yes, ma'am." Luke cracked it open and studied the laminated picture of the professor from the Web Detectives forum.

Claire's stomach twisted. Luke was capable in so many areas—professionally, sexually, home improvements. But he failed miserably at being a misogynistic asshole. Did he really have what it would take to blend in?

There was too much riding on this. Millions of women were at risk every single day while ESA was still at large, not just her and her family. If they messed this up, they would never find the professor again, and their only named lead would disappear to some other ESA stronghold.

There was no choice but to succeed. And while she was there, she was going to find out if they sent the fricken mountain lion. Those evil zookeepers were going down.

Two hours later, Claire descended the steps, disguised from head to toe. Luke was in the foyer, staring at his watch. He looked up at her.

"You look ridiculous," they said at the same time.

"Me?" Claire asked. "*You're* wearing a fedora."

"Isn't that part of the uniform?" He crossed his arms, and his biceps strained against the Mountain Dew T-shirt he was wearing. He had never looked less like himself.

Mindy appeared from the kitchen with Sawyer in tow. "Aren't his sideburns great? I glued them on."

"They do look good," Sawyer mused.

Mindy came up to inspect Claire. "Damn, Bri did a way better job than me. It's like you don't even have forty pounds of hair hiding underneath that wig."

"Or boobs," said Luke. "How did you pull that one off?"

Claire unbuttoned one of the buttons on her maroon

dress shirt and tugged her white T-shirt down to reveal a sweaty mass of Saran Wrap. "I told you."

Luke came toward her and peeked down the neck hole. "It's like marine animals in an aquarium that's too small."

The fake mustache tickled Claire's nose, and she sneezed. "All right, enough chitchat. Let's get our weapons and meet back here in five."

She ducked into the downstairs bathroom and inspected herself in the mirror. Okay, maybe she did look ridiculous. The maroon button-down she had borrowed from Luke was too big, as was the suit jacket she had bought to go with it. Newspaper was stuffed in the tips of her dress shoes. The sandy-colored wig and facial hair looked natural enough, but she still felt like a child playing dress-up. Maybe she should have gone more casual, like Luke. It was too late to turn back. She straightened her ankle holster and flung the door open.

The threshold nearly tripped her as she crossed the foyer in her too-big dress shoes. She dug in her purse until she pulled out pepper spray and three Tasers. One Taser went in her ankle holster. The other items went into her surprisingly large pants pockets. Why did women's clothes have such ineffective pockets? It was probably also somehow ESA's fault.

Everyone had returned to the foyer. Since Mindy, Sawyer, and Bri weren't going inside, their disguises were minimal. Bri donned the classic anti-paparazzi outfit of an oversized hoodie, baseball cap, and big sunglasses. Mindy and Sawyer had slightly altered their usual attire to fit the California vibe.

It was now or never.

Claire turned to Luke and took a deep breath—as deep

as the plastic wrap would allow, anyway. "Let's do this. Code Purple on three?"

She put her hand palm-down in the middle of the group. Mindy and Brianna joined her without hesitation. Luke shook his head and put his hand in a second later. Sawyer enthusiastically threw his on top and nearly dislocated all their elbows.

"One, two, three, Code Purple!" They shouted in unison.

CHAPTER FIFTY-THREE

To Do:
- *Find the professor*
- *Bring him down*

THEY STEPPED OUT OF THE CAR A BLOCK FROM THE HOTEL. Luke locked the vehicle and Claire grapevined her way to the sidewalk.

It was strange to not have her gigantic purse. How did men even get by with just their pockets? What if they needed a bottle of water, or an aspirin, or a breath mint? Going out like this was wildly irresponsible.

The hotel loomed down the block. Her heart pounded, but the panic stayed at bay. Maybe there was something to this whole medication thing.

She set her shoulders back and lifted her chin. She could do this. All she had to do was sneak into the convention, infiltrate one of their obscene presentations, and then maybe if there was time she would casually track down the professor, follow him to his hideout, give the information to the FBI, and make a big batch of popcorn while they brought this organization down.

"Okay. Let's go over the ground rules," Mindy said. "Mandatory check-in from you two every five minutes. Green check emoji if all is well."

Sawyer nodded. "Code word platypus if there's trouble. And if you find the professor?"

"We follow him," Brianna said.

"Be careful. I'll be watching the perimeter," Sawyer said.

The air shimmered with possibility as she clomped down the sidewalk, Luke at her side. Dr. Taylor was the first domino. Was today the day? Would ESA finally pay for what they had done to her life over the last year? If they caught him, could the FBI crack the professor and bring the whole thing down?

A rhythmic chanting reverberated off the storefronts around her. She turned the corner by the hotel and came to a full stop. In front of the hotel, dozens of women were protesting. Some held signs, others had microphones. One girl was wearing a pink, uterus-shaped hat.

"Equality, not patriarchy" was written on one sign. That was going to piss off the convention-goers. Claire bit her lip, and the adhesive on her mustache tugged at her skin. How was she going to sneak inside without crossing the picket line? Drawing a bunch of attention to herself in the midst of a crowd of angry feminists that she would frankly like to join was not a great idea. Maybe there was a service entrance somewhere.

"Hey," a gruff, masculine voice said from behind a tree.

Claire jumped. Was someone about to try to sell her drugs? Alice had warned her about this since middle school.

She peeked around the tree. A skinny man with cheekbones like the top of a shovel pulled a cigarette out of his mouth and nodded at her.

"You guys here for the convention?"

"Yeah," Luke said in a deeper voice than usual.

"There's another entrance around the back. Crazy fuckin' women," the man said and spat at Claire's feet. She fought the urge to kick him and instead muttered a quick thanks.

There it was. A service door propped open by a trash can. A suitable entrance for such a shady gathering. They exchanged a look and walked down a long, beige hallway, passing the kitchens and housekeeping closets. Finally, she emerged in the foyer and spotted a sign for the convention center. She beelined toward it.

Damn it. Dozens of men were pouring out of what looked to be the main conference room. They had missed the opening remarks. She scanned the crowd. Greasy guy, greasy guy, ancient guy, probable Neo-Nazi. Men streamed past her, some cracking jokes, others staring darkly at their phones. How many of these men were in ESA? Was her abductor here right now? She shuddered. She was going to have to make a donation to a women's shelter after submerging herself in this toxic stew.

Luke nudged her and pointed his chin at a large board. They approached together. A list of speakers and topics littered the board.

There were three lectures scheduled for the same time slot—Involuntary Circumcision: Male Genital Mutilation and You, Reclaiming the Male Space in Your Home and Beyond, and Restoring the Balance: Taking Women Out of Power. She didn't recognize any of the keynote speakers. Which one would the professor go to? Which one would

Luke go to? Taking women out of power seemed to be the organization's primary goal. But who was to say he wouldn't want to learn about man caves or foreskin? Time was running out. She needed to choose.

"I'll take Restoring the Balance," she whispered to Luke.

"Man caves it is." He looked at her with an intensity in his eyes, and she hesitated. Would he be recognized? He could only hide so much under a fedora.

"See you later," he said with a fist bump.

Claire took a deep breath and moved toward the conference room, but something on the wall caught her eye. Posters ran the length of the hallway.

What the hell? Smack in the middle of the posters was a picture of Brianna. "Dangerous Feminist" was branded above her headshot. A description below listed her upcoming movie and how it furthered the "feminine agenda." A dozen other posters with similar women covered the bulletin board around her. Tingles ran up and down her spine. She studied each name and face. These women were bound to be ESA targets. Would anyone notice if she took pictures?

She took her phone out and surreptitiously snapped a couple of photos. Jack couldn't be too mad at her for going to the conference if she identified some future targets, right?

The next set of lectures was about to begin. She made her way to Conference Room C and settled into a seat in the back row on the end.

Men slowly filtered in. Some looked perfectly ordinary, in suits and ties. Others wore what looked to be pajama bottoms and T-shirts featuring cartoon character with references she didn't understand. Still others dressed in regular street clothes and hunched over in their chairs, staring at their phones. One man dressed in baggy jeans and gold chains took a seat in Claire's row. The scent of his cologne was overpowering—cedar and balsam. She could practically taste it. He slouched down in his chair, dark sunglasses covering his eyes. A couple of the men turned around to look at him. Great, he was probably some idiot celebrity.

She decided to ignore the potential celebrity and shifted her attention to the rows in front of her. Two men in suits began a loud conversation about the opening remarks and the dangers of putting a woman in charge. Claire stiffened but kept her mouth shut. Her life may depend on her silence.

The speaker took the podium, and her breath hitched. Holy shit. There he was. Professor Taylor. His salt-and-pepper hair had been dyed jet black, and he had grown a handlebar mustache, but there was no denying that menacing sparkle in his slate-colored eyes. She hadn't seen it since he had handed back her last term paper in business class. The same class she shared with Barney. He nodded at someone in the audience. The poorly dressed man next to her with the chains nodded back.

Her heart thumped against her ribcage. Cologne guy was definitely in ESA. Measured breaths crawled out of her. Thank god she had taken her meds earlier.

She pulled her phone out of her pocket and sent a quick green check emoji to the group. Should she text Jack now? But what good would it do for the FBI to catch him here? If she could follow him and find out where he was staying, they could watch his house to see who came in and out. Either way, Jack was going to want a picture.

Glancing around to be sure no one was watching, she rested her arm on the back of the chair and dangled her phone in her hand like she was just holding it. She opened the camera app and triple-checked that silent was on before snapping a quick picture and closing the app. It was side-ways, but better than striding to the front of the room and capturing him in portrait mode.

She snapped one of the guy in her row too. The more faces she could provide, the better.

"Gentlemen. Thank you all for being here today. Today I'm going to talk about a subject that's more important than anyone realizes. For decades now, women have been forsaking their divine duties and flooding the halls of higher learning in order to 'better themselves,'" he said, throwing up air quotes.

"Did you know that women currently make up almost sixty percent of total college students? The balance is shift-ing, my friends, and we need to be very worried."

Several of the men in the audience shifted. One was staring at him, open-mouthed. It wasn't that crazy of a state-ment, but okay.

"Women haven't stopped there, though. Let's back up a bit. Let's say, to the decades following World War II. Unsatis-fied with their sacred duties of homemaking and child-rear-ing, women started demanding jobs. Instead of applying their nature-given abilities in the home where they're meant to be, suddenly they were in the workforce. Sure, some moved into appropriate careers, like nursing or waitressing."

Her ears perked up. He was talking about the acceptable five!

The guy in her row shifted, and he pulled something out of his pocket. A second later, he was doodling on his program with a pen. A very familiar pen, in fact.

Her breath caught in her lungs. That was absolutely an ESA pen. Silver, weighty, expensive-looking. She still had the one she had found in the woods in a drawer at home. She slunk down in her seat and adjusted her suit jacket. If he recognized her as one of their failed targets, it was game over.

The professor's droning crept back in. "And we applaud those women for wanting to contribute to the household income. But suddenly, women were moving into inappropriate roles. Instead of changing diapers and cooking dinner, they were answering office phones and making presentations. They were making decisions and taking clients. And finally, slowly but surely, they started to take jobs away from men who need them. Promoted above their male peers. Above men who are the head of their household and need to provide for their families."

A man in the front row harrumphed.

Dr. Taylor folded his arms on the podium and stared into the audience. "Having a woman in charge is incredibly dangerous, friends. They are fundamentally, hormonally unstable. They take months off at a time to care for their newborn children, expecting others to pick up and shoulder the burden of their work. Instead of leaving things the way they have been proven over decades to work, they come in and change things. They bring dangerous new ideas, and worst of all, once they're in power, they promote more women. And then you have companies like Grenfell, whose entire advisory board is made up of women. Can you imagine that place one week out of every month?"

Several of the men laughed. Claire's fingernails bit into her arms. Who had emasculated this tool so badly that he was lumping every single woman with a job into the same category?

"As men, it is our right, it is our obligation, to work," the professor continued. "To be the heads of our families. Just as it is the obligations of our wives to stay home, tend the house, and raise children. Now that model doesn't always work for every family. Sometimes a supplemental income is needed. Women have a proficiency in certain careers, that much is true. But should they be leading Fortune 500 companies? Can they be trusted to run a hospital or a bank? Will they be able to make the hard decisions and sacrifices?"

Several men shook their heads. Claire's hands balled into fists. The coppery taste of blood stung her tongue. This motherfucker needed a swift punch in the dick.

"How many of you in here know a woman who has a job opportunity that she hasn't earned?"

Several hands shot up.

"How many of you have been passed over for a promotion in favor of a woman?" Three or four hands remained in the air.

"Herein lies the problem, gentlemen. These women are not worthy. They have stolen the American workplace from us. And it's time we take it back."

Several members of the audience applauded.

Claire unfolded her arms and clenched the seat of her chair until her knuckles ached. And there was another sensation that she hadn't counted on—the Saran Wrap stranglehold on her torso was squeezing her very full bladder. If she didn't do something about it, she was going to pee her pants in a room full of misogynists. She crossed her legs and squeezed, then immediately uncrossed them. Mouth-breathing misogynists probably didn't cross their legs.

Stupid, stupid. She could barely even focus on whatever crap the professor was spouting. Could she sneak out to pee and come back? The professor had been notoriously long-winded at Venor—not even pausing his lecture when a power outage had shut down the entire business building. What were the odds that he would wrap things up quickly during a convention about his favorite subject?

This idiot wasn't worth a urinary tract infection. Claire rose to her feet as silently as possible. Her slightly oversized shoes caught the corner of a chair and she pitched forward, barely catching herself. Heat rushed into her cheeks, and she hurried out the door without looking behind her.

The hallway was empty. Perfect. She pulled up her baggy pants and shuffled as quickly as she could to the bank of bathrooms. She barged inside and finally, mercifully, relieved herself. After sending a quick check-in text, she washed her hands. As she looked in the mirror, her stomach dropped into her butt.

She had waltzed right into the women's restroom without thinking. At a men's rights convention. While disguised as a man. Panic fluttered in her belly, and her throat tightened like she was coming down with something. If someone caught her coming out of this bathroom, she would absolutely be stopped and questioned. What if they noticed that the mustache didn't match the wig? What if they recognized her?

Her stomach was in a vise as she gripped the handle. She pressed her ear to the door. There was a shuffling sound in the hallway. Footsteps thudded outside. Maybe three sets. Shit. If she didn't get back to that conference room, she was going to lose the professor.

"It's him. Hartley's boyfriend," a gravelly voice said.

Blood froze in her veins. Her heart pounded so hard it ached. Someone had recognized Luke.

"He's in the last row. Pull him out," an oily voice commanded. "Do it now. The boss will tell us what to do with him."

Footsteps retreated.

Claire pulled out her phone, ears ringing in panic. She dialed his number. It rang three times, then went to voicemail. It wasn't like him to not answer. She dialed again, free hand twisting in the wig that was bobby-pinned to her real hair. The phone rang and rang, mocking her. Back to voicemail. She should have brought her anti-anxiety medication.

There were voices in the hallway. The sound of a struggle.

"Where do we put him?"

There was a pause.

"The pigpen. We don't wanna be disturbed."

Her heart rate spiked again. A pigpen? Shit, they must mean the women's restroom. She threw herself across the room and darted into the handicapped stall. The lock on the door clicked as she crouched on the toilet. The seat wobbled and slid beneath her. One bolt was gone entirely, and the other was almost out. She felt underneath the seat and twisted at the nut that barely held it in place. It rotated three times and fell out in her hand. It was better to have another blunt weapon, even if it was a super gross one.

The door to the bathroom banged open. A shuffling ensued.

"You're going to regret this." That was Luke's voice.

She peeked through the crack between the door and the stall, heart hammering in her throat. Two men had Luke's arms pinned behind his back. Veins stood out in his neck from the grimace on his face. He twisted violently and nearly dislodged both of them.

Her hand froze on the door lock.

"We need another. Get Barnes. Come here," the portly captor on the left said. A sheen of sweat glistened in the fluorescent lighting. The portly one and his greasy-haired colleague marched Luke to the end of the bathroom. They pinned him to the floral wallpaper directly outside Claire's stall.

Panic flared anew in her stomach. They had him. She needed to do something. Her free hand snaked into the pocket of her blazer and pulled out the first of three Tasers. Alice would be upset about Claire going to the convention, but she would have been furious if she had gone unarmed.

Two more men entered the bathroom. Through the crack in the door, she could only just see Luke's Mountain Dew T-shirt. She ached to touch him, to comfort him. To defend him. Labored breathing came from outside, and it was impossible to tell if it was Luke or one of the men holding him back.

"We can't hold him," the gravelly voice from before grunted. "What does the boss say?"

A blow landed, and there was a grunt of pain.

"He said to take care of it," the oily-voiced man announced. His voice was eerily calm, like he was making a To Do list. What did he mean by "take care of it"?

An unseen gun cocked. Her heart leapt into her throat. Every muscle in her body tensed. Tunnel vision struck, and before she could consciously decide what she was doing, Claire jumped down from the toilet seat and kicked the stall open.

CHAPTER FIFTY-FOUR

To Do:
- *Save Luke*
- *Kick some ass*

Everything moved in slow motion. Luke's eyes widened as Claire emerged from the stall, Taser and toilet seat blazing. Claire swiveled, taking in the scene, barely registering the five other men, until she zeroed in on the one with a gun. Surprisingly good-looking, dressed in a three-piece charcoal suit. She swung the Taser up just as he aimed his gun.

She squeezed the trigger, and electricity crackled as prongs traveled the length of the narrow bathroom. They bit into his chest. He collapsed to his knees and seized. The gun fired with an ear-shattering *bang*.

Claire screamed and ducked. Her ears rang, vision still fuzzy. She waited for the pain, but it didn't come. She turned, quickly scanning the length of Luke's body. He wasn't hurt. She breathed a sigh of relief, then someone grabbed her shoulder.

"*Aaahhh*," she screamed. She used the attacker's momentum and flipped him up and over her body. He crashed through a stall door and cracked his spine over a toilet. He lay on the floor, unmoving. She chucked the toilet seat at him for good measure.

The floor was wet. Like, way wetter than a normal bathroom floor. Her damaged ears caught the sound of a rush behind her. The stray bullet had shattered a sink and lodged itself in a pipe. Water gushed out like a geyser.

She turned back to the men who held Luke, but he had freed himself and was already fighting one of them.

"It's her," one of the men behind her grunted. She whirled, mustache dangling over her upper lip.

Fear gripped her. She pulled her phone out and pushed the button for the virtual assistant. "Call Jack Hartley," she commanded, then stuffed the phone down into her plastic wrap bodice. The phone rang.

A man who looked like he wanted to sell her a used car took a step back. His eyes widened, and he darted out the door.

She dug her second Taser out and clutched it. A solid right hook from Luke sent another man spiraling, and he flashed a grin at Claire.

"Claire?" a quiet voice in her cleavage called.

At the same moment, a third man drew his arm up behind Luke. A hunting knife glinted in the light.

"Luke—" The warning had barely sounded before her second Taser fired, finding purchase on the nipples of the greasy-haired knife wielder. He jerked and crumpled, dropping his weapon. Claire snatched it and whirled around.

Her pants were wet to her knees. She was sweating profusely, and on her last Taser.

She spun, searching the bathroom, but the used car salesman had not reappeared.

"Claire?" the voice repeated, louder this time.

"Shit. Jack, I'm at the convention."

There was a hefty sigh on the other end.

"What did you do?"

"I need backup. We're in the women's restroom on the first floor. Several members of ESA are incapacitated. Luke was—"

Suddenly, the fire alarm in the corner of the room began to flash. A piercing siren wailed in the hallway.

She met Luke's eyes. "The professor," they said in unison.

They ran from the bathroom, stepping over limbs of incapacitated bad guys.

"This one." Claire forced her way through the throng of bodies pouring out of Conference Room C. By the time they fought their way inside, the room was empty.

"Shit!" She buried her hands in her hair. "Which way did he go?"

There was an emergency exit at the back of the room.

They looked at each other. Luke pulled her into him and drew her into a desperate kiss. Heat washed through her, and then they broke apart. There was ice in his eyes as he gripped her arms like it might be the last time.

"You take that way," he said. "I'll hit the lobby. I love you. Go."

Without pausing to answer, she turned and sprinted for the emergency exit. Splitting up was their only choice. She hurtled through the door, looked left and right, and chose a path. Soon she was following the hallway she had originally come in. She was close. She could feel it. Just a right at the employee elevator, then a left after the laundry room and—

She ran smack into a man in a black suit. They bounced off each other, him staggering against the wall and Claire tumbling to the floor.

"Claire?" Jack Hartley's impeccably sculpted hair caught the fluorescent lights overhead. A clear earpiece snaked up his neck.

"I gotta go." She scrambled to her feet, ignoring the piercing pain in her side. "The professor—"

"This way?" Jack followed after her. They sprinted together, her clomping along in oversized shoes and Jack leaping over janitor's buckets and ordering hotel employees out of the way. Their heads on a swivel, they ran for another fifty yards before bursting through the emergency exit into sunlight.

"Fuck." Jack buried his hands in his hair. "God damn it."

Claire stopped in her tracks. She had never heard him swear before. Tanya would have scolded him.

There was a veritable sea of sweat from her boobs to her belly button thanks to the Saran Wrap bindings. Her thighs ached from her marathon bike ride the day before. And the professor was nowhere to be found. Now what?

Jack pulled a walkie off his belt and barked into it. "I need two agents to sweep the hotel top to bottom. The rest of you need to head for the streets and stop cars. We can't let him get away."

"Isn't there a perimeter set up?" Claire's question was nearly a whisper.

"No, Claire, there isn't. We didn't want to tip them off that we were here. We could have had him. We *should* have had him. If you hadn't attacked those men, he'd be in custody right now. Fuck." His voice cut like a knife. There was a hardness in his eyes that she hadn't seen since she was a child.

She recoiled, a memory creeping back in. A cold-eyed Jack shaking his finger and shouting at Claire in kindergarten for forgetting her sweater at school. Her toes curled in her massive shoes, and she took a step back. She fought for words. Was he *blaming* her?

At another point in her life, she would have stood down. Accepted responsibility and put together an apology basket. But so much had changed since she was a six-year-old girl.

"No." The word escaped from her like the bark of a chihuahua.

Jack turned to her, eyebrows raised. His knuckles were white where he clutched the walkie talkie.

She took a deep breath. A river of words threatened to escape. If this exact interaction had happened two weeks ago, she would have slid into a full-blown panic attack. But now she was Medicated Claire. She was Cognitive-Behavioral-Therapy Claire. And Medicated, Cognitive-Behavioral-Therapy Claire was pissed.

Even though her insides squirmed, she made firm eye contact and stood her ground. Maybe it was the fake mustache and men's clothing, but she was raging with confidence.

"I know you're frustrated, Jack. But you don't get to blame me for this failure. They had Luke. He is always going to be more important to me than catching these idiots. I will choose him every time. If they had Tanya, you would have done the same thing I did, no matter the cost to your 'operation,'" she said, throwing up finger quotes.

Jack opened his mouth, but she cut him off.

"In fact, you wouldn't even know he was in California if it wasn't for me. I am a goddamn *proposal planner*. I shouldn't be better at tracking down serial killers than the FBI. Every day that he's out there—that they're out there"—she pointed to the street as if expecting to see a pile of them wielding machetes in a Hummer limo—"every woman is in danger. You need to do better. This isn't my fault. Good day."

She turned on her heel and ran smack into Luke. He was still wet from their fight in the bathroom, but there weren't any visible gaping wounds or lacerations. Relief flooded her. He was safe.

"Let's go home," she barked at him and strode off in the direction of the car. The oversized shoes nearly tripped her, but she kept walking. Anything to put distance between her and Jack. Her insides were tangled up like yarn. So much for her dream of a united family. How *dare* he blame her?

They rounded a street corner. The hotel was hidden from view. Her shoulders relaxed by a centimeter.

Luke, who was almost jogging to keep up with Claire's rage-induced stride, grabbed her wrist.

"What?"

"You just yelled at your dad."

"No, I yelled at Jack." Jack may have saved her life the previous summer, but it didn't make up for two decades of silence. Roy was her father.

Luke raised one eyebrow. "Are you okay?"

"Of course I'm okay." She resumed stomping back to the car, then stopped. "I mean, he tried to blame me for blowing his operation." She waved one hand back at the hotel. "Of all the shitty things that man has done in his life—which is a long list—that's one of the worst."

"I heard." His voice was soft, his lagoon-green eyes more relaxed than they should be after nearly dying at the hand of half a dozen madmen. "I also heard you say you'd pick me."

She drew herself up to her full height. "If you're about to make fun of me for having feelings, I need to warn you that I am pumped full of fake masculine energy and I will drop-kick you straight back into ESA custody."

He cupped the back of her head with one hand and drew her roughly to him. Fireworks exploded behind her eyes when he crushed his mouth to hers. Her toes curled in her shoes, and warmth ran like lightning through her body straight to her crotch.

After a beat, he broke apart. "I'd pick you too. Let's go. I'm sure the cops need to talk to us, and then we have to pack."

CHAPTER FIFTY-FIVE

To Do:
- Keep eyes open for William Hickory
- Contact manager of ice skating rink for D proposal
- Meet up with Nicole

WEST HAVEN GREETED CLAIRE AND LUKE LIKE OLD FRIENDS when they touched down on the tarmac and climbed into their car. Beyond the grid of the city, rolling green farm hills on either side stretched as far as the eye could see, dotted with wildflowers. Not even the redeye they had taken to West Haven International Airport could dull Claire's enthusiasm for her hometown.

She pressed herself to the window. Maybe it was Tanya's influence, but she needed to feel that grass under her bare feet.

"Can you pull over?" she asked. They were less than a

mile from home. He looked at her like she had just asked him to perform open heart surgery. "Just for a second."

"Okay," Luke said, braking and shifting onto the shoulder of the road. He put his hazard lights on while Claire unbuckled her seatbelt.

She flung her car door open and kicked her shoes off. The air was clean and light here, if a bit tinged with manure from the farm to their left. She lifted her face to the sun. It was more humid than Los Angeles, that much was true. But she was home. She closed her eyes and just took a moment to simply be. Dr. Goulding would be proud.

Glancing back at the car, she dropped to her knees, then to her side. She flung her arms until she started rolling down the hill. She laughed as the grass tickled her toes and a wildflower nearly went up her nose. It was a short hill. Rosie's head popped up in the back seat. Winston joined her. She barked, clearly anxious to be home. Or maybe just annoyed that her mom was adventuring without her.

"All done communing with nature?" Luke asked when she climbed back inside.

She shot him a dirty look. "It's just so beautiful. I had to feel it."

"Okay, Tanya." He patted the top of her head and pulled back onto the road.

Claire glowered at him. Judgey Luke was back. At least he hadn't yelled at her for tasering those men. Any argument would have been short-lived since she had one hundred percent saved his life.

The daffodils that lined the driveway bobbed in the breeze. The grass was sorely in need of mowing. There was always something to do at the Islestorm Compound.

"I have never been so happy to be home. Even if it's just for a few days," she announced as she threw the front door open and tossed their bags inside. The dogs darted in next to her. Winston tiptoed across the kitchen and found his favorite bed. He circled several times before settling down. Rosie yawned and crawled in behind him.

Luke glanced at his phone. "I'm glad we were still able to make the trip. I thought the cops were never going to let us go yesterday."

Claire sidled up to him and looped her pinky through his. "How are you feeling today? Sore?"

He had barely said a word about the assault since the incident. The police had opened an investigation, but little could be done without a name of the perpetrator.

He shook his head. "I'm fine. I have some work emails to go through. Should we ignore the unpacking for now?"

She nodded. "I have to get Heather's onboarding documents together anyway. Come get me when you're done." She stood on her tippy toes to kiss him.

"Will do," he said before disappearing down the hallway into his office.

Her phone buzzed. Brianna had texted and confirmed she was alive and still filming in Palm Springs—part of the mandatory check-in policy Claire had established while they were separated. Brianna was surrounded by coworkers, but Claire couldn't shake the feeling of unease. Her premiere was on Friday. If ESA was going to make a move to stop it, it would happen this week. They planned to head back to Los Angeles on Thursday when Bri came home for the weekend, but maybe sooner would be better.

Claire ran one hand fondly over the kitchen island. She needed to go grocery shopping and do a thousand other house-related things. But first, she should probably make sure no one had tried to break into the house while they were gone.

She went outside and carefully inspected all the exterior doors. None of them looked like they'd been forced. There were no broken windows, no mysterious footprints in the flower beds, no menacing messages written in blood-red paint. What a nice change.

She went back inside with a happy heart. Even with the jet lag, it was going to be a great day. She would get some work done, drop off an extra couple of months' loan payment at the bank thanks to Brad's cash tip, and meet Nicole at their favorite taco truck later.

Her desktop computer greeted her like an old friend. The dogs tippy-tapped their way into the office and settled in their respective beds. Claire cracked her knuckles and jumped into work.

Two hours later, there was a knock on her office door. It swung open, and Luke stared back at her with an unreadable expression.

"It's done."

She stared at him quizzically. "What's done?"

"The documentary. They just sent me the final, official cut."

"Holy shit." She jumped out of her chair. "Luke! This is huge!" She leaped into his arms and kissed him. The day's growth of beard scratched her skin. "How do you feel?"

"I won't know until I watch it."

"This is incredible. I'm so proud of you." She tugged him in and kissed him again, deeper this time. He put a hand on her lower back, pulled her even closer. His other hand snaked into her hair. He broke away to kiss her neck, then lower.

Claire strained toward him. Good lord did that man have a mouth. She released one of her hands and felt around behind her for the ceramic jar of dog treats on her desk. She nearly knocked it to the floor, then dug two out and threw them into the hallway. The dogs scampered after them. Luke slammed the door behind them. He carried her back to the desk. With one swift motion, he shoved everything off her desk—keyboard, wireless mouse, new employee binder.

She bit her lip. Sure, he was in the moment. His testosterone levels had probably skyrocketed after finishing this huge project. But did he have to throw everything on the floor? She had just alphabetized the binder tabs.

Luke sat her on the desk, and his hands moved to her shirt. He tugged at the buttons of her blouse, planting kisses as he slid them open one by one.

Screw the binder tabs. Her shirt slid down her shoulders until it fell away. He pressed her back until she lay flat on the desk, then he kissed the swells of her breasts and moved lower.

She unbuttoned her pants herself and wiggled them off before groping for Luke. If this wasn't a brand-new shirt, she would have simply ripped it off him.

He kissed her like they were the last two people on earth, a desperate hunger coming through as he plundered her mouth with his tongue. His grip was so tight that there were sure to be bruises, but she didn't mind.

Rrrrrip. Her shredded panties fell to the floor.

She barely had time to catch her breath before he was inside her. He crashed into her like thunder. Something fell off a shelf. The desk, a secondhand purchase from a thrift store with a cartoon sticker on the corner that she could never quite get off, creaked underneath their weight.

Was this going to be how he reacted every time he finished a major project? If so, she was going to insist he get started on the next one ASAP. She might need to do some Kegels to prepare for the Emmy ceremony this fall.

Her bra strap slipped off her shoulder as he moved with her. The desk wobbled beneath her. The dogs whined at the door. It wasn't the most romantic lovemaking they'd ever had. But damn it if it wasn't hot.

He pulled back to stare into her eyes, so deeply it was like he was seeing her soul. The afternoon light drifted in through the window, painting the curves of his shoulders and lighting him up like a Greek statue. Minute by minute, the fire in her grew until it was almost unbearable.

As they plunged over a crest together, something popped underneath Claire. Her back still arched, she pulled away breathlessly.

"Maybe we should—"

Crack.

Something gave way beneath her, and she fell hard onto the floor, nearly hitting herself in the face with her knees as her body crumpled like an accordion.

"Shit. Are you okay?" Luke's face appeared behind the splintered wood that used to be the end of her desk.

"We broke my desk." Her knees were still in her face.

"I told you it was a shitty desk."

"Just because it wasn't made from the rarest, most deforested tree in the rainforest doesn't mean it wasn't a good desk," she said indignantly. It was hard to be dignified when she was flashing her vagina to the ceiling.

Luke sighed. "Why do you always act like I'm some bougie asshole? My desk is from Costco."

"Can you stop arguing with me and just help me up?" She stuck her hand up and glared at him.

"Are you okay?" He helped her to her feet.

Claire rubbed at the scrape on her back. "I'm fine. I can't believe your project is done. *Wait.*"

She took him by both shoulders and stared into those

infuriatingly beautiful green eyes. "This means we can finally, officially have your premiere."

He crossed his arms. "I told you I don't need a premiere."

"Yes, you do. Now talk to your agent or Streamster or whoever you need to and get permission. Two weeks from now sound good? That gives us a week after Bri's premiere. I have the perfect place." Her mind ran full steam ahead, ideas flashing in and out like news bulletins. "I need the binder." She whirled around. Splintered wood and a mess of pens covered her rug. "Shit. I forgot everything's broken."

Luke frowned. "You can use my desk."

"Really?" She almost gasped. Sneaky McSecretFace had never let her use his desk before. He protected his office like a mama bear guarding a pack of cubs. He had only just started leaving it unlocked.

"Yes. Just don't touch anything or delete anything."

"Like your super-secret porn?"

"Especially my super-secret porn," he said, pointing at her as he walked out of the door, naked as the day he was born.

CHAPTER FIFTY-SIX

To Do:
- *Contact manager at drive in*
- *Shop for a new desk*

"HERE, LOOK AT THESE." NICOLE DRAGGED HER TABLET OUT and foisted it at Claire. "Previews from Brad's proposal."

They had met up for dinner at the park where Claire had tackled someone she thought might be the Widow-maker the year before. She had been wrong, but at least the park still had tacos. Gnats bobbed irritatingly overhead. Children passed a soccer ball back and forth on a green patch of grass. A spicy aroma wafted over from the taco truck in the parking lot. The weathered boards of the picnic table creaked beneath her as Claire shifted.

She wiped the taco grease off her hand with a napkin, then gasped when she focused on the photo. It was perfect. Joy sparkled in Karen's eyes. The Hollywood sign glowed behind her. Peonies wound through the altar behind her.

"Coli, they're perfect. You're a prodigy. How do you do it?"

Nicole smiled. "I'm not. It's just light, aperture, shutter speed. It's practically science."

"Shut your beautiful mouth, you magnificent humble genius." She flicked through a couple more pictures. The sunset ones were striking. Even the drone pictures of the couple huddled together in a Ferris wheel car were flawless.

Claire pulled Nicole into a hug. "I love them. Thank you so much for flying all the way out there. Especially while feeling like a hot bag of garbage."

"It's starting to get better," Nicole said, shrugging. "I ate a whole roll the other day without vomiting."

"Small miracles," Claire said with a smile.

Nicole sipped from her water bottle. "Mindy says the proposal's already starting to blow up."

Claire nodded and sipped from her to-go margarita. "Yeah. Who knew a plug on *Good Morning America* would be all it took to crash our website and fill our inbox? I would say it was nice of Brad to do that, but honestly it was the least he could have done after everything he put us through."

"Amen," Nicole said. She dipped a tortilla chip into a plastic container of queso. "How do you feel now that it's over?"

Claire's gaze swept across the park out of habit. Sure, she had traveled a few thousand miles away from the West Coast. But ESA always seemed to know where she was.

She mentally cataloged all the men within eyesight, just in case. Handlebar mustache dripping taco juice on a baby's head. Two elderly men playing chess. Guy in a suit jacket shouting to someone on the phone about the market price of lobster. No one seemed to be paying them much attention, but that didn't mean anything.

A chilly wind whipped across the parking lot, and she shivered. "Good, I think. It's definitely going to be an adjustment having Heather in LA. It's just been Mindy and me for so long. But I think it's meant to be. She was such a huge help the day of Brad's proposal. I can't believe Wendy almost snatched her out from under us."

"I was impressed with her too." Nicole crunched into another chip. "She just handled the whole traffic situation like it was nothing. We'd probably still be sitting on the Pacific Coast Highway if it wasn't for her."

Claire nodded. "She earned that sign-on bonus. And I used most of the tip Brad gave me to pay a couple extra months of the loan."

"Look at you, Miss Responsible," Nicole said, nudging her.

The shadows were growing long around them. "Not that responsible. I did save some for a new pair of shoes."

"I wouldn't even know who you were anymore if you hadn't."

Claire smiled. "Are you guys free next Saturday? I want to throw Luke a premiere party. I can't believe he's finally done with the doc. I imagine we'll just play the first episode, but of course that'll be up to him. So long as it's not my episode." Her smile turned to a grimace.

"Of course we'll be there. Have you started planning?"

She shot Nicole some side eye. "Obviously. I just want it to be really special for him. We had such a rough time in California. I let work take over every aspect of my life, and it almost destroyed us. I wasn't there for him in the ways that he needed me to be. I'm committed to doing better. Starting with throwing him a hopefully awesome—but also reverent —party."

"Tell me everything." Nicole crumpled up their trash and threw it in a nearby bin.

Claire launched into all the details she had considered for Luke's premiere. If all went as planned, the event would take place at the drive-in movie theater next to her favorite state park. In her youth, money had been tight after Jack left. On special occasions, she and Alice would hike up the overlook at the park and watch the drive-in movies with binoculars from across the highway.

"And I want a fleet of food trucks so that everyone can get whatever they want. It has to be tastefully done, though, because of course we're inviting the families of the victims. Sometimes I forget that we're celebrating the completion of a project that showcases their...you know."

"Murdered spouses and children?" Nicole grimaced. "Everything you're planning sounds really beautiful. Luke will love it. And you'll find a way to honor the victims and their families. Will you speak?" Nicole raised her eyebrows and sipped a thermos of ginger tea. Perhaps the queso hadn't sat right with the baby after all.

Claire paused and sloshed the ice in her to-go margarita. "You know, I hadn't really thought about it. I don't think it's my place. This is Luke's night. It's not about me."

"Well, you *are* responsible for putting their killer behind bars. The families might want to talk to you. Didn't the Herrolds send you flowers after Barney's arrest?"

Claire frowned and looked over her shoulder. "Sure. But at the same time, every time those families see me, they're reminded of their wives and daughters who didn't make it. I don't want to draw any attention to myself."

"They don't hold your survival against you, you know." Nicole bumped Claire with her shoulder.

Claire fiddled with the cap of her water bottle. "I wouldn't blame them if they did. There's no reason why I should have been the one to live. I only survived because of dumb luck. And Alice drilling personal safety advice into me for as long as I can remember, I guess."

Nicole flicked her on the nose. "Stop it. Don't make me call Sawyer's mom so she can explain survivor's guilt to you again."

Claire snort laughed. "I'm a mess, aren't I?"

"We all are. I locked my keys in my car this morning *and* shrank Kyle's boxers in the wash."

"Damn. That's impressive." Claire tucked Luke's to-go meal in her purse. Her fingers brushed against a binder. She glanced at her watch. Luke was watching his episodes back-to-back and was unlikely to emerge for hours. An empty evening stretched in front of her. Although they were only in West Haven for a couple of days, there was plenty of time to investigate the whole William Hickory thing. Maybe if she could find another victim and bring that family closure, she could look them in the eyes at the premiere.

"I should probably get going." Claire hopped off the picnic table. "Thank you so much for meeting me." She pulled Nicole in for a hug and then crouched so that she was speaking to her belly. "This is your Auntie Claire speaking. You are perfect exactly the way you are, Baby Collins. You are so loved and I can't wait to meet you. But not too soon," she added.

Nicole smiled. "I'll see you again before you go back for Bri's premiere?"

Claire nodded. "Are you sure you don't want to come?"

"It's Kyle's parents' thirty-year anniversary, so we kind of have to go. Since I'm the one throwing it."

"Of course. Give them a hug from me. Love you." Claire waved as she walked away.

She could have closed her eyes and walked back to her old apartment, where Mindy and Sawyer were probably tangled together in her old bedroom. She knew every brick of Market Street, every crack in the sidewalk. Her favorite florist was six blocks down on the right. The bodega with the best price on dog food was around the corner next to the health food store. It was so good to be home, away from the overpriced hummus and confusing parking laws of LA. There wasn't even a single influencer on the sidewalk Instagramming street tacos or climbing their ex-boyfriend's drainpipe.

In the morning, she would have to cram as much planning for Luke's premiere in as she could. But, for now, maybe it wouldn't hurt to do some investigating. She fired off a text to Luke and let him know she was going on a walk alone, but that she had three new Tasers and a fresh can of mace on her person.

She glanced underneath her car out of habit before sliding into the driver's seat. The dying sun glinted off the shiny and very official binder she had put together to investigate Barney's latest riddle. She flipped to the first page. There was no record of any William, Will, or Bill Hickories buried in West Haven. That eliminated the cemeteries.

Barney's only victim to be discovered, Kayley Herrold, had been buried along a stretch of road he drove almost daily. If he kept to that pattern, there was a good chance the other victims were buried near his frequent haunts.

Her stomach twisted at the thought of Barney stepping out of his favorite café and visiting the resting place of a victim. Those families deserved answers. They deserved to have a funeral, a chance to say goodbye. If she could find another victim, it would have to help the FBI with their case. Maybe he'd finally be put away for good. And with all hopes of getting out of prison gone, maybe Barney would turn on ESA.

Claire's phone vibrated, startling her out of her reverie. Mindy was calling.

"Hey. What's up?"

There was a clatter on Mindy's end of the phone. "Just baked some cookies. Down, Diesel."

Claire smiled. "Nice. Are you bringing them to the meeting tomorrow?"

"Of course. What did you think about those three West Haven couples I sent you?"

"Claudia and Tyrell are delightful. It's been so long since we did a female proposal. It's long overdue."

"Great. I'll pull their information together and we can get started tomorrow. Where are you going?" She asked sharply. "I hear your seatbelt thing chiming."

Claire squared her shoulders. "Just doing a bit of driving. I missed West Haven."

"Bullshit. You're looking for Bill Hickory, aren't you?"

Claire frowned. How did she know?

"Nicole said you looked suspicious when you left. You're not going by yourself," Mindy said firmly. "Don't go anywhere. I'm coming to you." There was the sound of a struggle on the other end.

"Ugh, fine. I'm at the park with the taco truck."

"I'll see you in five."

The line disconnected. So much for an hour of alone time. But maybe it was best to have some company. Only an idiot would attack her with Mindy in tow. She was basically a chihuahua in stilettos.

Claire flipped to another section of the binder. Thanks to her intense cyber-stalking of Barney and Victoria during his proposal planning phase, she had a spreadsheet of all their favorite places. His barber, his tailor, their favorite restaurant, even the stadium of his preferred sports team. Her skin crawled as she read over the names. She had watched him and Victoria on a date at that restaurant. Picked up a coffee from his favorite café before proposal practice. She had catered to a serial killer, and she had no clue.

West Haven businesses stared back at her. Nothing online connected any of these places to William Hickory, but maybe in person she'd be able to spot something. She'd investigate them all if she had to. She pulled out a high-lighter and set to marking the most likely ones.

Ten minutes later, someone rapped on her window. Claire jumped like she had been electrocuted and smeared orange highlighter across her thumb. The Taser was half out of her purse when she recognized Mindy's green eyes peeping at her through the glass. Phew. Not a murderer. She unlocked the doors, and Mindy jumped in.

"So," Mindy said, immediately handing over a bag full of cookies. "Where do we start?"

"Where do you think he'd be most likely to hide a body?" Claire plunged her hand into the cookie bag. There wasn't any room in her stomach after the fleet of carne asada tacos and extra guac she had eaten, but she'd always make room for Mindy's cookies.

"Barber? Tailor? The quad at Venor?" Claire added.

Mindy grimaced. "Isn't the suit guy down the street from

the Heirloom? Let's start there." She twiddled Claire's radio dial to a pop music station, and they set off.

Once parked in front of Barney's tailor, Hammond Brothers, they climbed out of the car and glanced up and down the street. At this hour, the dinner crowds were dispersing and people were going home. Two couples walked toward a sports bar a block over. For once, there were no creepers hiding in the shadows. None that Claire could see, anyway.

She caught a glance of the Heirloom Hotel as she surveyed the street one more time. The sign blinked on, a sinister red in a sea of concrete. She shuddered from head to toe. What should have been a blissful evening celebrating Kyle and Nicole's wedding had turned into the scene of a nightmare. She had avoided this part of town for the better part of a year, and now Barney had dragged her back into his web.

Claire redirected her attention at the store and put the hotel firmly out of her sight. If she could just solve the riddle, another family would have answers. *That* was what was important. Her heart skipped a beat, and an ember of anxiety stirred deep in her stomach. She closed her eyes and counted to ten.

Dr. Goulding's advice echoed in her mind. Deep breaths, ground yourself in reality. The streetlights buzzed to life overhead. An overripe dumpster must have been nearby as the smell was making her eyes water.

"All good?" Mindy's voice was gentler than usual.

Claire's eyes popped open. Her heart rate slowed, and she nodded. Maybe there was something to this anti-anxiety medication after all. Barney's hold on her had just lessened another notch. It was time to focus.

She turned back to the window. Good lord, even the

mannequins looked pretentious. Was that a pocket watch? Who carried a pocket watch anymore?

"If only we had a cadaver dog." Mindy squinted at the ground as if expecting to see a shinbone jutting out of the small planter surrounding a red maple tree.

"I know, right? Detective Smith had the audacity to say 'the police station is not a dog library, you can't just borrow one.' It's like they don't *want* to find the victims." And there hadn't been enough time (or corpses) to train Rosie or Winston.

Mindy squatted to inspect underneath the store's dumpster. "And here we are, doing their job for them. Again."

"Yep," Claire said flatly.

They scoured the front and back of the store, but everything was asphalt and concrete. No patch of dirt to hide a body, no hickory tree, no curious graffiti, nothing.

The same was true for his barbershop, favorite café, and gym. Dead ends were everywhere. Her new jeans were covered in dirt. The ends of her hair had dipped into a dribbled milkshake outside the café dumpster. Could William Hickory have just been a red herring? Was she wasting her time? But he had told the truth before. Barney wanted everyone to play his game. Why lie now?

"I don't know where else to look." Claire's shoulders slumped as she crossed off Buff Bros Gymnasium. "You pick."

Mindy closed her eyes and pointed to a random location.

"*Chez Louis* it is." Claire activated her turn signal and pulled out onto the highway. It was Barney's favorite restaurant, the one Claire had sent him to after getting engaged. It was on the edge of the business district, near the park that was the site of his flash mob proposal.

Storefronts flashed by and a sense of unease crept in. Her stomach was in knots. If she failed, she would have to face the families of the victims empty-handed. Sure, her abduction had culminated in Barney's arrest. She had debased herself to get him to reveal the location of Kayley Herrold's body. But nothing was going to change the fact that she lived while their daughters died. Some closure was all she had to offer them. But they wouldn't get it if she couldn't find William Fricken Hickory.

They rolled up to the restaurant. The inside was dark, chairs already stacked on tables. They were closed on Mondays, but it wasn't like Barney was going to just chuck one of his victims in the basement anyway.

She and Mindy exited the car and surveyed the area. Barney had always insisted on getting the window table at the restaurant. Claire shivered and drew her jacket more tightly around her. She backed up to the glass and panned slowly around the area like a human security camera. Was it someplace he could see from his favorite table? Something about this place felt different. The air was thick, almost heavy. The back of her neck prickled. Was someone watching them? Or was she onto something?

She leapt to the edge of the building and whipped her head into the alleyway. A sudden crick in her neck almost made her cry out, but she clutched a hand over the source of the pain and probed the darkness. A squirrel darted out from the dumpster. There were no footsteps. No movement in the shadows.

"Something's different, Mindy." Claire turned back to the street.

"Is it?" Mindy closed the chute of the mail collection box she had been peering into.

"You don't feel it?" Claire swept her gaze over the

surrounding area. There was a dry cleaner across the street. A law office to the right. A bank at the end of the block.

Inspiration struck like lightning, sending goosebumps down her arms. There, in a small courtyard behind the bank, was a towering tree.

"Mindy. William Hickory paid the ultimate price. *Paid*. Like a bank." Was Barney's riddle just a stupid pun?

Something inside her propelled her down the street. She crossed the street without looking, earning an angry beep from a Mini Cooper. The courtyard grew closer. Her heart hammered in her chest. Was it a hickory tree?

When she and Mindy approached, they took a small concrete path that curled toward the back entrance of the bank. A flower garden surrounded the tree and a simple iron bench stood at one end. Claire reached up and pulled on a branch. The rounded leaflets looked just like the picture of hickory leaves from the internet. She took a step closer and banged her shin into something hard.

"Damn it." She clutched at her shinbone. It stung like she had punted a beehive. What had she hit? She crouched down and brushed away the thick green leaves of a clump of daffodils. There was a small, tarnished brass plaque hidden underneath.

"Mindy. Flashlight."

Mindy's phone illuminated the small plaque. They crouched together, reading breathlessly.

"The Colonial Bank was rumored to be a station on the Underground Railroad in the mid to late 1840s. John Bledsoe, the owner of the bank, was a secret abolitionist. He would leave one lantern lit at the base of this hickory tree on nights when it was safe for slaves to enter. They called it 'waiting for Bill Hickory.' Fugitive slaves were fed and sheltered before moving on."

Tingles exploded up and down Claire's spine. The plaque wasn't one of the official Pennsylvania historical markers. That must be why it wasn't on the website.

Was this the final resting place of one of Barney's victims? Had he sat on that bench and reminisced about her murder?

"Does that mean...?" Mindy pointed at the flower garden that surrounded the tree.

Claire ripped her phone out of her purse. Her hands shook as she dialed Jack's number. She was still mad at him over the whole convention thing, but this trumped her issues.

"Don't tell me you tracked down the professor again." Jack sounded annoyed.

"You mean you haven't caught him yet? I'm so surprised," Claire sniped.

There was silence on the other end. She took a deep breath and took another step away from the tree. "Listen. Mindy and I solved the riddle."

"What? You found William Hickory?" The annoyance had vanished from his voice.

"Yes. There's a tree at the Colonial Bank in West Haven. There's a plaque—not an official one, I guess because it was only a rumored stop on the Underground Railroad." Her words were tumbling out too fast. "Anyway, there was something about a lantern and the plaque says former slaves called it 'waiting for Bill Hickory.' How quickly can you get a cadaver dog here?"

"Stay right there. I'll send Detective Smith."

"You're not coming?"

"I'm still in Los Angeles. It'll be hours." The phone disconnected.

Claire and Mindy stepped to the sidewalk and shivered under a streetlight. The night was too cold for spring. A sliver of moon peered out from behind a wispy cloud. Her eyes were drawn to the flower bed beneath the tree. The hair on the back of her neck stood up. This tree had once stood as a symbol of hope and freedom. Would Barney really be so uncouth as to commandeer a historical landmark and dump a body?

Mindy's thumbs were firing away on her phone. "Sawyer's not going to believe this."

"Won't he, though? This is kind of our thing. Doing the police's work for them." Her tone was light, but it didn't unravel the ball of anxiety in her stomach. She pulled out her phone. Luke would probably like to know about this turn of events.

Claire: *Will be home slightly later than I thought—might have found one of Barney's victims.*

Thirty seconds later, her phone buzzed.

Luke: *What?! Where?*

She hastily responded that she should probably wait for permission from law enforcement to divulge anything else. Luke sent a swearing face emoji.

The seconds stretched like hours as she stared at the garden. Leaves rustled in the tree.

Finally, two cop cars and a black sedan pulled up. Detective Smith jumped out of the sedan and slammed his car door. Latex gloves slid on with a snap.

"I think you should look here," Claire addressed the detective, pointing to the base of the tree.

"Seal the perimeter," he said over his shoulder to the cops.

"Thank you for the tip, but I need you to get off the bank grounds. This is a potential crime scene."

Claire sighed. She had basically wrapped the professor up with a bow and handed him to the FBI, and they still couldn't catch him. Now she was being banished from another break in the case.

"That's Barney's favorite restaurant on the corner right there. Perfect view of the courtyard from the table in the window. I'm just saying." She pointed at the restaurant, then walked off, too irritated to stick around and snoop. It could be hours before they actually did any digging.

When Claire and Mindy got back to her car a few minutes later, a note was sitting on her windshield. Either someone was trying to tell her about a sale on Polish pottery, or ESA knew she was back in West Haven. Claire looked up at the stars.

"Why?" she half-yelled at the Big Dipper. She looked down at the stupid piece of paper, ready to just throw it in the trash. Knowing the contents of this note would change nothing. But if she did that, she'd be driving back here in the middle of the night and digging through the trash can. You never knew what you'd find in a West Haven trash can. One time, an unhoused person searching for food had found a dismembered finger.

"Not another note." Mindy groaned. "Should we call the police?"

"What's the point? At best, they'll check traffic cams and find some faceless hoodie-wearing idiot dropping this note." Claire turned counterclockwise, staring slowly into each dark corner. There wasn't anyone lurking behind the concession stand at the park or staring at her from outside the shoe store on the corner. The taco truck had disappeared.

"Screw it." She dug in her purse and pulled out a pair of rubber gloves. At this point, they were a permanent fixture in her purse due to the sheer number of times she was required to handle potential evidence.

She clumsily unfolded the note and held it up to the streetlight. Magazine letters were cut out and pasted onto a piece of paper. What was this, an old-timey ransom note? Someone had too much time on their hands.

Blood is thicker than water.

A smudge of red liquid clung to the bottom of the note. She rolled her eyes. "Thanks for the science lesson, idiots," she called to the empty parking lot, just in case someone was listening. A couple walking by with a Shiba Inu exchanged a concerned look and quickened their pace.

She sealed the note in a plastic sandwich bag and threw it in her purse with a mind to take it to Detective Smith tomorrow morning. She already knew what they would find —absolutely nothing.

CHAPTER FIFTY-SEVEN

To Do:
- Follow up with Detective S
- Pick up Heather from the airport

"What is the minimum length of time a couple needs to have dated before applying for our services?" Claire rapid-fired the question at Heather over the top of her menu.

An impressive chandelier hung above them. The scent of garlic and cream clung to the air. Couples chatted at the white-linen-covered tables around them. Claudia and Tyrell, their latest West Haven couple, sat a few tables away, staring dreamily into each other's eyes as they shared a cala-mari appetizer. Candlelight flickered between them.

"One year," Heather said.

Claire nodded. Heather had clearly read the employee handbook and guidelines. Claire hadn't managed to stump her once.

Heather acted like she was trying to catch the overhead light to read her menu and stole a glance at the couple. "Oh good, he's been so polite to the waiter."

Claire nodded and lowered her voice. "Her too. They're honestly adorable. I just want to take them home with me."

"What do you think they're talking about?" Heather whispered.

Claire glanced down at the laminated sheet she had tucked in her menu. "She said they hadn't broached one of the big five—which are?"

"Finances, children, division of household chores, communication styles, love languages."

Claire held out her hand for a fist bump. "You've clearly done your reading."

"I want to do this right," Heather said, casting another glance at the couple. "It's so important."

Claire nodded. "It's not just about the proposal, you know. Obviously that's where we make the splashiest impact. But the reason why we make our applicants talk to each other about the hard stuff is to set them up for a healthy and successful marriage. The proposal and the wedding are just a day. Marriage is for life. Or at least, it's supposed to be."

Heather nodded and looked pensively into the distance. "What's Luke's love language?"

Claire took a sip from her water glass. "Quality time. I really sucked at meeting his needs over the last few months, which is one of the reasons why I've adjusted our company hours and some of our policies. Work was everything to me for a long time. But things have changed." She smiled.

Heather nodded. "I think that's amazing, and not only because you're my boss. Life is about balance and you have to decide where you want to spend your energy."

"Exactly. Oh, they're bringing out the entrées. Let's watch in the least-creepy way possible."

Claire watched their reflection in the glass-fronted fireplace. Tyrell offered his plate to Claudia before taking a bite. She sawed herself off a piece of steak and squeezed his hand. He lifted it to his lips.

"Oh my god, they're so cute. Is it possible to have cute aggression for a couple?" Heather's eyes were misty.

"It is now. Speaking of marriage," Claire said, adjusting her fork. "Legally I couldn't ask you before, but is there a special someone in your life?"

Heather wrinkled her nose. "Nope. I'm single as they come."

"By choice?" Heather was sweet, gentle, and an amazing listener. There was no way she didn't have a fleet of suitors waiting to woo her.

"I haven't had a serious boyfriend since college. I thought things would change when I moved to California, but apparently my true love doesn't hang out at The Last Bookstore or the grilled cheese truck on La Cienega."

Claire nodded. "For what it's worth, you are a beautiful and amazing woman and you deserve the best. As such, I will be informally vetting all future love interests to make sure they deserve you. Background check, the works. It's just one of the services we offer here."

A very new and overdue service, especially since the last person Mindy had dated before Sawyer had turned out to be a member of ESA.

"Oh, of course," Heather said with a smile. "Oh shit, she's coming over here."

"What?" Claire said sharply. Clients didn't usually come over to chat during their stalking sessions.

Claudia cast a glance over her shoulder before crouching down next to their table. "Two kids, Claire! He wants two!"

"That's exactly what you hoped for! That's amazing. How do you feel?"

"So relieved. That was the last big one. Last week, we talked about joint bank accounts since we're moving in together anyway, and I already told him I don't do the ironing. It's perfect. I love him so much and I just want to marry him and have his babies." Claudia sighed and looked longingly at the bathroom door.

Claire smiled. "I'm so happy for you. Now go back to your table before he comes out and finds you planning his proposal with the people who have been creepily staring at you all night."

"Right, right. I'm just so excited. You'll let me know tonight if you'll work with us?"

Claire nodded, and Claudia rocketed back off toward her table, nearly knocking over an empty chair on the way. She had the ambling confidence and slightly clumsy joy of a golden retriever. Warmth grew in Claire's heart. As far as she was concerned, they would sign a contract tonight. All signs pointed to a beautiful marriage for Claudia and Tyrell. But she wasn't the only one involved in the decision-making process. Happily Ever Afters was bigger than ever, and maybe it was time to loosen the reins a little bit.

"So, Heather."

Heather's blue eyes shone back at her. She looked like she was anticipating another quiz question.

Claire rolled her shoulders back and straightened her spine. As difficult as it was going to be, she needed to learn to start giving up control. "I'm going to give this one to you.

You get the final seal of approval. Do we work with Claudia and Tyrell, or not?"

Heather blinked. "You want me to decide? Are you sure?"

Claire nodded. Her heart beat faster than normal, and blood whooshed in her ears. "I trust you. What do you think?"

Heather sat back and looked pensive for a moment. She slid a checklist out of a binder in her purse and studied each item. The binder closed with a snap, and she made steady eye contact across the table.

"Let's do it."

"Good choice." Claire smiled. Sure, she had lobbed her a softball. But Heather had good instincts. She would rep the business admirably in LA. And besides, Claire had totally put an absolute veto power in her contract. But still. Baby steps.

They ate a celebratory meal of lasagna and gnocchi. It was a fabulous day to be a proposal planner.

"So," Claire said as they walked into the parking lot. "I'm going to walk you through sending out the welcome packet and have you run the first brainstorming session."

"This is all so exciting!" Heather's eyes sparkled in the dim light. "Thank you so much for bringing me on board. I'm really excited to get to work."

"Me too," Claire said. "Let's swing by the warehouse site to check on the construction, and then I'll drop you off."

Claire gave the parking lot a cursory glance before dropping to her knees beside the car and inspecting the tires. ESA was *not* going to abduct her again.

"Sounds good," Heather said from the ground on the other side of the car. She had picked up on Claire's safety habits immediately and integrated them into her own routine. "All clear on this side."

No trackers, no rusty nails. It must be their lucky night.

They climbed into the car. As Claire backed out of the parking spot, Heather withdrew a binder from her purse. "The sound equipment was finally replaced. It's in storage at Luke's. We're still waiting on all the other electronics, the décor, moving equipment, office furniture. Hmm."

In addition to learning the ropes as a proposal planner, Heather had also taken over the inventory replacement project.

"It's not much, but it's a start," Claire said as she turned out onto Main Street. Things were looking up. They had a new, competent employee. Their inbox was positively exploding with proposal requests from all over. The top Google search result for Claire Hartley was an article about Brad's proposal instead of her abduction. Brianna's premiere was in two days, and the strong message of female empowerment was sure to piss off ESA. Luke's premiere party was ninety percent planned, and he had even begrudgingly listened to some of the details.

"Forgive me if I'm speaking out of turn," Heather said softly, startling Claire out of her reflection. She hovered on the edge of her seat like a hummingbird thinking about landing. "But you're still set on having this dinner tomorrow?"

Claire cracked a smile. Already getting involved in the personal lives of her coworkers. She really did belong here.

Luke and Claire were flying back to LA the next day. A sure-to-be-disastrous family dinner with Jack, Tanya, Brianna, and Charlie awaited them. Charlie and Jack hadn't shared a dinner table in two decades. Even at Thanksgiving,

Charlie had disappeared into the closet in the basement with a plate of turkey and a bottle of wine.

"For the record," Claire began, "I fully recognize that this is a terrible idea. But my family's been broken for so long. Especially now that I have Luke, if we have children someday, I want them to know their family—aunts, uncles, grandparents. I want us to be able to get together for the holidays without all the adults screaming at each other. You'll understand when you meet them someday," she added, glancing in her rearview mirror as she switched lanes.

Heather nodded and leaned forward, seeming to sense that Claire wasn't done.

"Charlie's never forgiven my dad for what he did. It's going to be very uncomfortable, if she even shows up. But she accepted Bri. I really think we can work through this and at least tolerate each other. Hopefully. And if not, Bri's premiere will be less fun than the average funeral."

Heather nodded and settled back in her seat. "And Luke's family?"

Claire wrinkled her nose. "That's a project for another year. I tried meddling already. Rachel jumped out into traffic and I threw Luke's brother out of my apartment after dropping him to the floor like a sack of flour. Separate incidents."

Heather whistled.

Family stuff was hard. Even at his best, Jack was still the man who abandoned her and missed twenty years of her life. In fact, he had only shown up to question her about the worst thing that ever happened to her. And Tanya, his wife, would forever be the woman who destroyed Alice's marriage. But Jack had taken a bullet for her, and Tanya had welcomed her, a product of her husband's previous marriage, with open arms.

The Hartleys were a fractured family, glistening fragments of a stained-glass window that hadn't been whole in decades. She couldn't choose her family. She couldn't fit the pieces back into the places they once held. But maybe she could make something beautiful with the mess.

CHAPTER FIFTY-EIGHT

To Do:
- *Unpack new Tasers*
- *Refill prescriptions*
- *Google red carpet etiquette*

"LET ME GUESS. MYSTERIOUS HOODED FIGURE. NO identifiable features. Emerged out of the shadows and promptly disappeared. He seemed to have an intricate knowledge of which businesses have security cameras, so it's impossible to tell which direction he came from," Claire said. It took every ounce of self-control in her body to not reach through the phone and strangle Detective Smith.

"Well, yes."

She could practically see the tips of the detective's ear reddening.

"Great. Thanks for the update. And the smudge of red fluid?"

"Initial testing indicates that it was ketchup."

"Awesome." Well, at least it wasn't actually blood. "Any news on the dig site by the Colonial Bank building?"

"I'm not at liberty to discuss—"

"I figured." What good was having a detective's cell phone number if they couldn't even tell you when a missing victim was located? Honestly.

"Never mind. Have a good day, Detective." She hung up without waiting for a response.

"Same shit as usual?" Luke asked. They were elbow to elbow in front of the master bathroom mirror. His California house was cute, but it needed some serious updates. His green eyes seared in the mirror as he fixed his bowtie. He looked like an international spy setting out to seduce a foreign enemy.

"Same shit as usual," Claire parroted. Yet another reason why catching bad guys couldn't be left to the men.

She leaned forward and brushed another coat of mascara over her lashes. The one-shoulder amethyst cocktail dress she had picked out for the occasion had better be comfortable to sit in. Or run away in, depending how angry Charlie got.

Their handful of days in West Haven had been a veritable whirlwind. She had managed to drop off her business plan for Tender Hearts rescue, locate a murder victim, test Heather's instincts, and plan the majority of Luke's premiere. There was no rest for the weary.

Luke grunted and frowned at himself in the mirror. "I don't understand your obsession with awkward family dinners. You don't think Charlie suffered enough at Thanksgiving?"

"You don't understand because you have a velociraptor instead of a mother and your brother...well, you know."

They were leaving in five minutes. It wasn't the time to remind Luke that his brother pulled the plug on their dad before he had a chance to say goodbye.

Luke grunted.

"Sorry. You're right. But family is very important to me, and now that I've been able to at least partially put my anger toward Jack aside, I want Charlie to try too."

He raised an eyebrow. "It was different for her, though. She was way older than you when she left. She was practically an adult."

Claire shot him a dirty look. "She accepted Bri after a little bit of persuading. They went out for sushi together while we were in West Haven. Whose side are you on, anyway? Stop trying to crap on my blended family fantasy."

Luke titled his chin toward the mirror and appeared to be inspecting for rogue nostril hairs. "Why is it so important for you that they all get along? Your dad cheated on your mom."

"Yes, and my mom was able to forgive him."

"Only after he jumped in front of a bullet for you."

She dabbed a bit of perfume on her wrists. The GPS watch she had been wearing since her first abduction didn't really go with the dress or the gold stilettos she was wearing, but thanks to the near-constant threats on her life, it was staying on.

"It was pretty decent as far as apologies go."

"And how does Roy feel about you starting up a relationship with your bio-dad?"

She turned to stare at him. Why was Luke being such a dick? "Why are you so upset about this dinner? Is it because I'm making you dress up two nights in a row? I promise we will veto dress clothes for a whole week after Bri's premiere tomorrow. Sweatpants only."

He shook his head. "I'm just trying to prepare you for all the arguments Charlie's going to fling at you tonight."

"Really? Because she already agreed to come, and it kind of just sounds like you have a problem with Jack."

He glowered. "I don't have a problem with Jack. Well, beyond the fact that you seem to be doing his job for him."

She groaned. "Don't remind me. Speaking of families, your mother RSVP'd 'maybe' to your premiere."

"Classic Rachel." Luke ran his hands through his hair once more and turned away from the mirror. "Are you ready for this shitstorm?"

Claire glanced at her clunky GPS watch. "I guess I have to be." She took his arm and followed him downstairs.

"Hang on." He pulled out his phone and opened the app for their security system. He studied the screen. Apparently ESA was not tailgating outside, as he ushered her into the car a moment later. With the dogs safely checked in at daycare, they set off for the restaurant.

Forty minutes later, the tension was already sizzling at the dinner table. Claire sipped the rest of her glass of wine and picked up a roll from the bread basket. Today was definitely an exception to cutting back on alcohol.

Charlie, looking like the President of the United States in a killer navy power suit, was staring daggers across the table at Jack, who was at least pretending to not notice. Tanya sat next to him, dressed in yet another one of her signature floral muumuus and gushing over every detail of the restaurant's decor.

"Oh, what a lovely centerpiece," she said, reaching out to stroke a rose petal with one finger. "We grow knockout roses at home. They're blossoming this year."

Brianna and Claire exchanged a glance. Pruning a thorny bush in the nude sounded terrifying to Claire, but according to Tanya, it was remarkably freeing and a way to commune with nature. What was an errant thorn to the nipple when there was nature to commune with?

Luke fiddled with his napkin. If they had been at home right now, he would almost certainly be oiling cabinet hinges or replacing lightbulbs. He was clearly uncomfortable being the only male besides Jack at the table. Bill, Charlie's husband, had been called in to a work emergency, and Charlie had refused to expose their son Ryan to Jack's "toxic influence." Brianna was still eschewing men after her last disastrous relationship.

Jack cleared his throat. "Claire, I meant to tell you. The dig went well. Jennifer Heiser's body was uncovered."

Claire's stomach clenched. She grimaced. The image of Jennifer, the beautiful basketball player who spoke fluent Portuguese, was burned into her mind. "I'm...glad?"

Jack nodded. "Because of you, her family can have some closure."

"Did Barney say anything else? Will he tell you more about—" A curt look from Jack cut her off.

"Why don't we discuss that later?" Jack said. "Charlotte, how's work going?"

Charlie wrinkled her nose. No one called her sister by her full name. "Busy. Lots of PR nightmares out here. I had TMZ quash two different stories about one of my clients just this afternoon."

"I think you need new, less problematic clients," Claire commented over a piece of bread.

Charlie shook her head and lowered her voice. "Big Z is a goldmine for a publicist. There's always something to cover up or spin, and at this point, I know so many of his secrets that he has to keep paying me to keep quiet. Same with Lady Larissa. If I went to the news and told them what kind of beauty treatments she was into, she would be cancelled before the end of this sentence."

Claire shuddered. What the hell was Lady Larissa doing for beauty treatments? Bathing in the blood of virgins?

"Sounds like very interesting work, sweetheart," Tanya said earnestly.

Charlie's eyes moved over Tanya's body like an X-ray machine at an airport. Claire could practically hear Charlie's internal thoughts about being called "sweetheart" by the woman who broke up her parents' marriage.

"It is," she said after a beat. "What do you do for work, Tanya?"

Tanya leaned forward. A bit of her blond hair dragged through the butter dish. "I'm a bit of an entrepreneur," she whispered conspiratorially. "How much do you know about essential oils?"

"Oh, look," Brianna interrupted loudly. "Food!"

Charlie, a carnivore through and through, dug into her prime rib. She made steady eye contact with Jack as she cut through it. Jack cleared his throat again and stuck a fork into his vegan pasta dish. Tanya took one bite and exclaimed for a full five minutes about the blend of flavors.

Luke squeezed Claire's thigh twice under the table—his agreed-upon nonverbal cue that she was making a stress face.

"I can see why this restaurant's your favorite, Charlie," Claire said, spearing some roasted chicken on her fork. "Is there where you and Bill had your first date?"

"You know that it is," Charlie said, sopping up some of the juice that had leaked out of the prime rib and shoveling it into her mouth. "You used to love prime rib, Jack. Didn't Mom make that on your birthday? You know, the last one right before you abandoned the family."

Jack wiped his mouth on his napkin and set it on his lap. "I've made a lot of changes in the past two decades, Charlotte. Go on and say what you want to say."

Charlie banged both of her hands on the table. She hit her fork, which spun into the air and clattered onto the floor.

Claire held her breath. Luke stroked her hand under the table.

"Didn't you ever feel guilty, even for a minute? Sleeping with the woman from the health food store." Charlie paused, stabbing a finger at Tanya. "Betraying your marriage to a hard-working woman, not even having the common sense to use protection, bringing this perfect human specimen into the world?"

Brianna's face flushed. She wasn't wearing any makeup again, and she was, as always, lovely. The makeup-free complexion must have come from Tanya.

Claire braced. Charlie was just warming up. This molten flood of feelings had been brewing for two decades. The only reason they hadn't come out at Thanksgiving was because of Claire's careful refilling of wineglasses.

"Did you feel nothing? Did we mean nothing to you?" Charlie leaned forward and stared Jack in the eyes with a look that made Claire's toes curl. "Didn't you care that you left your wife and two daughters all but destitute in a stupid apartment full of spiders? I had to start working another part-time job to help pay the electric bill. I was sixteen, Jack. You stole my teenage years from me."

Jack dropped his fork and sat back in his chair. "As I have explained to your sister—"

"Don't interrupt me." Charlie's nostrils flared.

People in the restaurant were still staring, and several of them whispered and pointed. It was hard to tell if they were looking at the shouting, emotionally battered publicist or Brianna, whom Claire kept forgetting was famous.

"You abandoned your family to start a new one. Tossed us out like yesterday's leftovers. And you disappeared from our lives."

"Charlotte, I emailed you several times—"

Charlie stood and planted both hands on the table. "So what? You think I wanted an email full of empty apologies from my biological father four times a year? I wanted a dad. By the time Roy came around, I was eighteen and headed to college. We have never asked for anything from you. And here you are, trying to tell me how to live my life because a bunch of serial killers are trying to—"

"Charlie," Claire whispered and tugged on her sleeve. "Not in front of the public."

"You're right. Sorry." Charlie took a deep breath and sat back down. She shifted her gaze back to her father. "You have no right to concern yourself with my welfare after two decades of neglect. I want you to stop putting agents outside my house and stop having me followed. You don't get to have an opinion on my personal safety. If I want to get drunk and stumble down the street naked with a backpack full of Girl Scout cookies, I'm going to do it. And I don't need your protection. So back off," she punctuated with a final jab. She picked up her wineglass and downed what was left.

"Well," Claire said, folding her napkin and tucking it underneath her plate. "This was really fun, guys. It's always great to get the family together. But we should probably get going. Check? For the love of god?" She frantically scanned the room for their elusive server. That was enough for one night.

"Charlotte," Jack said, staring at his daughter. "Please stay for a few minutes. I want to talk to you. Everyone else is free to go," he said to the table. That was all the excuse Claire needed.

"Thanks for dinner, Jack. Tanya. See you all tomorrow." Claire jumped out of her seat. If Jack didn't smooth things over before Brianna's premiere, it was going to be a very uncomfortable event. Brianna had worked so hard on this movie. There was no way Claire was going to let the Hartley dad drama overshadow her special night.

"Oh my god," Brianna whispered behind them as they walked out into the cool night air. "I thought she was going to pull out a sword and decapitate him."

"Honestly, I think it was a productive dinner." Claire checked her phone for messages.

"In what way?" Brianna raised her eyebrows.

"Charlie's been waiting to say all that to him for a long time. She's like a little tea kettle. She gets super angry, boils over, then simmers down in time to make a delicious beverage. Seriously, her apology sweet tea is the best. She makes it with mint from her garden."

"Anybody want subs?" Luke asked as he unlocked the car door. "I'm still starving."

"Yes," Brianna and Claire said in unison. She had barely touched her chicken during the shouting match.

"Let's pick up some more wine too," Claire said. "I have a feeling we're going to get a visitor."

CHAPTER FIFTY-NINE

To Do:
- Order high capacity thumb drive for Luke
- Limo pump-up playlist?

"I REALLY SHOULDN'T BE TAKING SHOTS TONIGHT," BRIANNA said with a groan. "I'm going to look like a puffy, bloated nightmare tomorrow. You have no idea how rude the press can be. I'm one unplucked armpit hair away from a scathing tabloid cover."

"It's just one," Claire said, dumping cinnamon whiskey into three shot glasses. "Think of it as a sisterly bonding ritual. But only if you're comfortable."

Bri shrugged and sniffed the whiskey. "This is probably a bad time to mention that I'm leaving early tomorrow morning. I have to go to my last fitting and spend the whole day getting 'cover-worthy,'" she said with finger quotes and an eye-roll.

Claire paused mid-pour. "Are you bringing someone with you?"

Bri nodded. "My assistant will be at the appointments with me. Why are you pouring three? Didn't Luke say he was heading up to watch one of his episodes?"

The knot in Claire's stomach released. She nodded. "It's not for him. Just wait. You'll see." She screwed the cap back on the bottle, and there was a knock at the door. "Told you."

She didn't pause to pull up the app before yanking the door open. There she was. Charlie stood with her arms crossed, tapping one foot against the stamped concrete porch.

"Come in." Claire stepped back.

Charlie all but stomped into the foyer and flung her purse and jacket at Claire.

"I can't believe you made me do that." She glared at her sister.

Brianna hesitated in the kitchen like a startled deer. She clearly wasn't used to sibling blow-ups. Claire had seen more than her fair share from Charlie before she had left for college.

"Do you want to talk about it?" Claire asked gently, as if she was questioning a child who had just woken from a nightmare.

"It's just—" Charlie paused to take in Luke's foyer as if she hadn't seen it before. "I like this flooring. Luke has good taste."

"Well, obviously. He picked Claire, didn't he?" Brianna called from the kitchen.

Charlie's attention snapped to the kitchen. "Oh, good. Shots." She strode into the kitchen like she owned the place. Her elbow lifted, head thrown back. Something glass clattered against the kitchen island. Then she strode over to the window above the kitchen sink and seemed to be composing her thoughts.

Brianna and Claire hurriedly took their shots and sat down at the kitchen table, where tall glasses of water were waiting. Claire's throat burned from the whiskey. Was Charlie about to confess to running Jack over with her car? That would really put a damper on things.

A second later, Charlie spun back around to face them. She looked a little more composed.

"So?" Claire prompted. She pushed the chair across from her out with her foot. Charlie sank into it and took a big sip of water.

"We talked. I didn't flip the table over."

"Always a good start," Claire said. "How do you feel about what you talked about?"

"I don't know. He hurt me—and you and Mom of course. I know you guys have both somehow found a way to forgive him. But I had him for sixteen years. He was teaching me how to drive when he left. I never really learned how to parallel park. I almost rear-ended a Tesla last week."

"Of course," Claire said, reaching over to squeeze her sister's hand. Roy had systematically taught Claire how to parallel park, and she could practically do it with her eyes closed. Maybe he could teach Charlie at the next uncomfortable family gathering. "It was different for you."

Charlie stared at the ceiling. "I knew what it was like to have a stable, two-parent household. Even though they fought, at least they were both there. And then one day he just wasn't. And everything changed. Our house, my responsibilities, everything shifted."

"But he reached out to you?" Claire asked. She had only recently learned that Alice had hid years of birthday cards Jack had sent.

Charlie shrugged. "Here and there. He emailed and sometimes called, but he told me Mom got upset and made him stop. I guess after a while he got tired of trying. I didn't really help things. I was so angry I never wanted to speak to him again."

"For good reason. What he did was super shady," Brianna said, throwing her own dad under the bus.

"Exactly. But there is a small possibility that I'm getting tired of being angry. I've been so focused on raising Ryan and making sure he never has to go through what I did that I didn't stop to ask myself if he would want to meet his grandfather. And maybe I did him a real disservice."

"You were protecting him," Claire said. "It's understandable."

"Anyway," Charlie said, shaking her head. "I told Jack he has one chance. If he screws it up, he's right back in the mental dumpster. He's going to come out for Christmas this year."

"We can all come out if you think that'll make it less awkward," Claire said without thinking. Crap. She probably should have made sure Luke hadn't already made holiday plans.

"I think this is something we should try just ourselves. You're wonderful, but sometimes you can be too much of a buffer," Charlie said, raising her eyebrows.

"That's fair." Something in Claire was glowing. Maybe, just maybe, her dream of a blended Hartley/Alejo family was becoming a reality. If only she could find the stick that was permanently lodged up Rachel's ass, maybe she could whip Luke's family into shape too.

"Do you want to drink a glass of wine and dance to some nineties music?" Claire asked when Charlie didn't respond.

Charlie shoved herself back from the table and downed her glass of water. "Will there be costumes?"

"Obviously. Come on." Claire led the charge upstairs.

Thanks to Claire's cache of emergency disguises, the three of them were unrecognizable as they thrashed around the living room thirty minutes later.

Charlie, in a lime-green wig with matching lipstick, sang into an imaginary microphone while Claire and Brianna did backup dancing. Brianna wore denim overalls and a clown nose while Claire had slithered into a replica of Sandy's final outfit from *Grease*. The wine was flowing—definitely more than just one glass now, and Claire's head was swimming pleasantly. She would do better at cutting back tomorrow.

At one point, Luke came down with his camera, but Claire chased him out.

Surrounded by her sisters, the warm feeling only grew. Because of her age gap with Charlie, Claire had practically been raised as an only child. Now that Happily Ever Afters had a branch in Los Angeles, maybe they could make up for lost time. Monthly dance parties, weekly dinners.

"Brianna," Claire said when the song stopped. She grabbed Brianna by both shoulders and shook her. "You are a magnificent beam of human sunshine. I'm so glad my dad accidentally knocked up your mom and destroyed our nuclear family. You are a brilliant, talented actress, and I am beyond jealous of your gorgeous complexion."

"Stop it." Brianna swatted at her, but she was smiling.

"And you." Claire rounded on Charlie. She poked her in the arm, where Charlie had applied a temporary tattoo of a butterfly. "You are a fierce, loyal lioness. I've looked up to you my entire life. No one can command a room the way you can. I'm pretty sure I've actually witnessed a man shit his pants because he was so intimidated by you. And beyond all that, you are an amazing mother. Ryan is the coolest kid ever in a generation of kids who are all-too-frequently little assholes."

Charlie's lower lip trembled. "Another song!" she demanded, turning away. Luke's stereo blasted with a summer pop hit, and they launched into another dance routine. As the song faded out, something clanged against the window outside.

Charlie and Brianna froze. Claire leapt across the room. *Scrrrrrtch.* A Taser separated from the Velcro on the back of the couch. She threw her shoulders back and pointed it toward the window. Brianna and Charlie fell in behind her.

"Do you think it's them? ESA?" Brianna asked.

"Turn that down," Claire barked over her shoulder to Charlie. She couldn't think straight with *Barbie Girl* blasting. For once, her older sister twiddled the dial without a fight.

Claire picked up her phone, then pocketed it. Luke was deep in documentary mode. There were three of them. Nobody would be stupid enough to abduct Charlie. In fact, out of the three of them, Charlie had barely been threatened at all. Her vast knowledge of the Hollywood underground must have kept her safe.

Claire twitched the curtain aside. A streetlight illuminated a patch of sidewalk that was in need of repair. No shadows moved across the lawn.

Claire turned to face the other two. "Let's go see what it was. Weapons first, though."

Charlie and Brianna armed themselves with a butcher knife and a corkscrew. Claire flipped the porch light on and flung the front door open quickly, as though she expected to see someone casually preparing a murder kit. The porch was empty except for the Adirondack chairs and a bag of vegetables that Mr. Nesbit must have dropped off. Maybe that was the noise she had heard.

She crept down the short flight of stairs to the walkway. Charlie and Brianna followed her. She swung her head from left to right, probing the dark yard.

"Could it have been Olivia?" Brianna whispered.

Claire shook her head. "According to her Instagram, she's at some wellness retreat in Santa Barbara."

"She could be lying." Charlie lofted her butcher knife. "Claire, do you recognize that car?" She nodded toward a dark gray sedan with tinted windows idling on the other side of the road.

"No, I don't. But I don't know all the cars in the neighborhood."

"Then let's go find out who's inside." Charlie drew herself up to her full height of five feet and ten inches. Her bare feet padded over the grass.

Suddenly, something rustled in the buckwheat shrub that had just begun to bloom. Charlie screamed and threw the cleaver at it like a medieval knife-thrower. Claire swung the Taser up and fired without a second's hesitation. *No one* was getting kidnapped today. A crackle of static split the air as the prongs went flying across the yard and buried themselves in the bush. A second later, a very startled-looking squirrel sprinted across the yard. It could have been a trick of the moonlight, but it looked like the end of his tail was slightly singed.

"You just tasered a squirrel," Brianna said.

"Oh my god. He looked like he was okay, right?" Claire turned and glanced at the upstairs office window. Luke was pressed to the glass, camera at eye level and body heaving with laughter. She flipped him off and turned back around. "You want to see who's in this creepy car or what?"

She marched across the grass and picked up the knife that Charlie had thrown. The wine and whiskey mix had had a peculiar effect. She felt invincible—dehydrated, but invincible. She'd find out who was in that car. And if it was someone from ESA, she'd punch them right in the face, drag them out of the car, and sit on them until the FBI arrived.

Knife in hand, she stormed across the grass and tiptoed across the asphalt in her bare feet. She rapped on the driver's side window until it rolled down. Claire gasped.

"Jack! What the hell are you doing here?"

Jack Hartley sat in the driver's seat, mug of coffee steaming in one hand. Tanya sat next to him, a pair of binoculars and a partially crocheted blanket in her lap.

"Hello, darlings!" Tanya called enthusiastically, even though they had all seen each other two hours ago.

"Charlotte forbade me from installing agents to watch out for you all, so I thought I'd do it myself. Thank you for all being in the same place, by the way, it makes it much easier."

Claire sighed. "You don't need to do that. We have a security system. And each other."

"You've also had..." He paused for a moment and sniffed. "Several glasses of wine." What was he, a booze-seeking bloodhound?

"Forgive me if I have less than complete faith in your self-defense skills while your blood alcohol level is elevated," Jack continued. "As entertaining as it was to watch you tase a bush. By the way, if you were wondering what hit your window, it was a bird."

Claire whipped around. Was it injured? She wasn't versed in bird CPR, but she had quick hands when it came to YouTube.

"It's fine," Jack added. "It flew north. Here," he said, reaching into his back seat and pulling out a new Taser. "In case the chipmunks stage an uprising next."

"Deadbeat Dad's got jokes." Claire snatched the stun gun from him. There were five more inside concealed beneath various pieces of furniture, but she wasn't going to turn her nose up at a free weapon. Not after everything they'd been through in the past month. She turned on her heel and cut across the yard. Charlie followed her, but Brianna stuck her head inside the car.

Even under the blue tone of the streetlight overhead, Brianna looked like an elf princess from a fairytale as she skipped lightly over the asphalt and came back with a gallon-sized storage bag that looked to be full of cookies.

"Mom made us cookies. They're vegan, but I can confirm that they're edible," she said, brandishing the bag.

"Let's go back inside. I don't want to shame-eat these where they can see us." Claire stepped into the foyer and snapped the door shut behind them.

CHAPTER SIXTY

To Do:
- Find a sneaky place to do Ted Talk power stance
- Make sure Bri's flowers were delivered

THE LIMO PULLED TO A STOP IN FRONT OF THE TCL CHINESE Theater on Hollywood Boulevard. Claire's heart thumped in her chest despite her anti-anxiety medication.

"Why am I nervous? This is Bri's movie. No one here knows or cares who I am."

"Well," Luke said, climbing out of the leather-padded seat and resting his hand on the door. "You are a nationally recognized proposal planner and the person who changed the Hollywood sign. And Bri's sister. And, you know, a surviving victim of a serial killer."

"Great. Thanks for the reminder." She flapped her hands at her side, but they were still numb. Maybe another round of yoga breaths would help. If she didn't get out of the car now, whatever Hollywood A-Lister was behind them would surely tell their driver to ram them.

"Deep breaths, Clairebear," Charlie said in her best Alice impression. She looked as bossy and unbothered as ever in her form-fitting eggplant cocktail dress. Bill had been called to yet another lawyer emergency, so she was third-wheeling for the night.

Claire straightened the shoulders of her glittering, champagne-colored evening gown. A pair of brand-new Manolos, thanks to her tip from Brad, peeked out from beneath the hem. She glanced out the back window of the limo. A line of identical cars stretched behind them. Brianna and her assistant were in one of them.

"We're going to be late," Luke said pointedly, glancing at his watch. "They don't appreciate it when you hold up a red carpet."

"Fine, fine," Claire said. She took a deep breath and scooted to the edge of her seat.

The door opened. Luke stepped out and held out his hand. When Claire didn't take it, Charlie did. The press that lined the red carpet shifted and zeroed in on the inside of the car, probing the interior for VIPs.

Claire took a deep breath and stepped out behind her big sister. The glittering hem of her gown almost got stuck on her Manolos, but she wiggled just in time to avoid falling on her face. The door shut behind them, and the safety of the limo disappeared into the night.

"Anyone know who they are?" someone called out.

"That's Luke Islestorm! Luke, over here."

Oh, hell. Someone actually wanted to speak to Luke. But he was tall. She could hide behind him.

Luke's eyebrows raised. He clearly wasn't used to being recognized. His hand found the small of her back, and he guided her gently down the red carpet. Claire glanced over her shoulder, but Charlie was oblivious to the spectacle—her nose was buried in her phone.

Luke had been stopped by a small-time publication with an online edition.

"Mr. Islestorm," a man with sandy brown hair and a sprinkle of freckles asked, "how do you feel about your recent Emmy nomination?"

"I'm very flattered at the attention *Suburban Hustle*'s received. A lot of great candidates have been nominated this year. I hope people feel as strongly about my next documentary on the West Haven Widowmaker. It'll be released on Streamster this summer."

Wow. Had a studio executive given him talking points? That was next-level professional.

"And who do you have with you?" The reporter diverted his gaze to Claire.

"Claire Hartley." Luke's grip tightened as if he knew she was planning on diving headfirst into the bushes. "She's the owner of Happily Ever Afters, a renowned proposal planning company. You might have noticed the Hollywood sign was different last week. That was all her."

"Can we get a picture?" The sandy-haired reporter asked as microphones were suddenly thrust in Claire's direction.

"Sure," Luke said, tightening his grip on Claire. "Breathe," he whispered in her ear. She smiled for the camera and leaned in to him. She hadn't anticipated that anyone would recognize them, let alone want to put them in their publication. She should have triple-checked her teeth for spinach.

"Miss Hartley," a woman with curly red hair and a matching blazer called as soon as the picture had been snapped. "How did you manage to escape the West Haven Widowmaker?"

Ah, shit. The blood ran cold in her veins. They must have Googled her.

Luke turned to step in front of her, but Claire stopped him. He had plugged her in his brief moment in the spotlight. The least she could do was return the favor.

"Well, if you want an answer to that question, you'll have to watch the new Lucas Islestorm documentary, *The Widowmaker*, coming to Streamster this summer. Thanks," Claire said, turning on her heel before anyone else could chime in.

"You handled that really well," Luke said.

"Hopefully people will stop asking after the documentary airs." She shook her head and took his arm. They set off down the red carpet. They were nearly to the end, and then they could skip to the fun part—celebrating Brianna's triumph and shoving the female empowerment in ESA's face.

"Can we wait for Bri? Just to make sure she gets here," she said as they stepped off the red carpet and paused before the golden double doors.

"Sure." Luke pulled off to the side with her. Charlie joined them a second later, frowning at her phone. Once inside, she'd have to secure it in a locked bag to prevent any details about the premier leaking, and Claire knew she was taking one last opportunity to check her email.

"Unbelievable." She shook her head. "Big Z's in trouble again. He roofied a girl at a club last night. I'm not going to be able to squash this one. I already called in too many favors this week."

"What an asshole." Claire shuddered. As soon as she was back in West Haven, she was going to have a stern talk with Mindy about her musical preferences.

She glanced down at her phone. Bri hadn't texted her back in a couple hours. Surely she was just busy getting ready and doing whatever pre-premiere ritual she had adopted over the years. But she couldn't ignore the anxiety that had settled in her stomach like a ten-pound kettlebell.

"I'm going to call her assistant and see where they're at."

"Famous people are always running late." Luke reached over to rub her arm. "I'm sure she's trapped in that night-mare of limos." He gestured to the road, where a dozen town cars and limousines were waiting to drop off passengers.

Claire shook her head. Dread was threatening to over-whelm her, growing inside her like a black hole. Something didn't feel right. She pulled out her phone and scrolled to Brianna's assistant, Natalie. She held her breath as she dialed.

"Natalie Stevenson," a cheerful voice answered.

"Hey, it's Claire. Brianna's sister. I was just calling to check on Bri. Are you guys almost here?"

There was a pause on the other end.

"Aren't you with her?" Natalie asked.

The bottom fell out of Claire's stomach.

"What's wrong?" Luke asked. His phone rang, and he took a step away to answer it.

"No, she told us she was going to be with you all day," Claire said.

Charlie threw her phone in her purse and stood next to Claire. She was much paler than she had been in the limo. Claire put Natalie on speaker phone.

"Well, she was, but then she said she wanted to catch the limo with you guys. She headed to your house about an hour ago."

"Oh my god," Claire said. "I have to go."

"Wait, are you saying she's—"

Claire ended the call and frantically clicked on Bri's contact. Her hands shook as they clutched the phone. No answer. She dialed again. No answer. She sent a text. No answer.

"Luke," she called out. Her whole body was trembling. Something was terribly wrong. Where the hell was she?

"Thanks." Luke ended the call he was on and turned back to Claire with an unreadable expression.

"I can't get in touch with Bri. I think something happened to her." The words tumbled out over numb lips.

"I know," he said, scrolling through something on his phone. "We need to call Jack right now."

"I'll do it." Charlie looked rattled for the first time since she was sixteen. She buried one hand in her hair and dialed.

"What do you mean you know?" Claire asked. Her vision was starting to blur at the edges. She took shallow, hurried breaths. Goosebumps ran down the length of both arms.

Luke showed her the screen. It was their security camera for the front yard. Something was flickering onscreen.

"Is that *fire*?" She leaned in and stared at the screen.

Luke nodded. "It's hard to tell from the video. Mr. Nesbit called and the fire department's on their way. But they left us a message."

"What does it say?" Her stomach roiled. She was going to projectile vomit here on the red carpet outside a historic theater.

"We warned you," he said quietly.

Thirty minutes passed in absolute panic. Jack launched an FBI response. The venue shut down the screening. Cops and agents buzzed around them. Eventually, they were shepherded to what appeared to be an FBI safe room not far from the theater.

"Okay," Jack said, a map of Los Angeles spread out in front of him.

Tanya paced in the corner, weeping and clutching a crystal. "Should have known. Mercury is retrograde again. Oh, my poor baby."

"What do we know?" Claire asked. There was a pool of sweat beneath the Taser she had strapped to the inside of her thigh. She was going to use it on whoever had taken her sister.

"Last confirmed location was her house in Burbank." Jack pointed to a spot on the map. "She left there at six thirty to head to Luke's house—"

"But we were already gone," Claire said. Of all the days to be on time.

Luke sat in a chair in the corner, combing through the security footage. "I don't think she ever made it to the house," he said. "Her car doesn't show up on any of the footage since we left."

Jack made a note on a piece of paper and turned back to the map. "So that means somewhere between here and there she disappeared." His shrewd brown eyes narrowed. "LAPD is checking traffic cameras and looking for her car."

Charlie sat on a futon in the corner, eyes watering and fist clenched around a scrunchie that Brianna had let her borrow during their dance party.

"She could be anywhere." Claire stared at the map. "We don't even know where the professor is staying. Anyone could have her." She turned away. Her hands twitched, ready to flip a table or strike a match to burn down a building. ESA had taken her baby sister. There was no doubt in her mind.

"What about her tracker? Don't you always put a tracker

in her car or shoes or something?" She had seen evidence of the tracker at Jack's house back east.

"She left the bracelet at home." His voice broke, and he cleared his throat. That was fair. It wouldn't have gone with her outfit.

"She told me she hired a bodyguard," Jack added.

"She didn't," Claire half-screamed. Her mind spun. She could see it, clear as day. Brianna, bound and gagged while a psychopath stared down at her. If they didn't find her, she would be dead before morning. For the first time, she understood how Luke and her friends had felt the night she had been abducted by Barney. Nothing but dead ends, seconds slipping away. Could they find her before it was too late?

"Someone should check the decommissioned ESA houses. I have a list on my phone. That's where they were going to take Wendy when they planned to kidnap her." She scrolled through her emails and sent the spreadsheet to Jack.

Jack nodded and addressed one of the other agents in the room. "Humbert, we're going to need LAPD to investigate every fraternity house that was once affiliated with the Greek organization Epsilon Sigma Alpha. I just sent you the list."

"On it." The agent disappeared into another room.

"Why don't we just put out a social media blast?" Charlie piped up from the futon. She looked slightly more composed than she had a minute ago. The borrowed scrunchie was now around her wrist. "Bri's a public figure. People know what she looks like."

"We don't want to cause a panic," Jack muttered. "Whoever has her could drag her further underground where we'll never find her. These next few hours are crucial."

"I have another theory," Claire said quietly.

Jack whirled around. There was a crazed look in his eyes. "What?" he barked.

"I think it's possible that whoever is in charge out here lives in the Hills."

"What do you mean?"

"A couple weeks back, I mapped out where missing women over the last two years had been taken." She scrolled through her phone and found the picture she had taken of the map. "See how the lines intersect over the Hills? And I was attacked at the ranch right within the same radius. I drove through a couple neighborhoods, but I didn't really see anything suspicious."

Jack wiped a hand over his face. "We can't waste time on unfounded theories, Claire." His voice cut like a knife. A pair of agents came in, and he stepped away.

Another hour passed. Claire paced the room, Manolos clacking across the hardwood floor. Tanya stared out at the barely visible stars and whispered tearfully to the crystal in her hand. Luke called everyone he knew who lived in Burbank and asked them if they'd seen an abandoned Subaru. A set of cold, untouched pizzas sat on a table in the corner.

Reports trickled in. Every ESA house they checked was abandoned, just like the West Haven chapter. It was a dead end.

The radio in Jack's hand crackled.

"We found the car."

Everybody stopped what they were doing.

"Where?" Jack barked into the radio.

"A Starbucks in Burbank."

Jack swore. "That's her pre-premiere ritual. She always gets an iced coffee. And that location's close to two major highways. There's no way of knowing where they took her. She could be anywhere." He slammed a fist on the table.

Claire finally stopped pacing and sat next to her sister on the futon. It was surprisingly comfortable for something government issued.

Charlie opened a text. The tiny circular contact at the top of the screen showed a white man in his mid-forties dressed in a black suit with gold chains. A distinctive gold tooth flashed at the camera.

Claire gasped. A lightning bolt might as well have just crashed through the roof and impaled her. She had seen him before, she was sure of it. But where? A tabloid? A magazine? But no—this felt personal. Something tugged at her memory, but she couldn't place it. She jumped up and began to pace. The vegan restaurant? No, that wasn't it.

"Charlie," Claire said slowly.

"Hmm?" Her sister was clearly only half paying attention.

"Who is that?" She gestured at the phone screen.

"This idiot? It's just Big Z. He doesn't even care about Bri, he just wants me to fix the roofie thing. Un-fucking-believable." Charlie threw her phone at the futon. It bounced off and hit the floor.

Claire froze, then dove for her phone. Her hands shook as she scrawled through her camera roll. She shoved it in front of Charlie's face.

"Is this him?"

The picture she had taken of the man in baggy jeans at the men's rights conference stared back at them. With Luke almost dying immediately thereafter, she had completely forgotten about the other member of ESA in the audience.

"Yes," Charlie said slowly. "I got him those diamond studs for Christmas. How did you—"

"Where does he live?" Claire interrupted.

"Why?"

Jack turned away from the table.

"Because we need to go there right now. He has Bri."

"What do you mean? How do you know?" Luke appeared at her shoulder.

Jack stared silently at her from across the room. The pencil he was clutching snapped in half. He calmly set the pieces down.

"At the men's rights conference. Big Z was in my row. I hate his music, so I think that's why I didn't recognize him. But it was him, I'm sure of it. He and the professor nodded at each other."

Jack picked up a walkie talkie and pressed the button to talk. "We're going to need backup."

CHAPTER SIXTY-ONE

To Do:
- Find Brianna
- Make them pay

"I don't understand why you can't just go in there guns blazing." Claire was going to wear a hole in the floor of the safe house. "Every second we waste here is another second Brianna could be killed."

"They need a search warrant," Luke said. He was paler than usual. "Right now, we have no evidence of wrongdoing beyond the fact that you think you saw Big Z acknowledge the professor at a convention."

"A convention where there was a literal poster of Brianna labeled as a 'dangerous feminist.' I know it was him." Claire bristled, stopping in front of the window and staring outside. The streetlight on the corner changed color. "If he doesn't have her, he knows who does."

Jack looked like he had aged a decade. "Try to under-stand, Claire. If you're right about this Big Z character, his house is a treasure trove of information on ESA. He could have a membership roster or email correspondence. I want nothing more than to get your sister back. But if we don't do everything by the book, we risk rendering all that informa-tion inadmissible in court. Every single one of them could walk free."

"We can't just do nothing," Claire yelled. One of the agents in the kitchen side-eyed her. "I don't know about you, but I don't want a dead sister on my conscience. What can we do? Do I need to go drag that judge out of his daughter's wedding? Because I'll do it."

Apparently part of the holdup was the judge who was on call to sign search warrants was attending his daughter's wedding downtown. Traffic was a nightmare. She would sprint there barefoot if she had to.

Jack shook his head. "Agents are already on their way."

Charlie stood up from the futon. "We don't need a warrant."

"What do you mean?" Luke asked.

"I just texted Big Z. I told him if he wants to fix this scan-dal, then I need to come over right now. You don't need a warrant if you're invited in."

Jack whirled around. "Charlotte, it's too dangerous. You're not going."

Charlie rolled her eyes and ignored him.

"Where does he live?" Claire asked.

"Mulholland Drive. Less than five miles from here." Charlie glanced in her compact and wiped a stray tear away. She smoothed her hair back and straightened up. "I can get an Uber and have them stop a few houses away. Are you coming?"

"Obviously." Claire held out her hand. Luke tossed her purse at her and she slung it over her shoulder. She pulled an even smaller bag out and changed into her emergency flats.

"Girls," Jack said sternly. "You can't do this."

"We're not agents. Charlie can let me in a backdoor, and I can sneak around and find out where he's holding her. You don't have to wait for a warrant if there's a nine-one-one call, right?"

"That's technically correct," Jack said. His normally perfectly smoothed hair was sticking up in the back. The knees of his suit were wrinkled. He had never looked so disheveled.

"Uber's here. Let's go." Charlie cracked the front door open. Luke and Claire hurried after her.

"Wait!" They turned.

Tanya ran toward them and gathered them all into a bear hug. She whispered something over them and flicked something from a vial at them. It smelled like cinnamon.

"Be safe," she whispered tearfully as they left.

"Okay, what's the plan?" Claire asked minutes later from the middle seat of an overly large SUV.

"We stop a couple houses away," Charlie whispered. "I go in first. I'll ask him to let me use the powder room, and I'll unlock the window. It's at the back of the house by the pool. Then Luke can boost you up and you can climb inside."

"Done." Claire said. She would rip her dress in half if she had to. "Did he sound suspicious at all?"

"He said 'Now's not the best time, but I'll make time if you can make this go away.'"

"I wonder if he has company," Claire said thoughtfully. "When ESA tried to kidnap Wendy, they made a big show of it. Everyone from the chapter was going to be there, alumni included. And Brianna's a much bigger target. They had a poster of her at the convention talking about how she earned more than her male co-lead for this 'pro-feminist' movie."

Anxiety still clawed at her like a wild animal, but now that they were moving and had a plan, it started to subside. The Taser pressed to the inside of her thigh felt woefully inept for such a dangerous plan. Even the backup one stuffed in her bra didn't bring much comfort.

Charlie sighed. "There's already buzz online about the premiere being cancelled. Apparently studio reps blamed a gas leak, but conspiracy theorists are spiraling."

"Are you okay?" Claire whispered to Luke. "You've been so quiet."

"Just worried about Brianna," he said with a humorless smile. He turned to stare out the window. The streetlights and marquees of the city faded away as they crawled into Laurel Canyon. "It feels the same as it did right after we realized you were missing. Back then, we didn't even have a hunch, not for hours."

Claire squeezed his knee. "We'll find her in time. Don't worry."

"Are you saying that to me or yourself?"

"Both," she admitted, sliding her clutch into its crossbody position. She was going to need both her hands free if the occasion called for dick-punching.

Her phone buzzed. A message from Jack.

"They got the security tapes from the Starbucks." She pressed play on the video.

In the ten second clip, Brianna approached her car. As she reached to open the driver's side door, two men wearing ski masks and gloves leapt out of the black Escalade next to her and clapped something over her mouth. She slammed her drink over her shoulder and directly into the face of the figure who had grabbed her. It was unfortunate that her pre-premiere ritual wasn't a scalding hot latte. Brianna's body went limp and they dragged her into the car.

"Freaking chloroform," Claire said, clutching at her throat. She could practically taste the sickly sweet liquid on her tongue. Her heart ached for her sister.

"We're here," Charlie said dubiously as the car screeched to a stop outside a mansion.

The trio filed out and waited for the car to drive away.

"Which way?"

Charlie pointed two houses to the north. Another mansion hulked out of the darkness. Behind the wrought iron gate, a circular driveway was lined with at least a dozen cars. Claire's blood ran cold. Two Tasers were definitely not going to be enough.

"Looks like you were right about company," Charlie muttered. "They'll let me in the gate, but I'm not sure how we'll get you inside. There are cameras along the perimeter too."

"There has to be a way in. Back gate, secret exit, gap in the fence?"

Luke put a hand on Claire's shoulder. "Don't worry about us," he said to Charlie. "Just focus on getting inside and opening the bathroom window. We'll find a way in."

Charlie nodded. "Wait until I go in, then walk past. Try skirting around the back. There's a house under construction next door. It doesn't have a fence yet. I was only in the backyard a couple times at night, I wish I could remember more."

Claire grabbed her sister's hands. "It's okay. Be safe."

"You too." Charlie turned away from them and squared

her shoulders. She put her fists on her hips and stood with a wide stance.

"Are you doing the TED Talk thing?" Claire asked. She did it herself on occasion. Allegedly, striking and holding a power pose gave you confidence and lowered your stress levels.

"Yes," Charlie said. "I do it before every important meeting."

Claire mimicked her sister's posture. Apparently not wanting to feel left out, Luke joined them. What a strange sight it would be for anyone driving by.

Eventually, Charlie pressed the buzzer and went inside. Luke and Claire watched from the shadows as the gate swung shut.

"I hate this," Claire said as her sister disappeared up the marble stairs. Both of her sisters were now in the lion's den.

"Me too. Come on, let's update Jack and find a way in."

Claire hastily texted Jack and took a picture of the cars outside. Hopefully the picture would be clear enough to get some license plates. She took a couple more for good measure. A potential goldmine of information sat behind that stupid gate. And she wouldn't rest until every member of ESA paid for what they had done.

"Let's go this way." Luke grabbed her hand and pulled her around the western side of the estate. Scaffolding and tarps covered a half-built structure next to them. The heavy brick fence seemed to surround Big Z's entire property.

Claire's stomach twisted. How high was it? Eight feet? If she could teach Luke how to do a quick basket toss, she was pretty sure she could make it over.

"Idiots," Luke muttered into the darkness.

"What?" She whirled around. Was someone else outside? Had they been caught?

He crossed the yard of the house under construction and moved a tarp to the side. An eight-foot ladder rested snugly inside.

"Oh, thank god." Her knees would have been skinned to shreds if Luke had tossed her.

"Back there," he said, gesturing at the back of Big Z's vast estate. "See those trees?"

The tops of what looked to be maple trees towered over the fence.

"You think they'll provide enough cover?" Claire eyed them dubiously.

He shrugged. "It's the best shot we have. Come on."

She trailed behind him as they approached the back of the lot. She glanced over her shoulder repeatedly, but the streets were quiet. One of the security cameras Charlie had mentioned was perched on the top of the fence, but it was pointing away from them.

Luke unfolded the ladder and turned to Claire.

"Don't even try," she said sternly.

"What?"

"You were going to try to talk me out of going inside. It won't work. And we're wasting time. Hold the ladder."

He frowned.

"Those are my sisters," she said with one foot on the bottom rung. "Unless Jack has a secret third family he's been hiding, they're the only siblings I have. I have to go." Her heart jumped erratically in her chest, but she ignored it. The second dose of her medication she had taken at the safe house was probably the only thing keeping her from dissolving into a full-blown panic attack.

"I figured you'd say that. Hurry up." He nodded at the ladder.

Claire took the rungs one at a time until her head

popped over the gate. This was no time to be hasty. If she tumbled into Big Z's garden with a crowd full of witnesses, she would ruin everything.

She peered around the branches of the maple tree. Other than a gently tinkling fountain and dreamy-looking pool, the backyard was empty. All the owners of the cars must be inside.

"What do you see?" Luke called from the ground.

"Backyard is clear. I'm going over." She put one foot on the top of the fence. Thank god for emergency flats. She managed to shift until she was sitting down, then dropped heavily onto the soil below. Her knees creaked, but nothing seemed to be broken.

"Come on," she whispered to Luke. She ducked behind a shrub and surveyed the back of the house.

A lavishly decorated patio connected the house to the backyard. A massive pool with a swim-up bar and hot tub stood to one side. Several phallic-looking metallic sculptures were sprinkled throughout the space. A statue of Priapus, a Greek fertility god with a monster dong, peed into a pool below him. Tacky.

She narrowed her eyes. There, toward the left side of the house, was a small window. It was hard to tell from this distance, but it looked like it was cracked open an inch. Luke landed beside her, as agile as a cat.

"How do we cross without being seen?" she whispered.

"I have an idea." He pulled a handkerchief and a lighter out of his suit jacket. "If we cause a distraction, we won't have to worry about them seeing us on the cameras."

"What are you planning to set on fire? And why do you have a lighter? You don't smoke," she said.

"I don't know yet. And you're right, I don't smoke. But all the big studio executives do. You always want to have a light for them at the after party, trust me. It's basically a networking tool."

Claire shook her head. Her eyes swept the yard for dry kindling or anything that looked flammable.

"Luke," she said as her gaze fell on the wet bar. "What do you say to a little feminist Molotov cocktail?"

"Can we get there without being seen?" He craned his neck.

"Let me." She eyed the back of the property. Trees and shrubs were planted all around the outside edge of the yard. It wasn't perfect, but they had no choice. Charlie could only stall for so long.

"I don't like this," he said.

"You're going to like it even less when I tell you what comes next." Claire hitched her dress up around her thighs and tied it into a knot. She got on all fours and crawled behind the shrubbery. A chipmunk skittered across her path and she nearly screamed.

With one eye on the cameras that continuously swept overhead, she crawled forward until she hit the next wall that flanked the property. She leapt behind a bush as one of the cameras swept toward her and prayed that it hadn't caught her. When no one came rushing out of the house, she crept forward. There was the wet bar.

She slithered inside behind the counter and popped open the cabinet door. Vodkas, rums, and tequilas lined the shelves inside. She grabbed a bottle of high-proof tequila and shoved it down the front of her dress.

She was considerably closer to the house now. Whose voice was that? Charlie? A feminine laugh came from inside, and Claire exhaled noisily. Charlie was still okay. Maybe this crazy plan would work after all.

Claire reversed her course and crawled back among the

foliage. She yanked the bottle of tequila out of her cleavage and handed it to Luke. He looked at it warily.

"You have to throw it in the front yard to draw the attention away from me," she said, but her voice shook. "You have to go back outside the wall."

He shook his head. "No way. If I throw it in the front yard, I won't have time to jump back over before they start searching the property."

"I know. But you have to do this. You've seen my hand-eye coordination. The chances of me throwing it over the fence, let alone in a good spot, is less than zero. Every second we waste right now is another second Bri could be tortured."

A shadow fell over Luke's face. He tucked the tequila into the inside pocket of his suit jacket—how was he still so clean? She looked like she had just crawled through a war zone. He grabbed her by both arms and drew her into him. Her arms snaked around his neck. He kissed her like it would be the last time—and if they weren't careful, it could be.

"Be safe," she whispered to him when they broke apart. "Here." She hiked her dress up even further and propped her leg out. "You need a boost. Put your right foot here, then I'll cradle your left foot at chest level."

"You sound suspiciously informed at scaling fences," Luke said as he planted one dress shoe on Claire's bare thigh.

"I did cheerleading in middle school." She grunted as Luke put his entire body weight on her. He weighed significantly more than an eighth-grade girl.

"I want to hear about this later," he said as he pushed off her chest and disappeared over the wall.

She took a moment to make sure her collarbone was still

intact. There weren't any bones protruding through her skin, so she crouched back down and waited. The minutes ticked by. Had Luke gotten lost? Had he thrown it yet?

In the distance, glass smashed on the ground. She peeked around a bush and craned her neck toward the house. Had they realized yet? The fire wasn't visible from here, but she could smell it. It wouldn't be long now.

Shouts echoed from inside the house. Was that the sound of the front door opening?

Claire's phone buzzed. A text appeared.

Luke: *Go NOW.*

Claire slung her clutch across her torso and sprinted across the dark stretch of grass. She nearly slipped in the dew but pressed forward. The panicked shouts grew louder.

Finally, she hit the flower bed that lined the back of the house. Adrenaline propelled her forward. Using every last ounce of strength she had in her, she put her hands on the windowsill and hoisted herself up onto the ledge. She slid the window open and slipped inside.

CHAPTER SIXTY-TWO

To Do:
- Punch some misogynist dicks

THE BATHROOM WAS DARK AND SMELLED STRONGLY OF cinnamon and cloves. Claire would have bet her last dollar that there was a container of artisanal potpourri some-where. Using her phone flashlight, she crept across the ceramic tile. She paused at the door and listened.

The house was quiet. There were voices, but they were muffled as though they were coming from somewhere else. She held her breath and cracked the door open a centime-ter. She was in a short hallway that seemed to run between the massive eight-car garage and the kitchen. Directly across from her was a Big Z concert poster in a diamond-studded frame. Was it safe to leave?

Footsteps approached. Adrenaline shot through her from head to toe. She opened the only other door in the bathroom and leapt inside. The potpourri smell was even stronger in here. The scent all but choked her.

"Fuckin' feminists," a male voice grunted. Shit. Was that balsam and cedar joining the god-awful scent party? Her fingertips went numb. It was the same as the cologne from the men's rights convention. Big Z was in the bathroom.

Heavy footsteps stomped across the tile. A zipper unzipped. Liquid splashed. Claire's heart was pounding straight out of her chest. Could he hear it? She gripped the wooden shelf behind her like a lifeline. If he opened the door, she would be dead in seconds. Jack's helpful probing had revealed over a hundred firearms registered in Big Z's name, which was legally Zedediah Nipple.

"Z?" someone called from the hallway. "We need another extinguisher."

"Yeah, yeah. I'm coming." The zipper re-zipped. The faucet didn't turn on, but the rumble of his footsteps shook the shampoo bottles behind her. Of course he didn't wash his hands. Nasty.

A door slammed a moment later. She took a hesitant step out into the bathroom. Where would she go now? Charlie had mentioned rumors of a secret room in the basement, but she didn't even know where the basement door was. How did Big Z have a basement, anyway? Luke said they were uncommon in LA.

"Claire?" Charlie's voice called in a whisper. It seemed to be coming from the hallway.

Claire wrenched the door open.

"Door's over there. Hurry." Charlie pointed at a set of double doors across the kitchen. "This could just be a rumor, but someone at the party said there's two secret rooms. One's a freaky sex dungeon and the other is some kind of secret observation room. I've seen a door with a keypad down there on the right behind the bar. His phone passcode is 2-3-3-4 so try that first, okay?"

Claire exchanged a terrified glance with her sister as she opened the door and paused to listen.

"Where is everyone else?"

"Most of them are still down there," Charlie whispered. "Please be careful. Don't burst in and raise the alarm."

"I won't." Claire closed the door behind her. She would rather cut her own foot off than burst into a room full of homicidal maniacs. She had a simple job to do. A bulleted item on her never-ending To Do list. Find Brianna and call 9-1-1.

As she crept down the carpeted stairs, her breathing was ragged, like she had just run a half marathon. The walls were painted a matte black, and every couple of feet recessed lighting shone down like spotlights. The slanted ceiling glittered like the night sky. She wasn't exactly an expert, but the whole setup seemed like a tripping hazard.

She hit the bottom of the stairs and scanned the room. Had she just descended into one of the levels of hell? Hardwood floors ran underfoot. The walls were covered in the same matte black from the stairwell. It was obnoxiously dark. A pool table with a black top was at one end of the finished basement. Behind her stood a dark recording booth. Movie theater seats were just visible behind a partially open door. And there in front of her was the stone-front bar.

She stepped around it and peered at the door. There was the keypad, just like Charlie said. Light flickered under the door.

Her hand trembled as she reached out to touch the keypad. Was she about to barge into a room full of people who wanted to kill her? What if the code didn't work?

She entered the code Charlie had mentioned, 2-3-3-4. The keypad flashed green and the door swung open. Thank god he was a creature of habit. She peered inside. Empty. She hurried inside and shut the door behind her. The first secret room was somewhere between a recording studio booth and police interrogation room. An eight-foot panel of what she desperately hoped was two-way glass lined the front of the room. Couches stood along the wall behind her. A wardrobe of some sort was at the far end of the room, next to a mini fridge and a water cooler.

How many body fluids had been expressed in this room? Her stomach clenched as she ducked underneath the mirror and crawled over to the wardrobe. She pressed herself between it and the wall and slowly slid her way up.

The view that greeted her was something out of a night-mare. Brianna sat in the center of the room, stripped down to her bra and panties, bound to a chair and gagged. Her hair was disheveled and matted with blood, and her eyes were open wide in terror. Mascara streaked down her cheeks. Her ankles were bound to the legs of the chair.

If Claire hadn't been medicated, the sight would have undoubtedly sent her into the worst panic attack of her life. She rubbed her wrists where Barney had tied her to the pillar, and then her most recent abductor had zip-tied her. She needed to focus and put the fear behind her. They had her sister, and they were going to pay.

A dozen completely naked men sat in a semi-circle around her, lounging and chatting as though a twenty-one-year-old girl wasn't being tortured in front of them. The number of wrinkly ball sacks was truly nauseating.

The room was painted black from floor to ceiling. Heavy red drapes lined the windowless walls. Penis-shaped candles were placed in sconces every few feet, the only source of lighting in the room. A sex swing hung in the corner. A free-standing saddle with a large dildo attached was in another corner. Some kind of torture rack stood off to the side.

Claire's stomach heaved, and tears pricked her eyes. Her baby sister. What had she been through? Thank god she was alive, but how was she going to free her from this place? She pulled out her phone and immediately dialed 9-1-1.

Or at least she tried to. She drew the phone away from her ear. There was no service. How? They were in the middle of the Hollywood Hills. Who would have better reception than some of the richest people in America?

She tried texting Charlie and then Luke, but her phone chastised her with "message failed." She was alone, and Brianna was in the next room surrounded by naked murderers.

Shit, were those footsteps on the stairs? Her heart flew into her throat. There was only one place to hide. She darted inside the wardrobe. Seconds after she stepped onto an unidentified pile of what seemed to be even more rubbery dildos, the door popped open.

"No, she needs to stay upstairs until this is done. She's not leaving until TMZ drops the story." There was the suffocating cologne again. That had to be Big Z.

"Couldn't she come down here where we can keep an eye on her? That's how you lost one of your Grammys."

Claire's mouth hardened into a thin line. That was Professor Taylor's voice. Something leathery brushed against her in the wardrobe, and she bit her lip to keep from screaming. Hopefully it was just a riding crop and not a live snake.

There was definitely the sound of skin slapping against

skin. The professor grunted. Did Big Z just slap her old, shitty business professor?

"Are you stupid?" The rapper's voice carried in the small room. "This is her sister. We'd have to take them both, and that's not on the agenda for tonight. I need her. She can't know this bitch is here. Not even Charlie would cover that up for me."

"What about the other one?" the other male asked.

"Hiding in a safe house with Special Agent Fuckface."

Claire bit her lip even harder. A copper taste filled her mouth. They were talking about her. The *other one*? That's all she was to these idiots who had tried to kill her multiple times? Fury was building in the pit of her stomach.

Professor Taylor sighed. "It's a pity the mountain lion didn't work."

Big Z grunted. "It was a foolproof plan. I don't know how that bitch got out of being mauled. I'm gonna be having words with Dick."

A zipper unzipped again. Was that the sound of pants dropping to the floor? Ugh.

"She'll be gone soon after we take care of this one. It'll be easier to finish this in Pennsylvania. We never should have sent O'Rourke to the ranch. He's too inexperienced."

There was a deep sigh. "She's a wily bitch, I'll give her that. We can't just keep messing with her shitty fundraising events and calling in bomb threats."

Claire inhaled sharply, then bit her tongue. Those fuckers. They had been behind the bomb threat. And the fundraising event? Did that mean they were the ones who let the dogs out of the cages? How did they have so much free time?

"It's time to end this," Big Z continued. "After this one's

done, I want our full sights set on her. She's not going to escape again. It's time to teach Agent Fuckface a lesson."

"He'll learn," the professor said darkly. "I have to be honest, though. I don't like this one, Z. It feels risky. She's the highest-profile person we've ever taken."

Claire wrinkled her nose. Listening to her middle-aged business professor call Zedediah Nipple by a nickname was just gross.

"They'll never find her. You know how careful I am. They have no reason to link me to the outreach team."

"What about the fire?" the professor asked.

"Probably just some feminist whore on a star tour. I'm not worried about it. Trent's in the office. He's going to keep watching the feeds to make sure nothing else happens. The hard part is done. And now it's time for fun." More clothing dropped to the floor.

Claire's hand froze on the inside of the wardrobe. Rage flooded her veins. It didn't matter that it would be fourteen against one. She would rip him limb from limb if it was the last thing she did.

"To restoring the balance," Big Z said. Two glasses clinked together. A door opened, and the voices were gone.

She took a deep, steadying breath. The 9-1-1 call was still a necessity, but there was no way to do that in this basement. Her phone had definitely worked outside, so she needed to get upstairs without alerting whoever the hell Trent was. Every second that passed brought them closer to starting whatever horrible thing they were planning to do to Brianna.

She popped open the door of the wardrobe and poked her head out. Big Z, with a giant birthmark the shape of a cheeseburger on his blindingly white left butt cheek, approached the chair where Brianna sat.

Claire's heart galloped in her chest. She needed to go, but what if they found a way to cover everything up? She pulled her phone out and quickly recorded a video, zooming in on each attendee's face. Asshole after asshole panned across her screen. Unsurprisingly, the attendees were almost exclusively saggy, middle-aged white men. Triple-checking that the video had saved, she hustled across the small room and wrenched the door open.

She almost ran headlong into a burly, six-foot man eating a sandwich. They both stopped, utterly shocked to see each other. The sandwich fell to the floor. The man reached for something at his side.

Claire tugged up the hem of her dress and pulled out her Taser. She fired it at him before he could remove the gun from his holster. Prongs buried themselves deep in his barrel of a chest. His body dropped to the floor behind the wet bar, jerking and seizing. It rattled the cabinets under the bar.

Should she run? What if the Taser wasn't enough and he ran into the sex dungeon while she was upstairs?

When the electricity wore off, Claire climbed on top of him and punched him forcefully in the nose. There was a crunching sound. Blood poured from his face. His eyes went shut, and his body relaxed. Using strength she didn't even know she had, she rolled him onto his stomach. She pulled his hands behind his back and searched the room. There weren't any curtains to pull down and turn into restraints. She was going to have to go back to the dildo wardrobe.

Heart hammering, she punched the code into the keypad again and hurried across the observation room to the wardrobe. Big Z stood next to Brianna, addressing the crowd.

"I'm honored today to have the twelve founding

members of our illustrious organization here to celebrate. Over the past decade, you have focused your tireless efforts on our solemn mission to transform the world back into what it's supposed to be. A man's world, where men who shoulder the burden of providing for their families are given the opportunities they deserve, and women are relegated where they belong."

What a slimy, conniving douchebag. In the few songs of his Mindy had forced her to listen to, she had never once heard him use a word with more than three syllables. He must have stolen this speech from the internet. Thank god he was long-winded. It would take him all night to kill her at this rate.

Among the confusing array of nipple clamps and restraints on the wall, a pair of handcuffs hung. She yanked them free and closed the cabinet doors before sprinting back out into the basement. Luckily the man who must be Trent was still on the ground. She slapped the handcuffs on him and threaded them through a cabinet handle before sprinting up the steps, taking them two at a time. She kicked the doors at the top of the stairs open.

Charlie screamed.

"Claire, what the hell?" She jumped up from the table. The padded chair tipped over behind her and clattered onto the tile floor.

"No service in the basement," Claire said, holding her phone up. Still no service. "Shit, I can't get a single bar. Do you have service?" She whirled on her sister, who still looked alarmed.

"Nothing," Charlie said. "There must be a jammer or something."

"She's here. In the basement. I don't think we have much

time. I need you to go outside and call the police, Charlie. Now."

Charlie ran for the front door. Claire opened the basement door and headed back down to the lion's den. She was going to have to watch and wait. And if the police didn't get here in time, she would go down fighting for her little sister.

She stopped halfway down the stairs, heartbeat pounding in her ears. She pulled out her phone and typed a message to Luke. It wouldn't go through, but if everything went south, Luke needed to know he was her last thought.

Claire: *I think they're jamming cell phone signals somehow. I'm not sure if we can wait for the police. If the worst happens, know that I love you forever. Even though you drive me crazy. Watch over the dogs for me. Don't feed Rosie anything with corn in it; she's allergic. Winston's new favorite toy is the squeaky hotdog. Tell my mom and Roy I love them too. And Coli and Mindy. Just everyone I guess. Be safe, and don't forget me.*

She slunk back downstairs. With any luck, Charlie would call the police and they would accept a secondhand account of a girl trapped in a basement in a Grammy-winning musical artist's house. This was LA—calls like this probably happened every week. The cops wouldn't be far behind. There was nothing to do but watch and wait. If things escalated, she would intervene, whatever the cost.

Trent was still on the floor, bleeding and moaning. She aimed a kick at his ribs as she walked by. Back in the observation room, things were getting even stranger. Big Z was now tilting one of the candles so that it dripped hot wax onto Brianna. She flinched and stared at him with pure malice in her eyes.

"Our special guest is one of the worst kinds of women,"

Big Z said, clearly in the middle of some kind of hateful diatribe. "She thought she deserved to be paid as much as the lead actor. She thought she needed to tell the story of some hormonal idiot who impersonated a soldier and took all the glory of war from a man who rightfully deserved it. The story is shameful, and she's trash. A Hollywood nobody who should have stayed in the kitchen. Of course, we couldn't let this movie premiere tonight. Not on the night of our most treasured festival."

What fresh bullshit was this? A festival? Were they going to roll out a bunch of summer-themed beers and make flower crowns before murdering her sister? Claire bit the inside of her cheek. One hand froze on the door handle that led to the inner sanctum. How much more of this could she take? Her sister was in agony. If this went on much longer, there would be no waiting for the police.

"Priapus," Big Z continued, "the god of fertility and the male genitals, among other things. Today we honor him and sacred masculinity with a sacrifice."

Shit. That did not sound good. Brianna glared at him, but her hand trembled on the armrest. Claire's grip tightened on the handle. She couldn't take this anymore.

Footsteps echoed outside the observation room door. *Damn it*. There must be more assholes afoot. She needed to hide again. Back to the depraved wardrobe. She had one foot in when the door flew open. Claire grabbed the closest thing, which happened to be nunchucks with latex dildos on both ends. Did the spa in West Haven have a treatment where attendants would wipe her down from head to toe with Clorox wipes for three straight days? If so, she was booking it after this adventure. Assuming she lived.

Charlie and Luke entered. Charlie carried a solid gold

fire poker while Luke wielded a butcher knife. Claire almost collapsed in relief.

"What are you guys doing down here?"

"Cops are on their way but there's some kind of truck blocking direct access from Hollywood. They have to go the long way around," Charlie said. Her eyes zeroed in on Brianna. She bit her lip. "This is awful."

"Big Z keeps talking about some kind of sacrifice, and I just don't—"

At that moment, Big Z pulled a long, slender hunting knife from somewhere in the room. He held it in front of Bri's throat.

"Oh, hell no," Claire said. She slung the dildo nunchucks over one shoulder and picked up one of the chairs in the room. "On three?" She looked at the other two. They nodded.

"Cover your eyes. One...Two..." She swung the chair with each count.

"Three!" Luke grunted and thrust open the door into the inner chamber. Claire was treated to two seconds of shocked naked men panicking before the chair crashed through the two-way glass and littered the room with glittering fragments. Unless they wanted to be cut to shreds, the naked assholes were trapped.

"What the fuck?" Big Z turned around, knife in one hand and candle in the other.

"That's my sister!" Claire leapt through the newly broken window. A jagged edge bit into her thigh, but she didn't stop to inspect the wound. She nearly slipped on the shards of glass, then charged forward and kicked as hard as she could. The knife flew out of his hand and plunged straight up into a ceiling tile. The candle rolled out of sight.

"You stupid bitch!" Big Z clutched at his hand and she

tackled him to the floor, aiming a punch at his stupid smug face.

To her left, Charlie wielded the fire poker to block two balding, saggy men from leaving the room. She whipped one across the face.

"Get on the ground," Charlie said in her most authoritative voice. It was almost enough to convince Claire to get down.

"On your knees," Luke commanded, brandishing the knife toward a group of three men who were trying to scrabble through the broken window. One of them lunged at him, and Luke punched him with his non-dominant hand. The man hit the floor, and his entire body jiggled like a platter of Jell-O. He cried out. Blood leaked from a series of small cuts on his back.

The remaining men stared in horror at the broken glass on the floor and their bare feet. There were almost certainly a few fragments in Claire's own emergency flats, but Brianna was alive. Nothing else mattered.

Beneath her, Big Z struggled like an animal caught in a trap. Claire brought her knee up into his completely unprotected groin. He crumpled like a dollar bill, and she flipped him onto his stomach. In seconds, she had wrenched his hands behind his back and dragged his legs back to meet them. She hog-tied him with the dildo nunchucks as best as she could and ran to her sister.

"Bri," she whispered, taking in the full damage that was done. She shuddered as she ripped at the gag in her sister's mouth. Had adrenaline not been coursing through her veins, she probably would have been crippled on the floor.

As Claire ripped at Bri's bindings, she glanced around the room. Charlie bounced on the balls of her toes, sending jabs and right hooks at the four attempted escapees. She had attended a kickboxing class twice a week for the last four years. Whoever crossed her was going to be sorry. Luke was still shouting at the other half of the cowards.

They had actually done it. They had trapped the head honchos of ESA in one room. If they could just hold on until the FBI arrived, justice would finally be served. These men were cowards. They would roll over and release their member rosters. Victory was nigh.

Tears streamed down Brianna's cheeks. The second Claire freed her hands, she threw them around her.

"Thank you," she whispered hoarsely in Claire's ear.

"I'm so sorry this happened to you. They're going to pay, I promise you."

"Do you smell smoke?" Brianna croaked.

Oh, shit. The candle.

"Luke—" Claire called out.

"I know." He gestured behind her. One of the drapes had caught fire.

"Shit. We need this house—it can't burn down. Can you help them watch the group so they don't escape? I'm going to find an extinguisher."

She slashed the bindings around Brianna's feet with Big Z's knife and crunched across the carpet of broken glass. Her heart was in her throat as she fled up the stairs to the kitchen.

"Come on," she said, ripping open cabinets. The smoke smell was getting stronger. Where the hell were the police?

Pounding came from the front door. She abandoned her quest and ran for it.

"Dad!" She called out when his familiar face greeted her. Shit, she always called him Jack. Roy was "Dad." There was time to worry about that later. "We need a fire extinguisher," she called to the agent behind him. He turned on his heel and ran in the direction of the street.

Sirens wailed in the distance. Red and blue lights flashed off the underside of the palm trees in the front yard, and for a moment sheer panic gripped Claire. It was just like the night Barney had kidnapped her.

"Basement," she said, snapping back to reality. She pointed to the open set of doors. Jack drew his gun and ran down the steps, Claire just a beat behind him.

He swung his gun from left to right as they entered the basement. He cast one glance at Trent on the floor before following the smoke and panicked yelling. He kicked open the observation room door and revealed Luke, Charlie, and Bri making a human wall in front of the room exits.

The room stank of sweat and desperation. The fire was bigger now. The naked men lurched forward, sweat beading down their bodies. Charlie's right fist came out like light-ning, and one of them hit the floor.

"FBI, on the ground now!" Jack barked.

The group of men looked at each other and panicked. One vaulted over Charlie's outstretched arm and came through the broken window. The professor dodged around Luke and opened the door. He was out in the basement before they could blink. He was fast for an old naked misogynist.

"He's mine." Claire pulled a mystery tool from the dildo wardrobe and chased after him. Glass crunched in her shoes, and her feet slipped inside. A trail of blood led up the stairs. Agonized grunts soon led her to the man's position. He staggered across Big Z's foyer, blood dripping from the cuts on his feet. One wrinkly, liver-spotted hand rested on the doorknob.

He was not going to leave this house. Claire threw her

weapon overhand at him without bothering to check what it was. There was a mighty *thwack*, and a dildo stuck to the front door like a dart finding a bullseye. It trembled from the impact.

"Going somewhere, professor?" she asked.

He turned and faced her. His face was contorted in hatred. There was malice in his eyes.

"I should have killed you when I was slamming your idiot roommate," he hissed at her. He took one step toward her.

"Please." Claire crossed her arms. "You've been trying to kill me for like a year and a half now because Barney couldn't do his job. You blew up my car and my warehouse, threatened my family. Tried to set a mountain lion on my clients. But I'm still here. How do you think this is going to end for you? I'm curious." She tilted her head. If she could just waste another few seconds, police would come stampeding through that door.

"You are *nothing*," he yelled. "A pathetic training exercise. Not worth the blood that runs through your veins."

Claire pretended to ponder for a moment. "If I'm so useless, why is it that I've evaded every attempt your pathetic frat boys have made on my life? Isn't this kind of your job? Other than being a shitty professor, anyway. I guess it makes sense that your eradicators are as poorly organized as your course syllabus."

The look in his eyes sent a chill down her spine. "You won't win. We will never stop. Not until you're all dead."

Claire scoffed. "Look around. I've already won."

He stalked toward her, hands outstretched like he was going to strangle her. She took two steps forward and punched him full in the face. He wailed like an animal and lunged for her. Blood dripped from his nose. He tackled her at waist height. She managed a scream before crashing to the floor, wind completely knocked out of her.

His fingers found their way around her throat. Claire gasped, but there wasn't any air to fill her lungs. She wriggled underneath him, aimed wild punches all over his torso. And still he choked her.

His weight pressed down on her like an anchor. Everything slowed to a crawl. The edges of her vision darkened. Voices echoed far away. Her heart beat in her ears. Was she going to die in Big Z's foyer next to a tacky zebra-shaped umbrella stand?

Suddenly, the weight vanished from on top of her. She sat up and scrambled into a corner, gasping for air. Her throat burned. What the hell had happened? The sirens were closer, but the police hadn't come in. Unless he practiced close-up magic in his free time, he couldn't have just disappeared.

A sound Claire had heard too many times from the punching bag in Luke's garage was now emanating from a few feet away. With one knee on the professor's chest, Luke pummeled him.

The front door swung open, and an agent ran in with a fire extinguisher. Claire pointed to the basement doors, and he disappeared. He was followed seconds later by a small battalion of cops. One dragged Luke off the professor and stopped, staring between the two of them, one completely nude and covered in blood, and one still looking impossibly put together in a tuxedo and bowtie.

Claire waved the other cops down the stairs. "It's him," she croaked to the female cop who paused with her hand on her radio. "Check the FBI Most Wanted list. He's an escaped felon from Pennsylvania."

The professor growled and lunged for the front door.

Claire stuck one foot out and managed to send him sprawling. The cop jumped on him and slapped on a pair of handcuffs.

"Bri," Claire said to Luke, struggling to her feet.

He dragged her up. "Wait. Are you okay?"

His hand lingered at her throat, and she flinched.

"My naked, bloody business professor just tried to strangle me. Let's go with 'no.' Come on." She pulled him down the stairs, back into the smoky basement.

A dozen naked men covered in fire extinguisher foam were lying face down on the hardwood.

"We need more handcuffs," an agent called.

Claire and Luke ran past them to the observation room.

Brianna sat on a couch, sipping from a water bottle. Jack and Charlie sat on each side of her. Luke shrugged off his suit jacket and draped it around her shoulders.

"Are you okay?" Claire dropped to her knees in front of her sister.

"I'm fine," Brianna said. She touched her throat and drew Luke's jacket tighter around her. "But I'd love to go home. It's been a day."

No freakin' kidding.

CHAPTER SIXTY-THREE

To Do:
- *Hound the LAPD day and night*
- *Make sure they're ALL in prison*
- *Figure out what comes next*

"I can't believe it's actually over." Claire's bruised knuckles curled around a wrought iron staircase spindle. Luke sat next to her, still looking way too put together for someone who had just brought down a serial killer ring.

Cool marble pressed against her battered legs. Streams of dried blood ran into her emergency flats. Every part of her body ached like she had run a half marathon while wearing a backpack full of toddlers. Not even the world's most legendary dry cleaner could save her champagne-colored cocktail dress.

Luke slung an arm over her shoulders. She leaned into

him, reveling in his warmth. A handful of cop cars, lights still flashing, littered the front yard. The naked ESA honchos had been marched out, one by one, and taken to the police station. There was a sizable scorch mark by a palm tree where Luke had tossed the Molotov cocktail. Brianna sat in the back of an ambulance, first responders falling all over themselves to take care of her. She laughed, a bright, silvery sound in the silence. Tanya flittered around her, continuously offering vials of essential oil to the paramedics.

Was it really over? Twelve chapter heads were in custody. Big Z, the unseen cult leader, had been dragged screaming into a cop car. The many heads of the ESA snake had been lopped off. Would the FBI be able to pressure them into giving up their rosters? At the very least, with no one around to give orders, hopefully her family was finally safe.

Her head popped off Luke's shoulder. "Do you think Big Z is going to sue me? I'm pretty sure climbing a ladder and throwing myself into his backyard is the textbook definition of trespassing."

Luke nodded in the direction of Charlie, who was standing underneath a palm tree talking to Jack. "Considering all the dirt that Charlie has on him, I really don't think he'd risk it."

"Let's hope. Do you think they'll let us go soon? I'm starving." A full moon shone brightly above them. Maybe that had something to do with the timing of the dick-worshipping festival.

"Probably. They can only interrogate us so much."

Claire and Luke had both been questioned, separately and together, no fewer than three times. They had been here for hours. She was tired of explaining how she recognized Big Z and knew where her sister would be. Luckily, Jack's presence had helped smooth some things over.

She pulled back a couple of inches and looked at Luke. Police lights flashed over his profile. Aside from his bloody knuckles and some slight rumpling, he still looked like he should be walking a red carpet somewhere. Meanwhile, from the state of her clothes and hair, anyone could assume that Claire had been sucked into a jet engine.

He turned to look at her. He smiled, and her heart thumped unsteadily in her chest.

Something had been bothering her for weeks. "Do you ever regret moving to West Haven? Meeting me? All of it," she asked before she could consciously decide not to.

If he had never left Los Angeles, he could be married to Olivia. He never would have been drawn into the mystery of ESA. They may have never crossed paths except for Kyle and Nicole's wedding.

Luke stared straight ahead. "Never."

"Even though I dragged you into a web of serial killers who keep blowing up our stuff and made you throw a Molotov cocktail at a bunch of naked penis-worshipping misogynists? And got abducted? Twice? And flashed my boobs at your mom? And adopted a special needs dog without asking you first?"

"I wouldn't change anything." He tilted her chin and kissed her tenderly. Warmth flooded her.

"Me neither. Well, mostly." She took his hand and looked him in the eyes. "I'm sorry. For everything—ignoring my obvious trauma, the sleepwalking, not listening to you when you just wanted me to be safe, working too much, not making enough time for us. I have really sucked this year."

His grip tightened on her. "You also saved my life. That makes up for a couple of missed dates."

Claire shook her head. "Still. Now that this is behind us, I'm going to focus more of my energy on being a better partner. Starting with throwing you the best premiere ever."

Luke sighed. "Can't we just do a private one at home? You, me, and some sushi? I'll wear the gray sweatpants."

She smiled. "As tempting as that is, no. You were nominated for a whole-ass Emmy, and we never even really celebrated that. Besides, the venue's already confirmed. I want you to feel even just a quarter as loved as you make me feel. Let me show you how much you mean to me."

"Fine." His voice was curt, but his mouth curved into a smile.

A disturbance at the gate had Claire lifting her head. Someone appeared to be arguing with one of the cops. If it was another member of ESA, she was out of Tasers.

"I'm Mr. Islestorm's attorney," someone announced loudly. "I have a right to consult with my client."

"Kyle?" Claire and Luke both stood. He took her hand, and they trudged over to the gate together. Nicole, Kyle, Mindy, and Sawyer stood at the gate with rolling suitcases behind them.

"What are you guys doing here?" Claire asked.

"Oh my god. I leave you alone for one weekend and you break into Big Z's house?" Nicole juked around one of the cops and threw her arms around Claire's neck.

"Where is he?" Mindy stood behind Nicole, nostrils flaring. Sawyer stood next to her, looking exhausted.

"Big Z? Or the professor? They were all taken to the station."

Mindy's hands balled into fists. "I'm going straight home to burn every album of his I own. Nobody kidnaps my best friend's baby sister and gets away with it."

"Easy, killer." Sawyer put a hand on her shoulder.

"We got on a plane as soon as we heard about Bri." Kyle thumped Luke's back in a bro hug. His horn-rimmed glasses flashed under the streetlights. "We didn't expect you to single-handedly solve the problem before we even touched down."

"I'm so glad you're here." Claire pulled all four of them into a hug. "Come on, you," she called over her shoulder to Luke. He reluctantly joined the group hug.

She could have stayed in that moment forever. Finally, on Big Z's scorched front yard surrounded by her friends, both of her sisters safe, the heads of a homicidal anti-feminist cult arrested, and her family begrudgingly reunited, she was at peace. The nightmare of the past year was coming to a close. She could finally get back to her world of happily ever afters. She might even be able to build a new office space without someone blowing it up. The dogs could frolic in the front yard without—oh, shit. The dogs. Thank god for twenty-four-hour doggy daycare.

"Well, I sold the story to TMZ," Charlie's voice announced. "As much as the FBI would allow. In about three hours when people start waking up, Big Z's reputation will never recover. And if he tries to pull any shit from jail, I'll release everything I have on him to the highest bidder. What do you say we take the proceeds and go get a kickass brunch somewhere? Oh, hey guys. When did you get here?"

Someone reached out and pulled Charlie into the group hug.

"Let's make it a brunch at Luke's," Claire said, voice slightly muffled against Mindy's hair. "I don't know about you guys, but I desperately need to wash the blood of misogynists off me."

"Preach," Brianna's voice came from behind them.

"Bri! Did the paramedics finally let you go?" The group

hug shuffled over and encompassed Brianna. The paramedics must have donated a pair of scrubs to her, because she looked like she had just gotten off a hellish shift.

"They were just being helpful."

"Uh-huh. How many selfies did they ask for?"

"Only a few. And some autographs. And I may have agreed to make an appearance at their daughters' soccer game this week."

Claire shook her head, and the group hug broke apart. Classic Brianna. "Can I talk to you?"

"Of course." Bri followed her out the gate and into the street. She looked visibly relieved at having some distance between her and the house.

"How are you doing? Really?"

"I'm fi—"

Claire cut her off. "Don't give me a sunshiney, bullshit answer. I know what you just went through."

Brianna took a deep breath. She was quiet. The silence stretched for nearly a full minute. Her lower lip trembled. A tear slid down her cheek, and she hurriedly wiped it away. "It was awful," she said in a hoarse whisper. "They grabbed me while I was getting my pre-premiere drink."

"I know, I saw the footage. Your aim was really impressive," Claire said gently.

Brianna's shoulders shook. "I woke up in the basement already tied to the chair. I was so cold and everything hurt. I don't know if they did anything to me before I woke up. I had only met Big Z once at an album drop party like two years ago. I couldn't believe it. The things he said they were going to do, all because of a stupid movie—"

"Look at me," Claire said, grabbing her sister by both arms. Brianna raised her watery blue eyes. "It's over. You're safe, and you're going to be okay. You will not allow this night to define who you are. But you do need to get a thera-pist. Like, today. Don't make the same mistake I did. You need someone to help you process this trauma, and that's something only a professional can do."

Brianna nodded tearfully.

"Also, don't let them stop the movie. Have your premiere. Keep taking roles like that if that's what makes you feel happy and fulfilled. Or take a break from acting entirely. Whatever you choose to do right now is the right choice. Except for getting back together with Sebastian Yearling. Don't do that. He's an idiot."

Brianna laughed and drew her sister into a hug. They stayed like that under the moonlight until Brianna stopped quivering.

"Do you want to be alone, or do you want brunch?" Claire asked quietly.

Brianna considered for a moment. "Brunch."

"Okay. Can you use your celebrity powers to get us a police escort home? I'm pretty sure our limos are long gone by now."

"Done." Brianna wiped away her tears, straightened her shoulders, and marched back through the gates like it was her house.

Claire's heart lurched as her sister disappeared. The emotional journey Brianna was about to take wasn't going to be pretty. Maybe she should invite her to come stay with them in Pennsylvania for a while. She resolved to talk to Luke about it and followed her back through the gate.

"Coming to brunch?" Claire asked Jack and Tanya. "I'm sure we could grab some vegan pastries from an all-night market somewhere on the way home."

"That would be nice," Tanya said. Her eyes were red, and her bush of blond hair had become even more unkempt.

It had been the longest of nights. It was almost impossible to believe that ESA had been caught. What started as one gentle rejection in college had transformed into a handful of near-death experiences and a straight-up Excel spreadsheet full of enemies. Would things ever truly go back to normal? How could they move forward? There was time to worry about all that later. Priority number one was food.

Two hours later, Claire carried a stack of dishes down the deck steps into Luke's backyard. The sun was creeping up into the sky, casting a golden glow over everything.

Rosie and Winston napped underneath a palm tree, worn out from doggy daycare. Jack and Sawyer were talking security tech. Brianna, freshly showered and wearing a pair of Luke's old sweatpants and one of Claire's Venor T-shirts, sat at the head of the table, reassuring her mom for the hundredth time.

"Are you sure you don't want some lavender oil for your bruise, darling?" Tanya reached out to stroke the discolored bit of skin around Bri's left eye.

"No, I'm fine, Mom. I just need some food and a nap." She smiled across the table at Claire.

Kyle was engaging Charlie in a spirited discourse about ethics. Nicole was unconscious, drooling slightly into his shoulder. Mindy typed something on her tablet.

Most of the people she loved were in one place, and they were safe.

Claire set the plates and cutlery down and returned to the kitchen.

"Hi." She slipped behind Luke and wrapped her arms around him. She was beyond exhausted, but he felt like home.

"Hi, yourself." He dragged her out from behind him and pressed her against the countertop. He kissed her deeply, slowly. A warmth rose in her from her toes to the top of her head. Eventually they broke apart. There was a smudge of waffle mix on his cheek, and she brushed it away. They were awfully lucky to both be alive.

"What are you going to do now that we're not devoting so much of our free time to bringing down ESA?"

He raised an eyebrow. "Make a documentary about it. Obviously."

Claire smiled. He hadn't even had his premiere yet, and already the next doc was in the works. Classic Luke.

"Maybe you should make a happy one after all this miserable true crime." Would he ever grow tired of taking a lens to the darkest side of humanity?

He raised his eyebrows. "Documentaries are not typically considered a 'happy' genre."

"I guess that's why I don't watch them," she teased. "Except yours of course. Are these ready to go out?" She picked up a plate of waffles in one hand and strips of bacon in the other.

"Don't drop them," he said sternly, waggling a spatula at her.

"I won't." She bumped the backdoor open and stepped outside.

The sun was shining. Fresh, hot waffles were in hand. Her family and friends were gathered around her. The only thing that was missing was—

"Claire Aurora Hartley!" Alice Alejo's voice boomed across the yard. A suitcase lay on its side in the grass. Roy stood behind her, eyeing a hole in Luke's fence.

"Mom!" Startled, she nearly dropped the plates. She set them down on the table and hurried to embrace her mother. "What are you doing here?"

"Both of my babies are involved in a dangerous FBI sting operation and I don't even get a phone call?"

Charlie sheepishly approached and hugged Alice on the other side.

"We didn't want to worry you. Besides, for once we weren't really the ones in danger."

Alice reeled like Charlie had punched her. "Not in danger? Charlotte, you were working for a homicidal cult leader for two years."

Charlie waved a hand. "It's LA, Mom. Everyone's a homicidal cult leader."

"And you," Alice said, rounding on Brianna. "You poor, dear girl. How are you?" She perched on the six inches of space that was left on the picnic bench and drew Brianna into a tight hug.

Luke, who had apparently heard the commotion and came outside, shook Roy's hand and began a conversation about the fence. Alice sprayed something over Brianna, which must have settled on Nicole because she woke up with a violent sneeze. The gate that led to the street opened suddenly. Claire grabbed a butter knife off the table and jabbed it in the direction of the gate.

"Morning, everyone," a sweet female voice said. Heather nudged the gate open and tugged a wagon laden with coffee drinks and pastries behind her. "Boss," she said, handing Claire the first cup.

"Heather! I'm so glad to see you. What brings you out at this hour?"

"Mindy briefed me on what happened last night. I thought you could use some comfort food."

"You are a godsend."

"Let's hope," Heather said with a smile as she tugged the wagon over to the table and began unloading.

What a day. ESA's leader turned out to be a rapper whose most quotable song chorus included three separate references to women as "hoes." Her entire family—including stepparents—was gathered together for brunch. Alice was fussing over the illegitimate love child that ended her marriage. Their brand-new employee was showering them with thoughtful carbs. It was a truly bizarre day. And yet, it was just about perfect.

CHAPTER SIXTY-FOUR

To Do:
- *Follow up with theater*
- *Take donations to Tender Hearts*
- *Deep clean guest bedroom for Bri*

"So how are you doing, Claire?" Dr. Goulding's voice was like oiled honey.

Claire snort laughed. What a loaded question. She leaned back into the faux suede couch and folded her hands in her lap. "Sorry. Um, fine. Good, I think. Happy to be home."

The doctor stared at her through her bifocal lenses. Her clock ticked audibly in the background. "I know you appreciate it when I get straight to the point. So why don't we talk about what happened to your sister?"

Brianna's abduction had brought up a lot of feelings, it was true. They had been back in West Haven for four days, but Claire was still exhausted, sore, and wound up from the events at Big Z's house. She couldn't be a good friend, daughter, or girlfriend with all these unresolved feelings swirling around. Maybe it would help to talk about it.

She took a deep breath. There was no point in sugar-coating things—Dr. Goulding always saw straight through her. "I think I've been having trouble processing it, to be honest. So many shitty things have happened in the last year."

"You've certainly been through a lot. More than most people go through in a lifetime. How did you feel when you realized she was missing?"

She twisted her hands together. "I was terrified. It felt like I swallowed a bowling ball and it fell out of my butt. Bri didn't have a mom who hammered her with personal safety tips every single day growing up. Not that she isn't feisty or capable. But I was so afraid that we would be too late, and she'd be dead before we found her."

Dr. Goulding's chocolate brown eyes poured into hers. She dangled a pen from one hand. "And you know firsthand what it's like to be in her position. It must have been hard for you to relive that, especially so soon after your most recent abduction."

Claire grimaced and drew a pillow into her lap. "Honestly, it was harder being one of the people who was left behind. When I was taken, even though I wasn't in control of the situation, I was in a position to do something about it. Fight the bad guy, escape. But when Bri was taken, we knew who had taken her, but we had no idea where she was. I think I finally understood what it was like to be Luke, or Mindy, or my mom the night of the Barney incident. Just utterly helpless. It was awful."

"You struggle when things are out of your hands. Even

when they're not your responsibility," Dr. Goulding observed.

"Of course I do. I mean, she's my baby sister. And knowing firsthand what she was about to experience—"

Claire faltered. Tears pooled in her eyes, and one escaped. Dr. Goulding handed her a tissue.

"I didn't know if we'd ever see her again. I know she only came into my life less than a year ago, but she's family. She's a piece I didn't even know was missing." Claire tapped her heart. "I don't know what I would have done if we hadn't found her."

Dr. Goulding nodded. "How is Brianna doing?"

"She keeps saying she's okay. She's seeing a therapist, and she's going to come stay with us for a little while when her shoot is done. I just can't stop worrying about her. I'm afraid that she's going to do what I tried to do. Ignore the source of the pain and bury herself in work until she alienates everyone close to her. Or, you know, starts sleepwalking into the Pacific."

Dr. Goulding shifted in her chair. A small smile appeared. "It sounds like you've had time to do some introspection."

Claire shrugged. "It was a five-hour flight."

"First, Claire, I want to remind you that you're in a unique position to help your sister. No one else in her life truly understands how she's feeling. I want to encourage you to be there for her as you're able. You seem to get a lot of joy from helping people. It might help you to help Brianna. As uncomfortable as it is to confront these emotions, to talk about the awful things that have happened to you, it's so important. Sometimes you need to make yourself uncomfortable in order to grow, or even just to cope. You've seen what happens when you try to keep everything inside."

She nodded. "There's nothing quite like being arrested for trespassing while dressed as a hotdog."

The doctor smiled. "How has your sleepwalking been?"

"Better. The benzos have really helped, though Luke says now I plan proposals in my sleep. He nudged me awake last night and told me to stop talking about taffeta."

"When we last spoke you were facing some challenges in your relationship. How are things going now?"

"Much better. We both have things to work on—obviously—but I'm feeling really connected right now. I'm trying to do better, to be more present. I've made some changes to my work schedule and office hours. And it's not because I feel like I have to, if that's what you're thinking. I wanted to. It was time. Brad's proposal really burned me out. It's time that I enforce some boundaries and prioritize the people who matter most."

"You're putting a lot of effort in. That's great to hear. I hope that Luke's reciprocating."

Claire unclasped her hands. "He's grumpy and opinionated, but annoyingly amazing as always. He plans date nights, cooks and cleans, listens every time I need to bounce something off him. I can't believe I almost lost him because I kept throwing myself headfirst into danger. He means so much to me."

Dr. Goulding nodded. "I hope you have some peace now that all those men have been incarcerated."

Claire shrugged. "It was the best possible outcome, of course. But I don't know if I'll ever feel truly safe. It's hard not to wonder if one of the lackeys will take up the mantle. I still wake up expecting to find some horrible message burned into the front yard or written in blood. There's probably another hundred ESA-affiliated murderers and stalkers out there who haven't been caught because they weren't important enough to be at the festival celebration."

Dr. Goulding nodded. "It's going to take some time to feel safe again. All you can do is take things one day at a time. You said your entire family joined you after Brianna was recovered. What was that like?"

"That part was amazing. Charlie's even started talking to Jack again. My friends came too. It was a surreal experience to have them all together without any fighting."

"Why do you think it's so important for you to have your family on speaking terms?"

What kind of stupid-ass question was that? "Why do any of us want to be on speaking terms with our families? It makes life easier, more rewarding. I lost my biological father for twenty years. And when we reconnected, I gained an amazing sister and a crazy—sorry, eccentric—stepmother."

Claire talked about her family for another thirty minutes while Dr. Goulding took intermittent notes. Daddy issues appeared to be her bread and butter, as she had a seemingly unending stream of questions about Jack. When Claire walked out after their hour was up, it was like a weight she had been carrying for a year and a half had slipped away. Was it her imagination, or was she taller?

Finally, things were getting back to normal. Okay, so a year ago she never would have imagined she'd be a footnote on a serial killer's Wikipedia page. And after Jason slept with Wendy at her awards ceremony, she had sworn she'd never let another man into her heart. She definitely never would have believed she'd be speaking to her biological father again, or that she would have been able to expand her business despite it literally being burned to the ground.

But now, she was living with the man who made a documentary about the most traumatic event of her entire life, running a bicoastal business, and hosting awkward family Thanksgivings with her entire blended family. Maybe now, finally, she would be able to hang up her amateur sleuthing trench coat and focus on her calling—true love.

The sunshine warmed her skin as she stepped cheerfully into her car and shut the door. She got out again almost immediately and inspected the backseat and the ground behind her tires. Couldn't be too careful.

With therapy crossed off her to do list, she only had a few appointments left for the rest of the day. A meeting with Mindy and Heather, who was staying with Claire for two weeks so they could train her in screening and selecting candidates, and a hot stay-at-home date with Luke before his premiere tomorrow. But first, she needed to drop off a bag of donations at the animal shelter.

She rolled her window down as she crawled through the familiar city streets. Flowers bloomed in window planters. Her car hummed as it drove over one of the brick-covered streets populated by beer gardens and trendy restaurants. She navigated her car around a pothole the size of a Vespa before pulling into the animal shelter.

"Anybody home?" Claire called as she pushed open the front door.

Sam glanced up from the counter. A pencil was shoved in her messy gray bun, and a worn calculator sat on the desk in front of her. "Claire!"

"It's so good to see you," Claire said, leaning over the counter for a hug. "I brought a couple bags of food. How are the doggy daycare plans coming?"

"Great. We open on Monday."

"That's amazing!" She hefted two bags of food onto the counter.

"I'll say. We already have thirteen dogs signed up starting next week."

"Room for two more?"

Sam smiled. "You want Rosie and Winston to come to daycare?"

"If you'll take them. Rosie will probably try to herd all the other dogs, though."

"We always have room for the Fun Police." Sam made a note on a sheet. "And we won't accept your money, so don't even think about it."

Claire sputtered. "The whole point of—"

"Save it. You've been incredibly generous. Let us return some of the favor."

Claire turned to leave. "Fine, but I'm doing a whole post on the shelter for the blog," she called over her shoulder. "Don't be surprised if Luke comes by to take some footage."

"Thank you. Make sure you get the new name right."

"New name?" She turned back around.

"Did you check the sign when you pulled in?"

What was she talking about? The sign had been the same peeling, weathered logo it had always been, hadn't it?

"I'll have to look. Have a good day, Sam. I'll stop in on Monday with the dogs."

"See you then."

The door swung shut behind Claire, and she crossed the parking lot. There, by the road, was a brand-new sign. There was a new name, and a silhouette of a woman in heels walking a corgi and a pug.

"Hartley Animal Rescue and Doggy Daycare," she read in a whisper. She bit her bottom lip as she took a picture with her phone and just stared at it for a moment. If she didn't get out of here, she was going to ugly cry and scare

Mindy and Heather. She sniffed and turned around. Sam smiled from the front window of the rescue.

Claire waved as she got in her car and backed out onto the road. Against all odds, she had accomplished the impossible. Saved the rescue, survived two abductions, taken down ESA, pulled off the biggest project of her career, expanded her business. And now a piece of her was immortalized, a lasting legacy in her hometown. Her heart grew in her chest as she drove. Twenty minutes later, she pulled up to the house with the smell of blueberries wafting from the paper bag on her passenger seat.

"Hey, guys. I brought muffins." Claire shut the front door with her foot as she balanced iced coffees in one hand and muffins in the other. Rosie and Winston ran to her and jumped on her legs.

Heather and Mindy whipped around. Mindy shuffled something into her binder. "Thanks, Claire. I was just showing Heather some stuff on red flags."

"Oh, great." Claire slid the food onto the kitchen island, then bent down to pet the dogs. "Super important, especially considering our rather unfortunate reputation. Now that we're only at a ninety-eight percent success rate."

"To be fair, Victoria did say yes to Barney," Mindy said. She ripped the paper liner off a muffin and stuffed half of it in her mouth. She moaned. "So we're still at a hundred percent proposal acceptance rate."

"But they didn't make it down the aisle." Claire sat on the bar stool next to Heather. "Thankfully. So, since we're talking red flags today anyway, I wanted to go over how we gently reject clients."

Mindy nodded and cleared her throat. "We do reply to everyone who applies for our services. In most cases, we reject the ones who don't pass the initial screening via email. And we do it as quickly as possible so we don't waste their time."

"We thank them for their interest in our company." Claire paused while Heather scribbled down notes in a composition notebook. "Then we provide a reason for the rejection—most of the time it's because our client roster is already full for their preferred engagement window. But sometimes it's because they seem like a giant creep. But we don't say that, we tell them that based on the results of the questionnaire they didn't pass our screening process. It's ruffled some feathers before, but I think it's better to be honest." She paused again as Heather wrote.

"If we're feeling particularly generous, we sometimes refer them to other services—Wendy would be shocked if she knew how many of her clients came from our reject list."

"What do you think Wendy's success rate is of getting people down the aisle?" Heather asked.

Claire and Mindy both grimaced. They had briefed Heather on their history with Wendy in case it came up on the job.

"I don't know if that's a metric Wendy keeps track of," Claire said carefully. "We just have different methods for selecting clients. She generally doesn't turn people away unless her roster is full. We turn them away if they don't seem like a sound couple or if they don't seem to be on the same page. I can't tell you how many times we've found our applicants on dating websites."

"That's terrible."

Claire shrugged. "That's why we're so careful. Happily Ever Afters isn't just a name. It's—almost—a guarantee."

"I love that." Heather scribbled away.

They talked for another two hours and went through their current list of applicants. Now that Heather was on board, they could take more than one client on at a time. Claudia and Tyrell's proposal was already half-planned. Darius and Nick would follow, and they would round out July with Todd and Leslie. It was time to choose the next clients. Excitement tingled all the way down Claire's spine when they finally settled on two couples.

"I love them. Tenth grade drama teacher and his high school sweetheart, mother of his child, and who also happens to be a feisty salsa dancing instructor. Heather, do you want to try writing our acceptance email? For practice?"

"Yes," Heather said, drawing the laptop toward her. "I'm so excited. What do I say?"

Claire and Mindy coached her through the acceptance letter and discussion of budget and collection of ideas. She had never realized exactly how many steps they went through unconsciously. The training binder needed a serious update. Maybe a PowerPoint.

When Mindy left to meet Sawyer and Heather drove off to spend the night with an old friend, Claire stepped outside and sat on the porch. Rosie settled at her feet and let out a hefty doggie sigh. Winston put his paw on her leg until she lifted him up into her lap. For the first time in a year, Claire didn't wonder if someone was peeping at her through the trees that surrounded Luke's property. Unlike the relentless police sirens and hubbub of Los Angeles, everything was still and quiet. The wind rustled the flowers Luke had planted in the front flower bed. Tiny green buds would become stargazer lilies later in the summer—Claire's favorite.

Where was Luke, anyway?

As if he was anticipating her question, he rolled up the lane at that exact moment and smiled at her through the windshield. He slammed the door of his late father's truck and crossed the front yard to bend down and kiss her full on the mouth. Her toes curled in her shoes.

"I love seeing you like this," he said, cupping her chin.

"Covered in dog hair and sitting on my butt?"

"Just at peace." He kissed her again and petted both dogs.

"Where have you been all day?"

"Working on something." He stepped down the stone path back to his truck.

"What's that?"

He released a ratchet strap that was securing a tarp to a large, rectangular bundle. "You'll see."

He undid another strap, then whisked the tarp off like a magician.

An intricate, hand-carved desk sat in the back of the truck. She set Winston on the deck and danced down the steps to the truck.

"You got me a new desk?" She gripped his arm.

"Well, we banged the other one to splinters."

"Do you think this one can hold our weight?" She ran one hand over the smooth oak surface.

"Only one way to find out."

CHAPTER SIXTY-FIVE

To Do:
- *Triple check EVERYTHING*
- *Pick up mom*
- *Remind Mindy to get flowers for the families*

CLAIRE ROLLED OVER IN BED THE MORNING OF LUKE'S premiere. Today marked two straight weeks of not sleep-walking. Heather was fully trained and would head back to Los Angeles to spearhead Darius and Nick's proposal after Luke's event. They had two West Haven proposals on the books—one board game themed and one sunset river boat proposal. They were both going to be stunning. Her blog post on Brad's proposal was so popular that her site had crashed four different times. The proposal supercut Luke had put up on YouTube had received over eight million views and was climbing by the day. Ad revenue was rolling in. Things were going suspiciously well.

Luke slept soundly next to her, spooning Winston. She poked him in the cheek until he woke up.

"Hey. It's premiere day. Are you excited?" She rested her chin on his shoulder.

He moaned and tugged the blanket back over himself. "I told you I didn't want to make a big deal out of it."

"Yes, and respectfully, I don't care." Claire patted the top of his head and flung the covers off. "There's so much to do! I have to check in with the food trucks and head over to monitor the decorating. I really should stop at the warehouse too and see how construction is going. I can't keep shoving speakers and tablecloths in our garage forever."

Luke grunted and put a pillow over his face. Winston huffed and ducked his snoot under the covers.

"You don't mind if we go separately?" Claire asked, digging through her jewelry box and laying a few choices in her travel kit.

"It's better if we go separately. I don't want to be there eight hours early." His voice was muffled beneath the pillow.

She rolled her eyes and zipped up her case. "Fine. Your tux is on the rack in the bathroom. I would go wingtip collar and bow tie, but I left a couple options out for you. And your dad's cufflinks are in the dish on the sink if you wanted to wear those."

"I still think we should have gone with a mandatory sweatpants dress code."

"That's for after." She swooped in and kissed him on the cheek. "I'm so proud of you. Your dad would be too." She turned to go, but Luke grabbed her wrist and pulled her back onto the bed.

"Thank you," he said before dragging her down for a kiss.

"You're welcome," she said with a stupid smile. Even

though he drove her insane sixty percent of the time, he still gave her butterflies.

She ran through a quick yoga flow in the master closet before climbing into a steaming hot shower. She needed to be focused and disciplined today. Everyone was going to be there—Luke's family, her family, some studio executives from LA, the mayor, most of the West Haven Police Department, friends. While today was primarily a celebration of Luke's achievement, all the victims' families were also coming. There would be no mountain lions, no bomb threats, no unexpected rickshaw trips. Everything needed to be perfect, respectful, and beautiful.

She threw on a quick base coat of makeup and towel-dried her hair. She would fix everything later, closer to premiere time. The chances of her sprinting around and sweating off all her hard work were extremely high.

Three dresses stared at her from the closet. Should she take the shimmering silver gown that was practically begging to go down a red carpet? But what about the slinky black number with the sky-high slit? And then there was the royal blue gown with the sweetheart neckline that had nearly made Luke's eyes pop out. Shrugging, she shoved them all into a garment bag with shoe options and lugged it over one shoulder. Mindy would give her the honest truth.

Luke and the dogs were asleep again by the time she came back out. That man could sleep through a tornado full of marching band equipment.

She tiptoed through the bedroom laden with half a dozen different bags and crept into the hallway. Downstairs, she made a nutritious breakfast and left an omelet on a plate in the refrigerator for Luke. Protein was mandatory today, especially if the studio executives tried to ply him with an excess of twenty-year-old scotch again. After the last studio event, Luke had spent two days in bed.

Two hours later, she stood in a field in front of a movie screen. The West Haven Drive-In Movie Theater looked exactly as she remembered it. The grass had been freshly cut. The ruts made by car tires were noticeable but didn't wreck her vision.

She glanced behind her, across the highway at her favorite state park. A mountain rose sharply above a lake, and just about halfway up was the small overlook where Claire and her mom used to watch the movies with binoculars. Her heart warmed. Who knew all these years later that she would be planning a premiere at the same location for her grumpy yet thoughtful boyfriend?

"Okay." Mindy appeared at her shoulder with a clipboard. "Edison bulbs are strung over the beer garden and all are confirmed functional. Bluetooth speakers playing Luke's favorite tracks—at least the ones that won't give anyone's grandmother a heart attack—are set up and ready to go."

"Great," Claire said, making a mental note. "Where are we at with food trucks?"

"I made contact with all of them," Heather piped up, lugging a stack of chairs behind her. She had volunteered to help with the premiere. "Everyone's confirmed. They're also sending a bonus gourmet whoopie pie truck. I know you said Luke doesn't like cake, but it's not really the same thing."

"Good enough," Claire said, sweeping her gaze over the space. "We didn't hear back from Victoria?"

Victoria was Barney's fiancée. Claire had planned a stunning flash mob proposal for them before Barney had turned out to be a huge dick.

Mindy shook her head. "Not that I blame her. She did

agree to marry the man who killed all these women." She gestured to the right side of the screen, where a technician was installing uplighting beneath poster-sized pictures and descriptions of the victims.

Claire's heart sank. "She was a victim too." Maybe Victoria would have dinner with her sometime.

"So," she said, refocusing, "the bar is getting set up along the western tree line." She jabbed one manicured finger that direction. "The signature drink is 'The Luke'—Jack and Coke."

"Classic," Mindy said, nodding and making a note. "The press is already buzzing about tonight. All three major newspapers mentioned the premiere and the documentary. Marnie had a sound bite too."

Claire smiled and clasped a hand to her heart. "I'm just so proud of him. He worked really hard on this."

"So did you," Mindy said, nudging her. "I assume we're not playing your episode tonight?"

Claire shuddered. "No. I haven't even seen it. I don't ever want to see it. He's showing Ariel's episode. She was the first victim. Well, apart from his dad, I guess."

"And Luke is bringing the thumb drive directly here?"

Claire nodded. "He wouldn't let me take it. So annoying. If he gets here and forgot it at home, I'm going to murder him."

"Well, we shouldn't be surprised. He's always been super secretive about his projects."

"True." Claire glanced at her watch. "Oh, Mom and Roy's flight will be landing soon. I'm going to head to the airport, and I'll be back by three. Will you help me decide what to wear then?"

"Obviously. We'll stay here for a bit and make sure

everything's getting set up correctly. Cocktail tables should be here any minute."

"Thank you so much."

Details buzzed through Claire's mind like a vacuum cleaner full of glitter during her short ride to the airport. As she idled outside of baggage claim, she made a few notes.

Someone rapped on her window, and Claire nearly lobbed her phone in self-defense. Alice waved and smiled. Her hair was Florida-big and she wore a violently pink power suit. Claire jumped out of the car and ran to hug her.

"*Mija*," Roy said as he wrapped his arms around her.

"Thank you for getting on a plane for me. Again. I know you hate it."

"Oh no," Roy said, casting some side eye at Alice. "The hypnotist your mom took me to really helped."

"I bet." Claire took their bags and heaved them into the hatch of her car.

"Well," Alice said as soon as the car was in motion, "I had a gift for you, but those idiots at the TSA confiscated it."

"What was it?" It wouldn't have been the first time Alice tried to sneak an economy-sized bottle of sunscreen through security.

"Some fresh sage and rosemary bundles. They thought they were *illicit drugs*," she said, dropping her voice to a whisper.

"Well, thank you for thinking of me anyway. Where would you like to go for lunch? There are a couple stores downtown that might carry sage bundles. I'm sure we could find a restaurant nearby." She could already tell her afternoon was going to be spent on a wild goose chase for herbs. When Alice had something in her mind, she held fast to it like a toddler with a spatula covered in brownie batter.

"That sounds lovely, Clairebear. You're the expert. Anything you're hungry for is fine."

Three aggravating hours later, Claire and her parents had shared tapas and sangria and had gone to three separate stores looking for sage bundles that had been sourced from Alice's preferred region. When they climbed back in the car, Claire glanced at the clock.

"I better drop you guys off so I can head back to the venue. I need to make sure the trucks are arriving and everyone has what they need."

"Oh, we'll go with you, sweetheart. No need to make a special trip."

"Are you sure?" she asked even though she had already pointed the car in the direction away from Luke's house. Thank god. There wasn't much time to spare.

"Of course, sweetheart. I'd like to prepare the space for Luke so that he has a good experience tonight. Drive-in theaters are notorious for inconsistent energy."

"Sure they are." Claire turned onto a highway that wound out of town. They passed an expansive graveyard, several gas stations, and a couple of housing developments before reaching the drive-in theater.

"Oh, hell no," Claire said as she parked her car. She jumped out and slammed her door. "What is this trailer doing here? I didn't approve a trailer."

Next to the entrance, a white trailer had been set up, completely compromising her aesthetic. Mindy stood nearby, talking on the phone.

"Claire, I don't know what the deal is with the trailer—"

"Oh, that was me, darling." Alice marched over the grass in her heels, not even sinking into the ground. "It was supposed to be a surprise. It's a trailer for Luke so that if he gets overwhelmed from the attention, he can duck in and decompress for a few minutes."

Claire paused and frowned. It was actually pretty thoughtful. Why hadn't she thought of that?

"And also, sweetie, there's one other surprise. I hired a hair and makeup team to get us ready in the trailer. Just for fun. A little celebration to chase away all the bad energy from the past year."

Claire glanced back at the trailer and deflated like a balloon. She had been fully ready to rip someone's head off, and here it had been a considerate surprise from her mother. Clearly she still had work to do when it came to releasing the reins.

"This sure beats getting dressed in a cinder block bathroom next to the suffocating stench of old popcorn. Thank you, Mom."

"Oh look, they're here! Aren't these the girls you usually hire for hair and makeup? I assumed they were the best."

Claire glanced over her shoulder. Two cars had pulled up alongside them as she'd raged about the trailer. "Sharice! And Judy. It's so good to see both of you." Claire smiled warmly. "It's been months. I'm so glad to run into you. I was actually hoping to talk to you about a couple proposals we have coming up."

As they started setting up inside the trailer, she nailed them both down for her dates and was delighted to cross something off a To Do list she hadn't even made yet.

"Thanks, girls. I'll be back in an hour. I better go check on a few things." She walked out tingling with excitement. Food trucks were starting to arrive, and her stomach growled at the smell of funnel cakes. The sun was dipping lower on the horizon. In just two hours, Luke would be surrounded by people he loved (or begrudgingly tolerated—

they still hadn't confirmed if his brother, George, was coming) and celebrating what was sure to be the biggest accomplishment of his career.

"No, no, no," Claire said and sprinted toward the bar. The bartender was hanging a signature drink sign below the bar, but it was the wrong one. "Those aren't the right signs. We nixed the scotch and soda. Let me just track them down."

It was a good thing she had left herself an extra hour. She couldn't trust just anyone to pull this off.

CHAPTER SIXTY-SIX

To Do:
- Give Luke the best night ever

"You're all set, sugar." Sharice spun Claire around in the chair.

"Oh, wow. You did such a great job with my hair. Thank you, Sharice," Claire said, leaning over to hug her and slip her a twenty-dollar bill. She glanced at her watch. "I better get out there. Thanks again, girls." She waved as she exited the trailer.

Golden hour was just beginning. Pink and gold light softly illuminated the rows of white chairs. The Edison bulbs gleamed. Music was already thumping. Her insides twisted. Would everything go well? Would Luke be disappointed? She stepped carefully down the stairs in the royal blue dress that Mindy had insisted on. Now she just had to focus on not getting whoopie pie on it.

Alice had already finished and left to mingle with the other guests. Claire spotted her talking to Nicole from a mile away thanks to her pink suit. She couldn't see Roy, but if she had to guess, he was probably assisting the team that was erecting a small stage in front of the screen where Luke would give his speech. Where was Luke, anyway? He was cutting it close. He was probably sitting at home second-guessing his dress shirt options or stress-cleaning the gutters.

Dozens of people dressed in black-tie evening wear milled around. One of the studio executives was talking to Sawyer. Who knew they made tuxes that big? Mindy laughed at something he said. She had managed to change into a glittering silver dress with matching heels. Her hair was braided on one side and left long and down her back. Heather was there too, in an emerald-green cocktail dress with a scalloped hem. Ruby slippers glittered on her feet. Where did this girl get all her adorable shoes? Claire made a mental note to ask.

The food trucks were all set. The beer garden was teeming with people she didn't recognize but assumed were friends of Luke's. Nicole and Kyle were there though. Nicole looked adorable in a drapey peach dress. Her camera was slung around her neck, and the slightest hint of a bump was appearing in her midsection. A dozen rows of seats were lined up in front of the still-dark movie screen.

She had texted Luke twice to remind him to bring his cut of the episode, but would he remember? He'd been ignoring her all day. Probably still salty about the premiere.

Roy was chatting with Jack and Tanya, who appeared to have brought a Tupperware container of their vegan snacks. Tanya wafted something under Roy's nose, and his head retracted into his neck like a turtle in his shell.

George, Luke's bullheaded brother, was engaged in a spirited conversation with Rachel. Even though Luke's mother was facing away from her, the rigid posture was unmistakable. Thank god they hadn't stopped to say hello. She turned away before George could spot her.

Her stomach dropped when she saw the front row of seats. They had reserved five seats for Barney's victims. Jennifer Heiser's mother was talking to Kayley Herrold's wife, and they were both dabbing at their eyes. Ariel Pullizzi's mom was standing in front of her daughter's portrait, clutching a hand over her heart.

Claire was drawn to them like gravity. Her feet carried her forward even as she stumbled over what she would say. What *could* she possibly say to them? Sorry for being alive?

"Hi. I, uh." Claire stopped. The families turned around. Anxiety scrambled her stomach like eggs in a too-hot pan.

"Claire," Ariel's mom said gently. She laid a hand on Claire's shoulder. "Thank you so much for inviting us. You made it really special."

"I'm sorry, I—" she broke off again and bit her lip. Her mother would be ashamed. But there wasn't a How to Speak to Relatives of People Who Were Murdered chapter in that book Alice had given her when she tried to convince her to be a debutante.

"We know. It's okay." Kayley Herrold's wife swung in and gave her a hug. She smelled like oil-based paint. Blue speckles dotted her hands.

"It should've been me," Claire said in a rush. The words poured out before she could even process them. "Not your daughters and wives." She looked at the posters of the women in front of her. "I'm not special. I was just—lucky."

And that was the truth of it. Claire wasn't spared because she had some divine calling in life that demanded to be fulfilled. She was just a regular girl in a terrifying world. And she had been lucky enough to have a mother who cared about her enough to teach her self-defense. And Sawyer, who saved her life when she was ready to give up.

"Stop that," Shawna Delong's dad said. "The blood is on his hands, and his alone. We are so grateful for you, you know that? Because of you, that idiot is in prison. We've already been contacted by the FBI about the case they're building against him. He'll pay for what he's done. And that's because of you."

"You've given us justice, hon," Courtney Stevens's mom said.

"Because of you, we get to lay our little girl to rest." Jennifer's mom dabbed a tissue under her eyes.

Claire sniffled. If she didn't get out of here right this second, she would ruin Judy's hard work on her makeup.

"Thank you. I think of you all the time. I hope the documentary helps you heal." She smiled sadly and walked off before she put her foot in her mouth some more.

She took a couple of steadying breaths and glanced at her watch. People were starting to take their seats. Luke should be here by now. The meager amount of press on the red carpet couldn't be expected to wait around all day. She gritted her teeth, almost welcoming the instant flood of annoyance. He was pathologically punctual. It was his most annoying trait. So why the hell couldn't he manage to show up on time for his premiere?

Mindy was chatting with Alice. Claire marched up to them. "Have you heard from Luke? He's never late."

Mindy shook her head. "Maybe he hit traffic?"

Claire glanced behind her at the highway. Not a single car went by in either direction. "He's doing this just to annoy me."

"Probably. I'm sure he'll be here soon."

A knot grew in her stomach. What if something had happened to him? What if a rogue member of ESA had decided to take revenge for dismantling their organization and found him home alone? She called him, but there was no answer.

She pulled up the app linked to the doggie camera she had installed when they returned to West Haven. Rosie and Winston napped soundly in their beds in the kitchen. There weren't any puddles of blood or sounds of a struggle. She switched to the video doorbell and checked the driveway. Luke's car was missing, so he had definitely left.

"Just relax, Claire," she said to herself, shoving her phone back into her clutch. "Everything's fine."

Maybe a corn dog would calm her nerves. She took half a step in the direction of the food trucks when a video flickered to life on the movie screen. The Edison bulbs strung over the beer garden dimmed. She stopped and whipped around. Light emanated from the projection booth. Had Luke shown up and snuck the disk to the theater staff? Where the hell was he?

The remaining people who were standing hurried to their seats. A couple of them glanced around, like they were expecting someone to make a speech. That had been the plan, but apparently Luke didn't care about the plan. It was the tandem bicycle all over again.

Claire scanned the dark field for him, but he was nowhere to be found. What an ass. Should she take a seat and watch the episode without him?

Wait a second. This wasn't the episode. This wasn't anything to do with the documentary at all. A video of Claire dancing at Kyle and Nicole's wedding was playing. Oh my god. The idiot had given them the wrong thumb drive. They were playing Kyle and Nicole's wedding video in front of the families of Barney's victims.

She sprinted for the projection booth and hammered on the door until it opened.

"Yeah?" A dazed-looking teenager with impressive chin acne asked. A faded red vest that read West Haven Drive-In Theater hung over his skinny shoulders.

"You need to pull this tape. It's not the right one."

The teen crossed his arms. "Mr. Islestorm assured me that it's the right one."

"How could he have? He's not even here."

"He dropped it off earlier. It's the right one." The teen slammed the door.

What the hell? This was humiliating. This was supposed to be a celebration of Luke's documentary and an opportunity to remember the victims. Instead they were showing a video of a wedding for someone the families didn't even know.

She glanced at the screen again. Now it was playing behind-the-scenes footage of Claire on location for Kyle and Nicole's proposal. Before she could blink, it switched to her pirouetting on the beach with an ice cream cone, laughing into the wind. A dozen more clips flashed—Claire rolling her eyes as her mother read tarot cards. Browsing the aisles at Sephora. Dancing in the living room with her sisters. Shuffling some papers into a fresh binder. Aggressively mashing potatoes on Thanksgiving. What was this? Was this some elaborate plan to humiliate her for making him have a premiere?

Hang on—was something falling from the sky? Brightly colored spots floated down from beyond the treetops. The drone of a plane hummed in the distance. She hadn't cleared a plane *or* random glowing debris. Was there some kind of sky lantern festival going on in West Haven? It hadn't been on the community calendar. And more importantly, where the hell was Luke? Everything was falling apart.

One of the lanterns drifted and settled on the ground at her feet. She bent to pick it up. Great, now there was refuse littering Luke's premiere. People should really be more careful. She was about to blow out the candle when the hand-painted image on the side of the lantern was thrown into sharp relief. It was her and Luke on his birthday, hoisting the beef jerky trophy. Her mouth fell open. Another lantern landed a few feet away. It was also painted, this time with a picture of them dancing at Kyle and Nicole's wedding.

Claire glanced up. A familiar redhead smiled at her from the taco truck. Jane and Aaron, former proposal clients, waved mischievously. She rolled the lantern in her hand. Jane's signature was scrawled at the bottom. She must have painted the lanterns. But why?

Claire waved back, dumbstruck. On the movie screen, the video flashed to a title card that said "The Proposal Planner." The image froze. What was that sound? An engine revved from somewhere in the woods. Suddenly, there was a smell of sulfur. Was the forest burning down? Did they need to evacuate?

At that moment, fireworks exploded into the air. Someone crashed through the movie screen on a dirt bike and roared to a stop just before the first row of seats.

Her heart fell into her feet. There was no way they were getting their security deposit back now. The screen gaped and flapped weakly in the wind.

The rider took his helmet off and waved. The crowd cheered. Hold on. The rider was Steve, another past client. Claire had planned a Jet Ski proposal for him last spring. It was one of the first things Luke had ever mocked her for. And those fireworks had looked identical to the ones they shot off to celebrate Tyler and Ericka's patriotic proposal not long after. What was happening?

Music started playing. Not just music—an instrumental version of Claire's favorite song from the heavy metal band Nightsmear. All through the audience, people got out of their chairs. Nicole and Mindy materialized out of nowhere and began to dance in front of her. It was a stupid, wiggly dance they had invented in college after too many shots of tequila.

"What the—" But a grin was growing on Claire's face. This couldn't have all been a wild accident. Something was happening.

Seconds later, Tanya and Jack swooped in. Jack spun Tanya out and performed an elegant dip before they moved off to the side, exposing Roy and Alice. They incorporated a quick salsa number. Alice's breasts nearly tumbled out of her low-cut gown. Their grins would have been visible from space.

Suddenly almost everyone was dancing in a great big mob in front of her. Kayley Herrold's wife waltzed around the perimeter of the crowd with Jennifer Heiser's husband. Marco, the pawn shop broker who often found specialty items for Claire, danced by with his wife. Even Rachel and George marched to the front of the crowd and did approximately two seconds of "the wave" before stomping off to the side.

As the song came to the last chorus, a horse-drawn carriage emerged from the crowd. Claire laughed and clapped her hands. This was absolutely insane.

Victoria, Barney's former fiancée, hopped down from the carriage and walked over. Claire's heart jumped into her throat. She hadn't seen her in person since the proposal, but she had wanted to reach out a thousand times. Even the sympathy basket she had sent was a poor replacement for a proper phone call.

Victoria handed over a single red rose and pulled her in for a tight hug. She said nothing, but Claire could feel the well of emotions inside her. The horse-drawn carriage clopped off. Something was falling from the sky again. A flashing light approached them at high speed. The Edison bulbs came back to full power, and light suddenly sprang up from the ground.

Claire glanced down at her feet. Yards of battery-powered fairy lights had been arranged in concentric circles. She was standing right in the middle of them without even noticing. She was losing her touch.

The blinking light drew closer. It crested over the tattered movie screen, and *finally,* there he was. Luke Islestorm in a freakin' tuxedo skydiving into his movie premiere. But it wasn't a movie premiere after all.

The parachute streamed out behind him as he drifted gently over the rows of seats. As the song faded out, he cut the cord on his parachute and stepped smoothly into the ring of lights. A double baby Bjorn was strapped to him. Rosie panted happily, a pair of miniature goggles on her furry face.

If they were with Luke, what dogs had been on the camera at home? She didn't have time to worry about it. Luke let her and Winston out of the harness, and they ran for Claire. He took two steps and dropped down on one knee in front of her.

"Oh my god," she said, and her hands flew to her mouth in a gesture she had witnessed and carefully cultivated a hundred times.

He laughed and took her hand. "Was this enough dramatic flair for you?"

"I—I don't even—you idiot!" She slapped him lightly on the shoulder.

The crowd chuckled.

"Do you have any idea how hard it is to propose to someone who plans proposals for a living? You should have seen the binder we had to make for this project." His green eyes shone brightly in the light from the fairy lights.

"This was supposed to be for you," she said, gesturing at the tattered screen. "We didn't even get to play your episode."

"I knew the only way to distract you long enough to plan everything was to let you think you were planning something for me. Incidentally, it worked."

"You're such an ass."

He shrugged. "So. My legs are falling asleep here. Claire Aurora Hartley—Jesus, I didn't even ask the question yet."

Tears had sprung into Claire's eyes the second he said her full name. She sniffed them back and composed herself. "Sorry, go ahead."

"Claire Aurora Hartley. You drive me absolutely insane. You work too much, you bend over backward for people, and you love so fiercely. You inverted my entire world when I broke into your apartment and found you singing to your dog."

"So you admit it! You did break in!" she cried.

He ignored her. "Somewhere down the line, between the arguing, cheating at video games, trips to Paris and the beach, I fell in love with you. And with your crazy family— don't even get me started on Jack, he took two full weeks to give me his blessing." He searched the crowd for Jack, who lifted a martini in a toast.

So *that* was why he had been so extra anti-Jack.

"Meanwhile, when I asked Roy and your mom, I didn't even get the full question out before they said yes. Anyway, we've been through more than most couples go through in an entire lifetime. We're partners in everything. I've never met anyone like you, someone who creates joy for a living and adopts special needs dogs and tasers bad guys like it's nothing. I love you, Claire."

He paused and gestured behind them. She looked where he pointed. Across the highway, on top of the overlook where she used to watch movies with her mother, were several glowing letters. They were arranged to spell out "Marry me?"

"So," Luke said, drawing her attention back to him. "What do you think? Be my wife?"

He reached one hand into his pocket and pulled out a small box. He opened it, but she didn't even glance inside. Her heart was so full it might actually explode. She lifted her gaze and took in the moment. She wanted to remember every second of this day for the rest of her life. Friends and family stared at her, excitement glistening in their eyes. Warmth and love emanated from every direction. There was no fear, no danger. Just one perfect moment with the promise of forever.

Mindy gestured at Luke and raised her eyebrows. Oh, right. He was still waiting for an answer.

"Yes." Her throat was so choked with emotion she could barely get the word out. She nodded emphatically.

Luke slid the ring on her finger and pulled her straight off the grass. He twirled her around and around. They spun under the star-strewn sky, just like they had in Paris, and in the parking lot of the hospital where she had fallen into a trashcan and he had said "I love you" for the first time. If he kept going, she might vomit all down his back and ruin the moment.

He set her on her feet, and she kissed him. She listed slightly to the left, but at least she didn't fall over. They broke apart, and she finally remembered to glance down at her hand. A massive three-carat cushion cut stone with a diamond halo was perfectly sized and nestled on her ring finger. It looked like it had been made for her. And it was so much better than a beer bottle cap.

She took another look at the people who surrounded them. Her entire extended family smiled at her. Kyle was jumping and screaming. Nicole was snapping pictures. Mindy and Sawyer were making out. Brianna and Charlie had video cameras pressed to their faces.

She kissed Luke again. He pulled her into his arms, and she breathed in his comforting scent. She was surrounded by the people she loved. Everyone was safe, and she had found her soulmate in the unlikely form of a grumpy documentary director who could master the hell out of a proposal.

All in all, the future was looking as bright as the diamond on her finger.

BONUS SCENE

Claire twitched the curtain aside. Her heart fluttered in her chest. It was finally here. The day she had dreamed of since she was a little girl: her wedding day.

Before long, family and friends would be congregating in the rows of white chairs spread out in her and Luke's backyard. The sun was shining and there wasn't a single cloud in the sky. It was the least the universe could do after personally victimizing her for the last two years. The tantalizing smell of hors d'oeuvres drifted up the stairs to the guest bedroom, where she had camped out to spy on the action.

Not long after their engagement, Claire had dragged Luke into a discussion of their dream wedding. She was surprised to find that her feelings had shifted significantly from her first round of wedding planning. As much as she wanted the day to be beautiful and memorable, she wasn't laser-focused on the flowers or the ceremony or table decor.

Their wedding wasn't going to be some stately affair covered by bridal magazines. It was designed to be relaxed, fun, and hopefully full of amazing memories. It was a celebration of the two of them, and the love that they had found against all odds. Would that celebration include fleets of tiny tacos and stations where people could play a video game depicting Claire and Luke's love story that she had commissioned as a wedding gift? Damn straight it would.

Even though she had officially handed the event planning reins over to Mindy for the day, the master timeline still ticked away in her brain. Seven minutes until first look photography. Somewhere in the fray, Luke was probably anxiously sawing down tree limbs or doing some flower bed redefining in his tuxedo.

The door opened behind her and Claire jumped. Charlie and Bri slunk into the room and shut the door behind them.

Charlie took one look at Claire and her bottom lip trembled.

"Hi," she said, throwing her arms around Claire's neck. Her cobalt blue bridesmaid gown popped against her skin.

Bri, in a matching dress, came to stand on her other side. "We just wanted to check on you before things get underway. Are you doing okay? Need anything?" she asked softly, like she was trying to coax a kitten down from a tree.

"No, I'm fine. Ryan's ready to walk the dogs down the aisle?"

Charlie nodded. "He's been practicing his detangling technique all week."

"Perfect." Claire reached out and took one of each of her sister's hands. "I can't tell you how much it means to me that you're both here. And for standing up there with me in case Luke gets cold feet."

"I will happily put him in a headlock until the final vows are spoken." Charlie sniffed and wiped a tear away.

"I'm so happy for you," Bri said and came in for a hug. "Both of you. You've been through so much together. If you can survive the last two years, your marriage can survive anything."

Claire pulled back and looked at both of her sisters. *Mindfulness*. Dr. Goulding's voice resonated within her like a gong. Everything she had read and heard about weddings told her today was going to fly by. She needed to immerse herself in every moment while she could. She allowed the day to settle on her like a blanket.

Charlie's floral perfume. The sparkle in Bri's eyes. The baseboards that she had completely forgotten to dust. Every snippet would be woven into the mental tapestry of her wedding day.

Mindy bustled into the room, resplendent in her blue gown. Her phone was pressed to her ear.

She offered a wave, emerald-cut engagement ring flashing in the afternoon sunlight. "Yes, the ceremony will end promptly at five thirty and everyone but extended family will go straight to cocktail hour. Snacks out right away. We don't want the groom's brother throwing up in the pool again. Great. Thanks."

Mindy dropped her phone in her clutch and turned to look at Claire. "How did you get away from Alice?"

Charlie chimed in. "She's doing a reading for Tanya."

"Genius." Mindy bustled over and fixed one of Claire's curls. When she pulled back, tears were in her eyes.

"Don't start," Claire ordered. "Judy worked really hard on our makeup."

"I'm sorry." Mindy dragged a tissue under her eye. "You're just so beautiful. I can't believe you finally got your happy ending."

Claire shook her head and dragged the curtain to the

side again. "You know as well as I do that this isn't an ending. It's just one day. A beginning."

Below them, Alice and Tanya huddled around a cocktail table. Tarot cards were spread out between them. Tanya was rapt with attention. Jack was in the far corner of the yard with Roy, hefting something into the reception tent. Was that Rachel sneaking away from the bar with a martini?

Claire turned away from the window, heart positively glowing. "And you're next."

Mindy and Sawyer were having a destination wedding in the Bahamas in September. It remained to be seen if hurricanes would impact their ceremony.

The door opened again, and Nicole came inside with her daughter, Harper, propped on one hip.

Nicole took one look at Claire and burst into tears.

Would the entire day be this full of weeping women? Maybe she should have installed tissue stations.

"No," Nicole said when Claire took a step toward her. "Don't come any closer. Gooey baby," she said, gesturing to Harper's runny nose. In her six months of life, the baby had spent approximately half of them with some form of respiratory illness thanks to daycare.

"I don't want to take any chances with your dress," Nicole added.

Claire brushed a hand over the lace on her A-line gown even though she ached to hug her friend. "Thanks. I think it's even better than the first one."

"Well," Mindy said, "this one's not covered in blood, so it's already a pretty big improvement."

"No attempted murder talk today," Nicole said sternly.

Claire grimaced and inadvertently flashed back to that night in the parking garage. All the trauma of her past two years had been knitted into her DNA. Barney, the abductions, ESA, the stalking, harassment, threats, and constant fear for her family's safety. Those experiences had fundamentally changed her.

She was still healing, still re-discovering what it meant to feel safe. The trauma was a part of her, as much as today would become part of her. But the blaring mental alarms of danger weren't as loud as they used to be. Here, surrounded by family and friends and waiting to say "I do" to the man of her dreams, they were barely more than a whisper.

Harper whined on Nicole's hip.

"We're officially approaching a meltdown. Let me find Kyle and we'll get started on the first look. I'll meet you at the rose tunnel in five minutes." Nicole ducked out the door and disappeared.

As a surprise to no one, Luke had been largely uninterested in wedding planning, but had insisted on having a hand in the cinematic elements—namely, a twenty-foot series of archways he had spent an inordinate amount of time with gardeners persuading climbing roses to grow over.

"You don't seem stressed," Mindy said with narrowed eyes.

"Must be the meds," Claire said with a smile.

But it wasn't. Or at least, not entirely. Today was the culmination of a lifelong dream, and no matter how many things went disastrously wrong, all that mattered in the end was that she and Luke were officially starting their life together. Who cared if someone threw up in the pool or a mountain lion wandered into their midst? The rest of her life was waiting for her downstairs.

Claire said goodbye to her sisters and slipped off her Jimmy Choo bridal heels (a broken neck was not on the agenda today). A delicious medley of smells greeted her as she and Mindy descended the stairs. Luke's niece, Sophia, ran past her, shrieking and giggling as Kyle chased her with baby Harper.

"Claire?"

Claire's shoulders hunched up by her ears. That voice belonged to her almost mother-in-law. Their relationship had improved significantly over the past year, but she still put Claire on edge.

She turned around and fixed a smile on her face. "Hi, Rachel. Thank you for being here today."

"I wanted to give you something. I should have done it sooner, since your hair's already done, but here." She stiffly handed over a small box.

Claire lifted the lid. A beautiful jeweled comb studded with sapphires was nestled inside.

"This was my grandmother's," Rachel explained. "All the women in my family have worn it on their wedding days. It's something old and blue, though I'm sure you already have those traditions covered."

Claire squeezed Rachel's hand. "Thank you. I would be honored to wear it. Mindy?"

"On it." Mindy beelined over and began carefully removing the jeweled comb Claire had bought from Etsy. It was pretty, but it didn't have decades of family history attached. In no time, the antique comb was nestled in place of the original.

Claire took a look in the mirror in the hallway. It was perfect.

"You look lovely." Rachel put her arms out at her side.

Claire faltered. Was this a trap? Was Rachel about to stab her in the back and proclaim she was the head honcho of ESA this whole time?

Mindy must have been thinking the same thing, because

she tensed up behind Rachel and stealthily drew a Taser out of her clutch.

Claire took a chance and shrank into the hug. It was like embracing a pine tree covered in ice.

When Rachel drew back a millisecond later, she held onto Claire's arms for a moment. Her eyes were softer than Claire had ever seen. That martini must have done the trick.

"I know I've given you some trouble in the past. But I'm glad Lucas found you. You've opened something in him that I didn't even know was there. Thank you for making my son so happy."

Claire smiled. Her eyes were watering again. She most certainly did not have "waterworks due to a Rachel compliment" on her wedding day bingo card.

"I'm so grateful to be joining your family. I'd better go. You know how Luke hates to be late."

Rachel smiled and released her. "We'll see you up there."

Claire nodded, then rushed through the foyer and out the front door. The end of the rose tunnel caught her eye. Nicole and the florists had carefully arranged movable, rose-adorned trellises joined by a rose curtain at the end. They would remove it afterwards so guests could walk through it to the ceremony site.

"You're sure you don't want to do anything about the scar?" Nicole's voice broke her out of her reverie.

Claire looked down at the end of the shiny scar that was only partially concealed by lace. "No. It's part of our story too."

"Okay. Ready?" Nicole asked. She lifted her camera, eyes misty again.

"Let's do this." Claire stepped into the tunnel and was immediately transported to a different world. Earthy, floral smells surrounded her. It pulsed with life and natural beauty. Tanya was going to *love* it.

Nicole's camera clicked away behind her.

There he was. Luke Islestorm, her very soon-to-be husband. His back was turned, and the tension in his body was palpable even from ten feet away. There was an 85% chance that he was annoyed because she was two minutes late. But it was her wedding day and she was, after all, the bride. There was no such thing as late.

Claire glanced over her shoulder at Nicole with a mischievous smile before turning back to Luke.

"You're late," he said, back still turned.

"It's your mom's fault," she said.

"Really?" His head cocked.

"Yeah. She had the audacity to offer me a priceless family heirloom on our wedding day."

She tapped him on the shoulder. He turned, and his expression instantly went from one of annoyance to joy.

He held her at arm's length and studied her like he had just unfurled a beautiful antique map. When his eyes met hers, she saw forever.

"You look incredible, Mrs. Islestorm," he said.

She shook her head but smiled. "Hartley-Islestorm. And you're looking pretty incredible yourself. Go on, spin."

He obligingly turned, and she took an extra second to admire his butt. *Mindfulness.*

"You're really going to make our kids learn how to spell Hartley-Islestorm?" His eyes narrowed, but his smile hadn't left.

"Of course. It's important to me that they know where they came from."

"You don't want to throw an Alejo in there too?"

"Don't tempt me."

Luke chuckled and pulled her in. Their foreheads pressed together. She put her palm flat on his chest. His heart was beating a little faster than usual.

"Well, even if they never learn to spell their names, there's no doubt in my mind that they'll know they come from the strongest, bravest, most hardworking and incredible woman I've ever met."

He lowered his mouth to hers and kissed her gently.

There had been a gigantic softie behind Luke's grumpy marble façade this whole time. Who knew? All she had to do was systematically pry it out of him over the course of two years.

She glowed from the inside. "Think they'll be workaholics or pathological people pleasers?" she asked when he pulled back.

He considered for a moment. "I'd bet both. They'll probably have enough combined anxiety to forecast every possible natural disaster for the next forty years."

"My mom will be so proud."

They smiled and just took each other in for a moment.

"I love you," they said at the same time.

Electricity passed between them. Who could have imagined that the grumpy pain in the ass who broke into her apartment to demand a meeting would end up being her true love?

"Okay, lovebirds," Nicole chastised from the tunnel. "We only have twenty minutes until guests arrive, so let's get some pictures with the families."

After nearly half an hour of various family portraits that had only gone slightly awry when Winston attempted to pee on Rachel, Claire was concealed upstairs again while guests arrived.

Everyone was in attendance. Friends, family, former

clients, even a couple of detectives from the West Haven P.D. filled the rows. Finally, it was time.

"I can't believe today is your wedding day," Alice said as they stood on the front porch. Her eyes sparkled with tears.

She took Claire's hands. "Clairebear, you are all the best parts of me—no, don't start."

Tears had immediately sprung into Claire's eyes. "Sorry."

"You are so resilient, so courageous, and so beautiful. I am honored beyond words to be your mother, and to have watched you grow into the amazing woman you are today. You deserve all the best things in life, darling. And I truly believe that Luke is one of them."

Claire threw herself on her mom. How many tears could there be on such a happy occasion? She would remember everything about this moment—the anticipation of meeting Luke at the altar, the smell of her mom's shampoo, the brush of lace over her skin.

"Ready, *mija*?" Roy held out his arm.

She was beyond ready to meet Luke and start this day of celebration. But something was missing.

"Almost. Hold on one second." Claire beckoned Mindy over and whispered something in her ear. Mindy pulled out her headset and barked an order into it. A minute later, Jack and Tanya appeared.

"It might be kind of a tight squeeze. But I was hoping you'd walk me down the aisle. All of you," she clarified.

Tanya sniffed and nodded enthusiastically. Jack smiled and held out his arm. Roy took her other one, and they approached the rose tunnel. It definitely wasn't wide enough for five people to walk abreast. Alice and Tanya hung back, and after the fleet of bridesmaids, flower girls, and ring bearers passed, they started their journey through the blooms.

Claire snuck a glance at each of her dads as they passed through a dappled beam of sunlight. On her left was Roy, the man who showed her what a life partner should be. He had treated her like his own daughter since the first day they met, even though they didn't share any blood. He had been there for field hockey games, cheerleading tournaments, first dates, driving lessons and broken engagements.

On the other side was Jack. Deeply flawed, but deeply feeling. Reserved, cautious, protective even when it was annoying. They had lost two decades together. But he had saved her life and was doing his best to make up for it.

She glanced behind her, and Alice and Tanya beamed at her. They were arm in arm despite all their differences. Against all odds, her broken family had come together for the most momentous day of her life. For a moment, they were whole.

They broke through the end of the tunnel, and everyone in the audience stood. Two hundred faces smiled back at her as the five of them stepped down the aisle to a violin version of her favorite Nightsmear song. And there, at the end of the tastefully decorated aisle, was her husband.

ACKNOWLEDGMENTS

Editor Jess for patiently helping me turn this book from a steaming, meandering pile of poo into a steaming, meandering pile of poo with a plot.

My dedicated ARC team who lift me up even when I probably don't deserve it.

Cupboard Maker Books for being the first to put my nonsense on their shelves.

Ray S. for answering all my questions about bridges.

Kyle W. for coming to my aid for all things car-related.

TWSS crew for being the best.

Ashley, Kayleigh, Alyssa, Chek, and Terry for being the vivid inspirations for all of Claire's friends.

Mike for locking me in his trunk when I asked him to for research purposes.

Oliver for being the cutest.

Baby Score, whose imminent arrival spurred the fastest rounds of copy edits I've ever churned out.

ABOUT THE AUTHOR

Madison Score is the author of the Claire Hartley Accidental Mystery series (and the younger, weirder sister of Lucy Score.) She lives in Pennsylvania with her husband, son, and perpetually shedding corgi. For some reason, her parents allowed her to get a degree in Creative Writing, which she now utilizes to craft stories with comedy, romance, and sometimes a hefty dose of crime.

When she's not writing, working at her real job in medical billing, or chasing after her tornado of a toddler (seriously, how many times can he upend our rubber tree?) you can find her blatantly ignoring recipes in the kitchen, flailing her body around in the gym, or bingeing true crime podcasts, TV, and movies.

Follow her on Facebook and Instagram if you want to see an excess of poorly photographed foods during her weekly Madison Tries It segment.

Website: madisonscore.com
Facebook: madisonscore
Instagram: madisonscore

Made in the USA
Middletown, DE
10 December 2024

66545537R00376